PRAISE FOR
LITTLE GIRL LOST
AND

WENDY CORSI
STAUB

P9-BYA-908

"If you like Mary Higgins Clark,
you'll love Wendy Corsi Staub."
—**LISA JACKSON,**
#1 *New York Times* bestselling author

"One of the best suspense writers we have today...
the suspense is so unbearable
you can't stop turning the page."
—**GREG HERREN,**
Anthony Award-winning author of
Garden District Gothic

The Good Sister

DEAD
SILENCE

By Wendy Corsi Staub

WENDY CORSI STAUB

DEAD SILENCE

wm

WILLIAM MORROW

An Imprint of HarperCollinsPublishers

Excerpt from *The Butcher's Daughter* copyright © 2020 by Wendy Corsi Staub.

DEAD SILENCE. Copyright © 2019 by Wendy Corsi Staub. All rights reserved. Printed in the United States of America. No part of this book may be used or reproduced in any manner whatsoever without written permission except in the case of brief quotations embodied in critical articles and reviews. For information, address HarperCollins Publishers, 195 Broadway, New York, NY 10007.

First William Morrow mass market printing: August 2019

Print Edition ISBN: 978-0-06-274206-3
Digital Edition ISBN: 978-0-06-274207-0

Cover design by Amy Halperin
Cover photographs © 4x6/iStock/Getty Images (silhouette); © Ebru Sida/Arcangel (background)

William Morrow and HarperCollins are registered trademarks of HarperCollins Publishers in the United States of America and other countries.

FIRST EDITION

19 20 21 22 23   QGM   10 9 8 7 6 5 4 3 2 1

For my Aunt Marian Corsi, a font of fascinating information and suggestions, including . . . a rooster; For my friend and fellow U2 fan Maureen Martin, who kept me sane this past year when the muse tried to do otherwise; For the three men who love me unconditionally, even on my most frantic "I'm on a deadline!" days: Mark, Morgan, and Brody Staub.

And in loving memory of my foundling great-grandfather, Vincenzo Tampio, abandoned on a doorstep in Valledolmo, Sicily, in 1869. We may never find out who his birth parents were, but he lived a long and rich life as the patriarch of an enormous family, raising seven sons and three daughters—the youngest, my beloved TT, Sara.

Acknowledgments

With deepest gratitude to you, my readers; to book-sellers and librarians; to my editor, Lucia Macro, who coaxed me through with infinite patience and encouragement; to all at William Morrow who had a hand in bringing this to life; to my literary agent, Laura Blake Peterson, who specializes in hand-holding over sushi and wine; to my film agent, Holly Frederick, and the gang at Curtis Brown; to Carol Fitzgerald and the Bookreporter team; to my Mystery Writers of America, Sisters in Crime, RWA, and Boucher-con colleagues; to the always warm and welcoming crew at the Ithaca Marriott on the Commons and the Ritz Carlton Amelia Island, particularly sweet Carolina; to my friends and family who stood by with the answers to all my research questions—or who simply stood by me: Anita Borgenicht; Nikki Bonnani; Pete Criscione; Alison Gaylin; Laura Himmelstein; Hannah Rae Koellner; Andrew and Jessica Krawitt; Suzanne Schmidt; Chris Spain; Brody, Morgan, and Mark Staub. A special shout-out to feline fan club Chance, Chappy, Sanchez, Pippa, and the *real* Clancy.

"Hope" is the thing with feathers
That perches in the soul,
And sings the tune without the words,
And never stops at all.
—EMILY DICKINSON

Chapter One

The vast sky had been black and glittering when the Angler cast off from shore with his tarped burden. Milky gray oozes now from the east, extinguishing stars and veiling the lake in rippling shadows.

Damp chill permeates his waxed cotton jacket. Even under the circumstances, he'd had the presence of mind to grab it from the car. He'd shivered through many a night-fishing excursion on this lake as a child, even in August. You learn. You remember.

Some things, anyway. The good things.

Precious few of those.

A crowing rooster scolds the songbirds' dawn chorus into a smattering of chirps as the Angler reaches the deepest part of the lake. He'd hoped to do this and escape under cover of darkness, before the old man stirs to awareness back at the house.

Hugo is ninety-two, though. How aware can his waking hours possibly be?

The Angler hasn't spent time with his uncle in decades but has glimpsed him now and again through a farmhouse window, noting the way he shuffles and stares. No evidence in that stooped, gnarled figure of the vibrant man who'd been saddled with an incorrigible great-nephew one rainy summer.

All his life, the Angler had been told that royal blood ran through his paternal family, courtesy of an ancestor illegitimately descended from the great Capetian Dynasty. He'd anticipated the worst of his father's authoritarian behavior in Hugo, but instead encountered a humble farmer with aristocratic bearing.

Hugo had taught him how to row in an old wooden kayak, and to swim after it capsized one terrifying morning, and most importantly, how to fish.

"Did you learn anything this summer?" his father had asked in September, driving him south back to Ottawa.

"*Oui.*" French had become second nature; Hugo had spoken no English.

"*Oui?*" his father echoed, flashing a rare grin of approval.

"*Parle-moi en français!*" he'd commanded for years, but the older the Angler had become, the more he'd resisted.

Yes. I learned something that summer, you miserable bastard.

I learned I never wanted to sound like you, or look like you, or become like you, and yet . . .

Tossing aside the oars, the Angler turns to the tarp in the bottom of the boat, picturing her under there. Not the way she'd looked when he'd shrouded her— blue eyes fixed in horror, mouth gaping with a silent scream, her blond hair and pale lavender blouse soaked in blood. No, he sees her as she'd been the night they'd met, an angel dressed in white, haloed by a streetlight.

She'd told him her name was Monique. Not true, he'd discovered weeks later, spotting her face on a Missing Persons flyer. Nor had she been eighteen, as she'd assured him when he'd invited her into the car. Nor twelve, as she'd later claimed when she'd begged him to let her go, promising she wouldn't tell anyone, calling for her mother.

"Je suis seulement une petite fille!"

"I'm only a little girl . . ."

Then, she'd been a fourteen-year-old freshman computer whiz who'd run away from home after she'd caught her boyfriend cheating on her.

Now she's—she *was*—eighteen.

"Oh, Monique," he whispers, reaching for the tarp. "You should have stayed the way you used to be. So innocent . . ."

He lifts the tarped bundle with a grunt. He'd wrapped her with a large rock he'd feared might swamp or tip the boat. Now he just hopes it will be heavy enough to sink her to the murky depths.

He heaves the deadweight overboard with a gentle splash and watches it descend.

As he rows back toward shore, daybreak reveals a tangle of flattened and broken weeds along the overgrown path where he'd dragged her corpse down to the lake.

He keeps his eyes on the dim outline of the henhouse in the distance, rowing in rhythm to the refrain in his head.

One down, one to go . . .

New York City

As SLEEP'S MELLOW hush lifts, Amelia Crenshaw Haines knows she's alone in her bed, in the room, in the apartment. She hears traffic honking on Amsterdam Avenue ten stories below, sirens in the distance, and the soft whir of the HEPA air purifier on Aaron's dresser. He'd discovered his cat allergy two months ago, after she'd rescued a little Scottish Fold kitten. She hadn't offered to return Clancy to the kill shelter. Nor had Aaron asked her to.

He hadn't offered to skip his client dinner meeting tonight. Nor had she asked him to.

She'd thought maybe, though, since it's their anniversary . . .

She opens her eyes.

Dayclean.

Even now, the Gullah word tends to pop into her head in moments like this, when she sees that last night's storm has given way to an incandescent autumn day. Her old neighbor Marceline LeBlanc had shared it with a young, grieving Amelia twenty-eight years ago. *"Dayclean means early morning, after dawn breaks. A fresh start. Yesterday's troubles scrubbed away."*

Amelia sees a gift sitting on the pillow beside hers. Drenched in buttery sunlight, the small box is telltale turquoise, tied with a white satin ribbon: Tiffany's. A year or two ago, her heart would have leapt. Today, it sinks.

She leaves the gift where it is, reaching past it for her cell phone to check her email. She scans the list of messages, searching the sender column for genetic genealogy website addresses, hoping one of them has informed her that there's been a hit on her DNA at last.

Not today.

She turns off the alarm that has yet to ring and slogs into the adjoining bathroom. Aaron's navy cotton pj's with the white piping sway on a hook as she kicks the door shut. Early in their relationship, she'd gotten a giggle out of his pajamas, the old-fashioned kind with matching top and bottoms.

"What else would I wear?"

"You know . . . boxers and a tee shirt or something, or . . . nothing."

He'd laughed and pulled her into his arms.

She reaches for her toothbrush, past his, back in its holder after a two-day absence. She'd slept soundly through Aaron's late-night return from taking a deposition in Chicago . . . or had it been Denver? Not LA. That trip is next week. She'd toyed with tagging along until he'd told her his schedule will be too jammed for time together.

So much for celebrating their silver anniversary there—or here—or anywhere.

She stares into the mirror above the sink, searching for some remnant of the luminescent young bride she'd been twenty-five years ago today. She's read that light-skinned Black women don't age as well as their darker counterparts. Maybe it's true. She notes the deepening lines around her eyes and mouth, the slight sag beneath her jaw. There are no wiry gray strands in her sleek shoulder-length hair, but only because she'd had it straightened and colored last month.

"Girl, you are getting old."

The woman in the mirror turns away.

She takes her steamy time in the new shower with gleaming white marble and dual high-end rain heads. "Plenty of room for two," the contractor had said with a sly wink, but she and Aaron have yet to test that. He's taken to showering when he gets home at night. She's tried not to wonder why and hasn't asked him. She has never been, and refuses to become, a suspicious wife.

Wrapped in a fluffy white towel, Amelia returns to the bedroom and lifts the shades. The tall windows face east, and the first beams of sunlight have cleared the building next door, spilling over the unmade bed and the turquoise box on Aaron's pillow.

She goes to her closet and pulls out a navy lightweight wool Brooks Brothers skirt suit and white silk blouse. She dresses quickly, adding panty hose, low-heeled pumps, a string of pearls, matching earrings. Boring, boring. She'd prefer jeans, boots, a splashy-hued fall sweater, and the chunky teal and purple beads she'd bought in Union Square last week. But she has a new client coming this morning, and when her wardrobe leans casual, newcomers—the ones who haven't seen her on television, anyway—don't seem to take her as seriously.

She turns to the bed, tucking in the sheets, smoothing the duvet, and aligning the pillows, though she'll climb back in tonight long before Aaron does. Making the bed is second nature when you grow up sleeping on a pullout couch in the center of a cramped apartment. There had been a time, though, after her mother had passed away and before Amelia had gone away to college, when she'd taken perverse pleasure in leaving a rumpled tangle of bedding in the living room every morning.

She'd been so angry back then—at her mother for dying; at her father for letting grief consume him; at both for not having told her she wasn't their biological child. She'd discovered that shocking truth the day she'd lost her mother.

A few years later, her father, too, was gone. She's been an orphan for most of her adult life—an orphan who might still have parents out there somewhere.

"You have me," Aaron says, when she grieves for what she'd had and lost.

"You're my husband, not my parent."

"You have my mother and father, though, and my brothers and sisters, and all the nieces and nephews . . ."

Yes, they're her family, and she loves them, and she knows better than anyone that familial bonds don't depend on blood. But she's the in-law. The connection would sever if she weren't married to Aaron.

Which you are.

For a quarter of a century to this very day.

Marrying a handsome, stable, upwardly mobile law school graduate had been the easiest decision she'd ever made. Their disparate backgrounds kept things interesting, but they were similar enough to want the same things out of life—except when it came to their wedding.

He'd wanted an extravagant affair; she'd have preferred to elope. She'd had no mother to help her pick a gown, no father to walk her down the aisle, no family to line the church pews on the bride's side.

The future litigator had gotten his way, and so her

friend Jessie had helped her pick her gown, and Silas Moss had walked her down the aisle. The groom had more than enough family to fill both sides of the church.

The large, loving Haines clan is part of the reason Amelia had been so drawn to him in the first place. She can't imagine life without her in-laws. As for life without Aaron . . .

He's abandoned her on their anniversary.

Well, that might not be entirely true.

Your birth parents abandoned you. Your husband has a business dinner. Big difference—unless Aaron is lying.

She picks up the shiny turquoise box. The white satin ribbon slips away with a slight tug. She lifts the lid, bracing herself for the sparkly diamond bracelet, sapphire earrings, some expensive bauble a possibly philandering husband presents to his supposedly unsuspecting wife.

But inside, she finds a silver Tiffany horseshoe key ring. It holds a set of keys.

What in the . . . ?

The heart-shaped charm is engraved with a Sutton Place address and *7:30 p.m.*

A slow smile spreads across her face.

Googling the address on the charm, she finds that it belongs to a luxurious garden town house along the river.

She opens the top drawer of her dresser and retrieves the velvet jewelry box that contains the simple gold wedding band Aaron had placed on her finger twenty-five years ago today. She usually wears the diamond-studded platinum one he'd given her on their fifteenth anniversary, after he'd made partner at his law firm.

"Now you can get rid of that cheap old thing," he'd said.

"It wasn't cheap. It's gold, and it matches yours."

"Well, it looks like it belongs in a hardware bin. And don't worry about matching. I got myself a new platinum band, too. Let's throw the old ones away."

"We can't just throw away gold! Those rings symbolize fifteen years of marriage behind us. Sometimes I wonder if you have a sentimental bone in your body."

He laughed. "I do. But the new rings symbolize all the years ahead, and they're going to be even better."

Some days, she isn't so sure about that. And most days, she doesn't even think about the old gold ring. But this is the perfect occasion to wear it in memory of all the reasons they'd exchanged rings and vows in the first place. She slides it over a simple gold chain and fastens it around her neck, trying not to remember another time, another ring on another chain . . .

She opens the door to the adjacent former nursery. Amelia and Aaron had agreed early on to be content with each other, their careers, and a dozen nieces and nephews, so the tiny room had served as her office until she'd moved her burgeoning business downtown. Now it's a kitten corral.

Clancy is perched on top of a bookshelf, swatting at the floor lamp's fringed shade.

"Good morning, Clanc—whoa!"

A grasping, fat little paw makes contact, and the lamp teeters. Amelia steadies it, then picks up the kitten. He protests loudly. As she strokes his pinkish-orange fur, she notes that his food bowl is empty. Aaron filling it on his way out the door would have been an even more welcome surprise than the Tiffany key ring.

One thing's certain: he didn't buy the Sutton Place town house as an anniversary surprise. They're not hurting, but they can't afford eight-figure real estate. This Upper West Side junior four had needed extensive work, even at the top of their budget in an ever-skyrocketing Manhattan market.

A plumber and several workmen arrive as she's leaving the apartment. They'd completed the bathroom renovation on the Friday before Labor Day and had begun kitchen demolition the Tuesday after.

"We should have the appliances in by next week," the contractor tells her. "Bet you'll be glad to get back to home-cooked meals."

She thanks him, not mentioning that those were rare around here even before her kitchen had been gutted and tarped off. Aaron dines with colleagues or clients most nights—or so he says; Amelia gobbles takeout in front of reality TV shows he finds ridiculous.

"Haven't you ever heard of guilty pleasures, Aaron?" she'd asked the other night, when he'd walked in on her in sweatpants, clutching a plastic container of greasy beef *chow fun*, riveted by a *Real Housewives* catfight.

"Sure I have, babe. But this would definitely not be mine."

What is yours, Aaron?

She'd been afraid to ask.

She's never been one to meet conflict with taciturnity. Theirs has not been a marriage in which questions are unasked or unanswered. She and Aaron have always aired their grievances and hashed out differences. But they don't talk much anymore, whether they're together or apart. Phone calls have given way to texts; conversation to coexistence; companionable silence to a disquieting quiet that permeates the apartment even when the workmen are there with hammers and power tools.

The doorman, Alex, greets her in the lobby and tells her he caught her on television last night.

For the past couple of years, she's been an occasional on-air consultant for *The Roots and Branches Project*, a cable program hosted by renowned African American historian Nelson Roger Cartwright.

"I know it sounds crazy," Alex says, "but I bawled like a baby when you gave that guy the document about his great-great-grandfather being sold as a slave when he was just a little boy."

"He cried, too. We were all teary, on and off camera."

"I bet that happens a lot." He holds open the door. "It's a beautiful day out there. Enjoy."

Her wedding day had been nice as well—Indian summer, with sunlight streaming in the stained-glass church windows, and an outdoor reception at her in-laws' country club.

She bypasses the subway, deciding to treat herself to a cab. *Happy anniversary to me.*

The driver signals to turn down Broadway.

"Sir? Can you take the Central Park transverse instead?"

"It's the long way."

"That's okay."

She pulls earbuds from her bag and scrolls through her phone's playlists, ranging from classical jazz to hip-hop. Music had been her first passion. She'd once hoped to make vocal performance a career, but now she's content singing with the Park Baptist Church gospel choir every other Sunday.

She settles on U2. Her friend Jessie's voice, girlie-giddy—drifts back over the years. *"Bet I can guess your favorite song on* Joshua Tree.*"*

Amelia doesn't want to hear that one right now, doesn't need any reminders that she still hasn't found what she's looking for.

She finds the perfect song and Bono's voice replaces Jessie's in her head, singing about a beautiful day as they cruise past horse-drawn carriages, joggers, and baby buggies. The park is a tapestry of gold leaf–dusted walkways and burnished foliage. Manhattan's skyline gleams, stone and steel rising against a cloudless blue backdrop.

Southbound traffic is heavy when they reach the FDR, and she arrives at the brick office tenement on Allen Street just ten minutes before her first appointment. Had she taken the subway, she'd have had time to go over the client's paperwork. Now she's going in blind.

She hurries up three narrow flights, fingertips skimming the wooden banister, its nicks and scars worn smooth by countless hands. At the turn of the last century, immigrants had jammed generations into tiny apartments beyond rows of transom-topped doors. Amelia likes to think the place remains charged with their optimistic energy.

As always, a wisp of wistfulness grazes her heart when she reaches the door bearing a brass placard AMELIA CRENSHAW HAINES, INVESTIGATIVE GENE-ALOGIST. Calvin and Bettina Crenshaw would have been proud to see how far she's come; famed Cornell

University professor Silas Moss even prouder. But her parents are gone, and her friend and mentor now resides in the Alzheimer's wing of an Ithaca nursing home.

She opens the door to her office. Sunlight falls through the tall window. Beyond a metal fire escape, maple boughs rise from courtyards below, swishing red foliage in the breeze. The tin ceilings, exposed brick, and hardwood floors are original, spared before her time in an electrical fire sparked by rats gnawing through first floor wiring.

"Whole place was infested when I bought it," her landlord had said—after she'd signed the lease. Seeing the look on her face, he'd assured her that he'd long since rid the building of rodents, but every time she crosses the threshold, she does a quick check for evidence. She knows what to look for, having grown up in a neighborhood where rats were the least scary thing that might leap out from a dark corner.

Amelia opens the window. A warm wind drifts in, along with distant sirens, as she sits at her desk skimming the client's electronic file.

Lily Tucker had been found as a toddler at a New Haven, Connecticut, shopping mall in 1990. She hadn't matched the description of any known missing children.

She and Amelia have a lot in common. Lily is also African American, and had been raised by loving adoptive parents. But she'd been older when she'd been abandoned, and might have some memory of—

Amelia's cell phone buzzes with an incoming call. She smiles when she sees who it is.

"Happy anniversary, Mimi!"

Jessamine McCall Hanson is the only person in the world who's ever called Amelia by that nickname.

"Jessie, I can't believe that with all you have going on, you never forget. You're amazing."

"Don't get too excited. This is pretty much the only thing I remember. I mean, last night, the power went out? And the first thing I thought was, 'Crap! I forgot to pay the electric bill again.'"

"Oh, no. They cut you off?"

"Nah, it was just a thunderstorm. But I do keep forgetting to pay it. This middle-aged thing sucks, Mimi. My brain is total mush."

Funny—whenever Amelia hears her old friend's voice, still with that giddy-girlie upspeak she'd had when they met, her mind's eye pictures a young woman on the other end of the line. Yet Jessie is in her late forties now, a wife and mother with a master's degree in social work and a busy career as a therapist.

And Jessie, too, is a foundling, a kindred spirit she'd met through Silas Moss.

Amelia asks Jessie how he is.

"You know . . . the same. He's been asking for you."

"Asking for me? Come on, he has not."

"Well, not asking. But he misses you. Whenever I tell him about you, he smiles, like he knows. He's still in there somewhere, Mimi. Come see him. All of us."

"I wish I could."

"Why can't you? We have plenty of room. Chip and Petty are away at school." Jessie's oldest son and daughter had been born Paul and Paige, long lost to their mother's penchant for nicknames.

"No foster kids?"

"Not right now. Theodore's been going through some stuff at school again, so we're taking a little break from fostering."

"Oh, no. What's going on?"

"He's just . . . it's . . . complicated, you know?"

"I'm so sorry. I thought things were better for him." Jessie's youngest child has special needs and has endured bullying and academic challenges over the years.

"They were, but . . . I wish I could talk to you in person."

"Let's plan a girls' weekend at my place."

"What about Aaron?"

"If he's not traveling, he'll make himself scarce. He's good at that."

"Mimi, are you guys okay?"

"Sure we are, we're just . . ." She settles on Jessie's word. "Complicated. I don't know . . . maybe it's just me, reading too much into things. I wish I could talk to you in person about this, too."

"Then come to Ithaca this weekend. It's Apple Harvest Festival, and you only schedule morning appointments on Fridays, right? Take an afternoon bus, and you'll be here in time for happy hour. Just like old times."

"Not this weekend, Jess. It's our twenty-fifth wedding anniversary. Aaron's planning some kind of surprise, and—" Hearing a knock, she curtails the call. "I have a client. We'll talk soon, okay? Thanks for calling. Love you."

"Love you, too, Mimi."

Tucking away her phone and her wistfulness, she opens the door to one of the most stunning young women she's ever seen.

Amelia is five foot nine. Lily Tucker is taller. A model, maybe. She certainly has the willowy build and the looks. Her hair is cropped short, enhancing her delicate facial bone structure, glowing ebony complexion, and exotic wide-set eyes. She's effortlessly glamorous in a simple white tee shirt, black blazer, designer jeans, and flats, with sunglasses on her head and an oversized leather bag over her shoulder.

"Sorry I'm late. Metro-North was running behind."

"And here I thought it was the only commuter line in this city that runs like clockwork. I guess I'm glad I never moved to Connecticut. Come on in. I'm Amelia."

"I know. I've seen you on TV."

Lily sets her bag on the floor and settles on the couch, lanky legs crossed. Amelia sits on the opposite end, her back propped against the cushy leather arm, like a friend settling in for a chat.

"First things first," she says.

"Oh, right. You take cash?"

Amelia smiles. "You can pay at the end of the session, and sure, that's fine. I'll give you a receipt. But that's not what I was talking about. The first thing for me is explaining what I do, and why."

She shares her own story with Lily, who asks about her home life, whether she'd been raised with siblings.

"No, it was just the three of us—my adoptive parents and me."

"What about aunts, uncles, grandparents, cousins . . ."

She shakes her head. "My parents had relatives back where they'd come from, but no one had money to travel and visit."

"So you never met any of them?"

"Just once."

Bettina's favorite Auntie Birdie had traveled to New York from Marshboro, Georgia, when Calvin had passed away in 1989. Birdie's grown daughter, Bettina's cousin Lucky, had scraped up the plane fare.

"We couldn't bear the thought of you handling this sorrow all alone, child," Auntie Birdie had told Amelia, sounding so very much like Bettina. *"At least when your mama died, you had your papa to lean on. Now, you lean on me."*

Amelia had taken comfort in the elderly woman's presence, sensing a visceral connection to a stranger with whom she didn't even share a blood bond. Auntie Birdie had invited her to visit her mother's hometown the following summer. But by that time, Amelia had met Aaron. He and her future in-laws had filled the gaping hole at last. For a while, anyway.

"Are you still in touch with them?" Lily asks.

"With my mother's relatives? No, her aunt died not long after I met her, and I never did meet the others." She shrugs. "Anyway, my adoptive parents loved me with all their hearts, and I miss them both every day. But I also miss the strangers who brought me into this world, and I've spent my entire adult life searching for them."

"Have you found any leads?"

She shrugs. "Not really. But I won't give up."

"Even after all these years?"

"Would you?"

"Never. But I'd think, you know, being on TV, you'd have an easier time finding information."

"I don't talk about my personal search on the show. I'm just a consultant, not a guest."

"Maybe if they featured your story on an episode . . ."

"They won't. I'm not a celebrity."

The Roots and Branches Project delves into the genealogical pasts of prominent Black people—mainly entertainers, athletes, and politicians. Her television exposure has brought her more new clients than she can handle, and greatly increased traffic to her website, where her own story is featured. Maybe one day, someone will see it and come forward with a relevant lead. Maybe not. But it's been gratifying to help others discover their own roots.

Amelia takes notes as Lily recaps a happy childhood in a wonderful home where she still lives with her adoptive family. She paints an idyllic picture, recalling backyard pool parties and weekly board game nights around the kitchen table, girl scout camping trips, high school clubs, college honors . . .

"You were really lucky, Lily. It sounds like you've had the perfect life."

"Too good to be true, right?" She looks down, toying with the piping on a throw pillow, probably staving off guilt over seeking the parents who'd presumably deserted her when she already has parents who love her.

"Does your family know you're meeting with me today?"

"No. I don't know what they'd say about it, but, you know, I needed to try." She reaches into the leather bag and pulls out a battered manila folder, handing it over to Amelia. "These are newspaper clippings about how I was found in the mall."

"Can I keep them?"

"Yeah. I brought the ring, too. Only that, you can't keep."

"The ring?" She really should have gone over that paperwork.

Lily hands over a small jewelry box. It's plain, white, not from Tiffany, not ribbon wrapped.

Amelia lifts the lid. A strangled cry escapes her as she recognizes the object inside.

It's a little gold initial ring, with tiny sapphires set on either side of an engraved letter *C*, filled in blue enamel.

Chapter Two

On the southbound approach to the Thousand Islands Bridge, mingling with the car radio's drone, the Angler hears—or does he merely sense?—movement in the backseat. Maybe it's pure paranoia-driven imagination as Customs looms around the bend. The dose of Rohypnol he'd administered back at the farm should last at least a few more hours. Long enough to get into the US so this second victim, if later found, won't be traced right back to Canada.

It had seemed like a good plan back at the farm, where he'd congratulated himself on his restraint. He could have killed the kid on the spot, but then what? He couldn't paddle back out in broad daylight and sink a second victim alongside the first. If Monique ever floated to the surface, the cops wouldn't find any obvious connection to him, but the kid is different. Dangerous. It would have to wait. He couldn't risk transporting a dead body across the border. Even a live one is dicey, unless he's sound asleep.

The Angler glances into the rearview mirror, craning his neck until he spots tousled blond hair against the seat.

"Hey. You awake back there?"

No response, but that means nothing. The kid never has much to say, even when Monique was around.

He rolls to a stop beside the uniformed border patrol officer and lowers the car window.

"Good morning. Where you headed?"

"Boston." The Angler hands him two passports and nods toward the backseat. He'd come up with the story listening to sports radio. "We're going to watch the Blue Jays beat the Red Sox tomorrow night."

"You sound pretty confident about that, eh?"

"Oh, yeah. Huge fan," he lies, watching the man examine both passports and peer into the backseat. "Poor little slugger was so excited about the trip he didn't sleep a wink last night. He's making up for it now, though."

The officer makes no comment.

The Angler is glad he'd thought to throw a blanket over the kid from the neck down. Not just so that he'd appear to be napping, but to hide the dirt cellar filth and the fact that his shoes had been lost somewhere along the way.

He sees the man glance at the tackle box on the passenger's side floor.

"Hoping we can do a little fishing, too, while we're there."

"You got a license for that?"

Damn.

"Don't need one when you take a charter." It's a guess, probably true, but if this guy knows anything about fishing in Massachusetts, he might question it.

"Mmm," is all he says.

He braces himself for more tough questions, but the ones that come are innocuous. No, he's not transporting anything into the country; yes, this is a short trip.

"I'm a welder at a sheet metal manufacturer," he says. "Taking a couple of days off from work to spend with him."

It's a semitruth. He'd called in sick this morning.

"And his mother?"

"Oh, she's . . . she passed away. I'm widowed. Just the two of us now."

He sees something flicker in the man's gaze. Not sympathy. Suspicion?

But it's the truth. Even the widowed part—in his heart, anyway.

The first time he'd seen Monique, she'd been dressed in white. Like a bride, he'd told her. All those years together—he could have ended it, but he'd chosen not to. Because he'd been committed. Because he loved her.

And now look. Look.

Tears sting his eyes and he swallows hard. He's going to miss her, dammit.

The officer hands back the passports and motions him to drive on, saying, "Have a good trip. Go Jays."

"What?"

"The game."

"Oh! Right! Go Jays!" The Angler drives on, exhaling only when the bridge has disappeared in his rearview mirror, and he's turned west to continue into New York State instead of east, toward New England.

He tucks the passports back into the glove compartment. One is his own; the other, his son's. No, not the sleeping child in the backseat, but a handsome blond boy who looks very much like this one, and lives, along with his mother and sister, in a comfortable suburban Ottawa town house.

PULLING A ROLLING suitcase, Stockton Barnes steps out of his Washington Heights apartment building onto the sunny sidewalk. All is quiet at the construction site across the street. The workers are on a break. So are the toast-nibbling trio of elderly neighbors who park themselves in a row of webbed lawn chairs every morning, like aging groupies awaiting a free Sheep Meadow concert.

Carl, Dabney, and Harvey are there to witness—and criticize—the erection of a new apartment tower that will block the sunlight from their rent-controlled apartments. Barnes, whose dim one-bedroom overlooks the air shaft, can live without the dilapidated coffee shop razed to make way for the tower. He can also live without the early morning jackhammers, but that phase should be finished by early next week, the three old men say, before peppering him—and each other—with questions.

"What's with the valise?"

"Yeah, are you going somewhere?"

"Of course he's going somewhere. Why else would he have the valise?"

"Who says valise anymore? Get with the times."

"Listen to Mr. Hep Cat over here."

Suppressing a smile, Barnes tells them that he's going on vacation, opening the door to fresh commentary.

"To the beach, in hurricane season? What are you, nuts?"

"Don't you watch the Weather Channel?"

"Did he say he's going to the beach?"

"He's wearing flip-flops. You're going to the beach, am I right?"

Barnes nods. "Yes, Carl, you are right."

"Well, I hope it's not in Barbados because there's a hurricane coming."

"Not a hurricane. A tropical storm."

"Eh, you're both wrong. It's a tropical depression!"

Barnes, too, has seen the weather report. "Don't worry, fellows. I'm not going to Barbados."

"Then where? Boca? No? But somewhere in Florida, right?"

Barnes shakes his head. "No, not—"

"Oh, I know—Mexico! No?"

"Bahamas?"

"Fiji?"

"Fiji? Who the hell goes to Fiji?"

"You got a problem with Fiji? Is it Fiji?"

Barnes just shakes his head again, and they keep guessing and he keeps shaking until—

"Hey, get a load of that!"

All three of them fixate on something behind Barnes. He turns around. Beyond a row of parked cars and double-parked delivery vehicles, an extraordinary vehicle has rounded the corner from Saint Nicholas Avenue.

Vintage Rolls-Royce. Gleaming turquoise paint job. Top down. Nice.

"Looks like a '57 Silver Cloud. That for you?"

"I sure hope so, Harvey."

"Guess the NYPD's handing out big fat raises to the Missing Persons Squad these days."

"Nah, I've just got friends in high places."

They don't come much higher than Rob Owens, founder and CEO of Rucker Park Records. He's perched in the backseat, wearing a snap brim Panama hat and pink guayabera shirt. Barnes is surprised to spot a familiar passenger slumped beside him. No tropical resort clothing on Rob's son, though—just the usual dark jeans, tee shirt, and sneakers. His eyes, like his dad's, are masked by designer sunglasses.

"Hey, Kurtis!"

He removes one earbud. "Hey, Uncle Stockton."

"I didn't know you were coming with us."

"Neither did I."

"Last-minute birthday surprise," Rob says.

"Not my birthday for a few more weeks."

Don't I know it. Barnes thinks of his own daughter, born the same day as Kurtis: October 24, 1987.

"Never too early to celebrate a birthday," Rob says.

No. Only too late.

Barnes's daughter, too, will be turning twenty-nine. Does she also dress in head-to-toe black? Does she, like Kurtis, spend more time looking at her cell phone than at people? Is she more interested in texting than talking, and perpetually wearing earbuds? Does she, too, resent her father? Not, like Kurtis, for what he's done, but for what he hasn't.

"Good morning, Detective Barnes." The silver-haired driver steps out to open the door and stash his suitcase in the trunk. His clipped British accent is intact, but he's replaced his usual dark suit with a fedora and open-collared cabana shirt that matches the splashy shade of the car.

"Flying to Havana with us, Smitty?"

"I'm afraid not, sir."

"I invited him, but his lady friend didn't go for that idea, right, Smitty?" Rob says around the cigar clenched in his mouth.

"No, sir, she did not." Smitty's *lady friend* is the formidable housekeeper at Rob's palatial Bergen County house.

Barnes says goodbye to his neighbors as Smitty slips back behind the wheel and they're off to the airport, bongo-punctuated salsa blasting from the speakers. They're flying to Cuba—a major bucket list item for Barnes, whose *abuela* emigrated from there back in the fifties.

"Did you buy this car?" he asks Rob, leaning back into soft leather.

"Nah, borrowed it from a friend."

Rob is no name-dropper, but in his world, the friend is likely a household name.

Traffic is heavy, even up here in Washington Heights. Smitty navigates 177th Street, entering the West Side Highway just south of the George Washington Bridge.

Glancing over his shoulder at the span, Barnes thinks of that pivotal October when he'd started his job as a detective with the Missing Persons Squad. Three days in, he'd had a near-miss with a stray bullet. A couple of weeks later, hedge fund tycoon Perry Wayland had disappeared in the wake of a catastrophic stock market crash he'd seen coming. Before the month was out, Barnes had worked that case, cared for a terminally ill friend, lost another to violent crime, and made a choice that's haunted him ever since.

Oh, and he'd met Rob at a Brooklyn hospital where they were both pacing, fatherhood imminent. Two babies and two days later, Barnes had held his little girl for the first—and last—time.

Yeah. Tough month, October.

Rob had caught Barnes in an emotional moment in the men's room after he'd left his newborn daughter in the nursery, certain he'd never see her again. He'd been right, and wrong about Rob, about whom he'd thought the same thing. His friend had later tracked him down and has been family ever since.

"Want a Cuban?" Rob asks.

"Sandwich or cigar?"

"Cigar, unless . . . maybe we have time to stop at Victor's on the way. I could go for some *ropa vieja* myself."

"Thought you were on a diet."

"Not a diet, Barnes. A fitness plan. It's about living an active lifestyle, physical wellness, making healthy choices—"

"Smoking?" The comment comes from Kurtis, who has plucked an earbud from his ear. "Yeah, that's healthy."

"So you *can* hear me when you want to." Rob shakes his head. "A cigar once in a while never hurt anyone."

"You got statistics to back that up? Because I know you like your statistics when it comes to this stuff."

"Yeah, well, this is nothing like what *you've* been smoking, son."

"Tell me you never smoked weed."

Ignoring that, Rob turns back to Barnes. "So you're hungry? Because I am *hungry*."

"I could eat."

"What do you say, Smitty? Do we have time to grab some takeout from Victor's?"

"Unfortunately, sir, we must make haste to the airport if you're to board your flight on time."

"Sorry, Barnes," Rob says. "Must make haste. You'll have to settle for a Cuban cigar. Unless you gave up these when you gave up the cigarettes?"

"Just cigarettes." It's been three years now since he kicked the habit, but not a stressful day goes by that he doesn't reach for the pack.

Rob hands him a fragrant Cohiba, along with a silver Puiforcat cutter and small box of wooden matches imprinted with the name of a downscale midtown pub.

Typical incongruity. Barnes has seen him wear a Burberry scarf over a Champion tee shirt while eating Popeyes fried chicken from nineteenth-century Limoges porcelain. And though he's flown with Rob on many a private plane, today, his friend informs him, they're on JetBlue, the first US commercial airline to schedule regular flights to Cuba now that diplomatic relations have been restored.

Kurtis looks up in dismay. "No first class on Jet-Blue. We're flying in coach?"

"Don't worry. We've got extra-legroom seats."

"Yippee."

"You're spoiled, son."

Kurtis shrugs. "Then you're the one who spoiled me."

"No, that was your mother. Though I will admit, I do like to spoil that woman. Mmm-mmm-mmm." Rob shakes his head behind a screen of cigar smoke. "That reminds me, I need to call her and say goodbye."

"You said goodbye at the house."

"Not the right kind of goodbye. I was in a hurry, and she was late for yoga. I forgot to tell her a few things."

Seeing the set to his son's mouth, Barnes wants to tell him how lucky he is to have two parents who are alive and well and crazy about each other. Instead, as Rob dials, he asks Kurtis how work is going.

"It isn't."

"What do you mean?"

"That place wasn't for me."

Barnes puffs his cigar. "Not the right company?"

"Not the right industry."

"Advertising?"

"That was last year. This was publishing."

"Didn't like that, either, huh?"

"Nope." He lounges back against the car seat, eyes closed.

"Hey, babe, guess you're still in class," Rob says into his phone. "Just wanted to say I love you. Because I forgot."

"You didn't forget," Kurtis mutters without opening his eyes.

Rob disconnects his call and looks at his son. "And you didn't give it a chance."

"What?"

"The job."

"I was there six months."

"Exactly. You were there six months. Tell him, Barnes."

"You were there six months?"

"Yeah, I got that."

"What Uncle Stockton *means* is, you can't learn anything about anything in six months. You have got to have patience. Give things time, son. Don't just bounce from one thing to the next. That's no way to live. Make a commitment, see it through. Right, Stockton?"

Barnes thinks of his brief failed marriage to a fellow cop, and the string of women in his past. And present.

Future, too, most likely. Not to mention the daughter who's a stranger. And Detective Sullivan Leary, his longtime partner and confidante, with whom he's all but lost touch since she left the force and New York in August.

But this isn't about relationships, is it? It's about work. And Barnes's devotion to the job has been steadfast all the way back to his days in the academy . . . with one blip.

He sighs a gust of cigar smoke and stares out the window at the Hudson River beyond the West Side Highway.

October 1987.

Damn. What he wouldn't give for a do-over.

Rob is lecturing Kurtis. Six years have passed since his son entered the business world with an Ivy League degree and a fierce determination to make his way without his father's help. Early on, Barnes had admired Kurtis for avoiding the career path of least resistance. Now he wonders whether he really is more lazy than noble, as Rob sees it.

"Listen up, son. If you don't want to be like me, then be like your uncle Stockton. He's the most positive role model you could ask for."

"Me?" Barnes forces a laugh.

Rob doesn't know about the misdeed that's haunted him for almost thirty years.

Misdeed?

It was a crime. You know it now, and you knew it then.

AMELIA STARES AT the ring she'd lost nearly thirty years ago, on the worst night of her life.

She'd last seen it in Harlem's Morningside Memorial Hospital, where she had discovered, in the midst of a sorrowful deathbed vigil, that the dying woman, Bettina Crenshaw, was not her biological mother. She closes her eyes, thoughts spinning.

"Are you okay?"

Lily Tucker's voice breaks through.

"No . . . Yes . . . I mean, I'm fine. I just . . ." She opens her eyes. "I got a little dizzy there for a minute. Low blood sugar, I guess. Happens when I skip breakfast."

Lily nods, but Amelia sees something unsettling in her expression—a flicker of mistrust, maybe? Does she smell a lie?

Amelia forces herself to look again at the ring. She doesn't dare take it out of the box, afraid that she'll burst into tears if she touches it. "This is exquisite. So unusual. Can you tell me about it?"

"I had it on the day I was found."

So had Amelia, according to her father's account.

She clears her throat. "Weren't you a toddler? It's so small . . . a baby ring, isn't it?"

"Well, yeah, I don't mean I was wearing it on my *finger*, because obviously it would be too small. It was on a chain, just like yours."

She gasps. "How did you know—"

"Uh . . . what?" Lily points at her neck.

She reaches up to touch her original wedding band dangling from a delicate gold strand. She'd forgotten all about it.

"Sorry, I . . . Man, I really do need to eat something. Get the blood sugar back up, you know?" She shoves the lid back on the ring box and thrusts it into Lily's hands.

Then she walks to her desk on shaky legs and opens a drawer where she stashes protein bars for days when she doesn't have time for lunch. Composing herself, she feigns a hunt through the drawer before she grabs a couple of bars. "Do you want one? I have . . . let's see, there's chocolate peanut and oat crunch."

Lily doesn't want one.

Neither does Amelia, but she tears the wrapper from the chocolate one and forces a dusty bite down her dry throat.

Should she tell her?

How can you not?

But how can you?

Lily has come here for help finding her roots. If they're entangled with Amelia's, the truth will likely emerge in the investigation. If it doesn't, Amelia can consider telling her about the connection then. She cannot, however, drop the staggering bombshell in the first ten minutes of the young woman's first appointment. Lily would be overwhelmed. She might leave, and never come back.

The news can wait.

She tosses the half-eaten protein bar into the garbage can and sits on the couch again. "So you were wearing the ring on a chain when you were found. Do you know anything else about it?"

"I don't know anything about anything. That's why I'm here."

Pretending she's any other client, Amelia gives Lily an overview of her ever-evolving search methods.

"You can't imagine how many libraries and hospitals and courthouses I've visited—especially back when I first started looking. Microfiche was as high-tech as it got."

"You mean Microsoft?"

"No, micro*fiche*." Lucky Lily, spared all those dusty hours she herself had spent hunched over yellowed archives in fluorescent-lit rooms, searching for clues to her past. "Strips of film that had tiny images of documents like newspaper pages. You had to scroll through them manually on magnifying readers. This was way before the internet and online databases and social media."

"You use social media?"

"All the time. Facebook is one of my most valuable resources. Are you on it?"

"Yeah, but . . . not often."

Noting her guarded expression, Amelia guesses what she's thinking. Younger generations had thought Facebook was cool about a decade ago, but changed their minds as it caught on with the older population.

"Grandma sent me a friend request," she'd overheard one of her nieces telling an older cousin a few Christmases ago.

"No! Don't accept it!"

"Too late. And now she keeps, like, commenting on everything I post."

"Girl, you need to block her."

Amelia tells Lily that more than two-thirds of Americans are on Facebook. "The more people who join, the better chance I have of making important connections. It's the same with the genetic DNA databases. Are you familiar with those?"

"You mean like Ancestry, 23andMe, Lost and Foundlings . . . ?"

She nods, pleased that Lily mentioned the last one. Silas Moss had established Lost and Foundlings back in the 1980s, part of a pioneering autosomal DNA research project aimed toward reuniting adoptees with their biological mothers. Si's mission to help Amelia find her birth parents had never come to fruition, but she'd worked part-time in his molecular biology lab throughout her college years in Ithaca. If Aaron hadn't come along, she'd probably still be there.

Lily shifts her weight. "Wait—you're going to put my DNA into those sites and see if I get any matches?"

"That's part of what I do, yes."

"Do I have to? Because I heard that they do all kinds of freaky sh—stuff with it. They're making human clones from the samples."

It's not the first time a client has brought up that well-traveled conspiracy theory. As always, Amelia acknowledges and respects the privacy concerns but does her best to debunk the myths, reassuring Lily that she only works with reputable companies and that laws regulate how the DNA can be used.

Still, she seems wary.

"I get it," Amelia says. "I do. But foundlings don't have much choice. Without DNA testing, it might be impossible to find out where you came from."

She continues the spiel she gives all her clients, struggling to keep her voice steady.

"Genetic genealogy has taken off over the last few years. Last Christmas quite a few companies offered bargains on autosomal DNA testing kits, and now we're really starting to reap the rewards. Have you ever tried online dating?"

"Not really. Why?" Again, the guarded expression as if Amelia is about to urge her to join a matchmaking website.

"Don't worry, just an analogy. Say there's a new dating app with ten or twelve members to start. Your pool of potential matches is going to be extremely limited, right? But the more people who join, the better your chances of making connections. This is the same. Your odds of finding a biological match increase exponentially as these sites build up their databases. And lately, they've been growing dramatically every day."

"Have you found any matches?"

"Plenty. There's a tab on my website about my clients' success stories, if you want to—"

"No, I mean, for *you*. You've put your DNA out there, right?"

"Oh, it's out there, and it has been for decades."

Out there and will inevitably—or so it's beginning to seem—come back with a match one of these days.

Amelia clears her throat, trying not to look at the ring box still clasped in Lily's hands. "Again, we're not here to talk about my journey. Just know that I understand how it feels to be in your shoes."

"Because you're a foundling, too."

"Exactly."

"When would we do my DNA?"

"Next week, if you decide you want to proceed. I'll give you the information packet and some release forms today. Take it home, look everything over, and let me know if you have any questions. If not, you can scan them and email them back so that I can get this moving on my end."

"Can I . . . I mean, I don't have a scanner. Not right now. I did, but it broke, and I haven't replaced it yet. Sorry."

"Oh, not a big deal. You can just bring the forms to next week's appointment."

"And then what? We'd go to some kind of lab, you said?"

"Oh, no, not for the test. I do it myself, right here, and then it goes to the lab for analysis."

"You do it?" She seems edgy—squeamish, maybe.

"Don't worry, it's just a simple saliva sample. No needles, no blood, nothing like that."

"How long does it take?"

"Less than a minute. You just spit into a little vial, and—"

"I mean, how long for the results?"

"Oh—it varies, but typically, six weeks to a couple of months."

"*Months?* So it's not . . . I mean, I had a test for strep throat last winter and they got the results right there at the clinic before I left."

"It's not the science part of this that takes a long time. It's the human part. The labs are swamped, and there are only so many technicians and machines. Basically, every new sample goes to the end of a long line. I'm no molecular biologist, but the analysis of autosomal DNA is far more complex than checking a throat swab for the presence of streptococcal bacteria. Did you have it, by the way?"

She makes a face. "Yeah. They gave me antibiotics. I was so sick, and I was out of work for over a week, and I lost my job."

"You lost your job! Because you were sick? That's not—that's—What do you do?"

"Oh . . . I . . ." She shifts her weight. "I'm a teacher. I was a teacher. Then."

"I'm pretty sure it's illegal for you to be fired from—"

"No, no, I don't mean I lost my job *because* I was sick. But, um, you know how you look back on some stupid random thing that happened, and it seems like it's the thing that made a lot of other bad stuff happen, even though it didn't?"

Boy, do I ever.

"So now you're unemployed?"

"Yeah. So, anyway . . ." She inhales, exhales, on a shrug. "I had the time to start thinking about my past. And that's how I found you. And I guess if you find my real parents, then that strep throat wasn't a bad thing at all, you know?"

"I do, but . . . I should mention, Lily, going into this search, that what I turn up may not be what you're expecting or hoping to find. Sometimes, it's the opposite. And there's always a chance that I'll hit dead ends no matter where I look."

Lily nods slowly, thoughtfully.

"The other thing is that if I do find living relatives, they might not be receptive to making a connection. Okay? So just keep that in mind. It's a lot, I know."

"Got it."

Before Lily leaves, they make an appointment for the following Thursday. Amelia closes the door after her and leans against it, exhaling at last.

Chapter Three

Interstate 81 bisects New York State, running south from the rolling hills on the Saint Lawrence River to Watertown, along Lake Ontario's eastern shore, then down through Syracuse, where it intersects with the thruway. Traffic picks up there, in the shadow of its industrial cityscape. Rain begins to fall, and the world swims in around him. Strangers' eyes seem to probe him as they whiz past—truckers, commuters, university students. They can't possibly know, he reminds himself, adjusting the windshield wipers as the downpour ebbs to a drizzle.

The kid, slumped in the backseat beneath the quilt, looks like any other sleeping toddler, though he isn't sucking his thumb. That's what he does, what he's done since he was born—always when he's sleeping, and in his waking hours as well.

He's dead. He must be. He'd barely had a pulse when the Angler checked him at a gas station stop nearly an hour ago. He's such a frail thing, it's not surprising that the medication could have been lethal this time.

The Angler remembers how the boy whimpered when he saw the spoon and plastic cup, its foil seal already peeled back. There had been a time when he'd have gobbled the treat, but now he knew that it was no ordinary chocolate pudding, knew that the Angler would command Monique to force-feed it to him. The first time, she'd refused, so the Angler held down the struggling child and jammed the substance down his throat as he choked and gagged. Now she was the one who lifted the spoon with one trembling hand and pried the boy's mouth open with the other, crooning to him in French as tears streamed down both their faces.

He thinks of his wife, Cecile, administering pediatric cough syrup droplet by droplet from a measured oral syringe the last time their son had been sick.

"Don't be so stingy with it," he'd said. *"Give him a little extra so he'll stop hacking and sleep."*

"You mean, so that you can sleep," she'd said with a glare and turned her back, cradling the boy and rocking him like an infant. Pascal is a robust four years old and their daughter, Renee, almost seven. She has her mother's black hair and fair skin, but her towheaded brother looks like the Angler had at that age. So very much like the child in the backseat.

Convenient, with the borrowed passport and all.

Cecile will never notice that he'd snuck it out of the house. She won't need it until next June, when she and the children depart to spend the summer with her parents in Paris.

He clenches the wheel, spotting a green mileage sign ahead. He's reached Cortland, and Binghamton is just forty miles down the road. Both, like Syracuse, are college towns. He needs to get away from them, from all these people, from the highway. He's unsure of the speed limit in kilometers, and the car behind him is tailgating. Because he's going too slowly? Because the driver is onto him? Can it be an unmarked police vehicle?

He veers off the next exit without signaling, and exhales when the other car fails to follow. His nerves are frayed, and exhaustion has caught up with him. The sooner he's rid of the body, the better.

The two-lane road veers southwest past fast-food restaurants, chain hotels, discount stores, and a turnoff toward campus. A little farther on, it's lined with houses. He brakes for several small-town stoplights, noting that a few roofs are tarped, and there are broken branches stacked along the curbs. Must have been a hell of a storm here recently. A flagman waves the traffic to a single lane. He twitches, feeling trapped as he crawls past a bucket truck crew working on damaged trees overhead. He clears that, only to become stuck behind a yellow school bus making every stop to dispatch middle schoolers.

He watches two long-haired girls stroll toward a gas station mini-mart, carrying backpacks that stoop them forward so that their short skirts ride up their thighs.

The bus moves on, and the road opens up at last. Here, it's comfortably rural, winding toward the Finger Lakes and yet another well-populated college town. A signpost warns him that Ithaca is a scant twenty miles from here. He has to get rid of the kid before he gets much closer.

At the moment, he's the only car on the highway. He can't just pull over and dump a corpse, though. Maybe he can find a nice little pond out here, a rowboat he can borrow . . .

Maybe, but not likely. Not in the middle of the day, by any means.

Coming around a bend, he spots a cop car parked on the shoulder. He hits the brakes, curses under his breath, and looks at the speedometer. He'd been going more than seventy kilometers an hour—what's the damned limit here? He holds his breath as he crawls past, feeling the cop's stare. But the dome lights don't glow and spin, and the sedan is still parked there when he finally rounds a curve and loses it in the rearview mirror.

Close call.

He makes the next turn, off the main road onto one dotted with fields and the occasional farmhouse. Too much wide-open space. He needs privacy.

He turns down another, narrower road, a tree-lined, winding country lane littered with fallen leaves. Ah, this is more like it. He slows, spotting a weathered wooden orchard stand off the shoulder ahead. That's the spot.

He pulls over, turns off the engine, and opens the car door. The rain has stopped, and the world is dripping, thick with humming insects and chirping songbirds. Branches bend in a damp breeze, laden with glistening foliage and coppery apples. The dilapidated fruit stand appears forsaken, with no sign of tire tracks in the muddy parking area littered with downed branches. One appears to have taken out a chunk of the stand's slatted roof.

He goes around to the passenger's side and opens his tackle box. Had that customs official decided to look inside, he'd have found the filet knife right on top. Would he have realized that its ten-inch blade is smeared with human blood?

Heart racing, the Angler removes the knife and snaps the lid closed. He needs to get rid of it—not here with the body, but somewhere along the way.

And then, when he's safely back home, he won't be so quick to find a new girl. He'll take some time away from all that. Time for *normal*.

He shoves the knife into his coat pocket and pauses to listen for cars approaching on the road, hearing nothing. He only needs a minute here, perhaps mere seconds, and he'll be on his way.

He opens the door and leans into the backseat. The kid is still and deathly pale. There will likely be no need to finish him off. He would if necessary, but it wouldn't be easy with a child. Especially one who so closely resembles Pascal.

He scoops up the boy. The small, dangling feet scrape along the edge of the car door as he maneuvers to close it, but the child doesn't flinch. He carries the lifeless body toward the trees behind the wooden structure. There, far more gently than is necessary, he sets him on the ground amid rotting fallen fruit. If he's not dead, he's about to be. He's frightfully pale. One bare, filthy foot is now smeared with fresh blood.

Something stirs as the Angler stares down at that pathetic face, now half-obscured by weeds.

Not just because he looks like Monique, or like my son.

Because he looks like me, as I was then.

Vulnerable. Motherless. Alone. Injured. Broken.

Blamed for something over which he had no control.

He doesn't like to look back on his grim childhood. When he does, he prefers to remember just the summer he'd spent in the Laurentians, fishing for northern pike with the only man he'd ever known who hadn't abused or assaulted him.

Hugo had always known just where to sink the bait for that sleek, silvery prey gliding in the reeds below the murky surface; just how to move the line to lure the fish and blindside it with a barbed hook.

"Faites confiance à vos sens," he'd said as if it were that easy.

Just trust your senses.

The Angler would watch in awe as his uncle tossed catch after wriggling catch into a bucket, and he'd salivate at the thought of savoring that tender flesh.

His own job had been to clean the fish. Sometimes, he'd close his eyes, blade in hand, hands slick with guts and blood, and he'd imagine . . .

La bête noire.

The black beast—his father—had died a satisfyingly violent death. Car accident, as opposed to any of the grisly scenarios the Angler had conjured in his darkest hours. The funeral mass had fallen on his own thirtieth birthday, a most welcome gift.

Uncle Hugo had traveled from Quebec to pay his respects. Nearly unrecognizable, having traded worn denim for a dark suit, he'd extended condolences in French and sat apart from the smattering of coworkers and neighbors obligated to mourn a man who hadn't a friend in the world, and didn't deserve one. The elderly priest, who'd inflicted his own brand of cruel tyranny during the Angler's school days, had delivered a perfunctory homily and no eulogy.

After the yawning earth had swallowed his father's coffin, the Angler had followed his uncle all the way back to the Laurentians, keeping a careful distance behind the pickup truck's taillights. He'd felt no affection for the old man after all these years, and no need to reestablish a connection. He only wanted to see the farm again, perched near a rural lake surrounded by forests and mountains.

He'd expected that it, like every other place in the world, would have changed over the years. But the old homestead had appeared just as it had been that summer. He'd prowled the property and crept into the house after his uncle had turned in for the night.

There, too, time had stood still.

In a spartan room at the end of the upstairs hallway, he'd surveyed familiar furniture. The bookcase was still filled with boyhood novels he'd read that summer. On top, he saw the tower of elongated wooden blocks he and Hugo had made to duplicate Jenga, a game the kids were playing back home. The object was to stack the blocks and then take turns removing them one at a time with painstaking care. If the tower falls, you lose.

Standing there years later, he remembered playing the game with his elderly uncle on nights when they weren't out fishing.

His father had refused to let him take the game home to Ottawa with him, just as he'd refused him the boxed toy store set that had been all he'd wanted the Christmas before.

You lose . . . you lose . . .

He'd stared at the worn patchwork quilt he'd needed every night but one that chilly summer, longing to crawl under it and go to sleep—here, on the farm. Longed to stay forever, never go back to his father.

And then he'd realized that his father was dead. And that he was no longer an incorrigible child who'd been kicked out of three schools. He was a man with a full-time factory job and a newly inherited house from which he could finally banish his father's presence.

Another decade has passed since that tentative nocturnal visit. Now the orchards are overgrown, the livestock reduced to a small flock of chickens and roosters, the empty barn stalls surrounded by fallow fields. Uncle Hugo sleeps long and often. His meals are delivered by volunteers from the local church. If he ever happened to spot the Angler prowling about the property, he likely wouldn't remember him, or might—God forbid—mistake him for his dead father. Or his dead father's ghost.

His head echoes with the crack of a belt, angry cursing, slamming doors, breaking glass, terrified whimpers . . .

And then, too late, he hears something else.

Out on the road, some distance away. Not a car, but . . .

The unmistakable clopping of a horse's hooves.

He looks wildly for a place to hide, then remembers the car parked right there in the open. He runs for it, reassured to find the parking area still deserted and the road empty. But someone is coming. He jumps behind the wheel and pulls out onto the road heading in the opposite direction, back from where he came, watching the rearview mirror until the orchard stand disappears around a bend.

Safe. If he didn't see the horseback rider, then the rider didn't see him or the car or the Ontario plates. Only animals are likely to find the boy's body anytime soon, and by the time they're finished with him . . .

He'll no longer bear any resemblance to Pascal, much less to me.

It's over.

For a good long time, anyway. Maybe forever. If he'd been caught back there . . .

Had someone come along in a car, he wouldn't have had time to escape. The driver might have noticed a vehicle parked in the middle of nowhere. Might have stopped to investigate, even, and then . . .

But you weren't caught. You're never caught. You do the catching.

He retraces his route to the highway. The cop is still there, but the Angler notes the speed limit this time and holds the speedometer to it. There are no more school buses.

He spies two familiar long-haired girls outside the mini-mart. Their backpacks are on the ground now, their skirts hiked even higher than before as they straddle a bike rack in a most unladylike fashion, talking while tapping away on their cell phones and slurping tall blue drinks through straws. They look about thirteen, maybe fourteen—Monique's age when he'd first got her.

She'd been glorious then, her skin luminescent; her body taut and supple. He'd marveled that it had sprung back so quickly after pregnancy. Cecile had struggled to reclaim her figure, and to this day bears unsightly traces of childbirth, concealed beneath a well-chosen wardrobe.

Lately, though, he'd noticed that his precious Monique, too, was ripening—not like a pretty pink apple on the bough, but like one that had fallen and begun to stink and rot. Her breasts sagged, her hips had widened; there was an unappealing ridge of fat below her navel. Her face, too, was aging—hardened, sunken, gaunt. Her skin was sallow. Her mouth smelled of decay; her molars were turning black and crumbling. In pain, she'd said she needed a dentist. He'd laughed. As if.

He'd known that their journey together would soon come to an end, though he hadn't expected it to happen so abruptly. He'd assumed there would be time to figure out how best to get rid of her and the boy, even bring in a replacement so that she could teach the newcomer how it goes here.

That's all right. When he finds one, she'll learn on her own, just as Monique had.

He takes one last wistful glance in his rearview mirror at the schoolgirls, and then they vanish.

He'll take a break for a while. Maybe even until next summer, with Cecile and the children safely overseas and cool, languid nights that belong only to him. Nights that are perfect for fishing.

AMELIA HADN'T INTENDED to walk all the way from her office to Sutton Place. But when she'd stepped outside into soft evening air, she couldn't bring herself to descend to the subway. She'd started uptown on foot, needing time alone to digest what had happened this morning, and to discuss it with the one person in her world who would not only grasp its significance, but who knows what it's like to be in her shoes.

Her shoes . . .

Oh, *ouch*, her shoes. Leather pumps weren't made for three-mile urban hikes.

As she walks, she scrutinizes likely strangers and eavesdrops on their conversations, hoping to trigger some innate recognition of her birth mother buried deeply in her subconscious mind. Old habit, though she's well aware of infantile amnesia, the phenomenon that precludes people from remembering their earliest years of life.

Back when Silas Moss informed her that a child can't retain autobiographical memory until at least three or four years of age, Amelia had protested. After all, if the human brain is developed enough for a baby to learn how to talk and a toddler how to walk, shouldn't it be capable of storing a birth mother's face or voice?

Si had gently told her that it is not. *"Talking and walking are procedural memories, my dear, as opposed to episodic memories. Science has yet to fully explain why they differ so drastically, particularly at the very beginning of life, or toward the end."*

A bittersweet truth, especially now that Silas is nearing the end of his, wheelchair bound in a rest home, his memories and brilliant mind corroded by Alzheimer's disease.

As Amelia waits for the light to change at Second Avenue and East Twenty-Third Street, Jessie returns her call.

"Mimi? I got your message. What's up?"

"I found my ring!"

"What? How? Where?"

Jessie doesn't ask "which ring," though Amelia had lost it long before they'd even met.

Someone bumps her from behind as pedestrians brush past her into the crosswalk. The light has changed. She crosses the street and hobbles on, telling Jessie about Lily Tucker.

"What did she say when you told her it was your ring?"

"I didn't tell her. I couldn't say a word, Jess. I—" Hearing the click of an incoming call on Jessie's end, she asks, "Do you have to get that?"

"It's just Billy. Probably telling me he's late coming home, which . . . yeah, I figured that out two hours ago. I'll call him back. Anyway, why didn't you tell her?"

"Because I was shocked. She was basically sitting there holding *my* ring telling me my own story. She said she'd been abandoned as a little girl, and that she'd been wearing the ring the day she was found."

"In New York?"

"Connecticut. She was three or four at the time, she said. She's in her late twenties now—maybe."

"Maybe," Jessie echoes.

Most foundlings never know the precise date or circumstances of their own birth. Amelia celebrates hers on the anniversary of the date Calvin Crenshaw, a quiet, hardworking church janitor, had found infant Amelia in a basket in Harlem's Park Baptist Church. He'd brought her home to Bettina, and they'd kept her, passed her off as their own.

Every year since 1987, Jessie has called her on May 12 to sing "Happy Maybe Birthday to You, Happy Maybe Birthday to You . . ."

"So, Mimi, this Lily person came to you to find her birth parents?"

"Yes, and all I could think was, 'How did you get my ring?'"

"I can't believe you didn't ask her."

"What good would that do? What more could she have told me? It's not like she knows where the ring came from. She doesn't even know where *she* came from. But if I can help her figure it out, it might tell me something about my past, too."

"That's why you should have said something."

"The last thing I want to do is scare her off by making a bizarre accusation—"

"*Claim*, Mimi. Not accusation. Having your ring isn't a crime."

"No, I know. But my new clients are fragile. They've already been through the worst kind of emotional upheaval. They don't need me to add my own to the mix, or complicate matters."

"Have you thought about . . . I mean, she could have been playing you."

Amelia stops walking.

The person behind her slams into her. The hit isn't nearly as jarring as Jessie's comment.

"*Playing* me? What do you mean?"

"You're on TV, Mimi. How many people know about your ring?"

"I've never once mentioned it on the show, or even that I'm a foundling. I'm there as a consultant, not to tell my own story."

"No, but people see it. That info is on your website."

"That I'm a foundling, yes. But nothing about the ring."

"Well, have you ever put the information out there on any database or social media?"

"Yes, I put it out there in the ad, but that was eight years ago."

"Ad?"

"Aaron and I placed it on the Lost and Foundlings website. I must have told you about it." Jessie is her prime confidante when it comes to life-changing moments, day-to-day minutia, and everything between.

"Eight years ago—2008? That's when Theodore came along. I couldn't keep track of what was going on in my own life, let alone anyone else's."

She tells Jessie about the advertisement, which had offered a significant reward for information leading to her birth parents.

"If you mentioned the ring in the ad, what makes you think this Lily Tucker didn't know that when she came to see you?"

Amelia pushes aside misgiving, reminding herself that she'd taken precautions. She isn't stupid. Like a cop withholding crime scene specifics from the press, she'd kept a key detail to herself.

"I'm a good judge of character, Jessie. She's not playing me."

"I hope not. I just worry that you're too vulnerable and trusting. Someone might take advantage of you."

"*You* worry that *I'm* too vulnerable and trusting?" Amelia laughs, shaking her head. "Hey, I'm the New Yorker here."

"Yeah, but I'm the one with the edge. You say it all the time."

"I used to say it, when we were younger. Not anymore." Marriage, motherhood, and career have softened Jessie. She's the kind of woman who doles out therapy on her own time and fosters children and strays.

"Just tread carefully, Mimi. That's all I'm saying."

"I always do."

"Not always. Not when it comes to the past. Sometimes, you have to let it be and focus on the present."

"Easier said than done."

"I know, but—" Her phone clicks with another incoming call. "Crap, it's Billy again."

"Better get it."

"Okay, hang on."

"No, I'll let you go. I'm about to meet Aaron," she says, though she still has quite a ways to go before she reaches Sutton Place.

But she can't take up any more of Jessie's time. Or maybe she just doesn't want to hear any more cautionary advice or doubt that the tiny gold ring is the same one Amelia had lost in Harlem decades ago, and that Lily Tucker is exactly who she claims to be.

A FEW HOURS after checking in to the oceanfront Cuban hotel, Barnes looks at Rob lounging beside him in a low sand chair, puffing a cigar. "You were right, *amigo*."

"You mean *acere*. That's *amigo* here."

"*Amigo* is Spanish."

"Yeah, but there's Spanish-Spanish and then there's Cuban-Spanish," Rob tells him. "You'll see. So what was I right about, *acere*?"

"That this place is incredible. I'm never going back. I'm staying right here."

"In Cuba?"

"In this chair. On this beach. With this . . . what do you call this?" He holds up the hollowed-out coconut.

Rob peers into his own coconut. "Beats the hell out of me. I'm pretty sure it's got papaya in it."

"And rum, and . . . definitely rum."

"Rum. Oh, yeah. Whole lotta rum." Rob sips his drink, dribbling a few drops onto his bare torso.

Barnes watches him swab his lean, sculpted abs with a corner of beach towel. "You sure did get rid of that beer gut you were lugging around. You are cut, brother."

"It's the climbing wall. I'm thinking of putting one in at the house. You should try it."

"Yeah, I don't think it'll fit in my apartment."

Rob smirks. "I mean climbing."

"No, thanks." Rob is one of those people who is forever throwing himself headlong into some newly discovered passion, and wants everyone else—or at least, Barnes—to join him. "Like I said, all I need from here on in is rum, and . . . what's the other thing?"

"Women? Song?"

"Women are nothing but trouble. Song—that's your thing, not mine. Me, I just need rum and this view."

"If you think this is magnificent, you just wait till tomorrow."

They're only spending this first night in Santa Maria del Mar, just outside Havana. In the morning, they're flying on to Baracoa, a remote eastern coastal town that lies in the shadow of a mountain Barnes has no intention of climbing.

"You've got to check out the view from the summit of El Yunque. You'll think you died and went to heaven."

"Put me on a mountain after all this rum, and I won't just be thinking it, I'll be doing it. How 'bout I just take your word for it, Spider-Man?" He sips his drink into a final slurp and looks around for Luis.

When they'd first wandered out to the beach, they'd been taken aback to find a twelve-year-old serving drinks. But Luis seems pretty happy-go-lucky. Even happier and luckier after Rob handed him a hundred-dollar tip to set them up with the sand chairs at the water's edge and fetch a trio of cocktails from the pool bar.

The third chair has remained empty, and Barnes and Rob had split the drink meant for Kurtis. He'd said he would come down in a little while, but that had been a long while ago.

Over by the pool, Luis is shooting the warm, briny, flower-scented breeze with Ana Benita, the gorgeous brunette female bartender, and a suave older gentleman with a thin mustache.

Barnes had shaved his around the same time he'd quit smoking. Now he's rethinking both those decisions. Rethinking everything.

He lifts his coconut cup and waggles two fingers at Luis. The boy nods, grins, and says something to Ana Benita. She turns and gives Barnes a languid, appreciative look, as women tend to do.

That's not his ego's perception, just the story of a life in which nothing has ever come easily, except the opposite sex.

He turns back to gaze out at the water. It shimmers gold in the late day sun, dotted with fishing boats, battered buoys, and fat white floating seabirds. "Geez. Remember New York?"

"Yeah."

"It sucks, doesn't it? Why does anyone even live there? Why doesn't everyone just . . ." He gestures with his coconut. ". . . live here?"

"Plenty of people do."

"Everyone should. I should."

"Your apartment is in New York. Your job is in New York. Your whole life is—"

"My whole life isn't my apartment and my job. There are other apartments. Other jobs. Other places."

"Placessessssss?" Rob mocks his slur.

"Come on, I'm serious." *Sssssserioussssss . . .*

Yeah, he's well on his way to wasted.

"I get it, man. I told you, the first time I came to Cuba, I felt this kinship. And now that I know what I know about my family here?" Rob pauses to exhale a pungent Cohiba cloud. "I just want to keep digging and finding surprises."

A year ago, one of Rob's hip-hop musician pals had done a guest segment on a genealogy television show *The Roots and Branches Project*. He'd introduced Rob to the host, Nelson Roger Cartwright, and the next thing you knew, Rob was taping an episode himself.

"I don't know if it's kinship I'm feeling," Barnes says, stretching his legs so that the turquoise tide licks his bare toes. "I'd say it's just more of a buzz."

"Yeah, that, too. But you've got roots here, just like me. And in this life, there's nothing more important than that. It's like I keep trying to tell Kurtis. You've got to know where you belong. Know who you are. *Why* you are."

Barnes remains silent, thinking of his daughter. What if she decides to find out who she is?

Why she is?

Two strangers walk into a bar . . .

If there's anything his work has taught him, it's that some family mysteries are better left unsolved.

"What about that DNA test I gave you for Christmas?" asks Rob, whose newfound fascination had him handing out genealogy kits last December like a mall Santa with candy canes.

Barnes shifts in his chair. Speak of the devil.

The devil being the vial into which he'd finally spit a saliva sample after Rob had nagged him about it all year.

"I can't believe you're bringing that up again," Barnes says. "You know damned well it could open the door to all kinds of complications for me."

"You're worried there might be a twenty-nine-year-old girl—*woman*—out there looking for you, right? But this is about finding your ancestors, not your descendants finding you."

"No, that's what it's about for *you* because you know where your descendants are. They know where you are. You married their mother. It's different for me."

"You don't want to be found, then, is that it?"

"No. I mean . . . I don't know if I do. But once my DNA is out there, I can't change my mind."

"You're crazy, Barnes. Your kid is Kurtis's age. All they care about is right here, right now. Themselves. If your kid wanted to find you, she'd have done it a long time ago. She doesn't need to order some fancy science kit. It's not like you're hiding. You have the same name, live in the same city, have the same job."

True.

But . . .

"I'd be a lot easier to find if my DNA is in a public database."

"So you're going to let that stop you from finding out where you came from."

"What I want to know is where I'm going . . . and right now, I'm not interested in going anywhere at all." He wiggles his toes in the warm seawater. Somewhere down the beach, a guitarist is picking out "Guantanamera," faint strains rising and falling between the waves. "Anyway, I already know my father's family was Cuban and Jamaican. My mother's ancestors came from Africa in the 1800s."

"Not by choice."

Barnes shakes his head. "No, definitely not."

During Rob's episode of *The Roots and Branches Project*, he'd wept when the show's genealogist presented him with antebellum records revealing that his third great-grandfather had been sold at a Georgia auction to a Virginia plantation owner in 1858. He'd been twelve years old, and had never seen his parents and siblings again.

"I know it's tough, brother, to face what our ancestors went through," he tells Barnes. "But don't you think you owe it to them to find them? I can put you in touch with the investigative genealogist I worked with on the show. She specializes in this stuff."

"Thanks, but no thanks. I spend every working day of my life looking for real people. I'm not interested in adding more to the list, especially when they've been dead for a hundred years, and I'm not getting paid for it."

"All I'm saying is that you should—"

"Rob! Enough." He shoots him a sideways glance. "Anyway, I already sent in the sample over the summer."

"Well, great! Good for you!" Rob pats his arm. "Did you get your results yet?"

"No. When I do, I'll let you know. Until then, case closed." Barnes leans back, feet digging into the wet sand until the tide swings in to wash it out from beneath them, exposing his toes and scattering shell shards in its wake. He scoops up a small, intact white one.

"That's a conch," Rob tells him. "The meat makes great fritters. We can get some for dinner at a little *paladar* I know, just down the beach."

A *paladar*, Barnes has learned, is a family-owned restaurant here in Cuba, as opposed to those that are run by the government.

He runs his fingertips along the shell's satiny pink lining, wondering whether its former occupant had chosen to move on, or been deep fried and served with dipping sauce.

Wondering whether his daughter might one day, years from now, care about her roots. She'll find him, or maybe just his name on a splintered branch of her family tree.

He shoves the shell into his pocket and the thought to the back of his mind as Luis arrives with the round of fresh rum drinks. Chatting with him in Spanish, Barnes learns that he doesn't have a mother, and his fisherman father is gone for days at a time. At twelve, he's pretty much on his own.

Barnes watches him walk away like he hasn't a care in the world.

"Maybe it really is time to get out of New York."

"You gave Sully hell when she left."

Sully—Sullivan Leary, his former partner.

"We're not talking about *Sully*. She moved to the middle of nowhere. This is *somewhere*."

He gestures at the wide beach, bordered by a stretch of pastel hotels populated by tourists and locals who'd spent the afternoon swimming and sunning nearby. Now that they've gone, it's peaceful, cast in a haze of late day sun and rum. Paradise. Not like Main Street, USA, where his former partner now lives, that's for damned sure.

"You know what I think, Barnes? I think you wish you'd gone with her."

"Okay, number one"—he counts off on his index finger—"this isn't about her and I don't wish that because the woman drove me crazy. She's nothing but trouble. And number two—"

"See, you admit it! She drove you crazy."

"Not in a good way."

"Yeah, in a bad one. You wanted her, *bad.*"

Barnes goes on, talking over him, "And (B) she didn't ask me. And I wouldn't have if she had."

"*B?* You mean, two."

"Right. She didn't ask me *to.*"

Rob grins. "You, my friend, are wasted."

Maybe. But Barnes doesn't want to think about Sully or the life he left behind. He's finally found the kind of place where you can lose yourself. Right now, that sounds like a damned good idea.

Chapter Four

"**S**ergeant Hanson?"

The attending physician emerges from behind the curtain and strides toward him. She's petite, with a bouncy black ponytail, and had introduced herself on her way in. What was her name? Dr. . . . something.

He stands, wiping chocolate-flecked golden crumbs from his navy uniform pants, almost expecting a reprimand from the physician. But she's not Dr. Varma, the cardiologist who's been keeping tabs on him since his chest pain episode just after Labor Day. This woman's only concern is the little boy on the other side of the curtain.

"How is he, Dr. . . . ?" He can't make out the name tag on her blue scrubs. Something that begins with a *B*. Maybe an *E*.

"Handler."

H? He squints at her name tag. Still looks like a *B* or an *E* to him.

Terrific. His eyesight is going, along with his memory and his ticker. Possibly his hearing as well. He can't always make out what sportscasters and actors are saying on TV, but Stevie Nicks's throaty voice is loud and clear in his head, crooning about how time makes you bolder and children get older. He's always loved that song, but hadn't grasped the lyrics until he'd turned fifty last year.

At this age, his own father only had a few years left. He, too, had been an accomplished athlete before the pounds piled on. He, too, had been a cop with the Ithaca Police Department.

You have to take care of yourself. No more candy bars.

He tucks the wrapper into his pocket with a mental note to toss it before he gets home. He knows what his wife would have to say about the candy bar he just scarfed down. But it's long past suppertime, he's famished, and the lunch she'd packed him had consisted of fewer green grapes than he has fingers, and a Tupperware container filled with what appeared to be wilted weeds. Plus, seriously, how often do you find a Zagnut in a vending machine?

"The boy is stable and alert," Dr. Handler is saying. "His vitals are good."

"How old do you think he is?"

"About three, give or take."

"That's what I thought." He writes it on his report beneath the physical description he'd jotted earlier. Fair skin, slender build, blond hair, and the bluest eyes he's ever seen—same shade as his favorite pair of jeans. The ones his twenty-year-old daughter had recently informed him are too bright.

"Dark denim is in style now, Dad," she'd said the last time she'd visited. "And those are cut way too wide in the legs."

"That's because *I'm* cut way too wide in the legs. And everywhere else."

"Next time I come home, I'll go shopping with you. We'll get you some fashionable stuff."

He'd looked at his wife, who'd laughed. "Come on, don't you want to be fashionable?"

"You, too, Mom. Time to lose the cargo pants."

"But . . . they're comfortable. And they have lots of pockets."

"Ugh. They're so 2012."

"I got them in 1996," she'd said after their fashionista had sailed out of the room. "Same year we got her."

"I think my jeans are older than that. Kids. One minute, we're changing their diapers and the next—"

"Don't you dare say they're changing ours!"

He'd laughed and put his arm around her. "I was going to say, the next, they're telling us we don't know anything about anything."

"Maybe they're right."

"They are. But we can never let on."

He sees Dr. Handler check her cell phone, bristling like she's about to dash away.

"Is the boy talking yet?" he asks her.

"No."

"Maybe he doesn't speak English."

"He seemed to understand me when I asked him to stick out his tongue and sit up."

"So is it that he can't talk, or do you think he's . . . you know, dumb? Sorry—that can't be the politically correct phrase, but . . . what is?"

"I refer to patients with this particular disability as nonverbal."

"Do you see a lot of them?"

"Very few. In this case, I'm inclined to suspect PTSD with selective mutism, depending on what happened to the child leading up to being discovered."

He jots that on his incident report. "PTSD—so he went through some kind of trauma?"

"At this age, just being separated from a caregiver can be traumatic. The sooner we can find his parents, the better." Dr. Handler looks at her phone again. "I'm sorry, Sergeant, I have a patient waiting to be discharged."

"Can you just give me another minute? The more you can tell me about this little boy, the better chance I have of finding out where he belongs."

"Is this part of the investigation? Or out of the goodness of your heart?"

"Both," he admits, and jumps back as paramedics rush past, pushing a bloody man on a gurney. A sobbing woman trails behind, grasping for him and wailing.

"Let's step into that office," Dr. Handler suggests, and leads the way into a closet-sized room. She flips on a light and closes the door. "I'd ask you to have a seat, but . . ." Both chairs are stacked with cardboard cartons, as is the desk and a good portion of the floor. "Medical equipment. It was delivered yesterday, but it's been too chaotic for anyone to unpack it and put it away. Happens a lot around here. Short staff, budget cuts."

"Happens everywhere. Especially CPS. You probably know how that goes."

"Oh, yes." She shakes her head.

Child Protective Services had promised to send someone over to the hospital for further assessment, but they, too, are overwhelmed tonight. The administrator who'd fielded the phone call had been pleased to hear that the Hansons are available to serve as emergency fosters if need be.

"That will help expedite things. We've worked with you and your wife enough times to know that he'll be in good hands. Are you sure, though? Because you'd said you were going to take a break for a couple of years."

"We were, but . . . this case is special. There's just something about this kid . . ."

"Enough said. We'll have someone there as soon as possible. Probably an hour or so."

More than two have passed since then.

He sets the clipboard on a waist-high stack of boxes, pen poised to write, and looks up at Dr. Handler. "Anything you can tell me about the child's condition that might help identify him?"

She flips through her file. "He's extremely pale, with poor muscle tone, but he doesn't appear to be malnourished. No head trauma. He has a few bruises and an open cut on his foot. Nothing that screams deliberate mistreatment, though. Kids that age—they fall, learning to ride a bike or climbing where they shouldn't, you know?"

"Oh, I know. I've got three of them. Not that age anymore, but . . . believe me, I know."

She nods, flipping a page. "Another thing—the child is filthy. His pajamas are caked in dirt. He's not wearing shoes. You said he was found on a farm?"

"Yes. I was in the area on speed patrol when the call came in. Levi Stoltzfus—do you know him?"

"No."

"He lives out on Cortland Hollow Road, has a big farm with an orchard. His wife, Anna, makes the best apple butter you'll ever taste, by the way. They'll have a table at the Apple Harvest Festival this weekend if you want to sample it yourself." His stomach rumbles in appreciation. "Anyway, that's where the boy turned up, by the old fruit stand. Levi was there to do some repairs—guess he had quite a bit of damage from that storm last week. He found the boy unconscious on the property, scooped him up, and went to the gas station to call for help."

"No cell phone?"

"Levi's Amish. A lot of people who live out in that area are. He was driving a buggy, so it took some time for him to reach a phone, even though his horse is a standardbred."

"Meaning?"

"Meaning it used to be a racehorse. A lot of the Amish use them, according to my teenaged son—he's obsessed with them."

"That's unusual."

"Obsessed with racehorses, not with the Amish," he explains, not adding that his kid has more than his share of unusual obsessions. "By the time I got on the scene, the boy was waking up. Groggy, not talking, seemed dazed. We're canvassing the area, but there aren't a lot of houses in walking distance of where he was found. No one recognizes him and no one has reported a missing child. There's a campground about two miles away, and we thought he might have wandered over from there, but the place isn't even open yet. Too early in the season."

"Two miles is a long way for a child that age to wander. And if he did walk that far, not wearing shoes, he'd probably have more than just one fairly superficial cut on one foot."

"I know. It's like he dropped out of the sky like a

baby bird. We've put out an APB, and we're checking the missing child databases. Nothing yet, but if—"

He breaks off as Dr. Handler's cell phone buzzes.

"Sorry, I have to get this."

She answers her call. He checks his own phone and finds a text that reads only, ETA?

Soon, I hope, he types back. Still waiting for—

He curtails the text as the doctor's terse conversation ends. "Okay, I'll be right there," she says, and hangs up. "I'm sorry, Sergeant Hanson, but I really have to dash."

"I appreciate your time. Do you think he'll be released tonight? Or do you need to admit him?"

"Ideally, he'll be released. We're waiting on CPS and a pediatric psych consult, but as you know, it's probably going to be a while."

"Can I see him?"

"Sure, go on in." She gives a little wave and disappears.

He deletes the second half of his text, hits Send, and heads back out into the corridor.

Crises are playing out in every direction. For many, the night will end in healing; for some, uncertainty; for a few, tragedy.

Which will it be for the lost little boy?

Poking past the curtain, he sees that the child's eyes are closed, his face pale as the pillow beneath his shaggy blond hair. His right thumb is in his mouth. A plump redheaded nurse in pink scrubs adjusts a tube in his scrawny left arm.

"IV fluids for nourishment and hydration," she says, seeing him without needing to look up, as women have a way of doing.

"Is he asleep?"

"He was awake just a second ago." She leans over the bed. "Sweetie? You okay?"

His heart stops the way it had when his own kids were toddlers, sleeping so soundly that he wasn't sure they were breathing. How many times had he poked them in their cribs to make sure, risking the wrath of a terrible two-year-old?

The nurse gives the blond hair a little pat and shrugs. "I think he's just resting."

Her tone makes it clear she doesn't think that at all.

"Um . . ." He tries to make out the nurse's name tag.

"Chess," she says with a smile. "Like the game. My full name is Francesca, but nobody calls me that."

"Mine is Willard. Like the . . . uh, guy in the horror movie about the man-eating rats—that's what my wife said when we met. She hasn't called me by my name since."

"What does she call you?"

"For the most part, you don't want to know," he says with a wry grin, and she laughs. "So how is this little guy doing?"

"Oh, he's terrific. We were having a nice little chat right before you came in."

"He was *talking*?"

"Not quite." She goes back to the IV tubes. "But I was telling him about my little boy, and how much he loves nursery rhymes. I sang a few and I thought he might join in. He didn't, but he smiled, like he knows them. Right, sweetie? Like this one—'*Mary had a little lamb, its fleece was white as snow . . .*'"

Ah, a ripple of awareness under the pale eyelids as she sings.

Someone shouts for help down the hall. Running footsteps, commotion.

This is no place for a frightened little boy.

Chess does her best to drown out the chaos as she works on him, singing "Jack and Jill," "Hickory, Dickory Dock," and "Baa Baa Black Sheep."

"There we go. All set for now," she says, finished with the IV. "I've got to move on to another patient. Did Dr. Handler tell you we're waiting on a psych consult?"

"She did. And a caseworker, too."

"That's going to be a while. Are you sticking around?"

"I am. My wife and I have volunteered to be emergency fosters if he's released before we find out where he belongs."

"That's a nice thought, but there's a lot of red tape to get approved for something like that."

"We're already certified. We've worked with CPS quite a bit."

"Fostering?"

He nods. "We've had quite a few kids over the years, and we adopted our youngest son through the system."

"That's a beautiful thing. The world needs more people like you."

"Really, more like my wife. She's the one who got us involved in this, years ago."

"I admire that. So many people are only interested in helping themselves these days. All right, make yourself comfy and I'll check back soon, but holler if you need me."

Chess disappears around the curtain.

"So, kiddo . . . you like nursery rhymes, huh?"

The boy is still. Asleep?

He keeps talking anyway, just in case he's in there somewhere, alone and frightened and needing reassurance.

"I happen to know a few nursery rhymes, too. I can't carry a tune, but they're not all set to music, are they?"

He reels off "Little Miss Muffet" and a few others he remembers from a Mother Goose book he used to read the kids—"Little Jack Horner," "Little Bo Peep," "Three Little Kittens." He's not sure, but the boy's eyelids might have fluttered a few times.

"Little. Why are so many nursery rhymes about *little*? That's what I want to know."

He reaches out to touch his shoulder. The child flinches and jerks his thumb from his mouth. His eyes open, and then close again.

"Where'd you get those beautiful blue eyes, kiddo? Oh, that reminds me of another good one for you. How about 'Little Boy Blue'?"

He recites it, sensing that the child is paying close attention.

". . . where is the boy who looks after the sheep? Under the . . ." He trails off as if he's forgotten the rest. "Under the . . . um . . . under the . . ."

The child's lips move. No sound comes out, but he mouths *haystack*.

So you are in there, aware. And someone read you a nursery rhyme somewhere in your past. Maybe someone who loved you.

The thumb is back in his mouth, and he's sucking it feverishly.

"How do you know that story, little guy? Who told it to you? Your mom, maybe?"

But it could have been the nurse. Just now, before he'd returned to the room. The recognition doesn't necessarily mean he has a mother who loves him.

Maybe you just want to believe that, for the child's sake.

A tear slips past the fringe of blond lashes and slides down the boy's pale cheek.

"It's going to be okay," he whispers, touching that fragile little shoulder. This time, the child doesn't flinch. "I'm here for however long you need me."

JESSIE HAS NEVER encountered a child who won't eat egg noodles, white bread, or chocolate pudding, but she'd recently rid her pantry of all three so that Billy wouldn't be tempted to indulge.

She'd dashed out for what was supposed to have been a quick supermarket stop, but it's impossible to leave Wegmans without a cartful of groceries and running into everyone you've ever known. Not fun when you're wearing ancient jeans that keep sagging down your hips because you didn't have time to find a belt, and you haven't picked up a brush since this morning.

Catching a glimpse of herself in the rearview mirror, she sees that her short, dark hair is slicked and spiky from the rain, and her eyeliner has smudged around her lashes. Precisely the look she'd been going for as a teenager in the '80s, but as a middle-aged mom? Not so much.

Thunder rumbles as she turns up North Cayuga Street and into her driveway. Home.

As a little girl growing up in the quaint gingerbread house next door, she'd thought this place, three stories with turrets and a mansard roof, looked like a cartoon mansion from which bats and ghosts would swoop as the clock gonged midnight. That was before the owner, Professor Silas Moss, covered the gloomy peeling paint with a fresh coat that had dismayed the neighborhood, especially her parents—which had in turn delighted Jessie.

"When he said yellow, I thought he meant a muted shade of ochre or vintage mustard, something like that," her mother had said, gaping out the window.

Her father had lowered the shade. *"I don't think Big Bird Yellow is in the historically accurate palette."*

Thereafter, Jessie had seen Si not as an aging neighbor, but as a kindred spirit. The garish yellow house had been her second home—and then simply *home*, after he'd moved out fifteen years ago.

She'd thought Billy might be back by now, but his car isn't here and the first-floor windows are dark. At least now she has time to pull herself together, get supper started, and warn Theodore. She sees lamplight in his bedroom window at the back of the house and a silhouette at the desk.

She grabs as many shopping bags as she can carry, along with the library book she'd picked up on the way home. It's about the *Titanic*, to help her better relate to an anxiety-ridden young therapy patient who's obsessed with the century-old disaster.

"It's common for kids to fixate on something when they're dealing with anxiety," she'd told his worried mother.

"Yes, like video games, or basketball . . . But a ship that sank a hundred years ago? Isn't that strange?"

"Not by a long shot," she'd said, and shared her own son's latest random passion for horse racing.

Inside the house, she flips the light switch with her elbow. No space for the bags on the cluttered countertops, so she dumps them on the floor, shouting, "Theodore? Can you come help me? It's about to pour again!"

Silence above. No surprise there. Chip and Petty, too, had often had selective hearing when it came to helping.

And you don't spring disruption on Theodore when he's doing his homework. Or ever, really.

I have to warn him before—

The lights flicker. Uh-oh. Jessie scurries back out for another load, glancing at the black storm clouds descending like a funeral veil. How much more rain, she wonders, can the leaky mansard roof take? Last night, she'd counted far more drips than there were strategically arranged third-floor buckets, and far too few emergency savings account dollars to repair the roof, let alone replace it. Another Ithaca winter is bearing down, with so much snow that it will be a miracle if the roof doesn't give way under the weight.

How many people had warned her and Billy against buying this place? Not just for the proximity to her parents' house, but because it was—is—five thousand square feet of fixer-upper.

I just couldn't let it go, though. I couldn't let strangers live here.

She'd had no problem when her parents sold her childhood home next door and moved away. She never had been able to shake the memory of what had happened there back in 1987.

Leaving the groceries on the floor, she hurries up the enclosed back stairway that had been used for servants in another century—not the one prior to this. The treads are steep and worn, the bulb long burnt out on a ceiling so high that replacing it is a death-defying feat. The house dates back to the 1870s, with original woodwork, tile, windows, doors, and fixtures—and the endless repairs that accompany them.

Theodore's room at the top of the flight had been built as a library. Overlooking the backyard and running the width of the house, it's spacious and inviting, with a marble fireplace, deep window seats, and two walls of built-in bookshelves.

Jessie and Billy had considered making it a master suite but had taken the smaller room at the head of the stairs instead, adjacent to their two older children. Petty had chosen the light-drenched turret room with the bay window seat. Chip had wanted the room with the "treasure cave"—a panel in the back wall of his closet that lifted off to access the ancient tub plumbing in the adjacent bathroom.

Chip had been six then, Petty going on five. Now he's got two more semesters at the University of Vermont; she has two years left at Northeastern. Jessie suspects that neither will ever be coming home again for a significant length of time.

Thank goodness they have Theodore. He'd been seven years old when he came to them; eight when they'd nearly given up on him; nine when they realized they couldn't let him go. Though hardly the only needy child who'd ever tugged at their heartstrings, Theodore is the only one they were meant to adopt.

His bedroom door is ajar, but that's not necessarily intentional. In this house, doors occasionally swing open and closed of their own accord. "Not haunted," Si had told her years ago. "Just old and off-kilter. Kind of like me."

She peeks in and sees her son sitting at his desk, typing on his computer. "Theodore? I need to talk to you."

"I'm doing my English homework. This is a stupid poem." He doesn't break the clacking rhythm. An open textbook sits to the left of the keyboard and a spiral notebook to the right, with three sharpened pencils aligned parallel to each other and the page.

"You're writing a poem?"

"No. Some lady did, and I have to analyze it."

"What is it? Who wrote it?"

"I told you, a lady."

"Does she have a name?"

"Everyone has a name."

She gives him a look, and he glances down at the book. "Her name is Emily Dickinson. The poem is about hope."

Jessie smiles. "Is it '"Hope" is the thing with feathers'?"

"You know this stupid poem?"

"I happen to love that stupid poem." She crosses the threshold into the only unfailingly orderly room in the house. Theodore's twin bed is made, his dirty clothes tucked into the hamper, clean ones organized in his drawers and closet. None of his shirts have buttons. Theodore hates buttons.

"Why do you love it? It doesn't make any sense. How can hope have feathers? And it isn't a *thing*, and things have feathers—like Petty's fancy bed, and Espinoza." Named after Theodore's favorite jockey, Espinoza is his pet rooster, and the root of her son's latest troubles.

"It isn't a *tangible* thing that you can see and touch. But the poem is a metaphor, Theodore. Do you want me to help you with it?"

She knows the answer before it comes, decisive as always.

"No. I can do it."

"What about French?"

"What do you mean?"

"Did you study for your French test tomorrow?" Foreign language is by far his worst subject.

"Not yet."

"Do you want me to—"

"No."

"Any other tests tomorrow?"

"Health ed. But I don't have to study. I'm great in that class."

Lightning flashes beyond the window.

"Better save your work, in case we lose power again."

Old house, old city, old trees, old wires. The electricity goes out a lot around here.

"The Wi-Fi isn't working."

"From last night's storm, or this one?"

"Don't know. I'm connected to the internet on my cell phone's Bluetooth hotspot. Can you call the repairman?"

"Yes, as soon as I get a chance."

Standing behind him, she resists the urge to smooth the tuft of hair sticking up on the back of his head. She learned early on that you don't touch him without warning or permission. And that sometimes, when you do touch him, he craves a squeeze so fierce that anyone else would scream. For him, it brings comfort.

"Theodore, I need you to stop typing for a minute and turn around so that I can tell you something."

She sees him clench and hesitate before he swivels in his chair.

He'd been an adorably roly-poly, round-faced little boy, but the extra pounds padding his frame now create an awkward bulk. His chin and jawline have all but disappeared, and his tee shirt clings to the rolls around his midsection. Angry red pimples spray his cheeks and forehead around the rims of his glasses, and a sparse slash of dark hairs lines his upper lip. His hair, once a sleek, golden cap, puffs out like a dandelion gone to seed. He balks about getting it cut, about shaving, washing his face, wearing new clothes that fit . . .

Let it go. Choose your battles.

It's just that the other kids wouldn't tease him so mercilessly if he took better care of himself or allowed her to.

Oh, come on, yes, they would. They always have.

It isn't about how he looks, though that doesn't help matters.

It's about his inability to fit in socially due to obstacles that accompany his particular diagnosis.

She'd had plenty of career experience with children on the spectrum before Theodore came along, but she'd never raised one. Compared to what she's been through so far with him, getting Chip and Petty through adolescence was like cruise control on a deserted country straightaway. Their mood swings and boundary-pushing escapades were nothing she hadn't expected, seen before, or done herself.

But Theodore?

Every day, it seems, he's waging battles on new fronts, from communication frustrations to academic challenges to severe sensory overload that can leave him in a crumpled heap.

Every day, she does for Theodore what she's done for her other children: embrace him for who he is, celebrate his gifts, protect him, love him. Yet she's also determined to show her son, and the world, that what some persist in referring to as his disability is a difference.

"Everyone is different, and everyone has their struggles, no matter how cool they appear to be on the outside," she frequently assures him.

Like me. I act as though I have all the answers, because that's what you need from me, and it's what Diane did.

When you've been raised by the most flawless woman in the world, after having been abandoned by a horribly flawed one, what kind of mother do you become? One who strives for perfection, ever aware of the gross imperfection inherent in your DNA.

"What's wrong?" Theodore asks, focusing on something over her shoulder as he often does when she's about to tell him something he doesn't want to hear.

"Dad called a little while ago. He's bringing someone home with him later."

Theodore stares fiercely at his bookshelves.

The titles are sorted not in alphabetical order or according to genre, but by size and color. Novels flank textbooks and children's picture books. Some had resided here long before Theodore had come along, when the majority of shelves had housed his siblings' trophy collections. Theodore scours tag sales for tall, skinny books with orange spines, or short, thick books with purple spines . . . whatever he "needs" to add to the rows on his shelves. It doesn't matter what's between the covers; he'll never open them. He just collects books the way other boys his age collect baseball cards.

Or girlfriends. That had been Chip's primary interest at fifteen. He hadn't been particularly mature for his age, but his brother seems years younger. The opposite sex isn't on Theodore's radar yet. Nor does he care about sports, friends, cars, a part-time job.

For Chip and Petty, those things had always come without a struggle. For Theodore, nothing ever will.

Chip had excelled at sports from the first time Billy tossed him a ball in the backyard. Intent on keeping up with her big brother, Petty had been a soccer standout and champion swimmer.

Theodore doesn't play sports or even watch televised games with Billy, unless you count the horse racing. Billy does not.

In August, they'd sat through hours of televised Saratoga races. When Theodore wasn't complaining about race coverage that had been preempted by the Summer Olympics, he was providing ongoing running commentary. Mostly, he was reciting from memory the statistics he's compiled in marble notebooks that occupy the entire top shelf in this room.

"I just don't get it," Billy told her privately. "It's not like the kid's an equestrian or has even been to Saratoga. Why the fascination?"

"It's his thing. Just roll with it."

"You know, Jess, if our lives had a theme, it's 'just roll with it.'"

"And that's why I love you. Nobody rolls with anything—everything—in this crazy world the way you do, Billy."

Theodore's eyes narrow as he processes what she told him, but they don't make contact with her own as he asks, "Who is Dad bringing home with him?"

She keeps her voice level and measures her words. "I know I told you we weren't going to be having any more foster kids for a while, but—"

"No!"

"—this is an emergency."

"No! No more foster kids!"

"Theodore, I know it's not what you want, but this little boy won't be here for long. He doesn't have anywhere else to go. He needs help."

"There are a lot of other places to go for help. He can go to the hospital. They help people. He can go to the police station. They help people. He can go to school. They help people. He can go to—"

"Theodore. He's coming here. He needs our help."

"I can't help him. I have to do my homework."

"And you can do your homework. This isn't going to change that. Everything will be"—she stops herself short of claiming things will be the same—"fine," she says instead. "Everything will be fine. You'll be fine."

"I have to do my homework," he repeats. "And I have to sleep in my bed. And then I have to make my bed, and eat my breakfast, and—"

"You can do all the things you have to do, Theodore. This little boy won't bother you."

She hopes he won't, anyway. She knows nothing about him, other than what Billy told her in their brief conversation.

It's not great timing. Not with Theodore's situation. But if Billy wants to shelter a child in need, there's no way she's going to say no. Not after all the yeses she's wheedled out of him over the years. Not after all the . . . rolling with it.

Theodore shifts his gaze to the ceiling, rocking in his seat, and for a moment, she thinks he's focused on the hard rain pattering overhead. Then he asks, "What about Espinoza?"

"What about him, sweetie?"

"I don't want the boy to see him or touch him."

"Don't worry. He'll be fine, too. Everything will be fine."

"You already said that."

"I know." She sighs. "Go back to your homework. I just wanted to let you know so that you won't be surprised if someone is here when you wake up in the morning."

"I have to make my bed. I have to eat my breakfast . . ."

"I know, sweetheart." She smiles at him. He doesn't smile back. Not this time, but once in a while he surprises her. Unlike Theodore, she likes surprises.

Surprises . . .

She heads back downstairs and puts away the groceries, thinking of Mimi.

Of course, her friend wants to believe that a new client showed up with the prized possession she'd lost back in 1987, but seriously, what are the odds? This Lily Tucker might be trying to take advantage of her. Nobody knows better than Jessie that when you desperately want to believe in something, find something—*someone*—all rationale flies out the window.

She drags a chair over to the old brown cabinets and climbs up to cram four boxes of cereal onto a crowded shelf. She closes the door. It swings back open again. She rearranges the cereal, trying to get the cupboard to stay closed, but it refuses until she removes two of them. Old house, old cabinets, old everything—including a landline phone that rarely rings anymore unless it's a robocaller.

I should just call Mimi right now.

She drags the chair to the refrigerator, shoves the cereal boxes on top, climbs down, and picks up the receiver. No dial tone.

Oh. Right. Theodore had mentioned the Wi-Fi is out. It must have impacted the landline as well.

She finds her cell phone and dials her friend's number. After a moment, the call is declined with an automated message: "Can't talk right now—I'll call you later."

Jessie hopes that for now, Mimi has forgotten all about the ring.

I get it. I understand how badly you want to know who you are . . .

So do I. But maybe you're better off not knowing.

Rain streams down the windows, thunder booms, and the lights flicker. Jessie heads for the basement. She has way too much to do before the new foster child arrives, and electricity is necessary for all of it.

Why, she wonders as she moves wet, clean sheets from the washing machine to the dryer, do she and her husband seem to attract so many lost souls? Maybe it's because they've both been there themselves, one way or another.

She'd grown up well aware that her parents were Good Samaritans who'd adopted her after she'd been found alone in the gorge on a frigid January night. They'd loved her. Because they were—are—wonderful people: supportive parents, welcoming in-laws, doting grandparents, not to mention successful Ivy League professors and ideal next-door neighbors.

"I'll babysit the kids while you plant your annuals," Diane would offer in July—as if planting annuals had even occurred to Jessie, while Diane's petunias had been blooming across the hedgerow since Mother's Day.

"Let me string your Christmas lights," Al would say around mid-December, when his had already been twinkling on the shrubs next door for two cheery weeks and Jessie hadn't gotten around to tossing the Thanksgiving leftovers.

"How can you resent them? They're trying to help," Billy had said in the beginning. But as time went on, he, too, had become awed—and agitated—by their flawlessness.

"How is your father's lawn not covered in leaves?" he'd asked the first October in the new house.

"He rakes."

"Me, too, but ours is always covered again right after." He'd gestured at their own yard, buried under foliage, and then at the unblemished green expanse next door. "Does your dad have magical powers?"

"My mom does. She just whipped up homemade peanut butter cups for her trick-or-treaters."

"Too bad she didn't make them for ours, too."

"She offered. I told her we're capable of buying our own Halloween candy." She'd held up a container—not a ceramic pumpkin-faced platter like her mother's, but a dishwasher-warped plastic Tony the Tiger cereal bowl. But it was clean. And orange, dammit.

Billy had peered at the individually wrapped disks. "Are those . . . breath mints?"

"The store was out of candy by the time I got there."

"So the kids get to go from homemade chocolates to Certs? Man. It's not easy living next door to perfectionists."

"Try being raised by them."

Imperfect Jessie had been secretly—and guiltily—relieved when her parents had retired and sold their home to a young couple with children Chip and Petty's ages. For years, a happy brigade of kids and pets had worn a path between the border hedges and traipsed muddy footprints throughout both houses.

These days, all is quiet. A little too quiet for her taste.

Not for long, though, with a little lost boy on the way, and Theodore protesting.

He'll adapt, though, and sometimes you just have to look to the greater good. Anyway, it may be good for him to have another child under this roof. And in a perfect world, they'll have an ID on the boy any second now, and his parents will show up, Jessie tells herself, wishing that darned thing with feathers would flutter just a little.

THE ANGLER HAD taken a circuitous route back to Ottawa. Instead of continuing northeast on Interstate 81 at Syracuse, he'd jumped on the New York State Thruway westbound toward Buffalo. It would be a good five or six hours out of the way, but he couldn't risk running into this morning's border patrol agent on the return trip. Not without having attended the Toronto-Boston baseball game, and without a striped bass, and without the boy.

Just past Rochester, he'd stopped for gas at a rest area, venturing inside to use the restroom and get something to eat. He'd left in a hurry when he'd spotted two uniformed sheriff's deputies standing at the fast-food counter. They were more likely to be waiting for cheeseburgers than for him, but what if the boy's body had already been found?

Rattled, he got back into the car and continued on, sticking to the speed limit, though his foot itched to gun it toward the border. After a brief, perfunctory interaction with the border patrol agent, he'd crossed the Peace Bridge at Niagara Falls.

Even back in Canada, he'd been clenched and paranoid, watching the rearview mirror for a whirl of red as Niagara Falls faded behind him.

He'd visited once, as a child. A school trip. He remembers standing at the brink, watching the water rush past and into oblivion, remembers Ralphie Michaels coming up behind him, nudging him in the ribs. He'd started, and all the kids laughed, with Father Hercule scolding him.

"This is not a place for monkey business! If you fall, you will die! Do you want to die?"

"Yes," he'd shot back, defiant as always. *"I want to die."*

But he hadn't. Not really. Not in that moment. He'd wanted Father Hercule to die, and Ralphie

Michaels, and the other kids, and his father—always, his father.

If you fall, you will die . . .

If the tower falls, you lose . . .

So precarious, this life he's built for himself.

The town house is dark when he pulls into the driveway. Cecile and the children will have been in bed for hours. Good. He isn't in the mood to interact with them after everything that's gone on today.

Are you ever, really?

He never misses them when he's away, nor when they are, even during the long months they spend in Paris. On the contrary, their annual summer sojourn is a welcome reprieve.

He unlocks the back door and crosses the shadowy kitchen to the refrigerator. Opening it, he's engulfed in a pool of light and a repulsive stench.

Damn Cecile.

Stomach churning, he slams the door shut and turns to the pantry cupboard, rooting around the white wire shelves for a box of dry cereal. He pours some into a bowl and stands in the dark, eating it dry. The milk, along with everything else in the refrigerator, will be permeated with the stink of Époisses, the smear-ripened French cheese his Parisian wife insists on buying.

He tosses the plastic bowl into the sink for Cecile to wash in the morning and climbs the stairs. He needs to shower, scrub off the stink of cheese and any traces of blood he might have carried home with him.

On the second floor, the three bedroom doors are closed. So, however, is the bathroom. He pauses beside it and knocks softly.

The bathroom door opens a crack. A face peers out.

For a brief, horrible instant, it's the boy, back from the dead.

The Angler can only gape, wondering how . . .

But of course, it's merely Pascal, hardly looking his usual robust, impish, handsome self. His blue eyes are sunken in a wan face, neatly combed side part lost in a blond tousle above his forehead. He looks so much like . . .

"What are you doing up at this hour?" he asks sharply.

"My tummy hurts. I've been sick."

He sees the other child, the one in the root cellar, blue eyes blinking up groggily into the flashlight's beam. He, too, had been sick, vomit caked around his mouth and oozing on the dirt beneath him.

"My tummy . . ."

Pascal. Not a ghost, haunting, taunting him.

"Go back to bed."

"I need Maman. Can you get her?"

"No. She's sleeping."

Cecile won't ask questions; it isn't that. Unemotional and independent, his wife had once told him that she preferred the company of her father's mistress to her own mother and made it clear that she doesn't care whether her own husband sleeps around, or with whom. She's content, as long as his paychecks go into their account and he allows her to make the parenting decisions.

But if he wakes Cecile, she'll make a fuss, up and down all night, turning on lights, maybe even calling the pediatrician.

"Please, I need Maman!" Pascal raises his voice, urgent. "My tummy—"

"All right, all right." The Angler pushes into the bathroom, closing the door behind them, and opens the medicine cabinet. "I'll find medicine."

"But Maman said—"

"Shush!"

The boy sinks onto the closed toilet seat, huddled in misery as the Angler rummages through the plastic bottles crammed along the glass shelf. Many are orange prescription bottles bearing Pascal's name.

He can't bear the way Cecile coddles their son. Their daughter, too, but to a lesser extent. Renee doesn't require—or desire—attention.

She's like me. She wants to be left alone.

But the boy . . .

If Cecile continues to treat him like the heir to some foreign throne, he'll grow up a spoiled, imperious man.

"What is that?"

Pascal points toward his jacket pocket. The forgotten filet knife has torn a jagged hole in the waxed canvas, honed steel tip poking through, smeared with darkened blood.

"Oh, that's . . . it's . . . I was fishing." He reaches into his pocket, giving the handle a hasty tug so that the blade no longer protrudes. He forces himself to let go when all he wants to do is—

"My tummy h—"

"I heard you!" He spins back to the medicine cabinet, yanks out a bottle, heart racing. He untwists the plastic top, connected to a measured dropper. Pumping the rubber knob a few times, he fills the tube with viscous liquid and turns to the boy. "Open your mouth."

"What is that?"

"Medicine."

"But it's purple. I don't have a cough. I have a tum—"

The Angler thrusts the dropper into the child's mouth and squeezes.

Pascal gurgles, gulps.

"There. Go to bed."

"Maman . . ." Pascal says miserably.

"I *said*, go to bed."

His fingers itch to grab the knife again. Or at least, to unfasten his belt and whip the boy as his own father would have done.

The child makes a whimpering sound and disappears.

Left alone in the bathroom, the Angler closes the medicine cabinet and stares at his reflection.

He may resemble his father, may have his blood running through his veins, may have been christened with his first name, but . . .

I am not like him. I am not!

"If not for you, my wife would be here with me," his father would snarl. *"For nine months, she was wretchedly sick, and then, the torture . . . She wasn't right afterward. Her body, in her brain . . ."*

He'd told his son that she had run away, made a fresh start in a western province without them.

How could she?

A flashback: a dark stain soaked into old floorboards.

How could she have left her own . . .

Another flashback, more recent: a small, still figure, the boy, lying on muddy ground thick with decaying leaves.

. . . flesh and blood?

Flesh.

Blood.

Again, he looks down at his torn pocket. This time, he notices dark staining around the frayed fabric.

Blood . . .

It's dried, and not his own, though he gives himself a quick once-over to be sure.

No. You can't stab yourself and not notice.

But you can stab someone else, someone you're carrying in your arms, their head dangling over your right arm, lifeless limbs dangling over your left.

Lifeless?

He remembers the boy's filthy foot, streaks of red smeared in the grime. At the time, he'd been certain he was carrying a corpse, but that damned horse had clopped along before he'd had time to make sure.

Can a corpse bleed?

He hurries back downstairs to the living room and sits at the desktop computer, not bothering to turn on a light. Fingers bathed in the screen's soothing glow, he types the question into the search engine and then waits for the answer.

It takes some time. The computer is old, without enough room in the hard drive for a software update.

He has plenty of time to decide that he'll get back into the car and return to the orchard if he discovers a person must be alive to bleed. It will take all night, and he's already delirious with exhaustion, but he can't take a chance.

The links pop up at last. He clicks the first, scanning forensic details that can't quite pierce the fog of fatigue.

He clicks another link and then another, searching for layman's terms: a simple yes or no answer. He finds only *inconclusive*.

There are too many variables to rule it out. It mainly seems to depend on how much time has passed since the time of death.

He was dead. I know he was dead. I could feel it . . .
Or maybe just feel it coming.

How long could he possibly have survived in that remote location? Alone, drugged, and bleeding, with a cold front rolling in, accompanied by more storms . . .

He's dead now, in any case.

The Angler pushes aside doubt, reminding himself that he'd escaped the scene—indeed, the country—without attracting suspicion. It would be foolish to risk going back there now. He wants only to sleep . . . preferably, straight through another night.

It won't happen if he stays in this house, with these people. He stands, rubbing his aching back, and heads for the door and the one place where he can recuperate, undisturbed.

Chapter Five

Friday, September 30, 2016

S he wakes to the bleating alarm, and a spikey "Amelia!" from Aaron.

She opens her eyes, caked with last night's makeup, and sees him at the foot of the bed, showered, shaved, and dressed for work.

She hits the snooze button. The room is bathed in soft gray; the window spattered with raindrops. Her eyelids close again. Eight more minutes . . .

"Too much champagne last night?"

Aaron again, pushing through the blackout curtains in her brain.

Champagne? Last night . . .

Right. The party.

Aaron had rented a luxurious mansion, hired world-class caterers, and invited a few dozen family and friends who'd yelled "Surprise" when she'd unlocked the door. He'd thought of everything, from filling the room with her favorite flowers to hiring a classical jazz pianist to offering a toast he'd written on an index card.

"Please raise a glass to my beautiful wife. She and I have gone through life together for a quarter of a century now, and if we're lucky, we're less than halfway

through that journey. I know Amelia shares my gratitude to each and every one of you who came to help us
celebrate tonight. You are the people who matter most
to us in the world, and we consider you all a part of
our big, happy family."

After a quarter of a century together, his words had
somehow seemed impersonal, more about the guests
than about their marriage. He'd talked about building
this big, happy family, but when she'd looked around
the room, she hadn't seen *all* the people who matter
most in the world.

Not in mine, anyway.

He'd invited colleagues, his second cousins, his
parents' neighbors . . . but not Jessie. How could he
have overlooked her dearest friend?

After the party, he'd had a black stretch limo waiting to drop him and Amelia back home on the Upper
West Side and then deliver his parents to Montclair.

"Man, you are just full of surprises," she'd said, trying to seem as delighted as Aaron's mother had been
to see the car.

But Amelia had been planning to tell him about
Lily Tucker's tiny gold and sapphire ring on the way
home, and hadn't wanted to mention it in front of
her in-laws. Aaron had been feeling romantic for a
change, so she hadn't told him when they'd gotten
back upstairs, either. He'd fallen asleep quickly afterward, and she'd lain awake until almost dawn, entangled
in the past.

"Amelia!"

"Sorry." She opens her eyes again and sighs morning breath. "What are you doing?"

"Sorting my clothes for my trip Sunday." He reaches into a basket of tee shirts and boxers she'd washed and dried a few days ago.

"You're folding them. I already did." She'd been meticulous, aligning seams and creating neat rectangles.

Not meticulous enough for Aaron. His seams are always straighter, rectangles more uniform.

"Aren't you going to be late for work?" he asks. His eyes aren't bloodshot or mired in purple trenches, even though he'd drunk a lot more than she had last night, had likely had a better time, and had managed to get up at five for his morning gym workout.

"I only have two appointments today, and the first one isn't until ten," she tells him. "Aaron . . . something really interesting happened yesterday."

"Mmm-hmm?" He grabs another white tee shirt, pinching the shoulders to unfurl it with a firm shake to rid the fabric of her clumsy creases. Morning has never been a good time for conversation with him, even when they'd had so much more to talk about. He's always been too preoccupied, strategizing the day ahead.

In a few minutes he'll be out the door, and she can't keep this from him for another day.

Sitting up, she tells him about her appointment with Lily.

He stops folding and looks at her.

"Amelia. It can't be *your* ring. Maybe it looked like yours, but—"

"It is mine. It was identical."

"Okay, here's the thing . . . the guy in the seat next to me on the plane home from Denver had on a watch identical to this." He waves his wrist, and then gestures at the mahogany watch box on his bureau. "I'd left mine at home on this trip. But I didn't see this guy wearing it and assume it *was* mine."

"Because there are tens of thousands of Rolexes in the world."

"And there are tens of thousands of baby rings."

"*Exactly* like mine? Same design, same gemstones, same initial engraved in the same font?"

"Maybe. But let's say it *is* yours. You lost it . . . when?"

How could he have forgotten that detail?

"March 7, 1987. Or maybe March 8—it was around midnight. Right after the nurse forgot my mother's file in the room, and . . ."

She pauses, remembering how she'd snatched up the paperwork, searching for some clue to how much time her dying mother had left. She'd found Bettina's medical history, including the fact that she'd carried just one pregnancy to term, back in 1957.

That was the year she'd delivered a son who'd lived for a few hours. Amelia used to visit his grave with Calvin and Bettina, now buried beside him.

"I found out my mother wasn't my birth mother about an hour before she died. I was wearing that ring when they found me. It was the only link to my past."

"I know all that," Aaron tells her—not with impatience, but not with patience, either. "What about the boxes from your parents' apartment that are sitting in the storage unit downstairs? They're filled with stuff from the past."

"Not *my* past. I mean, that was my past, too, but . . ." She shouldn't have to explain this. Not to him. Not after half a lifetime together.

Sometimes, she's tempted to visit her childhood belongings in the building's basement, thinking she might pull out some old photographs to frame, maybe wear her father's old plaid muffler on a cold day, even fry up some chicken in her mother's cast-iron skillet.

She never does, though. The scarf had moth holes even when Calvin had worn it. And Aaron doesn't eat fried chicken. Nor does he like clutter. He grumbles that her books, magazines, and research materials take up too much space.

He wouldn't dare complain, though, about the two most meaningful possessions from her past or expect her to relegate them to storage.

A tiny blue dress is mounted in a shadow box that hangs on the living room wall.

A tightly woven sweetgrass basket sits like a prized trophy on an adjacent shelf.

Calvin had confirmed that he'd first found her lying in the basket, wearing the dress—and the tiny ring etched with the blue enamel *C*.

She reminds Aaron how she'd worn it on a chain around her neck until it had disappeared the night her mother died. "Losing the ring on top of everything else, all at once . . ."

"It was hard, baby. I know." A hint of the old, empathetic Aaron.

"Not just *hard*. It seemed like some bizarre supernatural punishment. Like it had been snatched away by God, or the devil, or my mother . . ." Seeing his expression, she shrugs. "Look, I wasn't completely rational about this stuff back then."

"Back then?"

"Or for a long time afterward," she concedes, but that's where she draws the line. She's rational now.

He's gone back to folding. "I don't think the devil snatched your ring, Amelia."

"I know you don't, and I know the devil didn't. Okay?"

"Okay. Sometimes I worry that you . . ."

"Don't worry." She looks to the ceiling. "The chain was cheap and flimsy. I always fiddled with it when I was anxious. That was the most stressful night of my life. Of course, it broke. If I hadn't been so distracted, I'd have noticed right away, and maybe I could have found it. But I guess it doesn't matter now."

"Good. Then forget about it." He adds a white undershirt to a clothing-store precise stack and reaches for another one.

"No, the point isn't that it broke. The point is, how did it end up with Lily Tucker?"

"How do you think?"

She frowns. "How do *you* think?"

He pulls his cell phone out of his pocket and stands, head bent, tapping his thumbs against the screen.

"Aaron, I've asked you so many times to please not text while we're—"

"Here!" He thrusts the phone at her. "I wasn't texting. Remember this?"

She looks down at the advertisement they'd placed eight years ago. The headline reads $25,000 REWARD!

That had been Aaron's idea. "You want to grab people's attention. Give them a reason to read on. They will, if they think there's something in it for them."

"Is there?"

He'd smiled and pulled her close. "I just want you to be happy, baby. And you said this is the only thing you want for your fortieth birthday."

"You mean my maybe-birthday."

Silas Moss had believed that milestones make people remember. Birthdays, anniversaries, holidays . . . if you've lost someone, you tend to think of them on those days. And they might be thinking of you in return.

She and Aaron had been rolling in money back then, and he'd been so supportive.

Man, how things can change in eight years.

They'd put her story out there, accompanied by photos of her at various stages of life, including her first portrait. She'd been about seven months old, the closest to what she'd have looked like when she'd been abandoned.

It pains her even now to see that black-and-white photo, snapped by a door-to-door photographer. Bettina and Calvin had scraped up the cash for a sitting, featuring a scowling Amelia in a droopy, stained, sad little dress.

She's always wanted, needed, to believe that her biological parents had spent every day of their lives wanting to find her. Even if they'd given her up as a baby—just left her there, all alone in the night—they might see that picture and regret it and reach out and—

All right, or maybe they'd see that damned reward and reach out. Maybe, if she can't forge a relationship with someone wonderful, finding an answer would be the next best thing. Even if her biological parents weren't looking for her, then maybe someone else, someone who'd known them, would stumble across her photos and think she looked familiar. Maybe Amelia, at twenty-one, had resembled her birth mother at that age. Maybe at forty, she'd had her birth father's smile. . . .

Aside from a couple of cruel scam artists, though, no one had ever come forward to claim the reward. Good thing, because a year later, the money had been swallowed by the worst global economic downturn since the Great Depression.

In the kitchen, she hears the clatter of lumber and whirring of a power tool. The workmen are here, embarking on their day of disruption.

She looks away from the advertisement, back at Aaron.

"The ring is mentioned there, Amelia."

"Yeah, I know."

He shrugs, taking the phone back from her, swiping away the screen, and putting it back into his pocket. "Okay, then. I have to get to the office."

"No, wait. You think Lily Tucker is a liar, is that it? You think she came across the ad from . . . what, eight years ago? And she had a ring made up based on my description? Well, guess what? I left a detail out of that description. The ad doesn't specify which initial was engraved on it. So, if the ring is a fake, Lily Tucker had a one in twenty-six chance of getting it right. Maybe she played the odds. Or maybe she's the real deal."

"If you believe it, then I believe it."

"No, you don't."

"You're right. I don't. Maybe if I met her . . ."

"You want to meet her?"

"Do I want to? No. Will I?" He shrugs. "I think I should. I deal with liars every day of my life. It's part of my job."

Lying is part of your job, too.

But she doesn't dare say it. Early in his career—in their marriage—a discussion about legal ethics had morphed into one of the worst arguments they'd ever had. Now the topic is off-limits.

"She has another appointment next week," Amelia tells him. "You can come and meet her."

"I'll be in California. Just be careful. I don't like the sound of this." He picks up his briefcase and heads for the door. "Oh, I'll be home late. That dinner meeting I told you was last night—it's tonight."

A crazy impulse flies into her head. "I won't be home tonight, anyway. Girls' weekend in Ithaca," she says as if she'd already told him about it, and he'd forgotten.

"Oh, right. Is that today?"

"Yes. I'm . . . taking a bus up after work. So I guess I'll see you Sunday."

"I leave for the airport at five that night. I'm in LA all next week. When are you coming home?"

"Not before five."

"I'll miss you." Aaron covers the distance between them and puts his arms around her. "Have fun with Jessie."

"I always do. Have a good trip."

"I always do."

The alarm bleats again as the door closes behind him.

Man, how things can change in eight years, she thinks, turning it off and taking a suitcase from her closet. *And in eight minutes.*

A JACKHAMMER BLASTS Barnes from sleep, and he's home in Washington Heights—until he opens his eyes to blinding sunlight and pastel décor.

Ah. This is Santa Maria del Mar, and that isn't construction noise. It's Rob, knocking at the door of his hotel room. "Barnes! You in there?"

"Yeah."

"Alone?"

He turns his throbbing head to make sure the adjacent pillow is empty. "Yeah."

"You going to let me in?"

"Yeah."

He staggers over to open the door.

Rob is dressed in white linen and dark glasses, clutching three grease-splotched brown paper sacks. "Breakfast to go. We leave for the airstrip in ten minutes."

"How about fifteen?" He swallows too much saliva. "Or tomorrow?"

"What the hell happened after we left the nightclub? I thought you were right behind me."

"I was, but . . ."

He slogs through the memory. Right, while Rob had been climbing the stairs to his ocean view room, Barnes had gone in search of a vending machine for bottled water. There, he'd run into a local beauty who'd invited him to share a beachfront nightcap. One thing led to another. He remembers lying with her in his arms as the sun came up, watching seabirds dip low to pluck fish from the sea, and then spotting a couple of fins in the curl of a wave. Sharks, feeding too close to shore for his comfort.

He'd staggered back to his room, scrubbed sand from his privates in a hot shower, and dropped into bed . . . what? Less than an hour ago, according to his watch . . . and if raising his wrist to check the time is making him this queasy, he can guess what's going to happen when he boards a small plane.

"Who was she? Juanita?"

"No."

"Elena?"

Barnes shakes his pounding head.

"Both? You dog."

"Come on, Rob."

"Wouldn't be the first time, my friend."

"It would in this century." Barnes retrieves his wallet and passport from the nightstand drawer where he'd left them for safekeeping.

"Then who was it?"

"Ana Benita."

"The bartender? Hope you got her recipe for that papaya coconut rum drink."

"Do not"—Barnes pauses to swallow, eyes closed—"mention rum. Please."

"You told me yesterday that it's all you need from now on."

"I don't remember saying that. And you shouldn't say that, by the way."

"Say what?"

"Papaya. Ana Benita said Cubans call it *fruita bomba*, because *papaya* translates into a nasty word."

"Which one?"

"She wouldn't tell me. It's not like we did a whole lot of talking."

"Really? Because you also mentioned yesterday that you're through with women."

"What I *said* is that women are nothing but trouble. That, I remember."

"You also said Sully is nothing but trouble."

Barnes ignores that, forcing his legs to start moving toward the bathroom. "I need to, uh, shave."

"Yesterday you told me you were going to grow your mustache again."

"What are you, my personal historian?" Barnes closes the bathroom door and throws up into the toilet.

"Doesn't sound like shaving to me," Rob calls from the other side of the door.

Barnes washes his face and brushes his teeth, careful not to swallow any water, having been warned about dysentery and even cholera. He smooths white foam over his stubbly jaw, remembering how Ana Benita had stroked it with shellacked red fingernails, and how devastated she'd been when he'd told her he was checking out in the morning. She'd reacted as though they were longtime lovers in some Turner Classic movie, clinging to him as though he were going off to war.

"Stay here with me," she'd begged in Spanish, "and I'll show you my country."

"Wish I could"—not entirely the truth—"but I'm traveling with my friend, and he's made the arrangements."

"Why Baracoa? No one goes there unless they want to get lost. You really want to get lost?"

Not like he has much choice in the matter.

The Roots and Branches Project genealogists had discovered that Rob is descended from the Taíno Indians, an indigenous pre-Columbian tribe that had populated Baracoa centuries ago. He's already visited, and now wants Kurtis and Barnes to see it.

Forty minutes later, Barnes is on the tarmac eyeing the plane Rob had chartered—not, he'd said, an easy feat even in this new era. He'd predicted it would be "vintage."

Decrepit is a more apt description.

"You sure this thing can fly?" Barnes asks him.

"Guess we'll find out."

Kurtis glares. "Not funny, Dad."

Barnes eyes the laid-back pilots, who could pass for singers in a boy band and greeted them with a casual *"Que vola?"*—the Cuban version of "What's up?"

"Rob, seriously, are you sure they're old enough for a pilot's license?"

"They're not old enough for a *driver's license*," Kurtis says. "And I heard that there's a hurricane coming. Some of the airlines are canceling flights."

"Not a hurricane, just a tropical storm, and it's headed for South America. That's way south of here."

"Not as 'way south' as it is from home. This is crazy. We should get out while we can."

Rob pats his son's arm. "Don't worry. We'll be fine."

"I'm not *worried*. I'm pissed off."

"There's not a cloud in the sky, and I want you to see where you come from, son."

"I come from New Jersey." At his father's look, he says, "What? That's home."

"You can't compare Saddle River to Baracoa. You're going to feel something when you get there, I guarantee it."

"You mean something other than pissed off? Because I—"

"*Pride*, son. You're going to grasp your roots, and you're going to understand who you are."

"I know who I am."

"I don't think you do. I'm talking about who you are in here"—Rob taps his chest—"and in your blood. Our ancestors were in Baracoa when Christopher Columbus showed up over five hundred years ago. And for centuries before that. It's the oldest town in Cuba."

"Does that mean they don't have Wi-Fi?"

"They do, in spots. But the place where we're staying doesn't. Trust me, you won't miss it."

Kurtis mutters something.

"Well, I won't miss it." Barnes pulls his phone from his pocket and turns it off as they board the plane. It's sweltering inside, somewhat battle scarred, and so grungy that the New York City subway is pristine by comparison. A few of the seats are broken and all are worn, the seatbelts so dated it takes some maneuvering to figure out how to fasten them. There are no safety instructions—not in English, anyway. Nor in Spanish. Barnes is fluent, but he has no idea what the pilots are saying as they chain-smoke their way into the cockpit.

"Isn't it illegal for the flight crew to smoke on a plane?" Kurtis asks Rob, who shrugs.

"Things are different in Cuba. More relaxed."

"More dangerous. I say we cancel this stupid trip."

"Come on, Kurtis, relax. It's going to be fine. You've never been a nervous flier, and—"

"I'm not nervous!"

"You seem like you are. Look at Uncle Stockton. He's cool as a cucumber."

Yeah. Sure he is.

"Dad, this is stupid. I just want to go back to the resort. This isn't fair! I want—"

"And I want you to stop acting like a five-year-old. Time to grow up, kid."

"Yo, I'm not a kid. I'm almost thirty."

"Yo, it's time to man up, man."

Barnes cringes, and not just because it's the wrong thing for Rob to have said in this moment.

"This is about the election again, isn't it?" Kurtis asks Rob.

"Of course it isn't about the election."

Kurtis rolls his eyes. "Okay. Sure. Whatever you say."

Barnes looks from one to the other. "The *presidential* election? What about it?"

"Yeah, we don't see eye to eye on a couple of matters," Rob says.

Barnes has a feeling that he and Rob don't see eye to eye on a couple of election-related matters, either, and he isn't interested in debating it. He's tripped and fallen into one too many political arguments at the pub and precinct lately. He'll be glad when the divisive election is over, and life can get back to normal.

"You voting, Barnes?"

"I always vote."

"So do I. But Kurtis here was all about Bernie Sanders, and since he's not running . . ."

"You're not voting, Kurtis?"

"For Hillary Clinton? No way."

Barnes, who is, doesn't ask him why not.

"She's not running unopposed," Rob points out.

"Yeah, I'm not voting for your golf buddy, either."

"You and Donald Trump are golf buddies?"

"Not buddies," Rob tells Barnes. "We *golfed* together—back when he was doing *The Apprentice*, he wanted one of my artists to be on the show."

Kurtis slouches in his seat, arms folded, sunglasses masking his glower, untouched breakfast bag on his lap. He, too, appears hungover this morning, though when his father had asked about his evening on the way to the airport, he'd said only that he'd gone "out."

The butter-grilled Cuban bread, guava jam, and sliced papaya—er, *fruita bomba*—Barnes had gobbled on the way to the airport had settled his stomach, but takeoff rivals any Coney Island thrill ride he's ever experienced. A fresh wave of nausea hits as the plane makes an arching curve above the cobalt sea.

"You okay, there?" Rob asks as Barnes gags and clasps a palm to his mouth. So much for cool as a cucumber. "Look, it'll be better when we level off and the cabin cools off."

Neither of those things happen.

He fans himself with a mid-twentieth-century travel brochure he'd grabbed yesterday in Havana: palm trees, sugary sand, and busty bathing beauties holding coconut drinks.

Rum.

Flies—actual flies—buzz around Kurtis's breakfast bag, and he tosses it onto the floor.

Forcing back bile-tinged saliva, Barnes shouts above the rattling engine roar, "How long is the flight?"

"Couple of hours." Rob pats his arm. "Why don't you take a nap? Looks like you can use it."

Barnes leans back, closes his eyes, and falls into a queasy, uneasy sleep. Ana Benita shows up in his dream—*nice*—but she soon morphs into a tiny red-headed spitfire. Sully? Dammit.

They're back in New York, on a case, trying to find a lost child. A little girl.

"Did you get a description, Gingersnap?" his dream self asks, using his cozy old nickname for his partner.

"She looks just like you," Sully tells him.

Just like me . . .

"How old is she?"

"Same age as I am, Uncle Stockton." Kurtis is there, wearing sunglasses and earbuds. "We were born the same day."

"What's her name?" Barnes asks.

Kurtis shakes his head.

Barnes turns to Sully. "Gingersnap! What's her name? Tell me her name!"

"You know what it is, Barnes. You know. Man up! You need to find her!"

He wakes with a start.

The cabin is still warm and thick with the pilots' tobacco smoke. The sky has gone from clear blue to foreboding, and there are rain spatters on the window. The plane is still flying low, tilting to and fro above a verdant landscape.

"Rob. Are we almost there?"

"Almost."

"You said that fifteen minutes ago," Kurtis mutters, and Barnes looks down at his discarded bag of hotel breakfast.

"You going to eat that?"

"All yours, Uncle Stockton. But I saw a couple of cockroaches poking around it."

Barnes doesn't doubt it. He grabs the bag with a clammy hand, trying not to think about roaches or the grease stains or food . . . rum . . .

The plane lurches and a choppy sea looms at a crazy angle beyond the window. Barnes turns away, heart pounding like those whitecaps.

Man up! Sullivan Leary says in his head, just as she had countless times on the job. Somehow, she'd always been tougher than he was, particularly when a missing child case ended badly. Especially when it involved a little girl.

The plane drops like a high-speed car into a pothole, and his breakfast lurches in the opposite direction. He dumps the breakfast bag contents onto the floor and uses the paper sack as an airsickness bag.

"Hanging in there, Barnes?" Rob asks.

"Oh, yeah. Doing great." He swallows. "You sure that hurricane's in South America?"

"Tropical storm, and I'm positive."

"Then are you sure we couldn't have driven instead?"

"There weren't even any roads to get here until the sixties."

"Yeah, but there are roads now," Kurtis points out.

"There's a road. You think this is bumpy? Do you know how long it would have taken us to—" The plane makes another arc in the gray sky, and Rob points out the window. "There it is! That's El Yunque!"

On the wildly diagonal land-and-seascape below, wisps of mist trail like streamers from an anvil-shaped mountain. As they fly on past, the clouds evaporate and the sky is brilliant again, sun twinkling on an aquamarine bay.

"That's Baracoa," Rob says. "See it there, spread out along the water?"

Barnes presses his forehead to the glass to glimpse a dizzying hodgepodge of vibrant-hued wooden structures and red tile rooftops. At least his stomach is empty, so he's no longer afraid of losing the contents.

The plane lurches.

No, he just has to fear losing his damned *life*.

He's used to that, though, right? He's NYPD.

He finds himself thinking of Sully again, wishing he'd told her about this Cuba trip. She'd have been happy for him. She knows how desperately he's always wanted to travel here, just like she knows just about everything else about him. More than Rob docs, and definitely more than Barnes's ex-wife has ever known. You get close to someone, working cases together year in and year out. But when one of you leaves the job . . .

It's *over.*

Just like it was over with Frank DeStefano, his first partner who'd promised to keep in touch after he'd retired to a Myrtle Beach condo, but hadn't, other than sporadic phone calls early on.

Barnes hadn't expected that to happen with Sully, though. They'd worked together far longer than he and Stef, with far more in common. For a while there, they'd been a two-member support group, simultaneously muddling through their divorces from fellow cops. He'd even wondered if maybe, eventually, their relationship could have evolved from friends and partners to—

The plane wobbles to a lower altitude, and the co-pilot speaks rapid-fire Spanish from the cockpit.

"Yo, Uncle Stockton, what'd he say?"

"I, uh . . . I think we're landing."

"Landing where? In the ocean?" Kurtis asks as they dip toward jagged rocks silhouetted beneath the translucent turquoise water.

"Guys, I've done this a million times. Everything's going to be—" Rob breaks off in a curse at a violent jolt, and his smile bares too many teeth when he concludes with a strangled-sounding, "—fine."

The pilot calls out unintelligibly.

Barnes thinks of Sully—

Gingersnap! Tell me! What's her name?

"Charisse," he breathes aloud.

"What's that, Barnes?"

Rob is looking at him, and so is Kurtis.

"Nothing." He turns away, leaning his head back, eyes closed, as the plane leans left, then right, then so hard left that his clenched fingers gouge the paper bag he's holding. Vomit oozes over his hand, but it'll wash away if the plane plunges into the ocean. Will it draw the sharks, like blood?

If they crash, his daughter will never even know. She might read about it in the papers, because Rob is a celebrity. "Record Mogul, Companions, Perish in Plane Crash," the headline will say, but his own child won't recognize his name. Unless her mother—

But if Delia had shared his identity with Charisse, wouldn't she have come looking for him by now?

No, because Delia sure as hell wouldn't have made him out to be some kind of hero.

And you weren't, were you? Aren't even now, are you? You could have looked for her again.

Man up, man! Man up!

If he makes it out of this alive, he's going to find his daughter. No matter what. Find her, and—

The wheels hit a sand-dusted runway that seems to rise from the sea. The plane blows past a ramshackle building decked in Cuban flags and screeches to a stop before a fringe of tropical foliage.

"*Bienvenido* a Baracoa!" the pilot calls cheerfully, removing his headphones.

Disembarking onto the sunbaked tarmac on shaky legs, Barnes tosses the bag of puke into a garbage can, suspecting—by the heap of garbage and the smell— that it isn't the first.

He tilts his face to the sky, watching a fat white gull soar. It disappears into blinding sun and he closes his eyes, gulping in sea air.

Someone touches his arm. Expecting Rob, he opens his eyes to see Kurtis.

"Charisse," he says in a low voice. "That's your daughter, huh, Uncle Stockton?"

Barnes nods, wondering how much he knows. It's a subject he's rarely discussed even with Rob.

"You know where she's at?"

"No, but I . . . no."

No, Barnes doesn't know.

And no, he isn't going to try to find her. That was just a frantic whim in a terrifying moment, and both have passed.

Rob strides over. "Let's go. There's a *camión* here."

"Is that food?" Kurtis asks.

"No, transportation. Who's ready to climb a mountain?"

Not Barnes. "I feel like I just did."

Not Kurtis, either.

Rob shrugs. "I'll have the driver drop you both at the house on the way."

"You mean resort?"

"I mean rental house, Kurtis. They call them *casas particulares*. No resorts around here."

Rob leads the way to the *camión*. The front part is an old bright blue truck cab with rust peeling through. The back is open air bus, painted the same verdant shade as the palm fronds kissing the yellow tarp stretched across the top. There are benches along the sides—a bonus, Rob explains as he settles in with one relaxed arm slung along the railing. "On some of these, you have to stand—kind of like the subway."

"This is nothing like the subway," his son mutters under his breath, and plunks himself down as far away from Rob as he can get.

Barnes, who's had a front row seat to father and son's seesaw relationship from Day One, positions himself between them, and the vehicle begins to jolt over roadway that's even rougher than the airway. At least this time, they don't have far to fall.

He sees Rob eyeing the young man with frustration, sees Kurtis glowering at his father, and is glad the *camión*'s rattle is too loud for conversation.

A FAINT SOUND reaches Jessie, drifting in a troubled haze of dream. She tumbles to consciousness and finds, not the water-stained ceiling above her bed, but an elegant, cobwebby nineteenth-century light fixture. Ah, yes, she's in the living room.

Billy had texted at midnight telling her to go to bed, but she'd settled here to read her book and wait for him and had eventually drifted off.

She hadn't slept well, not just because the couch cushions are too spongy for her middle-aged back and the crocheted afghan is too thin to stave off the damp chill. Throughout the night, she'd dreamed she was on the *Titanic*. Every so often, thunder had made its way into her nightmare to become another iceberg striking the ship like a missile. Shivering, she clung to the deck, draped in this same thin afghan, watching the lifeboats depart without her.

At dawn, Espinoza's crow jarred her fully awake. But through the restless hours since, the rooster's troubling saga has looped through her brain as though his squawk had triggered a Play button.

She keeps seeing Theodore on a warm May afternoon, cradling a tiny bird he said he'd found in the park. After fashioning a makeshift nest in a shoe box lined with a frayed hand towel, Jessie had called the veterinarian.

"What is it this time, Mrs. H.? Lost puppy? Stray dog? Pregnant cat? Litter of kittens?"

"None of the above." She'd explained the situation to the vet, who'd sighed.

"Happens a lot this time of year. People buy live chicks for their kids' Easter baskets, then let them go when they get tired of them."

She could have told him that people have babies and do the same thing. Instead, stroking the creature's bedraggled feathers with a tender fingertip, she'd asked the vet about animal shelters that might take a chicken.

"Off the top of my head, I don't know of any. Your best bet is probably a farm."

"Should I just, what? Drive him out into the country and knock on doors?"

"You might want to call first."

"Call whom?"

"Farmers," he'd said simply.

"Terrific. Thanks."

As she'd waited for Billy to come home with a better idea, Theodore had bonded with the chick. Which had turned out to be a rooster. Which they didn't find out until a few months after they'd decided to keep him, and Theodore had built a little coop out back, bonding nicely with Billy in the process.

Pets can be therapeutic for troubled kids. Theodore is afraid of dogs, doesn't like cats, has no interest in aquarium fish, and is too squeamish for a hamster, turtle, or anything else she'd suggested over the years. A horse was out of the question. Fowl had never occurred to Jessie, but she's since read several studies about children like Theodore who had bonded with roosters and chickens.

Espinoza had been the perfect pet . . . at first.

But chicks grow. Roosters crow. Neighbors complain.

Espinoza is now ensnarled in long-brewing civic turmoil about a growing population of backyard chickens in Ithaca. Theodore had recently shown up at a livestock ordinance meeting and afterward had inadvertently given an impassioned statement to a local newspaper. The bullies are now having a field day— and this time, not just the ones at school. She's read the newspaper's digitalized comments section.

"Jess?"

She cries out, jerking upright.

"Sorry! I didn't mean to wake you."

It's just Billy.

"No, I thought I heard something, but . . ." She realizes he isn't holding a child in his arms. Her heart plummets. "You didn't get him."

It's for the best, of course. If they've found the boy's parents, then maybe his story had a happy ending without the role Jessie had been preparing to play. She's so busy with work these days, and so is Billy, and he should be taking better care of himself, and Theodore doesn't need the complication, and . . .

"No, I got him."

He gestures, and Jessie sees a small boy in the shadows by his side. His hair is a damp tangle of blond. He's sucking his thumb, one cheek pressed to his shoulder, hiding his face. A blanket slips off his frail frame to reveal grimy pajamas. He's wearing thick white athletic socks wet, muddy, and far too big for him.

"His feet—"

"I know," Billy says quietly. "It's pouring out and he doesn't have any shoes. I didn't want him to walk, but he wouldn't let me carry him. One of the nurses found socks for him."

"He must be freezing, poor little thing." She longs to sweep him into her arms but knows better. "Hi, sweetheart. I'm Jessie. What's your name?"

"We don't know that yet."

She looks up at Billy. "He's still not talking?"

"No."

"And no one has reported—"

"No."

They exchange a long, sad look. If no one is frantically looking for a child this age, then to whom—and where—does he belong?

"Are you hungry, sweetheart?"

The boy doesn't respond, just stands with his head bowed.

"They pumped him full of fluids at the hospital," Billy tells her. "He might not be hungry, but he's probably exhausted. I know I am. Good thing I'm off work today."

"Get some sleep. I made up beds in both Chip's and Petty's rooms with clean sheets for him. He can choose where he wants to be."

"What about Theodore?"

"He left for school about . . ." She looks at the antique mantel clock. "An hour ago. He got himself out the door, same as always. I heard him go, but I don't think he realized I was here on the couch."

"He wouldn't have liked that, or . . . Does he know about—"

"Yes. I told him last night."

"And?"

"He'll come around." She shrugs and turns away from her husband's misgiving.

Theodore isn't the kind of kid who "comes around." He needs stability.

But right now, this little boy needs a lot more than that.

"Let's go upstairs." She stretches, presses her palm into a kink above her hip, and starts for the archway to the foyer, hobbling a little.

"Are you okay, Jess?"

"I'm fine, just getting old and creaky. Are you guys coming?"

"We are." Billy follows, coaxing the child along. "We have a cozy room all set for you, Little Boy Blue."

"Little Boy Blue?"

"That's what I've been calling him. You'll know why when you see his eyes. And he likes nursery rhymes. Remember that Mother Goose book I used to read to the kids when they were little? Do we still have it?"

"Somewhere. Probably in Theodore's room."

"Good. I'll read it to you, okay?" Billy tells the boy around a deep yawn. "Not now, though. Let's go get some sleep. Sound good?"

Still the child stands staring at the floor with his right thumb in his mouth, not moving.

Billy gives him a slight pat and he flinches, skinny shoulders hunching beneath the blanket, bracing himself.

Jessie has seen it before, knows what it means.

Somebody hurt you.

She goes to him, crouching at his side without touching him. "Hey, it's going to be all right."

"That's what I've been telling him. It's been a rough night."

"Rough day yesterday, too, I bet. And God knows what else, and for how long." She looks down at the wet, oversized, filthy socks. "But you'll feel better after you sleep in a real bed. You can choose one of our older kids' bedrooms. And I bought lots of food for breakfast. Do you like Lucky Charms?"

No response.

After a moment, she dares to reach for his left hand. To her shock, he doesn't just allow her to grasp it, he grips her fingers like a lifeline. When he looks up at last, with enormous cobalt eyes swimming in tears, it's all she can do not to burst out crying herself.

She manages only a soft, "You're safe now, Little Boy Blue," and leads him to the steps, with Billy right behind them. Unlike the back stairway, the grand and formal one in the foyer had been built to impress visitors, but it dwarfs and intimidates this one. He gawks at the carved mahogany newel post, the polished banister with ornate spindles, the antique wall sconces that light the wide, windowed landing, the vintage bronze wallpaper, and the crystal chandelier overhead.

He shrinks back in the doorway of Petty's room. Perhaps he's startled by the butterfly mobile slowly stirring despite the closed windows, or the antique dolls Diane had given Petty on every birthday of her life, though Jessie has never been in favor of gender-specific toys and had scolded her.

"Mom, you shouldn't do that. It's like you're hoping she'll grow up to be a girlie girl."

"There's nothing wrong with being a girlie girl."

"Or with being a tomboy, like I was."

Her daughter had turned out to be both, hence the childhood nickname Petunia, shortened over time. Like her grandmother's favorite flower, Petty possessed a hardy resilience that belied the pretty pastel ruffles on the surface.

Seeing Little Boy Blue gape at the doll collection, Jessie can imagine that a child might be spooked by the glassy-eyed stares and fixed smiles. But then he seems to fixate on the vintage iron bed, with her daughter's lacy lavender robe draped over one of the posts.

"Come on," Billy says. "Let's show you Chip's room. It's better for a boy."

"Billy! Boys don't have to be masculine. You know that I don't believe in—"

"I know, I know. I'm just saying, it might be more familiar for him, and we want him to be comfortable."

Yet he seems equally hesitant when they lead him into the room down the hall, with its pale blue walls, plaid quilt, and sports posters.

"Maybe we should just put him in bed and see if he falls asleep," Billy says in a low voice. "He has to be exhausted. I know I am."

But when he starts to reach for him, the boy jolts and backs away, into the hall.

"Aw, sweetie, it's okay," Jessie says, and turns to Billy. "You go to bed. I'll take care of him. We'll be fine."

"Okay. Holler if you need me."

He retreats into their own room at the top of the stairs and closes the door.

After a moment, Little Boy Blue looks up at Jessie. Then he starts walking.

Following him, thinking he's gone after Billy, she finds that he's returned to Petty's room.

"So you are choosing. Do you want to sleep in here, sweetheart?"

No reply, but he doesn't protest when Jessie takes his hand and walks him to the bed.

He gazes at the lavender robe as if concerned that the room's occupant might not want him here.

"It's all right. That belongs to my daughter, Petty. She's far away, and she'd be glad to have you sleep in her bed."

Thinking of the many times her huge-hearted daughter had taken a foster child under her wing, Jessie wishes Petty were here now to help break the ice. Or Chip, with his easygoing charm and perpetual willingness to play with the kids who have come through this house.

Now there's only Theodore, wrapped up in his own world and resenting the intrusion.

Jessie feels Little Boy Blue stiffen as she hoists him up onto the bed, but when she guides him under the soft white comforter, his little body sinking into the mattress and pillow, he seems to relax.

She tucks the covers around him and resists the urge to kiss his pale forehead. "I'll be right downstairs if you need anything at all, okay? You just . . . come get me."

She'd been about to tell him to call for her.

As a therapist, she's familiar with selective mutism, but she needs to refresh her memory and figure out how to untangle the knot of trauma and terror that have a choke hold on his voice.

Back downstairs, she makes a pot of coffee and then sits at her desk in the living room to see what the internet has to say.

Oh, right—the Wi-Fi. She sighs and finds her cell phone. After a hunt through a stack of bills that need to be paid, she also finds the number for the repair service, and goes through a frustrating round of "If you are calling about . . . press one for . . ."

All representatives are busy—imagine that—and she's placed on hold long enough for the coffee to brew, and to finish her first cup while tidying the house. She pours a second cup and then goes to the basement, folding a load of laundry and starting another.

At last, a real live person comes on the line.

"A lot of customers are out in the area, ma'am. We'll try to get a technician there today if someone will be home, but I can't promise you anything."

"I'll be home. All day."

Home, waiting . . .

Waiting for the repairman, waiting for the boy to wake up, waiting for word on his identity, waiting for the caseworker who's supposedly coming to check in on him—though she certainly knows how *that* goes. Child welfare agencies are perpetually understaffed, caseworkers spread too thin and operating under constant duress, between the demands of the job and the inability to make ends meet on the salary.

She'd launched her career as one of them, toughing it out for a few years until Chip had come along, with Petty only eighteen months behind. Full-time child care for two would have cost more than she was earning, so she'd become a full-time mom until the kids were in preschool. That's when she'd changed career paths to become a part-time therapist. It was around that same time that they'd begun fostering children in addition to shelter animals.

With her house and schedule and heart crammed full, those years had been Jessie's happiest—years when she didn't have the time or energy or even the motivation to look back on the past or worry about what might happen down the road. There's something to be said for living in the moment.

Lately, though, the moments are so darned . . . complicated.

The house needs work, money is short with two tuitions, she misses her older kids, Theodore is a challenge, Billy's health worries her, and yet . . .

Right here, right now, you have everything that matters.

Chapter Six

Amelia closes the door after the day's final client and sits at her desk, longing to take off her shoes. The flats had felt a size too small when she'd pulled them on at home, her feet still swollen from last night's uptown hike in pumps. Despite two layers of bandages, the leather edges have been digging into her raw blisters. And despite her attempt to focus on her clients, her own past has been jabbing her thoughts all morning.

Unlike Amelia and Aaron, Calvin and Bettina Crenshaw hadn't been childless by choice. A full decade after losing an infant son, they'd failed to conceive again. Working five jobs between them to afford the subsidized Harlem apartment, they'd accepted that fertility specialists and adoption were out of the question.

They'd believed Amelia had been sent by Jesus, the answer to their prayers—because of the ring, Calvin had told her. "It was etched with a *C . . . C*, for Crenshaw. You were meant to be ours. Who were we to question His gift?"

But Amelia had questioned him, trying to grasp how they'd managed to pass her off as their own.

"It was 1968—we had the war, assassinations, protests, riots . . . the whole city was on edge. The whole

world. But especially in this neighborhood. We didn't
go out for a long, long time after we found you in May,
except to work."

"Because you were hiding me."

"A lot of folks stayed locked away inside that summer,
out of trouble—or what the cops might decide was
trouble. Terrible times for the black man back then."
That fall, he'd said, when they'd finally taken the baby
outdoors, people had just assumed Bettina had given
birth to her. "Back then, folks didn't ask nosy personal
questions like they do now. Pregnancy and childbirth
were nobody's business but the parents'."

Only one person in their lives had ever seemed privy
to the truth, likely not because Calvin and Bettina had
ever shared it. Amelia's parents had wanted nothing
to do with their exotic neighbor Marceline LeBlanc,
who'd come from a southern coastal island and had
spoken in a thick Gullah accent.

Amelia opens her laptop. It's been a long time since
she's scoured the internet for Marceline. She's not
likely to turn up now; she can't possibly still be alive,
but it wouldn't hurt to try again.

Amelia opens a search engine.

One thing is certain—Marceline couldn't have been
Amelia's birth mother. She'd been an old lady even in
1987. When you're young, even middle age seems old,
but Marceline must have been well past her forties or
even fifties when Amelia had known her. More like
pushing seventy, or beyond. She'd likely forgotten
all about Amelia after she'd left New York, carrying whatever she'd known about Amelia's past to the
grave.

Before she looks for Marceline, though, she needs

to check the bus schedule to Ithaca. In her flurry to pack a weekend suitcase and get out the door, she'd left her phone behind, plugged into the charger on her nightstand. She'll have to go back to get it before heading to the Port Authority.

There's a bus leaving at two twenty.

She looks at her watch. The renewed search for Marceline will have to wait. She needs time to get uptown and then back down again on aching feet.

There's no landline in her office, so she has yet to call Jessie and let her know she's coming to Ithaca this afternoon. But if there's anyone in this world who'd welcome unexpected—albeit invited—company with open arms, it's Jessie.

She also has to ask Aaron to take care of Clancy in her absence. That request, she suspects, won't be met with nearly as much enthusiasm.

Amelia hadn't consulted him before volunteering to foster the orphaned kitten. He'd been on an extended business trip when Amelia came across Clancy's plight via social media. He'd been placed in a shelter, developed a respiratory infection, and been listed for euthanasia.

Struck by instant kinship with the abandoned little soul, she'd taken him home.

"It's temporary," Amelia had promised Aaron. "I couldn't let them kill him just because he was all alone and sick in that awful place. Just for a few months, until he's old enough to be placed in a permanent home."

"And you're actually going to let him go?"

"Of course. That's what fosters do, Aaron. Jessie said—"

"I know what fosters do. I'm just not convinced you're capable of doing it."

She'd protested. Two months later, she hates that he might have been right.

She'll email Aaron, she decides. A call or text might invite an argument she isn't in the mood to have.

> A, forgot to tell you to make sure you feed the kitten while I'm gone. Leave him enough food and water when you go to the airport and he should be fine until I get home Sunday night. Love you, A

After sending it, she writes one to Jessie.

> Hope the offer is still open, because I'm Ithaca-bound! Will text you the arrival time. Xo Mimi

She hits Send, hoping her friend will see it. Jessie's never been diligent about checking her email.

The split second before she closes the laptop, she hears a new message clicking in. Maybe Aaron. Probably spam. It can wait.

She hurries for the door, anxious to start the weekend and forget about real life for a while.

THE ANGLER AWAKENS to the distant chiming of the Peace Tower carillon bells on Parliament Hill, across the Rideau Canal. The hour strikes once, twice, three times.

He stretches his arms and rolls onto his back, opening his eyes. He hadn't slept through to evening as he'd intended, but his slumber had been blessedly un-disturbed. Before turning in, he'd called in sick again, leaving a message for his shift supervisor. Well aware that it probably hadn't gone over well, he'd turned off his phone.

He reaches for it on the nightstand and waits for it to power up.

The small back bedroom is bathed in afternoon light. The smallest of the three rooms on the second floor, it's the only one that has access to the attic; the only one that holds no unpleasant memories.

The largest had belonged to his father. Upon inher-iting the house, the Angler had planned to claim that room for his own. The smell of sweat and booze had lingered there, though, long after he'd stripped away the personal effects and scrubbed it floor to ceiling with bleach. He'd thought removing the furniture might help, and then he'd torn out the ugly striped wallpaper and brown carpeting. The hardwood floor near where the bed had stood had been stained as if someone had spilled a can of brown paint. It had soaked so deeply into the oak that he couldn't sand it away.

He'd moved on to his own childhood bedroom across the hall. There, too, he'd gotten rid of every-thing, had ripped the light fixtures from the ceiling and walls, had all but gutted the room. Yet still his dead father wafted as palpably as the traces of his own terror. He'd tried, though, to banish him. He'd spackled and sanded walls scarred by hurtled objects. As he'd painted the oak baseboards spattered with his own blood, he could hear his father's belt cracking.

In the end, he couldn't erase the violence, and so he closed the doors on those empty rooms forever. He padlocked both and stashed the keys in a drawer back at the town house, lest he ever find himself tempted to revisit the past.

The phone buzzes to life and presents him with a series of missed calls, not from his supervisor, but from Cecile. Why is she bothering him when she thinks he's at work?

Unless somehow, she knows . . .

How much can she possibly know?

He scowls, sits up, and toys with the phone, belatedly wondering whether he'd remembered to clear his history on the desktop computer at home. She has a newer laptop, and never touches it, but what if . . .

No. Even if she'd come across his search about whether a corpse can bleed, she can't possibly suspect about Monique and the boy. She has no idea that he even owns this house in the city, inherited upon his father's death a decade ago, before she'd come into his life.

Liberated at last, he'd believed at that time that he might actually be able to live life just like anyone else. Instead of going home alone after his shift, he'd started frequenting pubs and wine bars, hoping to make friends. He'd never had any, unless you counted his school classmates or coworkers—none of whom had ever really known or cared to know him.

But it wasn't easy for a man alone to connect with other men. Women were easier—not as potential friends, but as potential mates. Wasn't that what he wanted? A wife, a family, an ordinary life?

It would mean quelling the inappropriate urges that had tormented him all his adult life. He'd tried, dating a few age-appropriate women who came on too strong too soon, asked too many questions. They all wanted to know about his past, wanted to see where he lived. He'd claimed that he had several roommates, not uncommon in this area populated by students, immigrants, and artists. Still, they'd persisted.

Not Cecile. While they were dating, they'd spent their time together at her place, never his. She had expressed no interest in seeing it, nor did she ask questions about his past. Maybe it was her youth or her aloof nature. The details of his past, or even his present, hadn't seemed to matter to her. She'd been focused only on the future.

She'd been eager to trade the crime-ridden neighborhood for their suburban town house. They'd bought it at a premium, and the market had plummeted soon after. It's been a financial burden from the start.

He'd never considered selling his father's house, though. Even now, he revels in the triumph of ownership, like a revolutionary who'd overthrown a cruel dictator.

Besides, it suits his purposes. He no longer curses the solid plaster walls through which no outsider would ever hear a cry for help. He's grateful for them, and for the thorny shrubs that have overgrown the property borders, keeping would-be visitors at bay. Grateful that there is no curb appeal, nothing eye-catching about the peeling paint and formidable gabled roof that protects not just the secrets of his past, but the present.

The house is built on a slope, with a steep, deep driveway running downhill along the foundation and curving around back to a single car garage built beneath the house. It enables him to come and go through the basement and load the trunk without witnesses.

Anyone on the street who's ever seen him drive past and given a second glance would have assumed he was alone in the car.

Thoughts of Monique stir him from his bed. He shoves his phone into his pocket and reaches for the chain dangling from the ceiling before he remembers. A crushing loneliness sweeps over him.

She isn't there. She's been relegated to the past with his other ghosts.

A sob threatens to escape his throat, and he pulls the damned chain. A panel drops, with a built-in wooden ladder to the attic. It squeaks loudly as he extends it to the floor, rungs creaking beneath his weight as he ascends.

"Ready or not, here I come," he calls the way he always did. For a few moments, he can escape the wretched loss. He can pretend he isn't alone, that she's still up there, waiting for him.

Yet the cavernous attic is unmistakably forlorn as he weaves a familiar path around forgotten household relics—a cabinet television, old-fashioned suitcases, boxes of books. Dull light falls through the small round window set in the triangular peak at the front of the house. High overhead, the rafters are strung with cobwebs, corners clumped with sleeping bats; beneath his feet, the dusty floor is littered with mouse droppings and heaps of guano.

He makes his way toward a wide rack against the far wall, hung with a woman's clothing.

His mother's, he'd suspected when he'd found it up here as a child. Nubby plaid miniskirts, long-lapeled blouses, dresses with bell sleeves—seventies styles popular around the time he'd been born. The colors have faded, and the fabric is filthy and decaying, shredded in spots by rodent teeth.

He rolls the rack aside, and the handcuffs clatter along the floorboards, one end clamped to the vertical pole, the other small enough—thanks to some considerable searching on his part—to secure a child's fragile wrist.

He turns back to the dark wooden plank wall. In the beginning, he'd needed a flashlight and pry bar to find and release the panel. Now he can do it in pitch darkness if necessary, his fingers gravitating to the precise spot, applying just enough counterpressure along the expertly concealed left-hand seam to move the right side forward. Only slightly, not so that anyone who accidentally bumped it might notice. He tucks his fingernails into the slight ridge on the right and gives a tug, freeing the panel. Behind it, there's a hidden door with a bolt on the outside.

He slides it and opens the door to a small room with a high ceiling, an identical bull's-eye window tucked beneath the tall gable. There's no doorknob or handle on the inside, and never has been as far as he can tell—which has made him wonder about the room's origin and purpose.

He'd wanted to believe that the false wall had been there since the house was built in the late nineteenth century. But if you looked hard, and from a certain angle, the wood seemed newer. Most likely, someone had added it later. A previous owner. Likely his own father. He'd been a carpenter. And he'd forbidden his son to enter the attic.

But once, as a young boy left alone in the house, he'd found his way up here regardless of his father's rules. Restless, lonely, he wasn't looking for anything other than adventure, but had found only uninteresting relics, including his mother's clothing and anything else she might have left behind. He'd had no more interest in snooping the remnants of her existence than he would a complete stranger's. How could he care about her when she hadn't cared about him?

The only noteworthy item on his first visit to the attic had been the circular window, its crisscrossed antique grille making it look like a bull's-eye. He'd imagined trying to hit it with his slingshot from the ground below but ruled it out after noting that it faced the street. Someone might see him and tell his father. There would have been hell to pay.

He'd climbed back down the ladder and forgotten about the attic for a few more years.

Then one miserable summer day, he'd been lying beaten and bruised on the grass in the backyard, watching a crow circling overhead like a vulture on carrion. It had landed on the roof's peak and cawed, trying to tell him something, he'd later thought. As he stared up at the bird, he'd noticed that there was a bull's-eye window beneath that gable, just as there was out the front.

Yet he'd only seen one in the attic.

The next time he was alone in the house, he'd ventured upstairs and discovered that the back wall was hollow. After some searching, he'd found the secret door. The chamber had been empty that day, other than the cobwebs, mouse droppings, and bats.

Those are long gone. The room's first occupant had stuffed every crevice with steel wool.

"Please, we have to block those holes," the girl had begged, early on. "I can't stand the thought of things crawling on me in the night."

"Anything for you, my angel."

"Anything? Please let me go . . ."

Ah, anything but that.

He no longer remembers her name, or even exactly what she'd looked like, other than that she'd been his type and had resembled those who'd come after.

And they had all resembled the vanished woman who'd worn the moldering clothes hanging in the attic.

Vanished? Or . . .

No, he doesn't allow himself to think about that. About how brown paint appeared to have been spilled here, too . . . directly above the stain on his father's bedroom floor.

Almost as if it had seeped down.

He used to consider tearing out the ceiling below, just to see, but maybe he doesn't want to know.

Or maybe you already do. Maybe you always have, deep down inside. Maybe you never believed what your father told you about how she'd walked away.

Before crossing the threshold into the hidden room, he drags a nearby floor lamp to prop open the hinged panel. It used to stay that way on its own, but something had shifted in the foundation following the 5.0 earthquake that had rattled Ottawa back in June 2010. No amount of hardware tweaking has remedied the door's ability to swing shut of its own accord, and if it were to close after him, he'd be trapped.

The room is long and narrow, running the width of the house. It holds just a mattress and bedding, a couple of folding chairs, and a toilet and washbasin. Before his first visitor, he'd installed the plumbing himself, running pipes up from his own bathroom below.

More recently, he'd welded an iron grid across the window's interior. It was a good twelve feet up in the wall, far beyond an occupant's reach, and too small for an adult to fit through. But when Monique's baby had begun to transform into a boy, the Angler began to worry. What if she stacked the furniture and climbed up with her son hoisted on her shoulders?

The cage ensured that if the window was ever within their grasp, they'd be able to do nothing but gaze out at the world like zoo animals.

"*C'est comme une prison*," she'd wailed in protest, as if it had ever been anything but.

Oh, Monique.

He appreciates the way she'd smoothed the quilt across the mattress on her final morning, two pillows juxtaposed at the top. Her belongings, too, are in order—cosmetics and toiletries aligned along the narrow sink, clothing, hers and the boy's, sorted and stacked on the floor. Her paperback novels are neatly piled on the floor beside one pillow. She'd lit up the day he'd brought them, an afterthought when he'd spotted a Free Books box in the break room at the plant.

"*J'ai adoré lire*," she'd told him in French—past tense, as though her love of reading had been a long-forgotten skill. She'd lovingly stroked the bindings, examining the titles in wonder. "*Merci! Merci!*"

He'd promised her that he would bring her more, reminding her that he wanted her to be happy there with him, that he wasn't *la bête noire*—her worst nightmare.

The way she'd looked up at him when he'd said it . . .

He'd often found her blue eyes impossible to read, and that moment was no exception. But her mouth had quivered ever so slightly, like she'd been trying not to laugh. Or maybe cry, happy tears over his thoughtful gift.

He reaches for a lavender pullover he'd bought to keep her warm when the bitter Canadian winter brought teeth-chattering drafts. Burying his face in the soft fleece, he breathes her essence.

What have I done?

It isn't that she's irreplaceable. In time, he'll find a new angel.

And he sure as hell won't miss the boy, or the way those big blue eyes had stared every time he'd entered the room—not warily, as Monique's had, but more intently, noting details. The way he'd sucked his thumb, making disgusting slurping noises.

"Get him to stop that," he'd warned Monique not long ago, in English. She'd been bilingual but had taught the boy only French.

She claimed to have tried to break the child's nasty habit, to no avail, and so he'd threatened to cut off the offending thumbs with his pocketknife.

"Please, no!" she'd wailed. "Please, he's just a baby."

"He's not a baby. He's a boy, and one day he'll be a man." He couldn't stand the way she'd coddled her son, very much as Cecile does Pascal. It's no way to raise a man.

Better, then, for a boy to have had no mother at all?

His jaw twitches, and he clenches it.

Better, in Monique's case, to have rid the mother of the boy. Why hadn't he taken him away, destroyed him, early on, when those blue eyes of his started staring, glaring?

Why, indeed? That would have been as foolish as tossing a flood insurance policy into a storm surge.

He'd needed the boy as a means of controlling Monique.

He can still hear her shriek the first time he'd ever snatched up her son and carried him from the room.

"What are you doing?"

"Just moving him out here where he can't disturb us. I can't close the door, and we don't need an audience."

It had been a clumsy solution. He could have locked the boy in the trunk of his car, he supposed. Or secured another room in the house where he could take Monique. But there was something powerful, oddly titillating, about enjoying his private time with her, while her child sat with his hands cuffed behind his back. What a pleasure to think that he couldn't get his damned thumbs into his mouth in that position, to imagine him contorting himself in futile attempts.

However, it seemed that the boy had never moved at all whenever he'd been left alone, had never tried to get away by dragging the rack so much as an inch toward the ladder. An imbecile, lacking basic self-preservation instinct. He wouldn't have left his mother any more than she'd have left him . . .

Ah, but she had, the other night.

After the kid had swallowed the chocolate pudding and slumped over, the Angler had told Monique to get ready while he carried him downstairs and dumped him into the car trunk.

She'd known where they were going, what was expected of her when they went out trolling for new girls. They were far more likely to trust him when they spotted a young woman smiling reassuringly from the passenger's seat.

Yes, Monique always smiled like she didn't have a care in the world. He'd been convinced she wouldn't dare do anything else.

Stupid, stupid.

Had she been planning, even as she'd dutifully put on makeup and gotten dressed for their evening out? He imagines her standing right over there, buttoning the silky blouse he'd told her to wear. When they'd first met, she'd told him lavender was her favorite color, and so all of the clothes he'd bought her were the same soft pastel shade. He'd been trying to make her happy, the ungrateful little bitch.

He'd locked her into the car trunk along with her son, same as he always did when they were coming and going, so that she'd have no clue to the whereabouts of Hugo's farm.

There were a number of outbuildings out beyond the weathered red barn. He'd parked by the old henhouse. Inside, he'd been greeted by a familiar stench and flapping and fluttering from the flock along the nesting boxes and roosting rails. The wide plank floor was thick with straw and droppings. You wouldn't see the iron ring unless you knew where to grab for it and lift the heavy trap door to reveal the nice deep root cellar beneath. Sometimes, as the Angler lowered him into it, the kid would stir to awareness and emit muffled screams behind the duct tape over his mouth. Not that time. He'd been out cold.

Had something felt off? Had he missed something, some sign that tonight would be different? Had she been planning, still locked in the trunk as he'd driven on toward Montreal?

He'd stopped on a deserted street just outside city limits to let her join him in the car. He'd reminded her, same as always, what would happen if she tried anything.

"Make one stupid move, say one word to anyone, and your son will die. I'll never tell you or anyone else where he is. Never, under any circumstances. And if anything happens to me, you'll never find him. Where I have hidden him, no one will ever find him. Do you understand?"

"Yes."

"Good. Behave, and you'll have him back when we're finished, same as always. Now let's go catch and release."

That's what he'd called their little missions.

"It's like fishing," he'd told her in the beginning. "Put out a line and see what we can catch. Sometimes, I get lucky, and it's a keeper, like you."

Except, when he's fishing, he dutifully removes the hook from a forbidden species and returns the wriggling creature to the water. The girls aren't swimming back to salvation when he's finished with them.

Monique had said she was hungry after he'd let her out of the trunk, so he'd stopped at a Tim Hortons. He should have used the drive-through, but he had to take a leak, so he'd left her in the car with the usual warnings.

Now who's the imbecile?

He'd left her unsupervised, though, so many times in the past. He'd always found her docile and submissive in the passenger's seat upon his return.

This time had been different. When he'd returned a few minutes later with two coffees and a bag of doughnuts, she was gone.

Stunned, heart pounding, he'd scanned the area. Would she have gone toward the road, or into the trees and undergrowth surrounding the empty parking lot? The road, he'd guessed, chilled at the thought of her flagging down a passing car for help.

As he turned in that direction, his ears had picked up a faint rustling back by the dumpster. He'd whirled back, expecting to see a cat or raccoon. All had been still, but the overhead light cast an unmistakable human shadow across the pavement. He'd pulled out his pistol and stolen toward it.

Expecting her to run, he'd been prepared to chase her into the tangle of foliage.

But she was a wilted, spindly weed, rooted to the spot.

"I'm sorry," she'd whispered. "I don't know what I was . . . I'm sorry. Please. I lost my head for a second there, I just didn't think. I didn't mean to—"

He'd shut her up with a pistol whip across the jaw. She'd gone down without so much as a whimper. He'd thrown her back into the trunk and returned to the farm. When he'd let her out, she'd scanned the rural landscape, perhaps memorizing the location for future reference, just in case . . .

Ah, but her future, at that point, could be measured in seconds. The devil that had gotten into her was gone. Her voice was small and hollow in the dark.

Ignoring her pleas, he'd taken grim pleasure in silencing her.

"Why?" he whispers into the empty room. "Why did

you try to leave me? Why didn't I realize you would do it?"

Stupid. So stupid.

He should have known. He'd spotted icy fissures in her blue eyes lately. When he'd visited, her energy had seemed different. Brazen, even reckless.

She'd been clenched with pent-up resentment, rage . . . a plan? Or had her digression been impulsive—a momentary lapse in judgment, a flicker of madness?

How could she have thought that if she'd managed to escape, she'd find her way back to her son? She'd had no way of knowing where he was. Even if she'd somehow managed to keep track of the time it had taken to travel to the farm, she couldn't know the direction or distance. He could have been anywhere within a three-hour radius of Ottawa.

The only thing that makes sense is her maternal instinct had finally given way to self-preservation.

He can only hope that his own reckless mistake won't come back to haunt him.

His life, after all, is built on lies, painstakingly layered and precariously stacked, one atop another, like the wooden blocks he and Uncle Hugo had carved that summer on the farm.

If the tower falls, you lose . . .

He could have, should have left the boy in the root cellar to rot like forgotten harvest. Yet he'd been worried that if remains had ever been found, they might be linked to Hugo's DNA, and traced right back to him, the bloodline's lone descendant.

It had been far riskier to leave the corpse out there in the open, where someone might come along and find him before he's unidentifiable.

Again, he assures himself that there will be no incriminating evidence even then.

A heap of dead flesh and bone in America will never link him to me.

And even if the child were alive, even if he were capable of speaking—which he'd never proven—what could he possibly reveal that would lead the authorities in this direction?

Monique herself had never seen the house or surrounding neighborhood, nor the farm. Nor had she ever even known his name. Still—

His phone buzzes in his pocket with an incoming call. He pulls it out.

Cecile . . . again?

Frowning, he answers the call. "Yes?" Greeted with a torrent of French, he interrupts, "You know I hate that! Talk to me in English!"

His father's voice echoes in his head. *Parle-moi en français!*

Only Monique had been allowed to converse with him in French. Her sweet accent had charmed him from the beginning.

Again, Cecile blurts a rush of information, this time in English. He discerns only, "Pascal . . . very sick . . . tests . . . hospital."

He closes his eyes and tilts his head to the ceiling. Damn her. Couldn't she have taken the boy to a pediatrician? She had to go to the hospital?

He counts to three before asking, calmly, "What's wrong with him?"

"His stomach. We have been here for hours. I have been trying to reach you."

"Yeah, well, I'm at work. You know that."

A brief pause. "*Oui*. But the doctor said you should come. It is not good."

He sighs. "All right. I'll come."

Hanging up, he turns abruptly to leave the room. His foot knocks the lamp in the doorway. It teeters, and he catches it before it topples out onto the attic floor. Close call, he thinks, shoving the lamp back out into the attic, stepping out of the room, and watching the door slam on its own.

A BLOCK FROM the beach and several from the heart of town, Rob's *casa particular* is a violet concrete box with splashes of red trim and slatted shutters on the open windows.

It's clean enough but smells faintly of mildew. Creaky metal ceiling fans push hot air around. The kitchen appliances are outdated, furnishings rudimentary, fabrics threadbare, electronics nonexistent. There's one shared bathroom—tub, no shower. The largest of the three bedrooms—or more accurately, the least tiny—contains a double bed and goes to Rob. Kurtis is next door in a room that barely holds a twin bed and dresser. Barnes is down the hall in a sunny space with just a twin bed. He has to kneel on it to close the door, and the mattress is lumpy but serviceable. He sinks onto it and closes his eyes. Ah . . . peaceful solitude at last.

He hears Rob leave, heading out to El Yunque.

A few minutes later, Kurtis knocks on the door. "Hey, Uncle Stockton?"

He sits up and opens it a crack. "Everything okay?"

"I'm walking into town to grab lunch at that *paladar* my dad showed us on the way in."

Probably, Barnes thinks, because Rob had mentioned

you can pick up Wi-Fi access in the nearby plaza. At least, he hopes that and maybe food are all he's looking for. Rob had warned him, on the flight over from the US, not to touch drugs here in Cuba, where punishment is severe and lengthy. Kurtis had assured his father that he wouldn't, but after the anxiety-ridden journey to Baracoa, a younger Barnes himself might have been tempted.

"You want anything, Uncle Stockton?"

He should probably eat, but he's far more exhausted than he is hungry. "Just a bottle of water would be good, thanks, Kurtis."

"Sure thing." He hesitates. "Do you, uh, have any money? They don't take American Express anywhere down here, and I . . . forgot to ask my dad."

"Of course." Barnes fishes some pesos out of his pocket and hands them over.

"Thanks." He shifts his weight. "Can you, uh, not tell—"

"It's our secret. Just be careful out there, okay?"

"Don't worry. I can take care of myself, no matter what my father thinks."

Barnes settles back onto the mattress.

Maybe he should have taken that private moment to tell Kurtis he and Rob are lucky to have each other, and not to take that for granted. Yes, Rob can be stubborn and controlling, but Kurtis is impetuous and idealistic.

He could have pointed out that Rob has been there from the start, stayed married to his mother, given him siblings, a luxurious home, a college education, everything money can buy.

My father only gave me a fraction of that, and he was my hero.

Yet there's no telling what might have happened had Charles Barnes lived until they could be men together. Maybe they, too, would be fractious as rival tomcats.

Barnes falls asleep to the sound of waves lapping and seabirds calling beyond a stand of banana fronds edging the back terrace. He awakens to the same, but long shadows now fall across the bed. He's soaked in perspiration, and ferocious hunger gnaws his stomach like a shark on chum.

He gets up, opens the door, and pads barefoot through the house, calling for Kurtis and Rob. The place is empty. So is his stomach. And the fridge. So much for the bottle of water Kurtis was supposed to bring.

He eyes the faucet, tempted to forget the warnings and drink some. Is there a thirst more urgent than this, born of sweat, liquor, and vomiting?

Throw diarrhea into the mix, and you'll find out.

He finds his flip-flops, sunglasses, and some cash, steps outside and remembers, belatedly, that Rob didn't give him a key for the door. Or maybe there isn't one?

He thinks of his duffel bag sitting there on his bed with his cell phone, wallet, keys to his Manhattan apartment, and passport zipped inside. The phone, credit cards, and keys are useless here, and it seems wiser to leave his passport in his bag than to carry it with him through unfamiliar streets.

But in an unlocked house? A hotel safe would be ideal. A hotel would be ideal, with locked doors and room service and pretty happy hour bartenders . . . though maybe he really should swear off women for a while. He isn't attracted to the weak ones—the ones who want him to stay.

And the ones who don't—the strong ones—demand, and deserve, far better than the likes of him.

He closes the door behind him and starts making his way on foot through the residential neighborhood. August in New York is downright brisk compared to this dense tropical heat. Mosquitos and gnats buzz around, nip at, and stick to his perspiration-slicked skin. After passing several shirtless men, Barnes takes off his own, uses it to mop himself, and drapes it around his neck like a gym towel.

Ramshackle houses cluster on inclines and cram along narrow dirt lanes. Some are low and rectangular, a few two stories with double-decker porches. Most are painted in a bright tropical palette, the flamboyant patchwork occasionally broken by monochromatic new concrete cinder-block construction or faded dilapidated relics.

In the heart of town, he crosses the triangular Plaza Independencia, teeming with activity as day fades to evening. Locals lounge on benches, smoking and drinking, arguing and laughing as children and dogs romp freely. He sees a few people playing checkers, others dancing without inhibition. Scattered musicians pluck guitars, beat bongos, and shake maracas, creating a glorious unsynchronized harmony. Street vendors weave among obvious tourists, focused on their cell phones in this rare Wi-Fi hotspot. One approaches Barnes, carrying a stick dangling with ice cream cone–shaped palm frond packets—*cucurucho*, he explains in Spanish, a unique local delicacy. Barnes buys one and strolls on, devouring the concoction of sweetened coconut, tropical fruits, and nuts.

Appetite raging, he locates the *paladar* Rob had pointed out—a lime-green shack tucked into a cobblestone courtyard in the shadow of an ancient church. About to pull his tee shirt back on, he notes that he and the waiter would be the only fully dressed men in the place.

No shirt, no shoes? Apparently, no problem here. You want an authentic travel experience, you eat where the locals eat—and dine as they dine.

Barnes takes a white molded plastic chair and table between a trio of elderly women arguing good-naturedly over pungent coffee and cigarettes, and a group of deeply tanned, shirtless men engaged in raucous conversation. At least ten minutes pass before a bearded young waiter strolls over with a basket of *chicharrones*.

Barnes asks him in Spanish whether a young man of Kurtis's description had been here earlier. The waiter shakes his head.

Barnes requests a menu and bottled water and is informed the restaurant doesn't have either of those things. Alrighty, then. "*Tienes arroz con pollo y una botella de cerveza?*"

Ah, yes, that, they do have: "chicken and rice and a bottle of beer."

He's not seeking hair of the dog or even a happy hour buzz, but when you're parched and can't drink the water, your safest bet is beer.

He leans back, crunching the delicious fried pork rinds, and takes in the rutted street, clogged with bicycles, pedicabs, motorbikes, *camiones*, even a horse and cart. There are a few cars, too—sherbet-colored American throwbacks, though not as well maintained as they'd been around Havana. Clothing flutters from clotheslines strung between the houses. Wandering tourists are distinguishable by their backpacks and sneakers. The air is thick with humid brine, lively conversation, fried and roasted food. "Guantanamera" is, as always, playing somewhere, everywhere.

It takes so long for his beer to reach his sweaty hands that he orders a second before he takes his first sip. It goes down easily, seeping sheer relaxation into his limbs.

He eavesdrops on a group of middle-aged men gathered around an adjacent table. The one with his back to Barnes seems to be an American expat. Like the others, he has shaggy hair and a beard, and is wearing only a pair of shorts. If not for his friends teasingly referring to him as a *yuma*, Barnes would never have guessed at a glance that he isn't a local. But now he notices the subtly accented Spanish, relatively fair coloring, and sun-damaged, thickly freckled shoulders.

Maybe Barnes, too, could live here. Maybe that wasn't just a drunken fantasy. Maybe he should give it a try.

Funny. He's been traveling for years, has never had second thoughts about going home to New York afterward to resume his life. But America is a hot mess right now with the election looming, and this is the country where his beloved *abuela* had been born.

"Pride . . . You're going to grasp your roots, and

you're going to understand who you are . . . in your blood."

He's always felt profoundly American, but Rob was right—about Barnes, though maybe not about Kurtis. He does feel connected to this place, and these people.

He sips his second *cerveza* and reluctantly orders a third, still thirsty, still starved, and hoping the food gets to the table before the beer goes to his head. Not likely, though. He still doesn't have a napkin or silverware, though the table is equipped with a bottle of hot sauce and an ashtray filled with red-lipstick-stained cigarette butts.

The sun has disappeared behind the palm trees and church steeple. Soft, warm light slips like a hug from the swooping, graceful arms of an old-world streetlamp. Salsa music, laughter, and conversation from a nearby nightclub float on the humid evening air. Passersby heading in that direction are younger and livelier, passing in groups. The women are scantily clad and wear towering stilettos; the men, guayabera shirts and linen pants. He keeps an eye out for Kurtis among the club-bound crowd.

A troubled young man might find trouble around here, if he were so inclined. Or anywhere, really. Barnes should know.

Been there, done that.

Again, he glances over at the American seated nearby, wondering how he'd wound up here. Maybe he can strike up a conversation, ask for some tips.

Yeah, and maybe you're starting to get drunk again.

He sets down the bottle and pushes it back . . . too hard. It slides right off the edge of the table and shatters on the cobblestones. Laughter erupts at surrounding tables, and a few onlookers raise their own bottles and glasses in salute, as though he'd offered some bizarre toast.

If this were New York, waitstaff would come hurrying over with a broom and dustpan to pick up the shards before someone gets cut and sues the place. Not here. He bends over to pick up the largest pieces, but it's shadowy down there. The first one he touches slices into his hand.

Terrific.

He sits up and checks the cut. Not deep, just a surface nick across his forefinger. If he had a napkin, he could wrap it and put pressure on it. Instead, he sticks it into his mouth and looks for the waiter.

The word *gringo* reaches his ears from the next table, and he feels the group looking at him. Glancing up, he finds one of the men leaning over, offering something. A red bandana.

"Aqui tienes." The man smiles. He's about Barnes's age, with glossy dark hair, crooked teeth, and eyebrows like black caterpillars.

"No, *gracias*." Barnes shakes his head and tells him in Spanish that he can't take it, that it'll be ruined with blood, but the man insists. Barnes thanks him profusely and looks again for the waiter, this time to request a round of drinks for the man and his friends.

Still no sign of the waiter. Barnes wraps the cut in the bandana, doubting its sterility. He doubts he'll find antibiotic ointment and bandages around here at this hour. Maybe Rob packed some in his bag.

And you think you're going to relocate to Cuba?

He's barely made it through the first twenty-four hours—drinking all the rum in all the land, breaking a heart, puking his brains out, nearly dying in a plane crash, sleeping the day away, and now drawing his own blood.

You'd make a lousy expat.

He finds himself grinning, and then, feeling someone's eyes on him, looks again at the next table. The American is watching him, and . . .

No. It can't be.

You're drunk. You have to be. Because there's no way that can possibly be . . .

But it is.

The barefoot, shaggy man is missing New York tycoon Perry Wayland.

Chapter Seven

Opening the door to the apartment, Amelia hears loud music amid the high-pitched whir of a wet saw. Vintage Eagles, one of Aaron's favorite bands.

She smiles. He must be home and blasting "Heartache Tonight," because . . .

Because he realized he's going to miss you this weekend?

Because your anniversary made him nostalgic, and he's remembering the good old days?

Because somehow, in the middle of a Friday afternoon, he's not at the office?

"Aaron?"

She leaves her rolling bag by the door and pokes her head into the rubble-strewn kitchen, where a pair of workmen are installing the new backsplash. The music is coming from an iPhone plugged into Aaron's high-end Bluetooth speaker.

Spotting her in the doorway, a workman jumps to lower the volume. "Sorry about that, Mrs. Haines."

"It's okay, Pete. I just stopped home to grab something. You can turn it back up."

He gestures at the section of white tile mounted to the wall between the white marble counter and white cabinets. "What do you think of the backsplash so far?"

"You mean the bland-splash?"

"Your husband likes it."

"No, I know, it's fine. It's beautiful," she adds, and he looks relieved. "Nice job."

Aaron had talked her into the classic white subway tile. She'd have preferred a herringbone mosaic in metallic coppery shades.

"We have to go basic, Amelia. Think about resale value."

"It's not like we need to worry about that anytime soon."

"You never know."

She'd frowned. "You never know whether we're selling our home and moving away? Didn't we say when we bought it that we were going to live here forever?"

"That was ten years ago."

"And . . ."

"Never mind," he'd said as if dismissing a half-witted stranger who hadn't grasped an obvious truth.

She opens the study door to find Clancy poised on the other side, tiny and expectant, tail in the air. She picks him up and he purrs. "Aw, somebody's glad to see me." Cuddling his warm, rumbly little body against the bare crook of her neck, she carries him to the bedroom, puts him on the bed, and picks up her phone.

She's missed several calls, all from Aaron.

No time to change into jeans for the trip, but she kicks off her shoes and finds a pair of shearling-lined sneakers in her closet. She dials Aaron and balances the phone between her shoulder and ear as she pulls soft yarn socks over her punished feet.

After a few rings, she hears Aaron's harried, "Hey."

"Hey."

"I just stepped out of a meeting. Are you on the bus?"

"I'm about to be. What's up?" She pushes her feet into the cushy sneakers, the edges hitting below her blisters. Ah, relief.

"I just wanted to let you know that I'm flying to California tomorrow instead of Sunday."

"What?"

"Yeah, I figured, why stick around home if you're going to be gone?" he asks as though he sticks around at all, lately, when she is here.

"But . . . I was counting on you to feed Clancy. Didn't you see my email?"

"What email?"

"The one I sent asking you to feed Clancy!"

"Why are you emailing me? Why not just—"

"Because I forgot my phone when I left for work this morning."

A pause. "Well, you're on it now."

She resists sarcasm. "I had to come home to grab it, and I'm going to miss the bus if I don't get out of here. Aaron, please don't go tomorrow. I need—"

"I already changed the flight."

"Are you sure you didn't see the email? Because I feel like maybe you read it and then changed your flight."

"Why would I do that?"

"You tell me."

She hates her petty, petulant self, but this isn't just about Clancy, or Aaron's disregard this morning for Lily Tucker and the ring, or even about his failure to invite her closest friend to the party.

"Amelia, what's going on? Why are you acting so . . ."

Because we're losing each other. The things that are important to me don't matter to you anymore. Did they ever?

"Sorry. Just . . . go back to your meeting. I'll call Jessie and tell her I can't come after all."

"Bring the cat with you. They'll never even notice with the menagerie in that house."

"Too late. I've already missed the bus. See you tonight."

"Yeah, I have that dinner, so—"

"See you whenever, then."

He starts to respond, but she disconnects the call, flecks of misgiving dropping like singular hourglass grains, contributing to the rising lump in her gut.

She looks at her watch. It's 1:52. The bus leaves in twenty-eight minutes. Chances are she really will miss it, but it's worth a shot.

"Hey, Clance, how do you feel about road trips?" She scoops him up and he mews loudly. "I'll take that for a yes."

At the Port Authority twenty-seven minutes later, she stashes her rolling bag in the luggage compartment and boards the bus with her laptop bag slung over one shoulder and Clancy's small canvas carrier over the other. She'd grabbed a few cans of his food, his little bowls, and thrown some clean litter into an empty plastic takeout container to serve as a makeshift litter box for the trip.

She makes her way toward the last available seat, against the window in the back row by the bathroom. The elderly man sitting on the aisle pretends not to see her, turning the page of his *Daily News*.

"Excuse me."

He looks up with watery blue eyes sunken in a liver-spotted face, mouth set as though he's just been force-fed a raw artichoke.

"May I?" She gestures at the empty seat.

He sighs and stands, allowing her to squeeze past. She plunks herself down with Clancy's carrier on her lap, wedging her other bag under her legs.

The man reclaims his seat, making certain that his slight build and open newspaper overflow onto hers. She resists the urge to scrunch herself closer to the window and validate his irritation.

The bus starts moving, navigating the maze of sloping ramps to street level and the Lincoln Tunnel. The air is close and damp. It's not raining in New York, but she doesn't need a forecast to predict that it will be in Ithaca. When she looks back on her college years there, memories often feature dramatic weather.

She unbuttons the khaki raincoat she'd thrown on as she'd left the apartment. She should have taken off the coat before she'd sat down. Now she's stuck wearing it until her seatmate disembarks—at the first stop, with luck.

The Burberry trench had been a gift from Aaron. "Timeless," he'd said, when she'd protested the extravagance. "It'll never go out of style, and it'll hold up forever." Fifteen years later, it's held up better than . . . a lot of things.

The old man taps her arm. "Is that a cat?"

"A kitten. Yes."

"I'm allergic."

"I'm sorry. But he's tiny, and pets are allowed"—she's guessing—"and I won't take him out of the carrier at all."

He glares. "How far are you going?"

"Ithaca. You?"

"Buffalo."

Stuck with each other. Terrific.

He crosses his leg with his knee to the aisle, his lug-soled shoe bumping her leg. No apology. Jerk.

She wriggles her phone from her pocket and sees that Aaron had called her phone twice while she'd been underground on the subway. He hadn't left a message. Probably calling to apologize. With a twinge of guilt, she wishes she'd told him she was going away after all.

She's not one of those people who makes phone calls on public transportation, though it appears that everyone around her, save the old man, is wearing headphones. A quick, quiet call probably won't disturb them.

She takes out her phone and feels the old man's shoe jab her leg again. She looks at him.

He points to her cell. "You aren't going to talk on that the whole trip, I hope."

"The *whole* trip? No." Tempted to ask him in return if he's going to be crowding her seat and kicking her the whole trip, she dials Jessie's number and gets voice mail.

"Hi, in case you didn't see my email, I'm on the bus. It gets in at . . . I have no idea. Around six thirty, maybe? Or seven? Oh, and I'm bringing Clancy. Is that okay? I'll call you when I get in."

She keeps her voice low, barely above a whisper. Yet her seatmate makes disgruntled noises and crackles his newspaper, his elbow digging into her ribs. She dials Jessie's home number, but gets voice mail there, too. She leaves the same message and then sends a text to cover all her bases.

A moment after she hits Send, her phone vibrates. That was fast.

But the incoming text isn't from Jessie. It's from Aaron.

Been trying to call you. Can you take my gray suit to the dry cleaner? Need overnight rush for trip tomorrow.

Seriously?

She turns off her phone, shoves it deep into her coat pocket, and stares out the window at the black tunnel looming ahead.

THE ANGLER SHOULD be heading south, toward the bridge and New York State, and the dead boy in the orchard. Instead, he's making his way toward the hospital in the western suburbs. The late afternoon sun is at just the right angle to produce a blinding glare, slowing congested traffic to a crawl.

He curses his wife. There's a name for this . . . this mental illness, or whatever it is that has her constantly worrying about the children. He'd recently seen something on the news about a woman who kept wanting to believe there was something wrong with her baby—or was it that she was actually making the baby sick?

Yet he can't alert the doctors to Cecile's condition

for the same reason he'll never be able to extract himself from his marriage. He can't have outsiders snooping into their private lives.

Reaching the hospital at last, he parks in the emergency room lot alongside a sign warning that cars will be towed after thirty minutes. That will be plenty of time to resolve this mess, get Pascal out of here, and be on his way to New York.

Hurrying toward the door, he passes a pretty brunette of about thirteen sitting cross-legged on a bench with a book. She's dressed in a hoodie, black leggings, and sneakers, and twirls a wisp of dark hair around her index finger as she reads.

He's struck by the resemblance to his wife, the first time he'd seen her in a café. Cecile, too, had worn glasses. She, too, had been engrossed in an open textbook, absently toying with her long hair. She, too, had stirred a familiar, forbidden yearning.

He'd assumed Cecile had been a teenager there to do her homework. He'd managed to drop several loose coins from his pocket as he walked past with his coffee. Cecile had glanced up, irritated by the rolling clatter, and he'd seen that she might be older than he'd thought. Sixteen, maybe seventeen?

He'd asked about the large textbook she was reading, and struck gold. It was about European monarchies. He'd mentioned his genetic roots in the Capetian Dynasty, and with minimal seductive effort on his part, wound up in her bed that night.

By then, he'd discovered that Cecile was of legal age, a university exchange student from the Sorbonne. She wasn't merely studying royalty; she was obsessed with it—and, in turn, with him.

He was under no illusion that an attractive co-ed would have been attracted to a thirty-year-old industrial welder if not for her desire to stay in North America—and her naïve fantasy that his royal lineage might one day lead to some kind of recognition or riches.

Marriage had been her idea, and for him, it had seemed the right thing to do. On the heels of an abnormal childhood, he'd needed to prove—to his dead father? His absent mother? Himself?—that he could be normal. That he could control his own destiny as well as his errant desires.

He walks on past the young girl on the bench and finds the emergency room hectic. Reminding himself that Cecile is a twisted woman and could very well have lied about the doctor summoning him here, he looks around the waiting area, half expecting to see her and Pascal among the patients waiting to be seen.

But they aren't there, and when he asks the woman behind the desk about his son, she immediately checks his ID and buzzes him through the locked door.

"Wait here," she says. "A nurse will come get you."

He leans against a wall, arms folded, toe tapping. He doesn't have time for this. He really doesn't. Every minute that passes could be carrying him back to New York State to cover his tracks.

Stupid, stupid, stupid . . .

Medical personnel rush past, pushing equipment carts and wheelchairs. Machines beep, a baby wails, a man moans, a young woman unleashes a shrill stream of cursing, and sirens of a departing ambulance meld with those of an arriving one.

A male nurse in green scrubs appears, asks him if he's Pascal's father, and instructs him to follow. He leads the way past the curtained treatment cubicles and into the main hospital, along a maze of hallways to a bank of elevators. He presses the button for the fourth-floor surgical unit.

For the first time, the Angler allows himself to doubt his instincts. What if something really is wrong?

He thinks of Pascal's wee-hour abdominal pain. Remembers, with a sickening twist in his own stomach, how he'd dosed—overdosed?—the boy with sticky purple medicine.

"What's going on?" he asks the nurse.

"They'll explain upstairs."

What if the cops are waiting for him? What if they know about the purple medicine? What if they know about everything else?

Thank goodness he'd been careful, resisting the urge to use something stronger on Pascal as he does on the other boy. No, he wouldn't administer Rohypnol to this child, even though he knows that it would never be detected in routine bloodwork unless it was suspected and sent to a forensic lab.

The doors slide open and several people get off. The nurse steps in.

"Coming?" he asks, a hand on the doors to keep them from closing.

The Angler nods, resisting the urge to bolt.

They ride to the fourth floor in silence.

Surely this isn't some kind of elaborate trap.

If it is . . .

I'll deny everything. They'll have no evidence. I've covered my tracks.

What about the computer search? He's almost positive he hadn't erased it. He'd been eager to escape the house, so exhausted, concerned that he'd left the boy alive out there in the orchard . . .

Dammit. Dammit!

He's always been careful to clear his computer activity, so cautious about where he disposed of the remains. The few girls who'd turned up over the past decade had been too decomposed for identification or had been such lost souls that not even the authorities seemed to care who they'd been or how they'd died.

It was different with Monique, though. She has a family, and they haven't given up on finding her. Early on, he'd taken great pleasure in lurking on their social media pages as they chased leads that would never go anywhere. Photos and sketches of the wholesome teen who'd disappeared four years ago bear little resemblance to the gaunt corpse he dumped into the lake.

There's no way, absolutely no way, that anyone could have found her there.

And her son . . .

No one on this earth knows she even had a child. Now that she's gone, no one cares about him—cares that he existed. No one is looking for him. If he's found, no one will ever know his name.

The elevator stops, and the doors slide open with a ding.

The nurse steps out, again giving him an expectant look. He forces himself to step out, to follow along another corridor. The nurse stops and opens a door, gesturing. "Go ahead in."

The room beyond is shielded from view, shades drawn over the wall of glass.

He has no choice but to cross the threshold, bracing himself for police.

But it's an ordinary waiting room—a wall television tuned to *CBC News*, a low table with magazines surrounded by a cluster of chairs, all empty. Cecile, the sole occupant, turns toward the door, hope and dread mingling on her face until she sees that it's only him.

She's impeccably dressed as always, in a black cardigan, dark jeans, and heeled boots. But she looks pale and washed-out—no cosmetics, he notes with surprise. She doesn't leave the house without eyeliner and lipstick—or accessories, for that matter. She's fond of hoop earrings and silk scarves, yet her neck and earlobes are bare.

"It took you so long."

"I came as fast as I could."

"The plant is fifteen minutes from here."

His house is thirty-five without sun glare and brake lights. It had taken him nearly an hour.

"There was traffic. Where is Pascal?"

"In surgery."

"Surgery!" He turns to the nurse, but the man has disappeared down the hallway. Slowly, he faces Cecile again. "Why is he in surgery?"

She says something, but her accent makes it difficult to comprehend.

"Did you say it's his appendix?"

"*Oui*. They are taking it out now. What if it is too late?" She clasps a fist to her colorless, trembling lips and spins away.

He turns to leave the room, notes that someone is

about to enter, and instead moves toward Cecile, placing his hands on her shoulders. She stiffens.

"It will be all right, my darling."

There had been a time when he might have said just that, perhaps even without benefit of a witness. But he's long since lost any affection he once felt—or at least feigned—for her.

He expects her to recoil, but her shoulders slacken beneath his hands. She turns slightly to rest her head on his shoulder, and there's nothing to do but embrace her. He pretends not to see the person in the doorway.

Whoever it is—a woman—clears her throat. Cecile pulls back, spots her, and is once again seized by that anticipatory expression of trepidation tinged with optimism.

"Dr. Lee. How did it go?"

The Angler turns to see a small woman in surgical scrubs and cap, a mask dangling from her neck. She strides toward them, briefly introduces herself to him as the surgeon who'd been about to operate on Pascal.

"*About* to operate?" Cecile sinks into a chair, braced for bad news. Her voice is high-pitched, frantic.

The surgeon turns to the Angler. "Please, sit."

He forces himself to sit beside Cecile and to place his hand over hers on the wooden arm between them in a show of husbandly/fatherly concern.

Dr. Lee tells them that Pascal's appendix had become inflamed and perforated, leaking pus. His body had sealed it off in an attempt to isolate the infection, resulting in a bacteria-filled abscess surrounding the organ.

"While the usual treatment for an inflamed or ruptured appendix would be surgical removal, an abscess creates a significant complication risk."

"But you cannot just leave it!"

The Angler resists the urge to slap Cecile.

Dr. Lee explains that they've started Pascal on triple intravenous antibiotic therapy. He'll remain hospitalized for at least a week, maybe longer, depending on how the infection responds. If all goes well, they'll schedule the appendectomy.

"Any questions?"

Cecile has many. The Angler remains silent, pretending to listen.

So he'd been wrong about Cecile's mental disorder. She hadn't exaggerated her son's illness—at least, not this time.

His thoughts drift back to the boy in the orchard.

Staggering coincidence. One son dead, the other clinging to life, all within twenty-four hours.

"How did this happen?" his wife is asking. "It was something he ate, *oui*?"

"No, that's very unlikely."

"He did not catch it from me," she tells the surgeon.

"Oh, it's not contagious. Nothing like that."

"It is hereditary, then? Because we have never had this in my family."

"We've never had it in mine, either." The Angler fights to keep his tone level, when he wants to spit at her.

"How would you know? You have no family."

The surgeon clears her throat. "Appendicitis isn't a congenital condition. There are only theories on what causes it."

Purple pediatric syrup can't possibly be one of them. If anything, the medicine had allowed the boy to get some sleep so that he'd been rested before this ordeal.

That makes two of us.

"I'll send someone to escort you to Pascal's room as soon as he's settled," the surgeon says, and is gone.

Left alone with Cecile, he watches her rub her eyes with both her hands. When she looks up, he is again caught off guard by her appearance. Her unblemished complexion is sallow in the fluorescent light, and a web of faint wrinkles surrounds her eyes.

He hasn't been attracted to her in years, nor, he supposes, has he truly looked at her. Now that he has, he feels repelled. She's transformed into a plain, middle-aged woman, the epitome of the very ordinariness he'd once coveted.

The novelty has long since worn off.

But she'll never give him a divorce without a bitter struggle—lawyers, financial disclosure, the kind of scrutiny he's managed to avoid thus far. She needs him—as provider, if nothing else.

He supposes he needs her as well. Needs what she and the children represent. No one would ever suspect a hardworking family man of what he's done.

"Renee," she says suddenly, looking up at him.

He frowns. Has she somehow mistaken him for their daughter? Is this some kind of mental breakdown? Ah, there would be his ticket out of this marriage, this life.

"I called the school earlier and sent her home with a friend. You will need to pick her up, make her dinner, check her homework."

He shakes his head. That's always been her department, not his—shuttling the children around, feeding them, anything to do with school.

"Go. She cannot stay alone, and I will not leave Pascal!"

"He'll be here for days. I have a job to go to." A trip to make; a body to bury.

"You do not work on weekends."

She's right. He'd lost track of which day it is.

He weighs his options.

He can walk out of here, get into his car, and keep right on driving. He can forget about Cecile and her demands, about Pascal, and Renee . . .

Forget all of them, and this life, forever. He can leave town, leave the country, start anew.

Five minutes later, he exits the hospital, car keys clasped so hard that his palm may be bleeding. Striding toward the car, he catches sight of the young girl, still sitting on the bench.

She's no longer reading, but has her phone in hand, texting.

His legs break stride of their own accord.

She looks up, seeing him.

"Are you all right?" he asks, and she looks around, uncertain whether he's talking to her.

"Me? Yeah. Why?"

He shrugs. "Just making sure. This is a hospital."

"I'm waiting for my mom. She's visiting my grandpa. I'm not allowed to—" Her phone buzzes, and she glances down. "Good, she's coming. About time."

She stands, gathering her book and backpack. When she shoots him a sidewise look, he realizes he's rooted, staring at her. He forces himself to walk on toward his car without a backward glance.

If her mother weren't coming . . .

There are others, though, out there. Others just like her.

Chapter Eight

Jessie looks up from her laptop as Billy descends the stairs for the third time in an hour.

"Still asleep?" she asks.

"Looks that way, unless he's faking it. How's the work going?"

"Oh, you know . . . it's work. But I'm done."

She'd spent today catching up on endless forms and paperwork, and finally just finished reconstructing the report she'd lost the other night when the power went out. She saves it to her hard drive, closes her laptop, and glances at her watch. It's well past six o'clock.

Theodore will be home soon. He stays late at school on Fridays for the computer club they'd convinced him to join in an effort to make some new friends. Well, any friends at all. When she asks him about the weekly meetings, he answers in broad terms and refuses to elaborate.

Oh, Theodore. Sometimes, I don't feel equipped to help you navigate this world. On days like this, I don't know how I'm doing it myself.

"Do you think he's okay, Jess?"

She looks up at Billy, thinking he's read her thoughts and is talking about their son until she sees his worried glance toward the stairs.

"Little Boy Blue? He's probably just exhausted after

all he's been through. But I'll look in on him. I have to go up and get my phone to check my email. Though I have to say, it was a nice afternoon without it. Amazing how much more productive I am when I'm not distracted by online stuff."

"Then you're going to get a lot done, because I doubt the Wi-Fi repairman is going to show today."

"You're probably right. Good thing Theodore can get online using his cell phone while it's down."

"And use up our entire monthly data allotment? No way. He'll have to wait."

"Come on, Billy, Theodore's going to have a hard enough time this weekend as it is, with . . ." She nods at the second floor. "He'll be even more upset if he can't escape to the internet."

"So you want to pay for something we can't afford because he'll be upset? Would we have done that with Chip and Petty?"

"He isn't Chip and Petty."

Billy sighs and settles into the worn recliner. "We always seem to be reminding each other of that, don't we?"

How many variations of this conversation have they had since Theodore came to live with them? Will they ever be able to define the line between accommodating special needs and spoiling him?

Billy is scrolling through his cell phone again. He's been compulsively checking it all day, and she knows what he's looking for. "Anything new?"

"Nothing. He doesn't fit any missing child reports."

"If nobody's noticed by now, then nobody cares. You know who we need? Mimi."

He blinks. "She's a genealogist, not a detective."

"Hello, she's an *investigative* genealogist? That *is* a detective. Figuring out where people belong is what she does for a living. I bet she'd be able to—"

"Whoa, we're just the fosters. I'm not working this investigation. And *you* are definitely not working it, with or without Mimi."

"Yeah, don't worry, Ricky Ricardo. We aren't going to barge on stage at the Tropicana and muck up your career."

"Not to change the subject, *Lucy*, but what were you thinking for dinner?"

"Broiled chicken and salad for us. A vegan hot dog for Theodore." He'd stopped eating poultry when Espinoza came along. "Oh, and I'm going to make some buttered egg noodles."

His face lights. "I love buttered egg noo—"

"Not for you, for Little Boy Blue. I'm hoping he'll be hungry when he wakes up."

"I am. I'm starved."

"Oh, for . . ." She shakes her head. "You just had a snack."

"You mean that tiny bag of microwave popcorn? It was only a hundred calories. I'm a big guy. I need—"

"To be a smaller guy. That's what you need, unless you have a death wish, and I swear to God, Billy, if you keel over and leave me now with this leaky roof and the rooster fiasco and no Wi-Fi, I will kill you. *Again*," she adds when he opens his mouth. "Just to make sure you're good and dead. And don't you dare even *think* about haunting me."

He flashes a wry smile. "So sweet. Love you, too, babe."

She sighs and heads for the stairs. "I'm just trying to take care of you."

Of everyone.

She shares with Little Boy Blue something that no other child who's come into this house—including her biological children and even her adopted son—can ever understand, something even Billy can't fully fathom, nor Si back in his lucid years. Of all the people she's ever known and loved in her life, only Mimi grasps the complex emotions that accompany being a foundling, and the irony in the term itself. Some days—most days—you feel far more lost than found.

As she puts her foot on the first step, she hears cellophane crinkling in the living room. She tiptoes back to see him pop something into his mouth. "Hey! What is that?"

The answer is thick with sticky-sweet crunch.

"Billy, are you *kidding* me? You're eating a *doughnut* after the cardiologist told you that's one of the worst things you can put into your body?"

He finishes chewing and swallowing. "No! You know I swore off doughnuts."

"Oh, good. You had me worried." Seeing a guilty tinge in his eyes, she narrows hers at him. "What was it?"

"Zagnut. They had them in the hospital vending machine. What? Don't look at me like that. It was a long night."

"And you're going to have a short life if you die of a heart attack."

"Yeah, well, I don't want to die of starvation, either."

"Believe me, you won't—" She breaks off at a knock on the door. "Theodore must have forgotten his key."

"He never forgets anything. It's probably the case-worker. Or the Wi-Fi repairman."

"Oh, right."

Someone is silhouetted through the frosted glass. She opens the door to an astounding sight.

"Thirty years, and the doorbell is still out of order?" Mimi asks with a laugh, and Jessie throws her arms around her.

"Holy crap—are you *magical*? I was just wishing you were here, and you appeared!"

"You invited me, remember?"

"Yes, but . . . what about your anniversary?" She holds the door open so that Mimi can step into the vestibule, with its ancient mosaic tile floor and cedar-lined coat closet that holds everything but coats. Those, they drape over the antique coat tree in the foyer.

"Aaron and I already celebrated. He, uh . . . threw us a party."

"That's . . . great. How sweet."

"I'm sorry, Jess. I wish I'd known about it. I would've made sure you were invited."

"If you'd known about it, it wouldn't have been a surprise party." She forces a smile, trying not to take the slight personally.

Jessie had gotten along well with Aaron in the early days, and she'd thought he was good for Mimi. But as his wife matured and became successful with her own business, Aaron had changed. Or maybe it's Mimi who's changed, and Jessie along with her. Maybe Aaron has always been somewhat rigid, self-satisfied, and a little too urbane for her taste.

The few times he'd accompanied his wife on an Ithaca "getaway," it had been pretty obvious that he couldn't wait to get home.

"He's a New Yorker," Billy had reminded her. "A commercial litigation attorney. Things are different there. To him, we're country bumpkins."

"Speak for yourself, Li'l Abner."

They'd laughed and dropped the subject. As long as Mimi's happy . . .

"I'm sorry, Jessie," she says again. "I mean, I'm sure Aaron thought it would be a pain for you to try to get to the city on a weeknight, otherwise . . ."

"Oh, it definitely would have been a pain. I have a lot going on here. It's totally fine that . . . you know." *That your husband snubbed me.* Needing to break the tension, she adds, "Really. It's okay . . . Tess."

"Tess?"

"*Working Girl*! The movie! With Melanie Griffith. Remember, we saw it together back in '88? Tess was our hero." Jessie gestures at the sneakers she's wearing with her suit. "That's what she wore. Don't tell me you forgot?"

"Never!" Mimi throws her head back and belts the first few lines of "Let the River Run," the movie's theme song.

Jessie grins. "Man, you can sing."

And she's beautiful as always, her black hair sleek and straightened, clipped back to accentuate her delicate bone structure and flawless cinnamon and sugar complexion. There are worry lines, though, around her large brown eyes. Maybe something went wrong with that new client, or with Aaron . . .

"Did Carly Simon drop in?" Billy asks. "I could've

sworn I heard her . . . oh, hey, it's Mimi! Even better!" He wraps his beefy arms around her in an easy bear hug. "I didn't know you were coming."

"Neither did I, until this morning. Jessie invited me, and I thought . . . what the hell. I missed you guys. Sorry to just show up, but I tried to call you, and text, and email . . ."

"The Wi-Fi is out, and the landline, too," Jessie tells her. "We had a couple of bad storms this week."

"Good old Ithaca. This house looks exactly the same as it did the first time I ever walked up this street, by the way. But the bus went past that fancy new Marriott, and I can't believe all the new construction on the Commons. Remember when it was a ghost town back when we were in college?"

"You took the bus from New York?"

"Yes, just like the first time," she adds with a nostalgic tilt of her head. "Only back then, I was nineteen and I'd run away from home. And Silas opened this door instead of Jessie."

"I showed up here right afterward," Jessie says with a laugh. "I remember that day so well. I was royally pissed off at my mother."

"And your father. And pretty much the entire world. Not just that day, but every day."

"Now she's just royally pissed at me," Billy says.

"Uh-oh. What'd you do?"

"He ate a Zagnut!" Jessie tells her.

"And you didn't divorce him then and there?" Mimi's grin is a bit drawn. "I love you two. You never change."

"Yeah, Jessie always was a tough little chick, and I've always been afraid of her." Billy steps out onto the wraparound porch and reaches to help her with her luggage. "Hey, is this an animal carrier?"

"Yes, I had to bring Clancy. I hope it's all right?"

"It's fine," Jessie assures her, sliding a *don't say anything* look in Billy's direction.

It escapes him, but not Mimi.

"Oh, no. I'm so sorry. I was thinking you guys have always had a menagerie, so I figured . . ."

"We used to, but . . . not since Theodore. He doesn't like animals."

"Except roosters," Billy adds. "Roosters, he likes. Did Jessie tell you?"

"I haven't had a chance, but I will." She leads the way to the stairs, with Billy hauling the bags along behind them. "Come on, let's get you settled before . . ."

Before Little Boy Blue wakes up.

Before Theodore comes home and sees the cat, or the kid . . .

Before all hell breaks loose.

Mimi is shaking her head. "You know what? I'll stay at the new Marriott."

"Nope. It's not even opening until December."

"Then I'll stay at—"

"All the hotels are full because of the Apple Festival," Jessie tells her, "so forget it."

"Come on, all of them?"

"Every last one."

"I don't believe you."

"You're staying here, in Chip's room. Just keep the kitten in there for now, and we'll be fine." She leans over to peer through the carrier's mesh panel at the sweet ball of orangey pink fur. "He's adorable. I hope you're keeping him?"

"I wish, but I can't. Aaron's allergic."

Guess that means you're keeping Aaron, huh?

At the top of the stairs, she gestures at Petty's closed door and tells Mimi in a hushed voice, "We have a new foster child. He's sleeping in there."

"I thought you weren't fostering anymore."

"Long story. I'm going to check on him while you get settled."

Billy and Mimi continue on down the hall as she opens Petty's door, trying not to let it creak. Impossible in this house. She slips into the room and winces as it creaks closed behind her.

The child in the bed doesn't stir. He appears even younger and more fragile than he had this morning, dwarfed in the queen-sized vintage four-poster Jessie's parents had left behind when they'd moved away. Chip had found it too "girlie," and Jessie and Billie already had a king-sized bed, so Petty got this, along with her grandparents' high-end mattress, Egyptian cotton sheets, lofty pillows, and goose down comforter encased in a silky white duvet.

"Mommy, I feel like an angel sleeping in the clouds," she'd told Jessie after her first night in luxurious comfort.

That's how Little Boy Blue looks now, curled on his side, sucking his thumb with the comforter bunched in a tiny fist beneath his chin.

No, not the comforter, she realizes, tiptoeing closer. Petty's lace-trimmed lavender bathrobe is no longer hanging from the bedpost. He's hugging it beneath the covers like a security blanket, a satiny scrap held just beneath the slightest hint of an upturn at the corners of his mouth. His features are serene, his breathing hushed and rhythmic.

She should probably wake him to ensure that he'll be able to sleep again overnight, but she doesn't have the heart to rip him from the safe, sweet dreamy haven.

Let him stay awhile longer. Reality will reclaim him soon enough.

Jessie tiptoes back out and closes the door quietly after her.

BARNES GAPES AT the shaggy-haired, bearded man.

At a glance, he bears no resemblance to the clean-cut blond Manhattan businessman who'd worn a black custom-made wool suit every day of his life, according to the wife he'd left behind. He's bare chested, and there's a tattoo over his heart. The shape isn't entirely discernable from this shadowy distance, but Barnes knows what it is.

A horse.

He impulsively opens his mouth to say something to Wayland, and clamps it shut again. He may not be on the job at the moment, but he's smarter, better trained, than to allow that mistake. You don't blindly jump in and engage, not even if you come across the suspect while vacationing in a foreign country several decades after closing a case.

Yeah. *Suspect.*

"It's not a crime to leave your wife and kids, Barnes," Stef had told him years ago, and he'd been right. It's not a crime to leave your family, even for another woman . . .

However, when that woman is a stone-cold murderer's daughter for whom you'd do anything . . .

Kill?

In the days after Wayland disappeared, evidence had linked him to a deadly homicide spree. Yet even Barnes had thought it was contrived . . .

Then, anyway.

And now?

"Arroz con pollo." The waiter pounces from the shadows with a steaming plate, utensils, napkins, condiments, yet another beer, which Barnes hadn't even ordered . . . had he?

Damn.

Things are fuzzy, and he needs clarity now more than ever before.

"Oh, no!" The waiter has spotted his bandana-wrapped finger and the broken glass on the ground. *"Te lastimas!"*

Yes, he tells the young man, he had hurt himself, but he's fine.

"Estás seguro?"

"Yes, I'm sure, really."

At the adjacent table, the group is disassembling, preparing to leave. The American's seat—Perry Wayland's seat—is already empty, its occupant vanished into the night . . .

Again.

IN THE UPSTAIRS bedroom, Amelia unpacks, changes into jeans and a sweater at last, and plugs in her laptop on the desk. She'd meant to get back to her renewed search for Marceline LeBlanc during the bus ride, but instead had spent it staring out the window, brooding about her marriage.

Toward the end of the trip, she'd finally turned on her phone again, bracing herself for more messages and missed calls from Aaron. She'd been surprised to find that there hadn't been another word from him. Somehow, that had bothered her more than a follow-up text about the dry cleaner would have.

The stroll along the familiar Ithaca streets had tamped down her marital unease, but had stirred the memory of an unsettling incident involving Marceline LeBlanc.

Throughout her childhood, Amelia had dutifully obeyed her parents' orders to avoid the elderly neighbor. But after Bettina died, she'd befriended the woman. Or had it been the other way around?

When you're desperate for answers, you look for meaning where there is mere synchronicity. She knows that, has seen it firsthand with her clients. You can't entirely trust autobiographical memory to remain unembellished. In her own, Marceline had been a guardian angel of sorts, always around, keeping an eye on things—or maybe just on Amelia. She'd even admitted having witnessed Calvin leaving Park Baptist with a baby on that Mother's Day in 1968, though she'd claimed to have known nothing more about it.

In October 1987, Marceline had left New York without warning, never to be seen or heard from again, unless . . .

Having impulsively run off to Ithaca to hunt down Silas Moss around the same time, Amelia could have sworn . . .

Come on, that's even crazier.

Marceline had told her she was going back home, down south. Amelia couldn't possibly have glimpsed her here in Ithaca, because that would have meant Marceline had followed her.

Why would Marceline have followed her?

It made no sense, unless there had been more to their connection. If, say, the old woman had not only seen Calvin carrying a baby out of the church, but had also seen the person who'd carried her in.

She'd often had a knowing look in her dark eyes, hadn't she? And she'd owned a woven basket very similar to the one in which Amelia had been found, hadn't she?

Well, hadn't she?

Returning downstairs, she traces the carved banister with her fingertips and thinks of Silas Moss. It's been twenty-nine years since she'd run away from Harlem to Ithaca and turned up unannounced on his doorstep, having seen him on television the night before. Yet no matter how many times she's visited Jessie and her family here, she always expects to see Si, too—there, by the fireplace with his gray head nodding off over a book or puttering in the kitchen from fridge to stove to sink, whipping up some delicious-only-to-him concoction.

Tonight, it's where she finds Jessie, reaching for the faucet to rinse cherry tomatoes. A pumpkin-scented jar candle burns on the windowsill above the wide white porcelain farm sink, its dancing flame reflected in the glass.

"You look comfy, Mimi. All settled in?"

"Yes. Billy said to tell you he's taking a shower, so don't run the water."

She turns it on anyway—not full force, just enough to rinse the tomatoes. The old pipes squeal and groan overhead, and Billy stomps his foot in the upstairs bathroom, where, Amelia knows from experience, his shower has just gone ice-cold.

"Hey, if you're going to take a shower while I'm making dinner, that's what you get!" Jessie tells the ceiling.

"Guess you guys never did get the plumbing fixed, huh?"

"Some things never change around here."

"Some things do, though. It's so quiet here now."

"I know, right? Too quiet. Empty. I try to convince myself that it's peaceful, but you know me."

Jessie has always thrived on a houseful of noise and chaos and people—her kids, other people's kids, friends, family, pets, strays . . .

"I don't know how she hears herself think in that place," Aaron had said the first time they'd come to stay—and that was before the extra kids and foster animals.

"Maybe she doesn't want to hear herself think."

"That doesn't make any sense."

No, it wouldn't, to a person whose thoughts are so streamlined and dispassionate.

Jessie opens the fridge, rummages around, and then closes it with her hip, arms filled with containers of mesclun lettuce mix, olives, cheese, vegetables, fruit. Amelia helps her set it all out on the counter, helping herself to a couple of distinctly round, deep purple grapes from the cluster.

The taut skins snap in her mouth, releasing sweet-tart juice, along with some of the day's tension. "I love Concords. I can't find them in the city."

"Tomorrow you'll find them in town."

"So it's the Apple and Grape Festival?"

"It's the Everything You Ever Wanted to Eat festival." Jessie flashes her deep dimples. "Tell me about your party last night."

"Oh, it was, you know . . . I'd rather not talk about it right now, actually."

Jessie hands her a couple of fat pears, a paring knife, and a small cutting board. "Here, slice these. *Please*," she adds. "Sorry, guess I even get bossy with house-guests."

"You're allowed when your houseguest shows up unexpectedly with a cat. I would have left him at home, but . . ."

It isn't the kind of *but* she intends to continue.

Jessie isn't the kind of friend to let her get away with that.

"*But . . . ?*"

"How thin did you want these sliced?"

"Medium thin. *But . . . ?*"

"Well, Aaron's allergic."

"I know. That didn't just pop up today."

"He's going away this weekend."

"And *that* just popped up today?"

"Well, he was supposed to leave Sunday night, but when he found out I was coming here, he changed the flight to tomorrow so that he wouldn't be home alone all weekend."

"Or have to take care of the cat."

Amelia shrugs, her marital anxiety bubbling back in.

"Mimi, you sure you guys are okay?" Jessie asks, arranging cheese slices and crackers on a plate. "And don't make excuses. It's me. You can tell me anything."

"We're supposed to be talking about your stuff."

"We will. I just worry about you. I feel like I've been neglecting you."

"Well, I feel the same way about you." Finished slicing the second pear, she asks what else she can do.

"Pour us some wine. Glasses are in the cabinet above the sink, corkscrew—"

"Second drawer." Amelia opens it.

"You remembered."

"Well, it's nice to know there's a place in this world where things stay the same."

"You just said it's different."

"The quiet, yes. But the way it looks, and the warm, welcome feeling . . ." She smiles. "That's the same, Jess."

"I'm glad. And I can't believe you showed up today, because I need you. So there's a dry red"—she nods at a bottle on the counter—"and I've got white in the fridge. But I know you've never been a white girl."

Amelia has to laugh. "No, that is one thing I never have been."

Jessie laughs, too.

Amelia twists the corkscrew into a bottle of Cabernet, opens it, and pours two glasses.

Jessie adds the pear slices and grapes to the cheese and cracker plate and puts it on the table. "You get to be a guest now. Relax."

Amelia sits down with her wine, comparing the outdated kitchen to the sleek modern one being installed in her Manhattan apartment. Somehow, she finds this one more appealing, despite its battle-scarred Formica, linoleum, and dinosaur appliances. Cereal boxes line the top of the fridge, and the front is covered in yellowed, faded crayon drawings secured by magnets.

Jessie is always talking about wanting to renovate, but they haven't gotten further than removing the adjacent sunroom's double French doors to create a wide archway. Amelia had assumed they were aiming to add natural light and open up the dark, cramped space, but Jessie's motive had been typically frank. "Nah, we're just getting ready for the kids to be teenagers, so we can spy on them when they're in there with their friends."

In Si's day, the sunroom had been "the conservatory" and housed only an array of plants that he paid Jessie to water. They invariably drooped and scattered dry, yellowed leaves across the old mosaic floor. Based on that, Amelia would never have pegged her as a future nurturer and nourisher to countless children and animals.

Watching Jessie chop tomatoes and cucumbers, she says, "You're so much like your mom—always doing a million things all at once and making it look easy. I can't believe you're putting out hors d'oeuvres when you're in the middle of making dinner and you didn't even know I was coming."

"You call that hors d'oeuvres? Diane would have whipped out shrimp cocktail and baked brie in one of those round bread loaf thingies. With homemade jam. Hey, don't laugh. You know I'm right."

"You're absolutely right. How *are* your mom and dad?"

"You know—perfect, as usual."

"Tell me about the new foster child before Theodore comes home. Billy says they don't get along."

"They haven't even met, actually. I've barely met him." She explains that the child, whom she calls Little Boy Blue, has been sleeping since his arrival this morning.

"Little Boy Blue? You and your nicknames, Jessie." Theodore is one of the few people in Jessie's life whom she hasn't rechristened—not that she hadn't tried. But even just shortening his name to Theo hadn't gone over well.

"This little guy has to have a nickname because he doesn't have a name—that we know of, anyway, or that he can tell us. He's a foundling. That's why I had to foster him. And I want to think his mother is out there desperately looking for him, but . . ."

"But she might be the one who left him there."

"If she didn't, she'd have reported him missing, right? Unless something's happened to her, too. I keep going over it in my head. The only thing I know for sure is that he's lucky we're the ones who have him."

"You and Billy are amazing."

"I meant you and me. Think about it, Mimi—we can do for him what nobody could do for us back then. I think we should—" She turns, head cocked to one side, and Amelia hears the front door open and close. "There's Theodore."

He appears, filling the doorway, and Amelia's jaw drops. The last time she'd seen him, he'd been a little boy.

Jessie's older children had been sweet-faced babies, cherubic toddlers, adorable schoolchildren, and had even escaped awkward adolescence. Theodore is in the throes of it, shaggy and disheveled, pudgy and pockmarked. Unlike Chip and Petty, he isn't blessed with a naturally lean body or symmetrical features.

One day, he'll be a fine-looking man, Amelia thinks, but her heart goes out to him now.

"Look who's here!" Jessie tells him, like he's a little kid and Amelia's the ice cream truck.

His eyes narrow behind thick glasses.

"Hi, Theodore!" If he were Chip or Petty, she'd approach with a hug, but she knows better with him.

"Hi." His voice is unfamiliar—a thin, lower pitch that is, like his fuzzy almost-mustache, on the brink of manhood but not quite there. "What are you doing here?"

Jessie answers for her. "Aunt Mimi's here to spend time with us."

"Why?"

"Because she misses us, and we miss her."

He opens his mouth, but Amelia cuts in. "Wow, Theodore, look at you! You're all grown-up."

He shakes his head, not in disgust at her corniness, but in literal-minded disagreement. "All grown-up is twenty-one. Chip is grown-up, and Petty will be grown-up in April. I'm fifteen. I have five years and ten months and . . ." Quick calculation. "Thirteen days."

"How'd you do on your tests today?" Jessie asks.

"I got a hundred and three in health."

"How is that possible?"

"Extra credit," he tells Amelia as if she'd asked how to navigate a staircase.

"Grades only went up to a hundred when I was in school. Hardly anyone ever got one."

"I got a hundred on my social studies quiz, too."

"Cool. You must be really smart, Theodore."

"I am. And a lot of the other kids are really stupid."

"How about your French test?" Jessie asks, and he scowls.

"It was hard. Madame Worst says I need to stay after for extra help all next week."

Mimi raises an eyebrow. "Madame Worst? She sounds German."

"It's what he calls his French teacher. Her name is Mrs. Best."

"Madame Best. She hates me."

"She doesn't hate you, Theodore. Why don't you tell Aunt Mimi about Espinoza?"

He brightens, turning to Amelia. "Espinoza is my rooster."

"Cool, you have a rooster?" *Stop saying cool. You're trying too hard. Kids hate that.*

Theodore gives a vigorous nod and goes on, recitation style, rocking back and forth on his sneakers. "He lives in his coop in the yard. My dad and I built it, and I painted it yellow, so his house would match our house. He eats chicken feed and vegetables and sometimes grass. He's named after Victor Espinoza. He won the triple crown last year on American Pharaoh. He's won the Kentucky Derby three times and the Preakness three times, and he was on *Dancing with the Stars* last fall, but he didn't win that. He was eliminated on the second night."

"Well, I wouldn't expect a rooster to be the best dancer."

Jessie laughs at Amelia's joke.

Theodore does not. "The jockey Victor Espinoza is the one who was on *Dancing with the Stars*. Roosters can't dance on TV."

"Aunt Mimi was just being funny."

"Not that funny. Anyway, Espinoza sounds like a—an awesome rooster." Not a cool one.

Her effort is rewarded with a grin. "Yeah, he is. I can show him to you. I have to feed him his dinner after I go wash up and change my clothes."

"I'd love that, Theo . . . *dore*," she adds, seeing the scowl flash again. No nicknames. No *cool*. She's got this.

Jessie flashes her a grateful smile and tells Theodore to hurry up because dinner will be ready soon.

"Is Aunt Mimi staying for dinner?"

"She is. She's staying for the whole weekend."

"Is that okay with you?" Amelia asks.

He weighs it, nods, and heads for the back stairway. "I'll be right back so you can meet Espinoza!"

"Well, that went well," Jessie says. "Good job. I'm sorry he's so touchy. He can't help it."

"I know, sweetie. All teenagers are like that."

"Yeah, but Theodore isn't your garden-variety teenaged pain in the butt. He's got so many issues. He's just not good with change or surprises or—" She throws her head back and curses under her breath.

"What's wrong?"

"I forgot to remind him about Little Boy Blue. He's not—"

A bloodcurdling scream erupts overhead.

Chapter Nine

The Angler had plugged the address Cecile provided into his phone's GPS app. It guides him in maddening, meandering loops through an upscale development that should be called Nine Circles of Hell instead of Evergreen Estates.

The winding lanes are filled with oversized new homes that are supposed to look old. Some are brick with stately pillars; some have gables and gingerbread porches. One ridiculous house is New England style, gray shingled with a lighthouse-shaped cupola and a widow's walk at the peak, though the ocean is nearly a thousand kilometers away.

Renee's friend lives in a white clapboard house with black shutters and a basketball hoop over the three-car garage. He pulls into the driveway behind two BMW SUVs. The yard is already decorated for Halloween— wheat sheaves wired to the glowing lampposts, and spotlit pumpkins and a scarecrow perched on hay bales in a pathetic attempt to duplicate a rural harvest scene.

It makes him think of his uncle's Quebec farm, and the country road in New York. Of Monique at the bottom of the lake, and her son left for dead in the dirt.

His fist finds the horn and he blasts it, good and hard.

Waiting for his daughter to come out, he opens a browser on his phone and types in several search terms. New York State, Cortland, Ithaca, dead child, body found . . .

About to hit Enter, he's startled by a rap at his window and turns to see a man there. Clean-cut and ruddy cheeked, he's wearing a navy crew neck sweatshirt and holding a rake, gesturing for the Angler to roll down the window. He obliges, shoving his phone into his pocket, wondering if the man could have glimpsed what he was writing.

"Hey there," he says. "Can I help you?"

The Angler gives a blank stare. "With what?"

"Are you lost, or turning around . . . ?"

"No, I was looking for my daughter. Guess I have the wrong address." He starts to shift the car into Reverse. "Sorry about—"

"Wait, are you Renee's dad?"

"Yeah. Is she here?"

"Inside playing with Melissa. I'm Bob Varner." He sticks his hand through the car window and the Angler shakes it with reluctance. "Sorry I mistook you for someone who was lost—happens a lot around here."

I'll bet it does. But do they all park in your driveway and honk the horn?

"Anyway, I figured you'd park and come in to get Renee," Bob goes on. "Cecile always does."

"That's Cecile." He pulls his false smile so taut that his face aches. "Can you tell Renee that I'm here? We have to get home for dinner."

"Oh, Sarah's making a huge meal, so you have to stay."

Sarah—his wife?

And they have to stay?

Yeah, I don't think so.

"We can't. I have to—"

"Aw, Sarah's counting on it, and she's whipping up Renee's favorite. Works out well for all of us, doesn't it?" He winks and leans on the rake, settling in for a chat.

Renee's favorite . . . what?

"Our girls are even making place mats for the table. They're such cutie-pies, you know?"

The Angler nods as if he knows, or cares. "Sorry, but we really have to get home. It's been a long day."

"Oh, right, I'm sure it has. Sarah just got off the phone with Cecile."

"What did she say?"

"She filled us in. Why? Haven't you talked to her?"

Noting the flicker of judgment, he says, "Of course I've talked to her. I just left the hospital."

All right, not *just*.

He'd detoured back to his father's house to pick up a few things he'll need if he does decide to flee. He'd been planning to tidy the attic, too—remove the evidence of the secret room's recent inhabitants, get rid of the handcuffs and a few other incriminating items, just in case.

But then Cecile had started texting him, asking whether he'd picked up Renee. He hadn't responded. She'd texted several more times as he drove over here. He'd ignored them all.

"We've all been so worried about Pascal the Rascal." At the Angler's look, the man explains, "That's what we call him around here. He gets a real kick out of it."

So. His own children have, without his knowledge or permission, become far too familiar with this stranger and his family. That this *Bob* has a ridiculous nickname for his son, that he knows his daughter's favorite—whatever the hell his wife is cooking . . .

It doesn't sit well with him. Not at all.

He pushes back his sleeve to pointedly check his watch and notices a small dark speck on the glass face.

Blood?

He yanks his sleeve back over it and looks up to see if Bob Varner could have noticed it.

But he's already turned away. "You're in a hurry, I know. I'll go get Renee."

She appears a full five minutes later, pausing in the doorway to hug a little blonde girl like a wartime soldier before trudging toward the car, lugging a backpack that's as big as she is and appears to be heavier. Bob Varner catches up with her, takes the bag, and carries it the rest of the way.

His lips are moving but the Angler had rolled up his window again and only catches the last bit of whatever he's saying when he opens the back door for Renee. ". . . save you some for next time, okay?"

"Yes, but . . ." She climbs in and asks in a whiny voice, "Papa, *s'il vous plaît*—"

"Talk to me in English, Renee!" he commands in his father's voice.

Parle-moi en français!

"Papa, please, can we stay for dinner?"

"No. We're going home."

"Where is your booster seat, Renee?" Varner asks.

"I don't have one in Papa's car. Only in Maman's."

"You're six years old," the Angler says. "You don't need one."

"She's very petite for a six-year-old, so she should probably have one, if you don't mind my saying."

I do mind.

He clenches the steering wheel. "Put on your seatbelt, Renee. Hurry up. We have to go."

"I want to stay to eat." In the rearview mirror, he sees her just sitting there scowling, arms folded across her chest.

"I said, no."

"Here, I'll help you strap in, Renee," Bob says.

"She can do it herself. Renee, close your door."

"But—"

He reaches back, grabs the handle, and gives it a yank, grazing Bob's arm before he jumps back out of the way. Shifting into Reverse, he backs out of the driveway, barely checking for cars or pedestrians.

"Papa, you hurt Mr. Varner!"

That's his problem.

"Stop! My seatbelt isn't on!"

And that's yours.

Grim, he drives toward home.

Fifteen minutes later, after a drive-through detour and a fast-food cheeseburger he'd gobbled on the way home, the Angler pulls into the town house garage.

His daughter remains silent and tear-stained in the backseat.

Cecile has spoiled both children. A long, challenging road lies ahead to undo the damage. With the boy recuperating from this appendix situation, there will be no end to the whining.

He gets out of the car. "Come on. Let's go into the house."

"I don't want to."

"Suit yourself. But you'll be locked in the car in the garage in the dark for the night."

She scrambles out and follows him.

In the kitchen, he tosses a white fast-food bag onto the table. "Sit down and eat your dinner."

Renee peers inside.

"This is not good for me. There are no vegetables."

"What do you think French fries are made of?"

"But Maman says—"

"Maman is French! They're French fries! Shut up and eat," he growls.

"What about my milk?"

He yanks open the refrigerator door and is assaulted by the stench of ripened cheese. He grabs the milk, pours some into a glass, and plunks it onto the table so that it splashes over the rim.

"Here you go. Are you happy now? Drink your damned milk, eat your dinner, and then go to bed."

"Mais je—" She stops herself, seeing him whirl back to glare, and begins again in English. "But I can't go to bed until I've done my homework."

"So? Do it."

"I need help."

"No, you don't." He takes a black garbage bag from under the sink.

"Mais—"

"Parle-moi en français!" he screams and sees the confusion on her face just before he slaps it.

She bursts into tears.

He stares, breathing hard.

Then he strides out of the kitchen and up the stairs, leaving his daughter crying inconsolably.

In the bedroom, he finds the bed unmade and Cecile's nightgown on the floor, indicating that she had, indeed, left in a rush this morning. Remembering the texts he'd ignored earlier, he looks at his phone. In addition to asking whether he'd collected Renee, and asking where he was, Cecile had written that the doctors had started administering the IV antibiotics and are optimistic.

"Pascal the Rascal," he mutters. "Pascal the Rascal. *Imbecile.*"

He strips off his clothing and throws it all into the garbage bag. Even his watch, and the waxed canvas coat he'd worn on so many fishing excursions. Now it's tainted and torn by the murder weapon he'd so stupidly carried home with him.

In the bathroom, he runs the water as hot as he can tolerate. Cecile's lavender bubble bath lingers in the air, along with burped-up raw onions from the burger he'd devoured.

Standing beneath the scalding spray, he scrubs his skin hard with a bar of strong white soap to rid himself of any trace of his father, and of blood.

He should have done it last night, but Pascal had interrupted that plan, along with today's. Why does his life have to be so difficult?

Children. They complicate everything. Remove them from the picture, and his life would become his own again. Cecile would let him go without a struggle if not for her twisted fantasy about royal heirs.

He has a twisted fantasy of his own, and it, too, involves his little heirs. One down, two to go. If Pascal doesn't survive, that would leave just Renee.

Accidents happen.

He might take her night fishing, out to the middle of a remote mountain lake . . .

JESSIE RUSHES FOR the stairs, Theodore's scream reverberating through the house.

It's Billy. His heart . . .

He'd been fine just a few minutes ago, stomping on the shower floor because she'd been running the water downstairs. The cardiologist had said his symptoms might be warning signs, yet he hasn't been taking proper care of himself. He'd started out concerned, committed to changing his eating habits, exercising, losing weight, reducing stress—doctor's orders. But the way he's been slacking off lately, she's certain she'll find him lying on the floor, Theodore standing over him . . .

When she reaches the top of the stairs, though, Billy is there, bursting out of the bathroom, a towel wrapped around his waist, and Theodore . . .

Theodore is howling, pressed against the wall, eyes scrunched shut.

"What is it? What's wrong?" Jessie grabs him, wrapping him in an embrace so tight it should hurt him. It's painful for her. Yet she knows it's what he needs right now.

She just grips him and shoots a helpless look at Billy.

"Did you get hurt?" he asks. "Theodore?"

"What happened?" Mimi is at the top of the stairs. "Is everything—Oh, no!" She scurries forward and scoops something from the floor. "He got out. I'm so sorry. I closed the door . . . oh, Clancy."

Jessie sees a wee kitten in her arms, and Chip's bedroom door ajar.

"It's okay, Mimi," Billy says. "The doors do that sometimes."

"They always did. I should have remembered that. I should have—I'm so sorry, Theodore."

He's shaking in Jessie's grip, his eyes still squeezed shut. "I hate cats!"

"Theodore, calm down," Billy says. "It's just a kitten. It's not going to—"

"Get it out of here! Get it out of here!"

Mimi closes the kitten in Chip's room and stands in the hallway holding the knob as though the tiny creature might break down the door. "Theodore, I feel awful. I'll pack him up and leave."

Jessie shakes her head. "No way. Billy will fix the door so that it stays closed. It's fine."

"Nooooo!" Theodore wails, wriggling from her grasp. "It's not fine! I can't be here with a cat!"

"Theodore!" Billy seizes his shoulders. "Open your eyes and look at me. Look at me!"

He does, trembling, his breath coming hard and fast.

"I know you're upset, but that kitten is harmless. It's the size of your—"

"Nooooo!"

"It doesn't matter how big it is," Jessie reminds her husband, hugging their son again with her arms wrapped around his thick middle like he's a life buoy bobbing on that wreckage-strewn sea in her nightmare. "He's terrified."

"I can see that. But he needs to get past this. He can't go through life freaking out every time—"

"If he could just 'get past this,' he would! And I

should have told him about it before he came upstairs," she says above Theodore's crying. "You know how he is about animals! You know he has . . . challenges."

Of course he knows.

That's why, when she'd first brought up the idea of adopting Theodore, he'd asked, *"Sure you don't want to quit while we're ahead?"*

The words had stung, though she'd secretly wondered the same thing. Not just before—but since, on days when she's convinced Theodore would have been better off with a younger, more patient mother. Someone who doesn't come with her own baggage and expectations. Someone who doesn't know what it's like to feel like the fifth wheel in a picture-perfect family.

I got over it. So can you, she finds herself wanting to tell him when he retreats, makes demands, acts out—as though his issues stem not from a medically diagnosed situation, but from resentment, as Jessie's own had.

No, Theodore's situation is different. His teenaged mother hadn't turned her back on him. She'd loved her son fiercely, had every intention of raising him, and would probably have done a good job of it, had the circumstances been different. She just hadn't been financially, emotionally, or intellectually equipped to handle a child with his needs.

But am I?

Are we?

Mimi dives into the fray. "Guys, it's my fault. I shouldn't have brought the cat without checking first. I'll get him out of here right away."

"That's crazy! You're our guest," Jessie says, "and you're not going anywhere."

"Yes, she is! She wants to go! Let her go!" Theodore protests.

"Absolutely not! There's nowhere to go, Mimi, even if we wanted you to!"

"We want her to, Mom!"

"Theodore!"

"No, it's fine," Mimi says. "I don't blame him, and there are plenty of places to stay around here. I'll find a pet-friendly—"

"Stop!" Billy shouts. "Everyone! Just stop and listen to me!"

Even Theodore falls silent.

"Here's what's going to happen. Mimi, you're not going anywhere. Theodore, you're going to go into your room and stay there until your mom tells you it's time for dinner. I'm going to put on some clothes and then I'll fix the door so that the kitten can't get out and terrorize anyone."

He utters the last part with an undercurrent of sarcasm, for which Jessie forgives him.

"Okay, good," she says. "That works. Let's all just . . ."

Behind her, a door creaks open. She turns to see a small figure framed in the doorway of Petty's room. She feels Theodore's body tense in her arms and looks at Billy. He's already on the move.

"Hey, there, Little Boy Blue," he says, going over to the child.

He's just standing there, looking tiny and unnerved, staring at them all with wide, groggy blue eyes.

"I don't want him here," Theodore tells Jessie. He doesn't shout, but the tone is vehement. "You said no more foster kids!"

"I did say that. But it was a long time ago. Last night,

I said that this is an emergency, and that he needed our help, and that he was coming. And now he's here." She keeps one eye on Billy, trying to keep his towel wrapped around his waist as he kneels beside the little boy. It would be comical if there were anything remotely amusing about any of this.

"I don't want him to be here. I want him to go away. And the cat. And her." He shoots an accusatory glare at Mimi.

"Theodore, that's enough. I know this isn't ideal for you, and I'm sorry, but—"

"This is *bad* for me. This is . . . it's so, so bad for me!" He breaks away from her and hurtles himself down the hall to his room, slamming the door after him.

Jessie exhales.

Mimi comes to her, putting an arm around her shoulders, leaning her cheek against the top of Jessie's head.

"Jess?" Billy asks in a low, composed tone, and she looks over at him.

He's crouched beside the little boy, who's clutching Petty's lavender robe against his heart. His head is bowed, shoulders hunched up as though he's trying hard not to cry. Her heart contorts.

"Listen, I'm going to take Theodore out for a while."

"Out . . . where?"

"To . . . wherever I can buy a doorstop. And then we'll get something to eat." Billy sounds like he's making it up as he goes along.

"I made dinner . . ."

"I know. But the caseworker is coming at some point, and I think it's best if Theodore's out of the house for that."

Her brain flies through various scenarios, none appealing, and she nods. He's right.

"That's a good idea. Can you also pick up some cat food and litter for Clancy?"

Mimi protests. "You don't have to do that. I brought—"

"You'll need more, though. And that way, Billy can pick up a few things for . . ." She gives a slight nod at Little Boy Blue and then turns to her husband. "Maybe some warm pj's? Socks? Sweats? Size 3T."

He nods, still crouched beside the child.

Jessie crosses over to Petty's doorway. "Are you hungry, sweetie? You must be."

No reply. He doesn't lift his head. She sees a wet droplet land on the top of his bare foot.

"Go, Billy," she says softly. "I've got this."

"*We've* got this." She looks up to see Mimi watching with tears in her own eyes and sends her a grateful smile.

BARNES TOYS WITH his chicken and rice, the fork clutched awkwardly in his wounded hand, thinking about October 1987 and the Wayland case.

The missing tycoon's Mercedes had been found on the George Washington Bridge. He wouldn't have been the first despondent person to kill himself that week, in the wake of Wall Street's Black Monday. Yet Wayland's assistant at the hedge fund had sworn he'd seen the market crash coming, and his financial records later revealed that he had indeed avoided catastrophic loss. His family insisted he'd always been terrified of heights and would never have jumped to his death. A tip line offering a large reward had yielded plenty of sightings—on the Long Island Railroad, out in Montauk, on Block Island across the sound.

Turned out Wayland had escaped his high-maintenance blonde wife and a match set of daughters to run off with his longtime mistress. Not quite the oldest story in the book, but damned close.

It's a hell of a lot easier for a gazillionaire to disappear without a trace than for the average man. Especially when he had no qualms about offering the NYPD a bribe to look the other way and the NYPD—Stef, anyway—had no qualms about accepting it.

And you had no qualms about accepting a cut. For your daughter, to save her life, but still . . .

If Barnes had known the whole story, known the true identity of Wayland's mistress—

"Señor? You don't like my food?"

He looks up. A middle-aged man stands beside the table, dressed in sauce-spattered white clothing with a dish towel over his shoulder. He's holding two open bottles of beer.

"It's delicious. Just a little awkward for me to eat it like this." He holds up the bandana-tied finger. Better to blame his lost appetite on the injury than on rattled nerves. The Wayland sighting had conjured a barrage of ugly memories.

"I am sorry. My son, he should have found bandages for you."

"Your son?"

"The waiter." He gestures at the young man handing out entrées at a nearby table.

"No, he was very helpful. I don't need a bandage. This is fine." Barnes takes a bite of *arroz con pollo*. It really is delicious. "Are you the chef?"

"*Si*, I am the chef, the owner, the host, the dish-washer, the bartender . . ." He grins, setting one of the beers in front of Barnes.

"Oh, I didn't order—"

"It is on the house, *acere*."

"*Gracias.*"

"*De nada.*" The man holds out a durable-looking brown hand. "I am Miguel Perez. My son, he is also Miguel Perez. You are . . ."

"*Not* Miguel Perez," Barnes says, earning a chuckle as they shake hands. "My name's Stockton Barnes. Nice to meet you."

"And you as well." Miguel pulls up a chair, takes a sip of the other beer, and pulls a pack of cigarettes from his pocket.

He offers it to Barnes.

Man, it's tempting.

He shakes his head. "No, thanks. I'd love to, but I quit."

"If you love it, why did you quit?"

"Because it's not good for me."

Miguel waves that off like it isn't true or doesn't matter. He lights a cigarette and leans back as if pre-pared to take a nice long break. A strange thing to do, Barnes thinks, in a restaurant with several occu-pied tables waiting for their meals. Oh, well. Different country, different culture.

"So you think you will live forever, eh?"

"Excuse me?"

"You deny yourself pleasure," Miguel says, gestur-ing at his cigarette, "because you believe your lifetime will go on and on and on. What if it does not? What if it ends tomorrow?"

"My life?"

"This life. The world. For everyone. Then what?"

"Then I guess I go to heaven and start chain-smoking Marlboros again," Barnes says with a grin and sips his beer.

Miguel isn't taking this as lightly. "You believe in heaven? You are a religious man, then?"

"Me? Not anymore," he admits. Before his father's death, he'd attended weekly Sunday services with his parents and *abuela*. "I mean, I believe in God, but I don't go to church anymore. Although I'll be going to one here tomorrow. Just sightseeing, though."

"Is this your first time in Cuba?"

Sipping his beer, Barnes nods. "I've wanted to visit for years."

"Many Americans, they are coming to Cuba now. But I am impressed that you have found your way to Baracoa, *acere*."

"Wish I could take credit, but my friend traced his ancestry here, and I'm traveling with him. In fact, he's the one who told me to eat at your restaurant."

"What is his name?"

"Rob Owens."

"The record producer. The last time he was here, he promised to come back and bring his family. Did they come?"

"Just his son, Kurtis."

"Ah, the *candela*. *El esta flama*."

"*Candela?* A candle? He's on fire?" he translates, puzzled.

"So you speak Spanish. Here in Cuba, it means troublemaker, messed up. Kurtis, I remember, he is the one who gives his father such problems."

Barnes shrugs, wondering how much Rob has shared. "He's not bad. Just . . . searching. A lot of kids are at that age."

"What age is he?"

"Almost thirty."

Miguel nods toward the waiter, bussing a nearby table. "Like my son."

"You know, Kurtis was supposed to stop in here earlier. By any chance, did you see him?"

Miguel is shaking his head even before Barnes describes him.

"So then you didn't see him."

"He was not here." Miguel's succinct tone invites Barnes to note the difference. "When the tourists come, I will know them."

"Like me."

"*Sí.*"

Maybe everyone gets a *cerveza* on the house. Barnes drinks some, considering. "So the locals . . . you know them, too, then? Everyone?"

"*Sí.*"

Pointing at the empty table, he says, "There was a group of men here before, sitting right there. Do they live here in Baracoa?"

"*Sí.*" This time, Miguel says it with a faint glimmer of mistrust in his eyes.

Barnes rethinks the question he'd been about to ask. "One of them gave me this bandana. I want to buy him a new one. Do you know where I can find him?"

"Give it to me, and I will give it to him."

"I'd like to thank him in person. Does he come in every day?"

"Some days."

"And his friends . . . one is American?"

Miguel regards him through a cloud of smoke, and shrugs. "I did not see who was here."

Sure you did. You said you know everyone.

Do you know everyone's secrets?

"I just thought I might have recognized him," Barnes goes on. "Do you know his name?"

"I did not see who was here," Miguel repeats. He stubs out his cigarette and gets to his feet, excusing himself to go back to work.

Barnes raises the beer bottle and thanks him again, watching him disappear into the kitchen.

He might simply be protecting Wayland because Barnes is an outsider, asking too many questions.

But Barnes wouldn't bet on it.

Chapter Ten

Sitting across the kitchen table from Jessie with Little Boy Blue between them on a plastic booster seat, Amelia forces salad and chicken past the lump in her throat. It's not that the food is inedible. It is, in fact, delicious.

Jessie has always been a good cook—though not, she'll say if you compliment her, as good a cook as Diane. After all these years, she continues to refer to her adoptive mother by her first name when talking about her, but never to her face. Same with her father—he's Al, unless he's present.

"Why do you only call your parents 'Mom' and 'Dad' when you're with them?" Amelia had asked her when they were young.

"Because it matters to them. In my head, they're Diane and Al, because I know I have other parents somewhere out there. It's how I keep them separate, for myself."

Yeah. That made a skewed kind of sense to the two of them, in their strange little corner of the world.

And then there were three.

She and Jessie limit their dinner conversation to small talk—the food, the weather, Ithaca. Little Boy Blue still hasn't uttered a sound and gives no indication that he's listening, but he might be.

Watching him gobble his second helping of buttered egg noodles as though he's never tasted anything so delicious before, Amelia wonders whether that might be the case.

Having never had children of her own, she's no expert, but circumstances aside, it seems likely that he hasn't led a happy-go-lucky existence until now. Pale, fragile, and skittish, he regards everything and everyone around him with a mixture of curiosity, circumspection, and fear.

He'd allowed Jessie to lead him to the kitchen but had shrunk from Amelia's attempts to engage him while Jessie was cooking. He'd stolen glances at her, though, and she'd caught him sneaking peeks at the cheese plate as well, though he'd refused to eat anything from it. He had, however, guzzled several glasses of milk before the food was ready, though he didn't seem to know what to do when Jessie set the first before him.

"It's a sippy cup, see?" She'd demonstrated how to use the spout, and he'd waited for her to turn her back before mimicking the action.

Such a basic element of American childhood, yet it was clearly a foreign object to him.

"Do you want some more?" Jessie asks as he sets down his fork, having cleaned his plate again.

He just looks at her and sticks his thumb into his mouth again, Petty's lace-trimmed lavender bathrobe clasped in his fist.

"How about dessert? Chocolate pudding?" Jessie gets up, and returns with a snack-sized plastic pudding cup and spoon. She peels back the lid and holds it out to the boy. "Here, sweetie. This is—"

He gasps and jumps back as if from a hairy black spider.

"It's yummy, see?" Jessie raises the spoon to her lips, pretending to eat some, making num-num-num sounds. She starts to offer it again, and this time he throws up his arms to protect himself, trembling.

"Okay, it's okay. I'm so sorry, sweetheart." Jessie throws the pudding into the garbage and the spoon into the sink and looks at Amelia with a slight shake of her head. What nightmare might a cup of pudding have conjured?

"How about some TV?" Jessie asks.

No reaction.

"Or maybe you'd like to play with some toys?"

Nothing.

"You actually have toys for him, Jess?"

"I have everything. I always thought we'd have another little one around here."

"Foster child? Or . . . wait, you're not pregnant, are you?"

"Pregnant!" She laughs heartily.

Amelia joins in. Jessie still has the best, most contagious laugh in the world.

The child looks up, startled by the outburst. After a moment, his lips curve. The expression is tentative, and fleeting, but it's definitely a smile.

Ah, progress.

"Come on, kiddo. You need to have some fun." Jessie leads him to the sunroom and flips a couple of switches. Lamplight glares off three walls of paned glass casement windows. Amelia recognizes the overstuffed floral print sofa and entertainment armoire from Jessie's parents' old living room next door.

Clearing the table, she keeps an eye on the sunroom. Jessie tunes the TV to a children's program with an obnoxiously lively host whose every comment is punctuated by *boing boing* sound effects.

The child shudders, hiding his face.

"Yeah, I don't blame you, kiddo. Here, let's find a cartoon . . ."

The more she channel surfs, the more frightened he appears, and she clicks off the television.

"It's okay. There are plenty of other things to do."

She rummages in built-in cabinets beneath the window seats that run along the room's perimeter, and finds a couple of wooden toddler puzzles with knobbed pieces, a coloring book, paper, and some picture books. She sets them out on the coffee table and rejoins Amelia in the kitchen, whispering, "I thought maybe some familiar things would help him relax a little."

"Maybe they're not so familiar."

The child sits on the edge of the couch, clutching the robe, sucking his thumb, staring at the floor.

"Why do you think he's so attached to Petty's bathrobe?"

"Maybe the silky fabric feels good against his face?" Amelia suggests. "Or does something about it remind him of someone who nurtured him? His mom?"

"I thought the same thing. Maybe she has a robe like it, or it smells like her. Petty's forever slathering herself in lotions and potions. The way he's holding it . . . it makes me think someone out there loves, or *loved*, him." Jessie opens a cabinet, takes down a couple of plastic food storage containers, and hands one to her. "For the leftover noodles."

"I don't think they'll fit."

"They will."

She's right. They just fit.

It must be nice to be Jessie, so self-assured and comfortable in her own skin. She always seems to know what to say and do, and exactly how to say or do it.

Amelia would like to think that she, too, has her confident moments. Back at home, anyway. Maybe not lately, with Aaron, but she's always in control where her work is concerned . . .

Really? So you're not wishing you'd confronted Lily Tucker when she showed you that ring?

"If his mom is out there, we've got to find her," Jessie says, layering chicken pieces in a Tupperware container. "This is our chance to do for him what nobody did for us."

There's that lump again, clogging Amelia's throat.

"Mimi? Are you in? Can you help me help Little Boy Blue?" She nods, and Jessie looks pleased. "Good. We just can't tell Billy."

"Tell him what?"

"You know—that we're helping. He'll get all judgy. He likes to play by the rules."

"Yeah, um, Jess? He's a cop."

"In Ithaca. This case isn't even his jurisdiction. The county sheriff's department is handling it."

"Shh." Amelia holds a finger to her lips, and they both glance into the next room. The child seems oblivious to the conversation. He's removed his thumb from his mouth and is toying with one of the knobbed wooden puzzle pieces.

"All I'm saying is that I can't not *do* something about this."

"You are doing something. You've taken him into your home."

"That's not what I mean."

"The sheriff's department must be issuing bulletins, searching the missing child databases, putting out Amber Alerts, getting it out there in the media, and—"

"Amber alerts are for kids who disappear, Mimi. This one *appeared*. It's the opposite, and he's safe and in good hands, so you can't assume the authorities are going to treat this as urgently as an abduction."

She suspects that's true, though in all her years working with adoptees and foundlings, she's never been involved in a case like this as it was unfolding. But she is well experienced in keeping zero-to-sixty Jessie in check.

"I know what you're saying, but I'm sure the police are doing everything they can."

"Everything they know how to do and have done before, but this is uncharted territory for them. A veterinarian would have more experience with this sort of thing than they do."

"What? Jessie—"

"No, seriously, think about it. A vet deals with abandoned animals all the time. But when kids get separated from their parents—like, in a store or something—it's usually by accident, and it's not for very long. If the cops get involved, they basically sit the kid down with a lollypop and wait for the mom to show up. It wasn't like that for me or you or Little Boy Blue."

Jessie sighs, and starts loading the dishwasher. "Anyway, the police were involved from the moment I was found, and didn't find my birth parents. I don't know how hard they tried, once Diane and Al had taken me in and I was safe. I think they just went back to focusing on other cases where lives were on the line."

Amelia understands what Jessie is saying. Anyone employed by any government organization has more work than they can handle. They can only do so much, and they have to prioritize.

"This seems premature, though, Jessie. He just turned up yesterday."

"Tomorrow, it will be two days. If you look at kidnapped child statistics, the first forty-eight hours of the investigation are crucial."

"I know, but like you said, this is the opposite. He's been *found*, not—"

"You can't be found without being lost, Mimi. We know that better than anyone. Unless he suddenly starts talking and tells us where he came from, the trail is going to go stone-cold in a hurry. Don't you think we owe it to him to do whatever we can to find out who he is?"

Amelia glances into the next room. Little Boy Blue is back in his own world, staring down at the lavender fabric.

She sighs. "What did you have in mind?"

"If we can get his DNA—"

"No! No way! You can't test DNA without consent. For a minor, you need a parent or guardian, and he's currently a ward of the state, so that means involving the foster system, lawyers, a judge . . ."

"I know all that. But if you can just get his DNA into a database and find a close enough match for him, we might be able to figure out where he belongs," Jessie rockets on. "We wouldn't tell a soul, Mimi. Not ever. It would be our secret. And you do this every day for people."

"For my *clients*. And what if we find his family? How do we explain it?"

"I knew you were going to say that, and it's simple. If we can link him to close relatives and a geographic area, we'll be able to sniff around online for birth records, pictures on social media . . . come on, I don't have to tell you all this. You do it for a living."

"It would be unethical for me to—"

"Seriously? Unethical? You can't tell me you've never bent the rules or snuck around to get information, like sealed adoption records!"

No, she can't.

Her friend closes the dishwasher and looks at her, eyes shiny with tears. "Mimi, kids fall through the cracks in the system every single day. I saw it when I was a caseworker, and I couldn't stand it. I did whatever I had to do to keep it from happening, and sometimes, that meant bending—or breaking—the rules. If we can save this child, and find his family, how we did it won't matter."

Amelia shakes her head, but she can't seem to form the word *no*.

"If he can't or won't tell us where he came from, and there are no witnesses to the abandonment, and he doesn't fit any missing child reports out there, and no one recognizes his photo in the press, then DNA testing is virtually the only way to identify him, isn't it?"

"Yes, it is," she admits. "And I'm sure the authorities will test him."

"But by the time they sort out the red tape—"

"I know." Her own eyes are beginning to sting. "Look, maybe if I talk to Aaron about it . . ."

"Mimi! Seriously? You swore you wouldn't tell anyone!"

Had she sworn? Or had Jessie simply asked her to? The day's stress is catching up with her, her brain functioning like a sieve capturing water.

"Jessie, it's not like I'm going to . . . I mean, Aaron is my *husband*."

"And Billy's mine, and I told you, if he—"

"No, I just meant that since Aaron's an attorney, I was thinking he might have some advice."

"He does commercial litigation! Plus, we said this is our secret."

No, you *said that, Jessie.*

It's like they're back in college, her friend talking circles around her, trying to convince her to go along with some elaborate plan. Only back then, it would have involved illegal beer or a cute older guy, not people's lives.

"I'm sorry, Jessie. I just need to . . . do you mind if I go upstairs? I need to feed Clancy, and Aaron doesn't even know where I am, so I do need to call him, but I won't—"

"Please don't—"

"—say anything about Little Boy Blue. I know, I know, I won't. I promise."

Amelia stifles a yawn, hugs her, and thanks her for everything, calling good-night to the boy whose sorrowful silence dogs her up the back stairs, chased by her own guilt.

But what am I supposed to do? My hands are tied. Jessie is trying to save the world, and I'm not even sure I can save my marriage.

Billy had given her some blue painter's tape to secure the bedroom door from the outside until he can repair it. She unfastens it and closes the door behind her, locks it, and wedges a shoe under it for good measure. Poor Theodore had been so traumatized by the kitten it might as well have been a raging lion.

The last thing this family needed was an unexpected weekend houseguest, even if she *had* been invited. This isn't the first time she's run away to Ithaca, but she's an adult now.

And all I want to do is crawl into bed and bury my head under the covers.

"Clancy?" She looks around the room, under the bed, the desk, the dresser. No sign of him. How could he have escaped again? "Clance? Where are you?"

There he is, having climbed into an open floor bin filled with sports equipment and fallen asleep cupped in a worn leather catcher's mitt.

She finds her cell phone and snaps a photo. Her smile fades when she realizes that there's no one to send it to. Jessie's under the same roof, and now isn't the time. Aaron isn't into cute kitten photos.

Aaron . . .

She checks and confirms that there are no missed calls or texts from him. Infuriating, though not unusual.

She tries his number and it rings into voice mail. Not trusting herself to leave a message without betraying her frustration and disappointment, she writes a text instead.

Came to Ithaca after all. See you next week.
Love you.

She deletes the last two words, adds them back in, deletes them again, and hits Send before she can change her mind.

It feels like the middle of the night, but when she checks her watch, she supposes he isn't even home from his dinner yet.

She climbs into bed, her thoughts turning back to Little Boy Blue.

Eventually, the official investigation will come down to searching the DNA databases anyway. As Jessie said, it's virtually the only tool to identify a foundling when there are no viable leads. But by the time they file the paperwork and jump through the legal hoops to get it done, the process could take months, or even years. And the results might not yield a conclusive match for a parent or sibling or even a close relative. It takes dedication, stamina, expertise, and considerable digging to follow all the less tangible threads—many-times-removed cousins, possible great-great-great ancestors.

Amelia chases down leads like that every day. What are the odds that some bureaucratic stranger who's never looked into those big blue eyes will go to such lengths for this lost child?

And even if someone is willing and able, even if a match is found . . .

How much time will have passed? In a few months, a year, the damage will have been done. By then, a child his age will likely have forgotten where he came from. He'll have settled into a new home, maybe even this one, and will have learned to rely on and maybe even love new caregivers—only to be wrenched from his life all over again.

If you're so worried about ethics, wouldn't allowing that to happen be more unethical than testing his DNA on the sly?

She turns off the lamp and lies awake in the dark, thinking about Little Boy Blue and then about Aaron. She imagines being dragged from a sound sleep later to face questions about why she'd ignored his texts about the dry cleaner, and why she'd left town without letting him know.

She reaches for her phone to silence it. The confrontation can wait until morning. By then, she might even have some answers.

Unless . . .

She'd sent him an email earlier today. Maybe he'd sent one in return. She hasn't bothered to check all evening.

She sits up, turns on the lamp again, opens her in-box—and finds herself looking at an email with the subject line she's awaited for years.

Amelia Crenshaw, you have a DNA match!

BETWEEN ITHACA COLLEGE and Cornell University, there are more than twenty thousand students in town. Billy finds a good many of them shopping at Walmart on this rainy Friday night, along with a mix of locals, alumni, visiting parents, and tourists. Theodore is always on edge in a crowd, so rather than maneuver him up and down the aisles, Billy rolls the cart directly to the book section.

"You can hang out here while I go grab the stuff we need, okay?"

"For how long?"

"Ten minutes. Maybe fifteen."

Theodore shakes his head. "I don't want to—"

"Pick out a new book and I'll buy it for you."

"Okay. Hurry up, though. I'm hungry. I want to go eat."

"You and me both. I'll be right back."

He heads first to the home improvement department. After five minutes of fruitless searching for the doorstop or a clerk who isn't busy with other customers, he comes across a gray-haired man wearing a store smock, stacking cans of paint.

"Doorstops? Couple of aisles over, with the door hardware. Come on, I'll show you," he says, and starts strolling in that direction like he has all the time in the world.

Billy, who does not, tells him he already looked there.

"Ah, we're probably sold out again. These college kids aren't supposed to prop their dorm doors open, but rules mean nothing to them. Not this generation. Back when I was—"

"If you're sold out, then I guess I'm out of luck. But thanks anyway, sir."

"Maybe you can just find a big rock or something? Save yourself a couple of bucks, too," the clerk adds conspiratorially.

"Yeah, I don't think my wife will go for that." Billy explains the situation.

"You need to take a screwdriver and fiddle around with the hinges. Door's not setting right."

"I've tried that. It never works for more than a day or so."

"Then why don't you just put one of those sliding bolts on it? That'll keep it closed."

Billy considers the idea. At least Chip and Petty are out of the house. In their younger days, they'd have locked each other in. Theodore is hardly a prankster like his older siblings, and it does seem to be the only foolproof solution.

He thanks the clerk, curtails another "back in my day," and throws a package of vintage-looking bolt hardware into the cart. Checking his watch, he weaves the cart back through the crowded aisles to the book section.

No sign of Theodore. He must have gotten antsy and come looking for Billy.

He sends a text.

Meet me in kids' clothing.

Keeping an eye out for Theodore, he picks out some clothes, undergarments, pajamas, and a warm down coat for Little Boy Blue. Then, remembering the child's bare feet, he sends Theodore another text.

Come to kids' shoes.

He picks out a little pair of sneakers, watching for Theodore, or at least an answering text. Nothing. He checks the book section again. Still not there.

Theodore must have gotten cranky about the delay, maybe so hungry that he'd gone off in search of food.

Billy texts him again, asking where he is, and works

his way toward the best bet—the grocery section. Passing a display of Halloween candy, he picks up a couple of bags of miniature chocolate bars. For the trick-or-treaters, he'll tell Jessie. Not like they're Zagnuts, or anything. She should be glad he's planning ahead, avoiding another Certs Halloween. For good measure, he throws some baby carrots into the cart, too. And some of those healthy protein bars she's always pushing on him.

Remembering Jessie had asked him to pick up some cat food and litter for Mimi's kitten, he moves on to the pet department. Enough with the texting. He dials Theodore's phone, but it goes right into voice mail.

He leaves a message. "Where are you? I'm going to the pet section, and then we're getting out of here, so meet me by the registers."

He sends the same information via text, starting to feel a little uneasy.

But this wouldn't be the first time Theodore has been unresponsive to texts that involve a change of plans. And this time, the plans involve the resented foster child.

Billy grabs what he needs from the pet department and goes to the front of the store. No Theodore. Now he's worried.

He wanders the aisles pushing his full cart with one hand, holding his phone with the other, texting, texting, texting . . .

Where are you?
I'm looking for you!
Time to go!

Finally, just ??????

"Hey, Sarge!" He turns to see a tall, gray-haired man in a starched pink shirt and dark suit. "Walk right on past me, why don't you?"

Dave Carver had gone through the local schools a few years ahead of Billy and had rubbed him the wrong way even back then, before they'd worked together on the local police force. Before Billy had been promoted over him.

Dave had retired a few years ago and is now working as a real estate agent, yet persists in calling Billy "Sarge" with the same old undercurrent of sarcasm.

"How's it going, Dave?"

"Can't complain, can't complain."

But you will, Billy thinks. And he does, about the store parking lot, the price of cereal, the upcoming presidential election, his sciatica . . .

"You know, those fuzzy footy pajamas look way too small for Theodore," he interrupts himself to say, scrutinizing the items in Billy's cart. "So I guess it's true, huh? You and Jessie are fostering the little kid they found out in the boonies yesterday? Saw it on the news last night."

"That we're fostering him?"

Dave's thin lips pull into a tight smirk. "That he was abandoned."

"And you heard that we're fostering . . ."

"Through the grapevine. How's that going?"

How do you think it's going? The child has been traumatized beyond belief.

"Great. It's going great. Speaking of going, I have to go find Theodore, so . . ." He starts pushing the cart away.

"Wrong direction. He's back there." Dave jerks a finger toward the book department. "Seems like a real bookworm type, huh? Not like Chip. Best Little League player I've ever coached."

Funny, he hadn't said that at the time. He was the kind of coach who'd started his own mediocre son every game, kept him in throughout, and never pulled the less skilled kids off the bench even when the team was up by fifteen runs in the seventh inning.

"Listen, Sarge, by the way, I've got a listing across the street from you . . ."

"The Hyland house. I heard Bob's retiring and they're moving to Florida. Well, I've got to get—"

"Just one sec," Dave says.

Billy sighs, knowing where this is going, based on the last time he'd had a listing on the block.

"Listen, Dave, Jessie and I have no plans to paint the house anytime soon." *And if we did, it would still be bright yellow because we like it, and even if we didn't like it, at this point, I'd keep it just to spite you.*

Dave rocks back on his heels. "Yeah, that's not the problem."

"The problem? So there's a problem?"

"Not the paint. It's like I was just telling Theo, the last thing I need is—"

"Wait, you were just telling who?"

"Whom. Your kid. Theo."

"He's Theodore."

Dave snaps his fingers. "Right! He did say he doesn't like to be called Theo."

And I'll bet you don't like to be called jackass.

"Anyway, we can't have potential buyers walking away because they're worried about getting woken up every morning in the dark by some crazy cock-a-doodle-doo."

His heart sinks. "You said that?"

"Of course I said it. Chickens belong on a farm—or in a deep fryer." He laughs. "Finger-lickin' good."

"Terrific," Billy mutters. He turns and pushes the cart toward the checkout, ignoring Dave's protest that he was only teasing.

After finding the shortest line—not short by any definition—he pulls his phone from his pocket to text his son.

I just ran into Mr. Carver.

He backs up, deleting the *Mr.*, tempted to replace it with a couple of choice words, but he refrains, thumb-typing on: I know he upset you & I'm sorry. Don't worry about anything he said. Where are you?

After a moment, three wobbly dots appear.

Good. Theodore is writing back.

The dots disappear. Billy edges closer to the register as the line moves forward, watching the phone. The three dots reappear at last, but it takes a long time for them to give way to a text.

I'm going home to make sure Espinoza is ok.

On foot, alone, at night, in the rain?

I'm sure he's ok. Come back here.

He waits for a response, rocking back and forth on his heels.

"Sir?" The woman behind him taps his shoulder.

"What? Oh—sorry." He closes the gap between him and the customer in front of him.

At last, Theodore pops up again: *He said don't be surprised if my bird flies the coop.*

Dammit. Dave is a bully, plain and simple. Always has been, always will be.

A knot tightens in Billy's gut. He'll deal with Dave later. Right now, he just needs to get out of here and track down Theodore, and the conveyor belt has edged forward enough that he can start putting his items on it.

He begins unloading the cart, then winces at a sharp stitch in his chest.

He takes a deep breath. The pain intensifies.

Strained muscle?

He exhales, feeling his legs tremble beneath him.

He must have pulled something. The cart is deep, the cat litter heavy, all that bending, lifting, and twisting . . .

It seems to be easing up a little, though. He stands, just breathing, in, out, gently, gently . . .

"Sir?" Again, the woman behind him taps his arm.

He sees that the belt has moved all the way forward, leaving room for the rest of his purchases. He resumes taking them from the cart. When he comes to the bags of chocolate bars, he hesitates, then deposits them on top of the rack of gum with other customers' last-minute unwanted items.

"Good for you," the woman behind him says, and her tone pings some irrational defiance in Billy.

He retrieves the candy and plunks it on the belt. Of course it's just a strained muscle. And he has plenty of other things to worry about.

* * *

Amelia Crenshaw, you have a DNA match!

SHE CAN'T BREATHE.

Her hand trembles as she opens the email to a message she's seen thousands of times before, addressed to her clients. This time, it's for her.

Dear Amelia . . .

She'd known it was coming, yet in its fruition, *inevitable* has transformed into *miraculous*.

The email expands upon the subject line, with an invitation to examine the match on the ancestry website. She clicks the link, logs in, and holds her breath, waiting, waiting . . .

Her account pops up. Another click. Click. Click . . .

There it is.

She scans the results.

Quinnlynn Johnson
Relationship Probability: 2nd or 3rd cousin.
Confidence Level: Extremely High.
282 Centimorgans shared across 15 DNA segments.

The only way to contact the match through the site is to message her through her account, but she hasn't logged in since August.

Not good, but not disastrous. Amelia takes the next step she'd take if the results were for a client: she Googles the name.

She knows that Johnson is the second most common last name in the country. It's turned up in countless clients' trees, always making for a difficult search. But in this case, she's counting on the unusual first name to help.

It does.

There is only one Quinnlynn Johnson in the world, assuming her name is spelled correctly on her DNA profile. She has a prolific online presence, including social media.

Amelia opens her Facebook page, hoping the privacy settings won't prevent a non-friend from seeing relevant information.

Quinnlynn Johnson lives in Atlanta. Her profile picture shows an attractive black woman who appears to be in her thirties. Studying it, Amelia notes that Quinnlynn's skin is much darker than her own, lips much fuller, face much rounder, and yet . . .

And yet . . .

She looks like me.

She stands and strides across the room, wiping tears, shuddering in a breath.

If she'd passed the woman on the street, would she have noticed the resemblance? Or does it seem striking because she's looking for it?

She dries her eyes, takes out her laptop, and checks to see if the Wi-Fi network is back up so that she can view the photo on her laptop. Nope, still down.

Aaron had once showed her how to connect through her phone's hotspot, but she doesn't have the patience to figure out how right now.

She enlarges the photo on her phone. There's something familiar about the slant of the young woman's smile, the expression in her eyes . . .

Sure there is, child, because she's your kin.

Bettina's drawl, in her head, makes her smile.

She scans the biographical information Quinnlynn has made public, needing to know more, needing to know everything.

Employment: Coca-Cola Company
Religion: Baptist
College: Georgia State
Hometown: . . .

That can't be right. It's impossible.

Marshboro, Georgia?

Bettina's hometown.

Chapter Eleven

Jessie seats herself beside Little Boy Blue on the couch.

The lavender robe is across his lap. He's sucking his right thumb, his left hand toying with a square red puzzle piece as he eyes the wooden board. It's simple, just five colorful shapes.

"Can you fit it back into the spot where it goes?" she asks him.

He glances up at her, then averts his gaze.

"Do you want me to show you how to do it?" She starts to reach, but he flinches.

She leans back, watching him stare at the board.

After a while, he extends the red square, poised to place it. But it's turned at the wrong angle.

"Just rotate it, like this." Again, she starts to reach; again, he retreats.

Giving him space, she picks up one of the other puzzles—also simple, with a transportation theme. She dumps out the pieces. He seems startled by the clatter, and for a moment she worries that he's going to bolt from the room, but he just slides a few inches away from her on the couch cushion.

Keeping the crazy lady at arm's length. Smart kid, she thinks, and pretends to be engrossed in her task. She can feel him watching her as she fits the pieces back in one at a time, trying several spots before finding the right one and murmuring the names of each piece.

"*Train . . . car . . . truck . . . boat . . . plane!* I did it!" She claps her hands, dumps it out, and starts again. "*Truck . . . plane . . .*"

After a few rounds of that, he moves his wooden square toward its space, turning, turning . . . it goes in, and she hears his breath catch in his throat. He gazes down at it for a long time, takes it out again, and puts it back, this time without effort.

"*Square,*" Jessie says quietly, resisting the urge to make a commotion. "Good job."

He casts a sidewise glance at her, and she averts her eyes.

She finishes her puzzle, gives herself another round of applause, empties her transportation shapes onto the table again, and starts over.

Little Boy Blue fiddles with the blue triangle piece. Then, he grabs the board, turns it over, and dumps the pieces onto the table. He seems shaken by the clatter, and she sees him shoot a glance at her as if to make sure he's not in trouble.

"Great," she says. "Now you turn them over and line them up so that you can see what they are, and you put them back one at a time, just like this, see? *Boat . . .*"

He just sits there for so long she's sure she's lost him, but when she steals a glance at him, she sees that he's engaged, studying the pieces, strategizing. Sure enough, he pieces it together quickly, and looks at her for a response.

She smiles at the obvious delight in his eyes, and claps. "You did it! See? *Square, triangle, oval, circle, diamond!* Want to try ag—"

He's already dumping out the pieces to start over.

Where have you been all your life, Little Boy Blue?

Noting his reaction to everything around him, to Amelia, Jessie wonders whether he's ever even seen a person of color before, or a toy, a television, a puzzle . . .

A knock on the front door startles them both.

"It's all right, sweetie. Someone's here, that's all." She stands. "Let's go see who it is."

He stays rooted to the couch. She glances at the double French doors to the patio, making sure they're bolted. The yard is murky in the weak glow of solar path lights. There's no way he'd leave his puzzle to venture outside, is there? She'll only be a minute.

She hurries into the front hall and opens the door to a harried-looking woman with windswept dark hair and kind eyes. "Mrs. Hanson? Laura Himmelstein. Sorry it's so late."

She shows an identification card—ah, the caseworker. Jessie had forgotten all about her.

"How's he doing?" Laura asks as Jessie leads her through the house.

"He's been sleeping and eating like a champ. He's very bright, and curious." She stops in the kitchen and they peer at him through the archway.

Head bowed, he appears to have gone back to his puzzle without noticing the visitor, but Jessie sees him steal a wary glance.

"Still nonverbal?"

"Yes," she tells Laura in a low voice. "I've been trying to make him more comfortable, reduce the anxiety level, but . . ."

"It takes more time to make a breakthrough with some children than others, especially in an emergency foster situation, when the separation from the home is still fresh and traumatic. Ideally, we'll find out where he belongs, and he can go home right away, but in the meantime, we'll be working to find him a longer-term placement."

She nods. They've been down this road before.

Theodore, too, was supposed to have been a temporary foster placement while his teenaged birth mother was hospitalized with pneumonia. The stay had turned into weeks, months, a year, as she'd regained her health, earned her GED, established herself in a job, and saved enough for a decent place to live. Visiting Theodore as often as she could, she'd turned to Jessie one day with tears in her eyes.

"He doesn't need me. He doesn't even care that I'm here."

"He does," Jessie had lied, as Theodore used tweezers to sort colored beads into slots in a tray.

"No, he needs you and your husband, your kids, your house. He needs a normal life. He'll never have that with me."

He'll never have that, period.

His mother had let go. Jessie and Billy could not.

Laura asks about the rest of the family, and she explains that Billy and Theodore are out shopping, neglecting to mention her son's adverse reaction to their new foster child. She also mentions that a friend is visiting from New York. Under ordinary circumstances, with a foster child in the house, she'd have had to give notice about a houseguest well in advance.

She assures Laura that she's well aware of the procedures—yes, Amelia is only staying for the weekend and no, she won't have unsupervised contact with the boy. Anyway, she'd passed the required criminal background check several years ago, during an extended visit while other foster children had been in the house.

They go over Laura's packet of paperwork and discuss what will happen if the child remains with them longer than a few days.

"I've already canceled my Monday appointments so that I can be home all day," Jessie tells her. "I can push back Tuesday, too, if it comes to that."

"Let's hope for his sake that it doesn't, and he's back home by then."

Hope . . .

Jessie looks at Little Boy Blue, trying to imagine him back in his mother's arms, but the thing with feathers just sits, weighted and withered, in her soul.

DRESSED IN AN old brown field coat he'd long ago stolen from Hugo's barn, hair still damp from his shower, the Angler pockets his keys and turns off the bedroom light. He picks up the garbage bag filled with discarded clothing and peers into the hallway. Deserted.

He'd heard a sobbing Renee stomp up earlier and close her door with a bang. All is silent now as he heads toward the stairway, past enormous school photos of the children. Every time he looks at Pascal's kindergarten portrait, he sees his own.

He, too, had worn a shy smile and a white dress shirt with a tie, the Catholic school uniform then and now. But he'd had no mother to purchase his own headshot and hang it on the wall, and so had glimpsed it only in the class composite hanging on the wall at that first of many schools he would attend.

In a box of old papers he'd found after his father's death, he'd seen childhood snapshots of his father— features identical to his own at that age, and his son's—no, his sons'.

They look like him. We all look like him.

He seizes Pascal's portrait from the wall and crushes the glass-framed smile beneath his boot heel.

Behind her closed door, Renee cries out. He continues on past without looking in or bidding her goodnight, congratulating himself on a solid step toward undoing his wife's coddling and pampering.

He'd whip both children into shape in no time if Cecile were gone from the house forever. With pleasure, he imagines bundling her into a tarp and sinking her to the depths of a cold Laurentians lake, but his grin fades when he realizes he'd then be responsible for the care and feeding of both offspring. Better to get rid of the children, one at a time. Make the first appear to be an accident or an abduction.

Cecile would go insane with grief. She might take her own life, and that of her surviving child, in a delusional attempt to join the first in the afterlife. That's what he'll make it look like, what he'll tell the authorities.

He pauses in the kitchen, seeing that he'd left the milk carton out on the counter. Renee should have known to put it away. He's tempted to drag her out of bed by the hair and make her pick up after herself, but that would invite another tantrum, and he might not be able to control his impulses this time.

Opening the refrigerator to put away the milk, he's

assaulted by Cecile's stinking slab of Époisses. He seizes it and throws it into the garbage bag. Let her wonder what happened to it. Let her dare to ask.

He ties the garbage bag tightly, carries it out to the garage, and pops the car trunk. It yawns open in the darkness, the interior light long ago disconnected.

It smells of damp earth and of Monique, pulling him back to the night he'd returned to his uncle's farm after her escape attempt. A knot of dread had clenched his heart as he opened the trunk and shined his flashlight into her blue-eyed terror. She'd known what he was about to do, what he had to do. There was no choice in the matter, no violent impulse.

"Get out."

She'd whimpered.

He'd yanked her arm, hearing her shoulder snap as he'd hauled her from the trunk. She'd yowled in agony, and he'd clapped a rough hand over her mouth to stifle her.

They'd been too far from the house for an ancient man to hear, though. The Angler had parked not in his usual spot behind the barn, but alongside the path leading down to the lake.

Monique had cried out again, softly, when she'd seen the tarp he'd already lain out on the ground beside the car, a coil of rope beside it. "Please, no . . . I don't want to die. Please don't—"

Her last words.

She'd spoken them in English, he realizes now, as if she'd believed that her son might be within earshot and hadn't wanted to frighten him.

He throws the foul-smelling garbage bag into the trunk and closes it. If he drives away now, his daughter will hear him and alert Cecile. He'll have to wait until she's asleep.

Back inside, he sits down at the desktop computer. Fewer than twenty-four hours have passed since he'd searched to see whether a corpse can bleed.

He waits for the computer to stir to life, remembering the boy, Monique, the farm . . .

Remembering Uncle Hugo, and all those nights spent fishing, reading, playing their homemade version of Jenga . . .

If the tower falls . . .

He opens his search engine and clicks on the history.

Can a corpse bleed?

There it is, like a wooden block snatched from deep in the layered foundation. The tower wobbles.

If it falls . . .

When he thinks of Cecile—of the lack of makeup, and the signs of her hurried departure this morning—he can't imagine that she'd somehow sat here and stumbled across this.

He erases the search, and after a moment's hesitation, begins another. This time, he won't be so careless when he walks away.

Boy's remains found in New York State.

Nothing of relevance.

He consults a map and tries again.

Boy's remains found in Tompkins County, NY.

Nothing.

Back again to the map, this time zooming in on the area where he'd left the body.

Boy's remains found near Cortland, NY.

This time, there's a hit. But not for remains.

Toddler Found on Cortland Hollow Road

The article, dated yesterday, reveals that a little boy had been found on property owned by Levi Stoltzfus, an Amish farmer . . .

He hears the horse's hooves clopping in his head, and he knows.

Even before he reads the description, he knows.

Two or three years old, wearing pajamas, shaggy blond hair, blue eyes, cannot or will not speak . . .

The Angler shoves back the chair. It teeters on two legs.

If it falls. . . .

The chair topples onto the parquet floor behind him.

You lose.

He yanks open the desk drawer and takes the passports—all of them, ensuring that Cecile won't be able to follow him, or leave the country in his absence.

Even before he steps into the garage, his nostrils pick up the stench emanating from his car. He can't possibly climb into the driver's seat, much less make a four-hour road trip.

Nor can he leave the bag with his bloodied clothes.

"Papa!" he hears Renee calling inside the house as he gets behind the wheel, and rage uncoils like a venomous serpent within him.

He begins to drive, fury building with every breath of foul air forced into his lungs.

ABOUT TO CLOSE the front door against the autumn chill as Laura Himmelstein's red taillights disappear down the street, Jessie pauses, spotting headlights coming around the corner from the opposite direction.

Billy's SUV.

She tilts her face to the sky. "Thank you."

She'd been praying they wouldn't come home before the social worker's visit was over, in case Theodore is still in a mood. She's certain it must have passed by now, though. A night out with his father is always a balm.

No, not always.

Billy has barely parked when their son throws open the passenger's door and storms down the driveway toward the back of the house.

"What's wrong?" she calls after him. "Where are you going?"

"To the coop! I hate him!"

"Theodore, you can't say that about your—"

"Not Dad!" he shouts, and disappears into the yard.

She turns back to Billy, unloading bags, his movements stiff and methodic. Something pretty horrible must be going on if he's not going to make Theodore come back and help. He lugs the bags toward the porch.

Jessie glances down at her sock feet, then at the puddle-pocked walkway. "Is there more? I'll come help you."

"Just the cat litter. I'll get it."

"No, I don't mind. Just let me grab my shoes and—"

"I've got it!" Billy snaps.

He deposits the bags on the floor just inside the door like a brick deliveryman, and trudges back out into the night.

What the hell happened?

She carries the bags to the kitchen and confirms that Little Boy Blue is still busy with his puzzles. He'd worked on them the whole time Laura had attempted to engage him in conversation.

"I think he'll come around, if you give him enough time and space," she'd said in parting. "I've seen worse cases."

So has Jessie, but this is her first foundling. Her other fosters have all had parents somewhere. Sick parents, addicted parents, violent parents, apathetic parents. Yet those children had known who they were and where they'd come from, even if there was no going back. It had given her something to work with.

She returns to the hall just as Billy closes the door behind him, plunking the box of cat litter onto the mat with a grunt. He pauses, head back, eyes closed.

"Are you okay? Is Theodore okay?"

"Not really." He sighs and looks at her. "And not really."

"What happened?"

"Dave Carver happened."

"Oh, crap. Did he bring up the damned election again?"

"Yeah, he did."

"I knew it." She'd run into Dave herself a few days ago. He'd badgered her about presidential candidates, then man-splained why her choice was all wrong. "Would you believe he told me that a woman can never be an effective president, and that—"

"Politics weren't the problem, Jess. It was about Theodore. That son of a bitch gave him a hard time about Espinoza."

"Crap."

Billy explains what happened and she shudders, imagining an angry, frustrated, frightened Theodore wandering alone into the stormy night.

"I picked him up before he'd crossed the highway. We went to get dinner, but he was too upset to eat, and I . . ."

"You what?"

"I didn't want to make him."

"That's not what you were going to say. You couldn't eat? Are you feeling okay?"

"I'm fine." Yet he grimaces as he picks up a shopping bag from the floor and follows her into the kitchen.

"Billy, you don't seem—"

"How's Little Boy Blue? Did he eat?"

"He ate, and we had a little breakthrough." She touches a forefinger to her lips and points toward the sunroom.

Her husband glances in. "He's doing a puzzle! And he's not sucking his thumb."

She smiles, filling him in as they put away the purchases—until she finds the chocolate. "Billy, you're not supposed to be eating—"

"It's for the trick-or-treaters."

"Halloween is a month away."

"And Amelia . . ."

"She doesn't like candy."

"Who doesn't like candy?"

"Come on, Billy, we both know this is for you. And it's the last thing you need in your condition."

"My condition? Here we go again. I told you, I'm—"

"What did you have for dinner?"

"Like I said, we didn't really eat."

"But what did you order?"

"A green salad and club soda." At her sharp glance, he says, "It's the truth! Ask Theodore!"

"Okay, I believe you, but . . ."

In a way, she'd almost wanted to hear that he'd ordered a cheesesteak and fries, same as always. A salad makes her wonder if he, too, might finally be concerned about his health. She doesn't like his pallor or the way he's wincing as he bends and stretches.

The back door opens with a loud squeak, and Theodore appears.

"Dad, we need to go back to the store. I need a padlock for Espinoza's coop. He's still there," he adds, sounding relieved. "But Mom has to watch him while we're gone. Come on."

Billy shakes his head. "Theodore, there's no way we're going to—"

"You said I can't bring him into the house, so I need to make sure no one can kidnap him."

Jessie puts a hand on his shoulder. "Honey, no one is going to kidnap him."

"But—"

"Look, I know what Dave Carver said to you," Billy tells him, "but I promise you that he's not going to—"

"You can't promise that!"

"I told you before, I won't let that happen, okay? That jerk will touch that rooster over my dead body!"

"Don't say that, Dad! It could happen!"

"It won't!"

"It might!"

Jessie shushes them, looking toward the sunroom. Little Boy Blue is sucking his thumb again, staring down at the floor.

"Come into the living room," she tells her husband and son. "We can figure this out in there. And keep your voices down."

"Why?"

"Because Aunt Mimi is trying to sleep and you're both too loud," she tells Theodore, who has yet to notice Little Boy Blue.

In the living room, she tells Billy to sit down. He can't quite seem to catch his breath.

"I don't want to sit down."

"I think you should."

"Why? I'm fine!"

"You're not fine, Dad," Theodore tells him. "You haven't been taking good care of your cardiac arteries. You have a plaque buildup."

"Who told you that?" Billy looks hard at Jessie.

She shakes her head. They'd agreed not to tell any of the kids about his emergency room episode a few weeks ago, or the follow-up visit with the cardiologist.

"My health ed teacher told me. He says people like you are at risk for a heart attack."

"People like *me*? He said that?"

"He said fat guys in their fifties who don't exercise are at risk for a heart attack."

"Terrific." Billy shakes his head. "Thank you, Dr. Theodore."

"I'm not a doctor. But I got a hundred and three on my test."

"Well, I feel like I've got a hundred and three fever right now. Not because I'm having a heart attack. Because this has been one hell of a stressful day—week—and I'm done. I'm going to bed." Billy heads for the stairs.

Theodore follows. "But what about the padlock?"

"There will be no padlock!"

"But . . ."

Up they go, bickering.

Left behind in the living room, Jessie sinks onto the couch. Billy isn't the only one who's *done*. She sits there, face buried in her hands, telling herself to just breathe.

Breathe . . .

Billy's breathing had scared her. She should have pushed him to sit down, maybe even called the doctor. But she knows he hadn't wanted Theodore to sense a hint of vulnerability.

Fat guys in their fifties who don't exercise . . .

She knows the words had stung Billy.

Tact has never been their son's strong suit. On a bad day, Theodore is temperamental. On a good one, he's exhausting. And on this day . . .

Hearing a faint sound, she opens her eyes and finds that she isn't alone.

Little Boy Blue has found his way to the doorway, right thumb in his mouth.

Seeing him, she thinks of the *Titanic* passengers in her nightmare. Petty's robe is wrapped around the child's shoulders like a blanket, and his desolate blue eyes stare at her as if she's the last lifeboat about to disappear into the black sea.

"Hey there, sweetie. I was just going to come and see if you wanted to have a snack and a story before I tuck you in."

No reaction, maybe because he doesn't know what any of those things are.

She stands and forces a smile. "Come on," she says. "I'll show you."

And I'll help you stay afloat. No matter how rough things get from here.

WHAT ARE THE odds that Amelia's first-ever biological relative comes from the same tiny town as her adoptive mother?

Impossible, that's what they are. Or pretty close to it. But there it is.

She stares at the screen, hearing Auntie Birdie's voice, back in November 1989, when she'd come to New York for Calvin's funeral.

"L'il old Camden County is growing," she'd bragged to her grand-niece. "Near thirty thousand folks livin' there now! I heard tell that Marshboro's population will be over five hundred by the new millennium."

"Your whole county could fit in a couple of high-rise blocks here in Manhattan," Amelia had pointed out with a grin.

"Oh, but they wouldn't like bein' sealed in and stacked up to the sky like that, child."

For the first time in her life, Amelia had wondered why anyone would.

Until then, she'd planned to return to New York after graduation. Someone needed to make sure Calvin ate properly, got enough rest, and monitored his blood sugar. She'd been racked with misgiving and worry when she'd left for Ithaca to begin her senior year, and he'd tried to reassure her, as always.

"Don't go fretting any about me, Amelia. I can take care of myself. Now shush and hear me out," he'd said when she'd opened her mouth to protest. "That is exactly what you told me when you went off to college the first time, remember? 'I can take care of myself,' you said. And so you have. And so I will."

But the next time she'd seen him, after an emergency trip home, he'd been lying in a hospital bed, blood sugar spiraling out of control. And the time after that, well . . . it had been the last time.

Then she'd been alone in the world, scrimping to pay for her education and basic necessities, wondering how she'd pay back her student loans, or where she'd live when she returned to New York after graduation. With Calvin gone, though, she could stay in Ithaca with Silas and Jessie and her college friends, or even move down to Marshboro to be near Auntie Birdie and Cousin Lucky . . .

Aaron had walked into her life a few weeks into her final semester, and her fate had been sealed.

Sealed in, and stacked up to the sky.

Eighteen months later, she'd sent wedding invitations to Auntie Birdie and her daughter Lucky, the cousin Bettina had affectionately remembered for their childhood escapades. Lucky had returned the RSVP with regrets and a newspaper obituary clipping dated a few months earlier. Birdie was gone.

The loss of a woman she'd met only once in her life had hit Amelia harder than . . .

Well, harder than Aaron wanted it to, or thought it should have. He hadn't said she had no right to grieve a woman she'd barely known, a woman who hadn't even been a blood relative. But he had pointed out that Birdie had lived a long, full life, and reminded her that she had him now, and his family—parents, even, at long last. Her soon-to-be mother-in-law had invited Amelia to call her "Mom." But she couldn't bring herself to do it any more than she could call Aaron's father "Dad."

It wasn't just that she'd already had a mother and father; no, she'd been thinking that if she ever solved the mystery of her past and found her biological parents, then they would become Mom and Dad. They'd share a blood bond with her, unlike anyone else she'd ever known. Looking back, it seems a foolishly optimistic notion, imagining that her birth parents—both of them, perhaps arm in arm and wearing gold wedding bands—would come along to pick up where Calvin and Bettina had left off.

That October, weeks before her wedding, Amelia had called her cousin Lucky to offer condolences, and to see what, if anything, she knew about Amelia's own past. Turned out that Lucky had no idea that Bettina's daughter had been "adopted"—her interpretation of Amelia's tale.

"I wouldn't go tryin' to dredge up the past if I was you. Just leave well enough alone. You had two parents who loved you. You were lucky. Me—that's just my nickname. I never had a father. I don't think my mama ever even knew who my daddy even was."

"Did you ever ask her?"

"No, child. Because there were certain things you

just didn't talk about back then. Shouldn't talk about them now, either, or ask questions. Just count your blessings and move on."

And so she had, occasionally reflecting upon her fleeting connection with Bettina's family, but no longer interested in visiting her Georgia hometown.

Now a quick Google search tells her that Auntie Birdie's prediction had come true, and then some. Marshboro's current population is 706.

Quinnlynn Johnson couldn't possibly have grown up in that town and not crossed paths with Bettina's relatives.

Amelia scrolls down the woman's Facebook page, trying to make sense of the bizarre coincidence.

Then she spots a photograph.

The image screeches through her brain, collides with the truth as told by Calvin Crenshaw, and shatters it.

It wasn't random at all.

There, on Quinnlynn Johnson's Facebook page, is a photo of Birdie.

She looks exactly as she had when Amelia had met her, accompanied by a younger woman she recognizes as Bettina's cousin Lucky, and a little girl whose broad smile revealed missing front teeth.

The caption reads: *Me, Mama, and Grammy. #ThrowbackThursday*

If Lucky is Quinnlynn's mother and Birdie had been her grandmother, then Bettina would have been her cousin.

Amelia doesn't merely have a biological connection to some random stranger down in Georgia.

She shares blood ties with Bettina's family.

With Bettina herself.

Chapter Twelve

Saturday, October 1, 2016

A damp chill permeates Levi Stoltzfus's denim trousers and jacket as he steps out of the house carrying a battery-operated lamp. This time of year, night lingers over the farm like a guest who's overstayed his welcome.

He thinks of his daughter Eva's fiancé, who had come for supper and hadn't left until nearly nine o'clock, ignoring Levi's yawns and the gentle hints of his wife, Anna. Being up so late had made it difficult to rise for prayer at the alarm clock's jangle.

Lantern light spills from the big red barn on a knoll behind the house. All five of his sons are already working there, including ten-year-old Jacob, who'd fractured his arm earlier in the week and now wears a sling. After feeding and watering the horses, the young men had hitched Dandy, his favorite standardbred, to the single-seat buggy. They'd loaded the back with jugs, jars, and tins—pressed cider, a fresh batch of Anna's apple butter, and the girls' pies and dumplings.

Levi climbs on board, sets the lantern at his feet, takes the reins, and instructs Dandy to be on his way.

They enter Cortland Hollow Road at a brisk clip,

heading toward the fruit stand to get the crates of apples the boys had picked. He's meeting two of his sons at the Apple Harvest Festival over in Ithaca. Yesterday's rain had dampened business there, and he's hoping to make up for it today.

Until recent years, the family had just sold their goods at their own stand. But he can no longer support the growing brood by relying on word of mouth, longtime customers, and folks out for a scenic Sunday drive to sustain the business. Now they compete with electronic advertising, entire supermarket chains devoted to wholesome produce and baked goods, and of course, the internet. While computer technology may not be the devil as Levi's elderly parents believe, and some Amish have even begun to utilize it, he has no intention of doing so. Such English temptations allow the outside world to permeate their own and may lead the young generations astray.

Shadows cling to the woods and fields along the road. There are no headlights at this hour, just woodland creatures that bolt from the buggy's path, and not a hint of pink in the eastern sky. Morning—as opposed to night, and Levi's future son-in-law—tends to lag, much like his first grandchild, due any day now.

"The baby will be born soon enough. We're enjoying these last few quiet days before everything changes," his eldest daughter had said yesterday, twinkling a shy smile at her husband, still captivated by the romance of it all.

"Das ist gut," Anna had later told Levi, and he'd agreed. The romance will fade when parenthood ar-

rives, and nothing will ever be the same for the young couple, though their lives will be enriched with every child who comes along.

Levi and Anna have been blessed with nine. Now the next generation is upon them, and there will be two daughters' weddings to celebrate in November, after the harvest season. Both girls will go to live with their husbands' families, making the women's work a looming challenge for Anna and their youngest daughter. Levi, however, has enough hands to help with the men's work—minus one of Jacob's.

This time, his son had been hurt falling from the hayloft ladder; last time, he'd sprained an ankle trying to hitch a ride on the wagon as one of his brothers was driving away. That boy has managed to get himself into trouble all his life. As an infant, he'd swallowed a whole cherry and turned blue. As a toddler, he'd wandered into the woods and been lost for hours.

The memory brings to mind another child, the one Levi had found at the orchard. Yesterday morning in town, he'd seen the child's face plastered on fliers. Someone had mentioned that Sergeant Hanson and his wife have taken him in until his parents can be located.

He senses a slight resistance in Dandy when he pulls the reins to turn off the road into the fruit stand's dirt parking area. The horse is picking up on his own tension.

Levi takes a deep, calming breath, reluctant to dwell on the reasons a child might have been wandering alone in these parts. He'll see what he can learn about the situation when he gets to town. Surely one of his English acquaintances will have heard updates on the television or radio or internet. Surely the boy's family has come for him by now.

He disembarks and ties Dandy to a post. Noting an anxious equine twitch, he looks around, wondering whether a black bear might lurk beyond the lantern's yellow glow.

It illuminates the wooden stand and the crates of apples his sons had stacked, but he sees nothing menacing in the fringe of trees. Leaving the lantern in the buggy, he begins loading in the heavy boxes, each labeled with the variety and the designated drop-off spot on the Ithaca Commons.

His back aches already with fatigue, and he again regrets his future son-in-law's extended visit, and the lost sleep. There is considerable work to be done today, despite Jacob's injury, Abigail's late pregnancy, and Anna coming down with a cold. All three will persevere as much as possible, and the others will pick up the slack.

As he returns to the dwindling stack to lift another crate, the light dims behind him, and the horse spooks. He turns back.

So much for the modern convenience of batteries—there's no way of knowing how much longer they'll last. At least with an oil lantern, you can see—

He hears a rustling in the dark and spots a large shadow looming. It isn't a bear.

"Don't move," a voice commands in English. "I have a gun. Where is he?"

A gun. Levi's heart slams his ribs.

The man steps closer. He's cloaked in a dark jacket, hood up, and he is, indeed, pointing a pistol at Levi.

"What did he tell you?"

He?

The man is clearly deranged. Levi stares in horror and confusion, stammers, "I don't know . . ."

"The kid!"

"The . . ."

Oh. The truth dawns, more terrible than he can fathom. This armed man has come for the little lost boy.

"He said nothing. I don't believe he was able."

A pause.

"Where is he now?"

Levi thinks of Sergeant Hanson. He lives in Ithaca, has a wife, children. He comes to the local farmer's market some Saturdays, always stopping to greet Levi and buy baked goods, with a chuckled warning not to mention it to his wife. Sometimes she joins him, a vibrant, friendly woman.

"I said, where is the kid?"

Sergeant Hanson has a son. He's far more reserved than his parents, and enamored with Dandy, asking countless questions about the horse's harness-racing past.

Levi thinks of his own sons—of Jacob, with his fractured arm. Last summer, he'd had a black eye courtesy of an English bully who'd jumped him while he'd been walking home from school, knowing Jacob would not fight back.

Matthew, 5:39. *"But I say unto you, That ye resist not evil: but whosoever shall smite thee on thy right cheek, turn to him the other also."*

"Tell me where he is," the man says in accented English, "or I will shoot you dead right here, right now."

Levi swallows hard, knowing what he must do.

It is God's will.

He can't bear to think of this dangerous man bringing violence to Sergeant Hanson's home and family.

He thinks of his own as he kneels, pressing his forehead to the earth, arms outstretched in submission.

AND SO, AFTER all these years trying to find her real parents, it turns out Amelia had had them all along.

Bettina Crenshaw, the woman she'd twice lost, twice grieved, on that shocking long-ago night, has come roaring back to betray her yet again, along with Calvin.

She's spent a sleepless night listening to the rain falling on shingles a floor above her, the occasional splash of tires on the street below, the kitten scratching litter in his carrier beside the bed, the echo of her father's voice.

"Back then, folks didn't ask nosy personal questions like they do now. Pregnancy and childbirth were nobody's business but the parents'."

"So that's why it was okay to lie."

"Ain't nobody went tellin' no lies."

But he had.

He'd turned her entire life into a lie once again.

How could he—why would he—have made up the story about finding her in the church?

No wonder he'd said they'd never even tried to find out who'd left her, nor sought medical attention, nor called the police.

She'd accepted his rationale. Yes, the country had been gripped by racial tension in 1968. A close friend of Calvin's had been murdered in cold blood by a gang of wealthy white kids the very week Amelia had been found, and the police and the media hadn't seemed to care. She could believe that an impoverished black couple had been reluctant to entrust the authorities with a precious, helpless infant.

But this new scenario? Nothing about it makes sense.

Why would a God-fearing, terminally ill Bettina, upon being admitted to Morningside Memorial Hospital, have given a false medical history? According to the records, she'd only carried one child—her dead son—to term. She could not have anticipated that an errant nurse would leave her file behind at her bedside after she'd slipped into a coma, and that Amelia would be there and sneak a peek at it.

And what about Marceline LeBlanc?

Had she, too, been part of an elaborate conspiracy to convince Amelia that she wasn't the Crenshaws' biological child?

Amelia can think of no logical reason for that, yet nor can she deny the truth. People might lie, but DNA does not.

She looks at the clock, willing the night to recede so that she can liberate Clancy, and absorb the shocking truth in broad daylight, maybe talk it over with . . . someone.

Her first instinct last night had been to tell Jessie, but when she'd started downstairs to do so, she'd heard her talking to the social worker. And then Billy and Theodore had returned, and she'd heard the three of them arguing.

She couldn't bring herself to burden her friend with one more thing—especially one that might dredge up Jessie's own wrenching past, on a night like this.

She rolls onto her back, eyes wide open. In the dark hush of an unfamiliar household, she hears the absence of sirens, people walking overhead, Aaron's even breathing.

Though he was the last person with whom she wanted to discuss what had happened, she'd made an impulsive attempt to call him at around midnight. He hadn't picked up, giving her more to fret about.

Was he punishing her?

Was he still out?

Was he asleep?

Was he *alone*?

After a sleepless night spent mulling all of that, and her own past, she feels as if she's dumped out a jigsaw puzzle, only to find that none of the pieces connect with each other or can possibly connect to create the image depicted on the box, except . . .

One piece, in all of this, *has* fallen into place.

When she was growing up, people had often commented that she reminded them of Bettina—not just her mannerisms, but the pitch of her voice, her facial features, some intangible evidence that had seemed to link them as mother and daughter long before she learned—or was led to believe—that wasn't the case.

Even now, she occasionally spots traces of her mother in the mirror but has chalked it up to missing her and longing to see her face again. Plus, women of a certain age tend to share certain physical characteristics. And sometimes, unrelated people who share a household do start to look alike or are at least perceived to. That phenomenon, she'd learned through her work, is surprisingly common among adoptees and parents.

Now it turns out that isn't the case for her. She looks like Bettina for the same straightforward reason most people resemble each other. They share DNA. They really are mother and daughter, unless . . .

A new idea pops into her head, so startling that she sits up in bed. What if—

A rooster's crow pierces the thought, so loud it sounds as if it's in the next room.

Espinoza. Now there's something you don't hear in Manhattan, or—

On its heels comes a child's terrified scream.

"BARNES!"

He opens his eyes.

The room is dark. Rob is standing over him. He looks fuzzy and sounds muffled, as though Barnes is underwater trying to see and hear someone above the surface.

He sits up, swiping his palms hard against his face, head throbbing.

Rob repeats himself, the words mingling with the sound of birds chirping beyond the window screen. Barnes concentrates, and comprehends, though he doesn't know the answer to Rob's question.

Has he seen Kurtis?

"I don't . . . I . . . What time is it?"

"A quarter after seven."

"In the *morning*?"

"Yeah. You were out cold when I got home around midnight. How much rum did you drink?"

Rum . . .

He thinks back. Dinner. Miguel. *Perry Wayland.*

"No rum. Just . . . dinner and a couple of beers at that *paladar* you recommended. Came back . . . went right to bed . . ."

He doesn't really recall the coming back or going to bed part.

He remembers finishing that final beer, paying his bill . . . thinking he should stroll around, keep an eye out for Wayland . . .

But when he'd gotten to his feet, it had hit him—the alcohol, the heat, the dehydration . . .

He'd fumbled home through dark, foreign streets, feeling as though he might pass out. He supposes he had, when he'd reached his bed.

". . . Kurtis?" Rob is asking again, and he shakes his head.

"I haven't seen him since . . ." He thinks back. "He went out to get lunch yesterday. And then I went out myself before he came back, so . . ."

"And he wasn't here when you got home?"

"No." He hesitates. "At least, I don't think so."

"You don't *think* so?" Rob peers at him. "You sure you didn't have any rum? Man, you look even worse than you did yesterday morning."

"I feel worse, too."

"What did you eat?"

"*Arroz con pollo*, but I barely touched it. Oh, but I did have some *chicharrones*, and I bought *cucurucho* on the street. Maybe it made me sick."

Rob waves a hand in dismissal. "No, that stuff's fine. Just don't tell me you drank the water at the restaurant."

"All I drank was beer. They didn't have bottled water."

"That's your problem. You were sick as a dog yesterday, dehydrated, with an empty stomach. You just need water. Here, finish this and I'll get you another one." Rob hands him a nearly empty bottle of water.

"Where did it come from?"

Rob points to the floor beside the bed. "Must be yours. There are a couple of empties, too," he adds, stooping to pick them up.

"But . . ." Barnes has a fuzzy memory of drinking water in the night. "Where did I get them?"

"There's a case in the fridge. You didn't buy it?"

"I don't think so." He's lucky he'd dragged himself home in that condition. No way he could have lugged a case of water, too. "Kurtis must have gotten it."

"But you didn't see him?"

"I don't know. I guess I could have, since I don't remember drinking that water, either."

"This is one hell of a beer hangover, Barnes."

Beer hangover? Yeah, no. He's experienced his share of those, and this is different. His bones have wilted, and his head doesn't just ache, it feels dense, as though his eyes and ears have been swaddled in a thick layer of foam.

Rob is gazing out the window, preoccupied with his son.

"Hey, he's a grown man. I'm sure he's fine. He's young, on vacation . . . he probably went out drinking, dancing, met a woman . . ."

"Probably. That's what I figured you'd be doing. I didn't expect to find you here when I got back. I tried to wake you up, but . . ." He shakes his head. "Like I said, you were out cold."

But not because he'd had too much to drink. Granted, he hadn't wanted that last one Miguel had brought over, but it would have seemed rude to turn it down, and anyway . . .

It would take more than three, or even four beers over a couple of hours to render a man his size unconscious. A lot more . . .

Like what?

It's almost as if he'd been drugged.

Perry Wayland hadn't been close enough to slip something into his drink without Barnes noticing, and anyway, it's not as though he'd have come prepared, expecting to run into Barnes there last night . . . or anywhere, ever again.

He hadn't started to feel woozy until after Perry had left, though not immediately after.

Barnes is streetwise, a New York City detective. He pays attention to details when he's in public, even when he's not on the job. He notices what's going on around him, who's in close proximity. He's well aware that a tourist, alone in a foreign country, is an easy mark for thieves.

Thank goodness he'd left his wallet, phone, and passport behind. He reaches down and finds that he's still wearing the shorts he'd had on yesterday, pesos still in his pocket. A quick count reveals that he's missing only what he must have paid for his dinner—not that he remembers how much it had been, or much of anything at that point.

At least no one had drugged and robbed him.

But had someone simply drugged him?

There had been other patrons. None had come near his table, other than . . .

He closes his eyes, seeing Miguel Perez senior holding two open beers.

"It is on the house, acere.*"*

What if . . .

But that's ridiculous.

The man owns the restaurant. He's Rob's friend. He'd have no reason to spike a customer's drink.

Rob goes to get him more water while Barnes sips the last warm bit in his bottle, feeling it splash into his empty gut. The fog is beginning to lift. He hears tropical bugs humming along with the bird chorus outside and is mildly surprised they're not singing "Guantanamera."

His ears pick up distant voices speaking rapid-fire Spanish, the rev of a far-off engine, a clanging school bell, and . . . a footstep?

It sounded like one, rustling just beyond the screen.

Barnes leans toward the window, surveying the yard—trees, grassy spikes poking through sandy dirt, garbage cans propped on cinder blocks. But there . . .

He squints at the undergrowth. Is that a person lurking in the tangle of vines and branches?

"Here you go. Drink up." Rob is back, handing him three bottles of cold water. Barnes glances again at the yard, confirms that there is no human silhouette, and focuses on gulping the water. He finishes one bottle and half of the second, then wipes his mouth and emits a quenched "Aaah."

"Better?" Rob asks.

"Much. How was your mountain climbing?"

Rob tells him about it, showing him several scenic photos he'd snapped on his phone, then asks about Barnes's adventures in Baracoa.

"I didn't get beyond the *paladar*. I met your friend Miguel."

"Yeah? He's a good guy."

"You sure about that?"

"Why? Didn't he treat you right?"

"No, he did. He brought me a beer on the house before he even knew I was your friend, actually. Offered me a cigarette, too. I didn't take it," he adds, at Rob's look. "He was smoking himself, drinking a beer . . . he sat down with me and we talked."

"So it wasn't busy?"

"No, it was."

"And Miguel *sat* and had a conversation with you? Wait, are you talking about the son?"

"No, the father. The owner."

"Huh. What'd you talk about?"

Barnes considers telling him that a missing person he'd chased in New York years ago had turned up here in Baracoa. He wouldn't have to mention Wayland's name.

But then Rob would ask questions, might figure out who Barnes was talking about, might mention it in front of Kurtis. In a future rum-fueled moment, Barnes might even feel the need to unburden his own guilty secret, the money and Stef, and then what?

Rob is a father. Maybe he'd understand, wouldn't judge, wouldn't tell . . .

But he'd *know*. Things would change between them. The shame and regret Barnes feels toward himself . . .

Could he bear to see it reflected in his friend's eyes?

Could he bear to hear Rob ask how the hell Barnes has lived with himself for all these years?

Same way you get through any day on the job, encountering good people in their lowest moments, and bad people at their worst. Compartmentalization. You lock away the things you can't face, and you hope they won't seep out until you've figured out how to resolve them and let them go.

In this case, it will be never, because every bad decision he'd made that fateful October has come back to haunt him now in a way he'd never expected.

"Barnes? What'd you talk about with Miguel?"

He clears his throat. "You know . . . just small talk."

"Small talk? That's surprising."

"How so?"

"He has his hands full with that place. He's friendly, but all business."

"Then how did *you* get to know him? He mentioned Kurtis, so you must have—"

"After hours," Rob says. "I'd hang out at the *paladar* at night to check email and take care of some work stuff because it's near a Wi-Fi hotspot. He'd come and sit with me after closing, tell me stories about the old days in Baracoa. You were home long before closing, though, and I can't imagine him taking a leisurely smoke break while he was working. So I guess you charmed him."

"Guess I did." Barnes rubs his morning chin stubble, staring into the shadowy yard.

JESSIE BOLTS FROM bed, maternal instinct and adrenaline propelling her into the hall even before she's cognizant of who is screaming, and where. She rushes to Petty's room, flipping the light as she bursts through the door. Blinded, she squeezes her eyes shut, hearing commotion behind her. Billy is coming, and

Mimi, and now Theodore is shouting from his room and Billy is telling him that it's all right . . .

Why is *that* the first thing people—parents—say at times like this? Why is it what she says to a child who's been through God knows what and is all alone in the world?

It's *not* all right.

Forcing her eyes to open again in the glare, she sees the shape of a child in bed, swathed in blankets and the lavender robe. A terrifying thought threads needle pricks of dread into her brain.

Then she spies a ripple of movement and exhales. He's alive under there. Alive, and shaking like crazy.

She sits beside him, resisting the urge to tear off the covers and haul him into a ferocious, Theodore-style embrace. "It's Jessie, honey. Did you have a nightmare?"

To her shock, she hears a reply. A single word, one that is muffled by the fabric and probably his thumb and makes no sense, but coherence doesn't matter.

"Was that *him*?" Mimi asks from the doorway.

"Yes. He said something!"

The word comes again—*Coke?*—and this time is followed by a whimpered, *"No, no!"*

Jessie's smile fades.

Out in the hallway, a fresh commotion erupts—father and son exchanging shouts. "Theodore, are you *kidding* me?"

"I was afraid he'd be kidnapped!"

"I told you he wouldn't be!"

"But you wouldn't get a padlock!"

Mimi peers back down the hall. "Uh-oh."

"Uh-oh, what?" Jessie asks.

"I think there might be a rooster in Theodore's room."

A squawk, beating wings, a crash. There is most definitely a rooster in Theodore's room, and it seems to have knocked over a lamp. Billy commands Theodore to take Espinoza back out to the coop. He grudgingly obeys, stomping down the back stairway.

Jessie turns back to the child in the bed. She gently pulls the silky bathrobe away from his face, just enough so that he can see her, the light, and that he's safe.

He shudders, eyes scrunched tightly, shielded by four small fingers, the thumb in his mouth.

"It's all r—" *No, it isn't.* She clears her throat, searching for a truth that isn't terrifying. "You're safe, sweetheart. I know this is a crazy house, but I won't let anything happen to you."

Eyes still closed, he whimpers another word, this one unmistakable to her ears. "Mama."

Does he believe that she's his mother?

But when his eyes open, they register no surprise. He was, she realizes, simply calling for his mother the way children do in the night, or when they're injured or afraid.

"I know," she says softly. "I know you're missing your mom."

"And we're going to help you find her." Billy is in the doorway behind Mimi, his expression revealing what he would never say aloud.

Or find out what happened to her.

For a long time, the room is silent.

Outside, Espinoza crows again.

The child flinches, but he doesn't scream. This time,

the sound is more distant, didn't startle him from sleep, and he's not alone in the dark.

He removes his thumb from his mouth, regards them all for a moment, and speaks. *"Coke."*

"What are you trying to tell us?" Jessie asks him.

"Are you asking for *Coke*?" Billy suggests. "Are you thirsty? Do you want a Coke?"

The child echoes the word, and it doesn't quite sound the same.

"Or maybe he's hungry," Mimi suggests. "Is he saying *cook*?"

"Cook?" Jessie repeats to him. "Do you want me to cook? Noodles? Do you want noodles?"

He seems to hesitate, then repeats the word yet again as the back door squeaks loudly. Theodore clatters into the house and up the stairs.

Jessie sighs inwardly. Just when they were making progress.

Her son appears in the hallway, launching another tirade.

Billy cuts him off. "Theodore, give us a minute here. We're trying to figure out what he's trying to tell us!"

"Is it *cook*?" Jessie asks the boy. *"Coke?"*

He shakes his head. At least they're communicating. *"Coke! Coke!"*

No, it isn't quite *cook*, but it isn't quite *Coke*, either. "Espinoza!"

Jessie turns to Theodore, summoning the patience to address his needs and rooster obsession in the midst of Little Boy Blue's breakthrough moment.

Her son is sleep rumpled, and he seems younger, more vulnerable, without his glasses. His expression is unexpectedly benign. Maybe he's progressed toward a breakthrough of his own—almost in the same room with the foster child he resents, interrupting, yes, but not causing a scene.

Billy glares at him. "Theodore, we're not talking about the rooster right now!"

"But that's what it is!"

"That's what *what* is?"

"The word he's saying." He points at the child. "Not *cook*, and not *Coke*. He's talking about Espinoza."

Billy is exasperated. "He didn't say Espinoza! He said 'Coke'!"

"No, he didn't! Espinoza crowed, and it woke him up, and he's French!" He palm-thumps the door frame. Like his father, he's rapidly losing patience.

Jessie musters what remains of her own. "What do you mean, Theodore?"

"*Coq*," he says in precisely the same accent and inflection the boy had used. "It means 'rooster' in French."

At Theodore's pronunciation, something shifts within the boy. He sits up. "*Oui! Coq!*"

"See? I told you." Theodore shrugs and turns to leave.

The child unleashes a full-blown sentence in French.

"Theodore, wait. What did he say?"

"I don't know. I stink at French. I'm tired. It's Saturday, and I don't have to get up. I'm going back to—"

"We need you, son." Billy stops him with a firm hand on his back. "He's trying to tell us something, and you're the only one who can understand what it might be."

He turns back, a bit grudgingly. "I only know some words and he talks too fast, like Madame Worst."

"Ask him to repeat what he said more slowly," Jessie suggests.

He yawns deeply. "I will later. I have to—"

"Now!" Billy commands in precisely the tone that will send their son into stubborn retreat.

Sure enough, he stomps off down the hall, saying, "I don't know how to ask him that."

"That's too bad," Mimi calls after him. "Because if you did, you and Espinoza would have been the heroes."

His footsteps pause. "What do you mean?"

"This child is lost, and he's stuck here with all of you because your mom and dad can't find his family if he won't talk to them. But I guess he likes roosters, just like you do, because Espinoza made him start talking. But since you're the only one who speaks French, you're the only one who can find out where he lives so that he can go home."

"I know how to ask him that," Theodore says, after a moment.

"Then maybe you should."

Seeing Billy open his mouth to chime in, Jessie cuts him off with a gentle, "Theodore, we're counting on you. Can you please help him?"

The footsteps return, slowly, and Theodore reappears. This time, he crosses the threshold into the room, bows his head to think for a moment, and then looks at the child. *"Ou habites tu?"*

"Je ne sais pas." The boy shakes his head, and adds, *"Avec Maman."*

"He just says he lives with his mother," Theodore relates.

"Ask him where she is," Jessie instructs, and her son obliges.

Again, the child replies that he doesn't know, and seems distressed.

"It's all right," she tells him, giving his shoulder a soothing pat. "Can you tell us your name?"

Without prompting, Theodore poses the question in French.

"Prewitt!" the child tells him, and returns, *"Quel est votre nom?"*

Theodore turns to Jessie. "He just repeated the question, but he didn't answer it."

"No, I think he did—it's *Pru-wheat*, something like that. And now he's asking you what your name is, so go ahead, tell him your name."

"Okay, but . . ." He shakes his head. *"Je m'appelle* Theodore.*"

"Thee . . . oh . . . door," the child echoes, smiling faintly and pointing at him. "Theodore."

"Oui. Mais quel est votre nom?"

"Je m'appelle Prewitt.*"

"Prewitt?" He shakes his head and presses a yawn. "I never heard of that name. Oh, well. Mom, now can I—"

"Theodore! Theodore!" The child reaches out, tugs his long sleeve, and says something else in French, distressed about whatever it is. Jessie recognizes only the last word—"mama," or something close. She looks at her son, who shrugs.

"Wait, what? Hey, Prewitt, slow down. Uh . . . *Ralentissez*. Slow down."

Again, the boy speaks, this time more slowly.

Theodore frowns. "I think he said something about being in the dirt, and a rooster, and his mother, and . . .

it sounded like on-de—something, or omm . . . wait, *homme*?"

"Oui! Homme!" A vigorous nod, and he repeats *homme*, along with another word that starts with a *d*.

Theodore's eyes widen in triumph. "I got it! *Homme dangereux*. It means 'dangerous man.'"

Chapter Thirteen

How convenient for the Angler that the crates Levi Stoltzfus had been loading into his buggy were clearly labeled.

He'd been bound for the Ithaca Apple Harvest Festival.

The Angler is headed there, too, westbound, following the highway signs. Maybe he'll find someone who knows the boy's whereabouts and share it for a price—or to save their own life.

"Imbecile!" he'd bellowed at Levi Stoltzfus when he'd knelt there, arms outstretched, praying softly, like he was ready to die, like he *wanted* to die . . .

Unnerved, he'd given the man one last chance to tell him where to find the boy. He wouldn't tell, so he had to die.

What a waste.

The Angler had dragged his corpse a little ways back, behind the stand, so that he wouldn't be visible from the road. He'd been planning to drive away in the buggy and abandon it elsewhere, but the horse had reared and kicked at him.

"N'aie pas peur. Il ne te fera pas de mal," Uncle Hugo had whispered back over the years. He'd wanted so badly for his nephew to learn to ride that summer on his farm.

Don't be afraid. He won't hurt you.

He'd been wrong. The horse had bitten the Angler's hand when he'd attempted to feed him an apple.

Disappointed by his refusal to try again, Hugo had agreed to leave the biting to the fish for the remainder of the summer, and the Angler had never gotten over his distaste for horses.

Distaste, not *fear*.

No matter what his father had said about the matter when he'd heard, calling him a sissy, a coward.

"T'es une poule mouillée!"

"Now who's the coward?" he bites out as if his father's ghost is tagging along for the ride.

The rising sun glares in the rearview mirror, but he prefers to focus on what lies ahead, and not behind him. The road is rural, forest and field broken every so often by a gas station mini-mart, a smattering of farms, or a crossroads community with a cluster of houses, a school, a church, a bank.

The car, a midsized maroon Toyota, is not his own. He'd left it back in Canada at an all-night supermarket near the border bridge, garbage bag still in the trunk, the stench of French cheese soon to mingle with rotting human flesh. The slender brunette in the trunk had looked a little like Cecile. But his wife would never have approached a strange man who called to her in a dark, deserted parking lot, his car hood propped open as if he'd needed a jump.

Crossing the border in a stolen car had been risky; leaving the corpse and evidence in his own car foolhardy. But simmering rage had clouded his judgment as he'd sped through the night toward the US, and it's hissing to a rapid boil.

Destroy the boy . . . destroy the boy . . .

AMELIA SITS AT the kitchen table clutching a hot mug of coffee in her cold hands. It's her third, or maybe her fourth. Jessie had brewed a second pot after Billy had poured the last of the first into a travel mug, on his way to share the new information with the Thompkins County sheriff's office. They're the ones working Little Boy Blue's case.

Prewitt's case.

Turns out the name is a fairly common French one, and its meaning had brought tears to Amelia's eyes.

Small and brave.

It certainly fits.

He seems okay in this moment, after devouring two helpings of the pancakes Jessie had made for him, drenched in butter and warm maple syrup and studded with chocolate chip smiles.

Multitasking as usual, she's frying another batch now while on the phone with the Wi-Fi repairman.

Earlier, she'd called social services, telling the child's caseworker what they've discovered, and that he'd started talking.

Started . . . and stopped, after Theodore had left the room.

The agency is working on getting an interpreter over here as soon as possible. Amelia has a foreign language translation app on her phone, but their attempts to question him in stilted French yielded no new information. He'd asked a question of his own: *"Ou est Theodore?"* Jessie had clasped flattened palms against her cheek, eyes closed, to indicate that her son was sleeping.

Hanging up the phone, she lets out a frustrated growl.

"What's wrong?"

"They're going to try to get a repair crew here today. *Try.* No promises." She looks at her cell phone. "And I just drained my stupid battery again. Remind me to charge it after we eat."

She grabs a spatula and transfers the steaming pancakes from the griddle to a platter.

"Let me do that," Amelia says. "Or give me your phone and I'll go plug it in."

"No, it's fine. These are only good when they're hot. I'm just frustrated. Someone has to be here all day just in case they show up, so there goes our Apple Festival plan. I thought it might be nice to take Prewitt down there for a bit."

"Let me wait here for the repairman while you two go."

"No, I'll stay with him. It's fine. You wanted to get your Concord grapes."

Yes, she had—but the Apple Festival is the last thing on her mind this morning. She hasn't told Jessie about the DNA match. It can wait until things settle down around here—*if* things settle down. Maybe by then, she'll have more information to share.

She checks her phone. It's not yet nine o'clock. Still too early to call her cousin Lucky in Georgia.

Google had shown her living at the same address she'd had thirty years ago, presumably with the same phone number as long as she still has a landline. If not, she should be easy enough to locate in a town that size.

Or maybe I should go directly to her daughter?

Quinnlynn, after all, is the one whose DNA had matched Amelia's. But she hadn't provided a phone number, and anyway, this situation is far more complicated than a genetic connection.

Jessie sets a plate of pancakes in front of her.

"Thanks. Hey—they're not smiling."

"I figured you wouldn't want a sugar overload."

"I don't, but the face ones are pretty adorable."

"Diane always made them that way, so I did the same for my own kids when they were little. How do you think Chip got his nickname? He'd eat just the chocolate, and then he'd pound his high chair tray shouting, 'Chip! More chip!'"

"I can picture that. He was the cutest little thing. Petty, too. The only time I ever questioned our decision not to have kids was when I came here and saw your two. Not that Theodore wasn't also a cute little thing," she adds quickly, "but I didn't know him when he was that age."

"Neither did we." Sitting across from her, Jessie looks at the stove clock as they dig into the pancakes. "I don't know whether to wish he'd wake up, or be glad that he hasn't. I'm pretty sure he won't be interested in hanging out with a little playmate today."

"He was great upstairs earlier."

"Because you made him want to be a hero. Thank you."

"Child Psychology 101. You and Billy would have said the same thing."

"Except that sometimes our patience wears thin, I'm ashamed to say. With Theodore, and with each other."

"It happens." She shrugs and gestures toward the sunroom. "Prewitt seems to be just fine entertaining himself for now."

Bathed in early morning light spilling through the

windows, the child is wearing new pajamas Billy bought him, the lavender silk draped like a lap robe. He's absorbed in fitting puzzle shapes into their wooden trays. Jessie had offered him other toys, but he prefers to do the same thing over and over again. He hasn't quite relaxed, and he isn't exactly content, but he no longer seems as anxious as he had yesterday.

That makes one of us.

"Mimi?"

"Hmm?"

Jessie has set down her own fork, elbows on the table, chin resting on her fists, gaze fixed on Amelia. "What's wrong?"

She opens her mouth.

"And don't you dare say it's nothing," Jessie says, "because I know you, and I can tell when you're stressing, and it's never over *nothing.*"

"I appreciate the concern. You have way too much going on here to worry about me."

"I always have a lot going on."

"Not like this. Not with . . ." She gestures toward the sunroom.

"That's no reason not to tell me whatever's bothering you. And don't say you're fine, because you obviously aren't."

"Okay. I'm not." Amelia leans back, arms folded and looks at her.

"I knew it." Jessie nods, picking up her coffee. "I already figured something was up with you and Aaron the other day when we talked on the phone."

"It's not me and Aaron." Maybe it had been then, but it isn't what's weighing on her in this moment. "I got a DNA match."

"What?"

"Yeah. I matched my mother."

"Your mother? That's incredible!" Jessie plunks down her mug, ignoring the coffee sloshing over the rim. "I don't care *what's* been going on around here, I can't believe you didn't tell me this the second you found her!"

"It just happened, and I didn't *find* her. I *matched* her."

"Same thing, as long as you can—"

"No, Jessie. It's Bettina. The mother I already had."

"Wait . . . *what?*"

Amelia explains, every word she utters widening Jessie's eyes like another breath into a balloon about to pop.

"This is insane! Why would your parents make up a story about finding you if you were their own daughter?"

"I don't know, but . . ." She stops, swallows hard, tears in her eyes. "It's like I've lost something all over again."

Jessie reaches across the table to clasp her hand. "Mimi, you've just *found* something. The one thing you've been searching for all your life."

"No, that wasn't me. It was you. *You* were searching all your life. I was pretty much an adult when I found out they weren't my parents. Even though, apparently, they were."

"Okay, but . . . what do you feel like you've *lost?*"

"My story. I've owned it for all these years. I've told it so many times to so many people, to *myself*—trying to figure out how it's going to end, where it began."

"Now you know."

Amelia leans back, staring at the ceiling, where a delicate cobweb wafts from the vintage pendant light. A thought gnaws at her consciousness like a rat bent on short-circuiting her brain.

"Tell me what's going through your head, Mimi."

She doesn't dare, saying instead, "I was horrified back when I found out that Calvin and Bettina weren't my biological parents. But now there's a part of me that's just as horrified to find out that they *were*. I'd already forgiven them for lying to me for the first twenty years of my life, and I guess it would be healthy to forgive them—*him*, anyway—for continuing to lie until the end of his, but . . ."

"It would be healthy," Jessie agrees. "And really hard."

"Yeah. Maybe not as hard if I at least knew why he did it. He had so many chances to tell me, especially at the end. It's not like he didn't know he was dying. It's not like he wasn't a God-fearing Christian. You'd think, after what had happened to me after Bettina died, he'd have wanted to confess the whole truth."

"Maybe he didn't think you'd ever find out after he was gone, so he thought it would be best for your sake to leave it alone."

"Maybe. Or maybe . . ." She takes a deep breath. "What if he didn't know it any more than I did? What if the lie was just Bettina's?"

"You mean, what if she gave birth to you without him knowing? That's . . . I mean, why would she do that? *How* would she do that?"

"Women have babies all the time without realizing they were even pregnant."

Jessie gives her a look.

"All right, maybe not all the time, but it happens. It's . . . I don't know, denial? You hear about teenaged girls who go into labor and they're so shocked, they don't know what to do with the baby afterward. Or some of them might know they're pregnant, but they hide it from their parents, and then afterward, they abandon the baby." She shrugs. "Oldest foundling story in the book."

"But your mother wasn't a teenager. She had to have known she was pregnant. She'd already had your brother," Jessie adds. "Plus, she was married, so she had no reason to hide it."

"Unless . . ."

Jessie stares. "Unless you weren't his baby."

Amelia nods, relieved Jessie didn't make her say it. The idea is upsetting, but it makes sense.

"I couldn't have loved you any more if you were my biological daughter . . ."

Calvin's words had brought such comfort over the years. How could they have been false?

"When he told me that they'd been longing for a child and couldn't have one, I got the sense that . . . well, that it was his fault," she tells Jessie. "That he was the one who . . . couldn't. At least, not anymore, after they'd lost my brother."

"Why? What did he say?"

"It's not what he said, it's the way he said it. It felt true. Just like when he told me about how he'd found me. I can't believe that was a lie."

"So if it wasn't, and he was telling the truth as he knew it, and your mother somehow gave birth to you without him finding out, then you think she . . . what? Left you in the church for him to find?"

"It doesn't make sense, does it?"

"Not at all."

But now that the idea has taken hold, it's as plausible as any other scenario she's managed to conjure. Especially if Bettina had had some help.

She looks at Jessie.

"What, Mimi?"

"I'm just thinking . . . what if Marceline LeBlanc had something to do with it?"

"The old voodoo woman?"

"Not voodoo. She was a Gullah priestess, but wow. I can't believe you remember some of this stuff."

"You're my best friend. Of course I remember."

Does Aaron? He's her husband.

But he's a man, and men don't remember details the way women do.

Even as the thought enters her head, she scolds herself.

Come on, girl. You know better than that.

"Why are you thinking about Marceline, Mimi?"

"Because when I got to know her, after Bettina died—it's crazy, and they were so different, but . . . Marceline kind of reminded me of her, in a way."

"She looked like her?"

"Not really, but she *sounded* a lot like her. She was from somewhere down south, too, so it's probably just the accent and inflection, but the way she looked out for me . . . not like a mother would, exactly; that's not why she reminded me of Bettina. It was like she cared about me, though. A lot more than the other neighbor women did."

"Maybe that's why your mother always wanted you to stay away from her. Maybe they'd been friends at one point. Maybe she knew something."

"Something Calvin didn't?"

"You could be wrong about that."

"Wishful thinking? But if they all knew, except me, then the thing in the church—Calvin finding me there, abandoned—it never happened. And to me, it really feels like it did."

She thinks of the basket, the dress, the ring . . .

Lily Tucker dances at the back of her mind.

"So let's say the church thing did happen," Jessie says. "Let's say Bettina had you and didn't tell Calvin for whatever reason. Where does Marceline fit in? Do you think she saw Bettina hide you in the church for him to find?"

"Maybe. Or maybe she was in on it."

"It seems risky, though. What if he hadn't found you? Or what if someone else had?"

"He'd been working that shift for years. He was always the only one there at that hour. I used to think that whoever had left me might have known that, and how badly he and my mother wanted children. I just never considered she could have had something to do with it herself, but now it seems pretty clear that she did."

"You might never get the whole story, Mimi."

"I know. And if I don't, I can live with it. At least I know the truth now. But as soon as it's a decent hour for a Saturday morning, I'm going to call my cousin Lucky, just in case she knows something."

"Lucky . . . and her mom was your auntie Birdie, right? The one who died right before your wedding?"

"Wow. You're like my family historian over here. What happened to the failing middle-aged memory?"

Jessie smiles. "Great nicknames, I never forget. I mean . . . Birdie and Lucky? How awesome are those names? Do you know what they're short for?"

"Do *you*?"

"No."

"Good. And I don't really know a lot about them—I kind of feel bad about that. I promised to visit them in Marshboro but then . . . I met Aaron, and he had this big, amazing family that welcomed me right from the start, so . . ."

"You didn't need to look further."

Amelia nods. "Between my in-laws, and you and Si, I guess I finally realized that family isn't just about blood ties."

Things might have been different, though, had she realized Bettina's Southern family had been her own biological relatives.

"What does Aaron have to say about all of this?"

"I haven't told him yet. But I guess I need to, before I talk to Lucky." She pushes back her chair and picks up her phone. "He might have legal advice."

"Legal advice?"

"Or . . ."

He might share in her excitement. Lend emotional support. Offer suggestions on how to handle the conversation.

Anything but indifference.

Avoiding Jessie's questioning look, her gaze falls on the little boy in the sunroom. She thinks of the wistful way he'd said *Maman*, and of the *homme dangereux*.

If his mother had taken good care of him, and he loves and misses her, then where is she now? If he has someone like that in his life, then this could only have happened to him if something had happened to her.

"Jessie?" She turns back. "I thought about what you said last night, and you were right."

"I'm always right." She pauses. "About what?"

"About testing Prewitt's DNA. When it comes to following rules versus helping a child . . ." Amelia gives a decisive nod, mind made up. "The child wins."

THE SUN RIDES high in a bright blue Saturday morning sky as the Angler drives into Ithaca. It's much larger than the surrounding towns, a small, hilly city of old architecture and older trees, with two campuses rising above it in the east and Cayuga Lake sparkling to the north. College students mill the downtown sidewalks as they do back in his neighborhood, wearing school hoodies—Cornell kids in scarlet and white, Ithaca College in blue and gold.

He passes the broad Commons, where vendors are setting up tables and awnings. He parks in a garage, buys a couple of local newspapers, and finds a diner. It's crowded—a good thing. He won't be conspicuous amid the bustle, and he can eavesdrop on the other customers. He dismisses the college kids, always caught up in themselves and each other and, mostly, their electronic devices.

Some of the locals are like that, but many greet each other and the waitstaff by name. They talk about the weather, the festival, the avocado toast, even each other, once certain people are out of earshot.

He orders a hearty bacon and egg breakfast and buries his face in a newspaper, searching the articles for information about where he might find the boy. And he listens.

He learns that Andy Cooper's family is looking for an au pair, that Beth Griswold's Bikram yoga class was canceled, that the Hylands are moving to Arizona.

But nobody mentions the child who'd been found and is being fostered somewhere in their midst. Nor do they mention that an Amish farmer has been brutally murdered about twenty miles outside of town.

That's the good news.

The bad is that sooner or later, he knows, someone is going to miss the man and go looking for him. When they do, they're going to find him pretty quickly. The Angler had considered hiding the body out back, but that hadn't gone very well with the boy, now had it?

At least Stoltzfus is good and dead, shot through the head and then stabbed so many times his light blue work shirt had been blood-blackened to match his suit.

Panting from exertion, the Angler had surveyed his bloody handiwork one last time before trekking back through the woods to the clearing where he'd parked the stolen car.

The Angler's breakfast arrives. The ponytailed waiter, a college kid with a pierced nostril and stoned, watery eyes, is already turning away as he asks, "All set?"

"No, I ordered toast and scrambled."

The kid peers at the poached eggs on an English muffin. "Oh, yeah. Be right back."

The Angler grits his teeth and toys with his place setting. The fork and butter knife are water spotted.

It had felt good to release the rage this morning, but it's building again.

Maybe it would be different if he'd killed the boy, or Cecile. Or even if Stoltzfus had fought back. But to execute a man who was waiting for it . . .

The two middle-aged couples in the booth behind him are still talking about the Hylands. "Dave Carver just listed the house."

"They're asking two hundred and fifty thousand. They'll never get it."

"Sure they will. It's huge, and it's brick."

"Yeah, but it's right across from the Hansons' house."

"Is that a house? I thought it was a school bus."

"Or a yellow submarine."

Laughter from some, but not all.

"The Hansons are lovely people. Who cares what color they paint their house?"

"Dave Carver cares. But it's not just the color. Did you hear about the livestock ordinance meeting last week?"

The ponytailed waiter is back. He deposits a fresh plate on the table in front of the Angler and again starts to turn away after a murmured, "Toast and scrambled. All set?"

"Wait!" He examines the offering. "I wanted white toast."

"I thought you said whole grain."

"I *said*, white."

Watching the kid carry the plate back to the kitchen, he clenches the butter knife, thinking of the blood-encrusted filet blade he'd again stashed in his tackle box on the seat of the stolen car.

Behind him, the couples are talking about a teenager and a backyard rooster.

"Is this the older son?" one of the women asks. "I thought he was away at college."

"No, he is, he's up at UVM. This is the crazy foster kid."

Foster kid?

The Angler's ears perk up.

"How many fosters do they have now?"

"Just the one, but they adopted him years ago. They don't foster anymore."

"Yes, they do. I heard they just got another one a few days ago."

"That's Jessie and Billy. Saving the world. They just can't help themselves, even though they have their hands full with the house and the rooster and the crazy adopted son."

"Yeah, and this new one is probably even crazier. I heard it's the little kid who was found out on Cortland Hollow Road the other—"

The Angler is on his feet, headed for the door.

"Hey, wait! Mister!" Ponytail comes barreling at him. "I'm getting your white toast."

"Changed my mind."

"But you had coffee! You can't skip out on your—"

"Here." The Angler thrusts a couple of bills at him. Canadian currency. Another block plucked from the teetering foundation.

If the tower falls, you lose . . .

AMELIA SITS ON the edge of the bed tying her sneakers with Clancy diving for the laces. She's covered her blisters in bandages, but they've already nearly healed. If only the rest of her were as resilient.

Jessie knocks. "Mimi?"

"Come on in. Just be careful because there's a kitten on the loose."

The door opens. Jessie is still in her red plaid pajama bottoms and thermal tee shirt she'd been wearing earlier, her dark hair a pouf of bedhead. She waves a white envelope.

"Here's Theodore's spit sample. Can you drop it off at the post office on your way to the festival?"

"Wait, *Theodore's*?"

Jessie steps into the room, pulling the door nearly shut behind her, hissing, "It's Prewitt's. I don't want you to get into trouble."

"Jessie . . ."

"No, listen, I was thinking we can fill out the paperwork like it's Theodore's, and I'll sign the waiver so that it's all legal just in case . . . you know."

"And what happens when it comes back with a match to Prewitt's family, wherever they are?"

"Happy ending. Who's going to press charges? But in the meantime, if anything goes wrong, I'll take the fall. I shouldn't have pushed you so hard. I don't want you to be an accomplice in this."

Amelia has to smile at that. "It's not a jewel heist."

"I know, but it's illegal."

"Well, like you said, it's not as if I don't already bend the rules to help my clients find answers. Anyway, when the Wi-Fi is fixed, I'm going to look up the name Prewitt on a few genealogy sites."

"Let's hope that's soon. When it's back up, our password is . . ." Jessie leans in and whispers, "*dimeys*2–1–1–9–9–0. No caps."

"Thanks. Why are we whispering?"

"Because the numbers also open Billy's gun safe in our bedroom closet. Do you want to write it down?"

"Nope, got it." She grins. "First time Billy kissed you, right? February 1, 1990, at the Dugout?"

It had been their favorite local dive bar. Tuesday and Thursday happy hours, ten beers for a dollar— *dimeys*.

"Mimi! Now who's got the amazing memory?"

"The next day, you told me you were going to marry him. You were so sure . . . I remember that you wrote it down and sealed it in an envelope and mailed it to yourself as proof."

"Yes! My Groundhog Day prediction. I still have it somewhere. Si called me Punxsutawney Phil for a while after that. Good times." Jessie's smile is wistful. She sighs, looking down just in time to spot Clancy about to dart into the hallway. "Hey! Where do you think you're going, little stinker?"

She scoops him up and hands him to Amelia.

"Sorry. I'll lock him in when I go."

"Thanks. And, Mimi—what made you change your mind? About Prewitt's DNA?"

"My own test results coming back with a match after all these years. I don't want him to go through the endless waiting, not knowing. Getting the paperwork and permits in order could take years, and by then, it might be too late. If we can send him back home before he's scarred for life—"

"If he has a home to go to."

"If he does, and if we can find it . . . we have to."

"How long will it take to get the results?"

"Normally? Months."

"Months?" Looking as though she might cry, Jessie buries her cheek against the kitten's head, stroking his fur. "It takes that long for a simple lab test?"

"It's not that simple, and no, but there's a huge backlog, but I'll see what I can do." Sneakers tied, Amelia stands and grabs a jean jacket. "Is there still a packing and shipping place down on the Commons?"

"Yes."

"I'll have it overnighted to the lab. And then I'll give my friend who works there a heads-up. Maybe he can expedite it."

"Thank you, Mimi. You're the most amazing person in the world."

"No, Jessie, you are. I wish I had a fraction of your strength and compassion. I've spent almost thirty years being self-obsessed."

"That's not true. You've devoted your adult life to helping people find out who they are."

"Because it's cathartic, not because I'm some noble heroine."

"Hey, I'm the therapist here. Don't be so hard on yourself. Look what you've been through."

"So have you. You've built this amazing life. You have a family, a home . . ."

A marriage.

Whose fault is it that Amelia's is faltering?

Not just Aaron's.

How much time has she wasted over the years, trying to figure out who'd left her in that Harlem church? How much time endlessly, fruitlessly searching—her own dimmest memories, strangers' faces, yellowed documents . . .

How much time speculating that someone out there

is just as desperate to find her? Weighing whether it would be better to discover that her parents hadn't come looking for her because they'd been dead, rather than that they just didn't give a damn?

It turns out neither is the case. She'd had them all along.

So, yeah. She doesn't want to look back, years from now, and realize that she'd also had—and lost—the love of her life.

She grabs her phone and heads for the door.

AFTER A COUPLE of hours at the county sheriff's office with Lieutenant Mai Xiang, Billy is no closer to the answers he'd hoped to find.

You'd think a name like Prewitt would be unique enough to turn up a missing persons report if one exists anywhere in the world, but so far, it has not. It appears that no one has reported Prewitt missing because no one is looking for him.

Billy's gut tells him that a crime led to the child's disappearance—or rather, his appearance; a crime that hasn't yet been discovered or reported.

He imagines someone—Prewitt's *homme dangereux*—breaking into a sleeping household in the dead of night, killing the mother, abducting the child . . .

Or a carjacking, maybe, where the perp didn't realize there was a child in the backseat . . .

Every time he thinks of something like that, he feels a twinge in his heart.

Not, he assures himself, in a medical emergency way.

In an emotional way. The kid tugs his heartstrings, that's all. He's worried. And he's exhausted. He'd had a hard time falling asleep and staying asleep. Indigestion had him tossing and turning—not from anything he'd eaten, because he barely had, but from all the stress.

Damn that Dave Carver.

He'd finally fallen into a sound sleep in the wee hours, only to be awakened by Espinoza's crow down the hall.

Poor Theodore. He shouldn't have been so hard on him, should have had more patience, like Jessie.

Usually she's the impatient one, in life, if not so much with the kids. In life, and with Billy.

He'd been glad to escape the house and her worried gaze this morning. She kept asking him if he was sure he felt okay as he'd knelt in the hallway, installing the slide bolt on the outside of Chip's bedroom door to keep the kitten confined.

"Don't you dare die on me, Billy," she'd said. "Don't you dare."

"Okay, for one thing, if I die, it's not by choice—unless you keep treating me like some kind of invalid and drive me over the edge. And for another thing, I feel fine."

And he does, more or less. He's just feeling anxious about the case, though it isn't his own—he doesn't work for the sheriff's department. Still, they're conducting a thorough investigation, and Lieutenant Xiang has noted even the most minor details he's provided. They've searched the local area and surrounding counties for children who share the name—first or last—and who might be roughly his age and fit his physical description. There haven't been many, and so far, all are accounted for. Now, as they await a call back from CPS about getting a French interpreter over to the house, the lieutenant is preparing for a press conference to release the new clues to the child's background.

They go down the list again.

He speaks French; he seems to have—or *have had*—a mother; he sucks his right thumb; he might come from a rural background, given his recognition of the rooster; and he's probably been relatively sheltered from the modern world.

"The hospital's immunity detection bloodwork indicates that he hasn't had routine childhood vaccinations, and that's not unusual in the Amish community," Lieutenant Xiang reminds him. "We have to consider that, and the fact that he's unfamiliar with everyday American foods or household items, you said?"

"Yes. My wife said it was as if he'd never seen a television before," Billy confirms.

Still, the Amish theory doesn't sit well with him. The child's clothing wouldn't support it, nor the fact that he speaks French, rather than Pennsylvania Dutch or German.

He shares his own theories with her—about a kidnapping, a carjacking.

"You may be right," Lieutenant Xiang says. "And if that's the case, we'll need to bring in the BCI." That's the state police department's Bureau of Criminal Investigation. "But let's see where this takes us first. Thanks to you, we have a lot more to go on now."

She puts aside her notebook and takes another can of Red Bull from the fridge—her third since he arrived. "Can I get you more coffee?"

He hesitates, considering. "I've had so much this morning that all that acid has messed up my stomach. But then again, I can use the caffeine."

"Why don't you go home and grab a nap instead of trying to stay awake?"

Home? Nap?

Sure.

Roosters, kittens, Little Boy Blue, a houseguest, repairs to be made, and Theodore, and Jessie looking at him like he's a gunshot victim about to keel over . . .

"Sergeant? Please go home." Lieutenant Xiang is not making a suggestion.

He bristles. "Look, I know this isn't my case, but—"

"It's not that." She pops the top of her can and takes a sip, regarding him. "You and your wife have a lot on your hands, and you just really look like you can use a break. I think you should take one. There's no telling what might happen with this case once we issue the press release. I'll text you if anything comes up. Meanwhile, keep your ears open and let me know if Prewitt tells you anything else that might help before I can get over there to talk to him."

"Will do." Billy stands and tosses his empty coffee cup into the garbage can on the way to the door.

Maybe she's right. He's completely wiped out, his legs a little shaky and maybe not just from all the caffeine.

In fact, he hasn't had as much as he usually does. Just the cup he'd taken from home, and the one Lieutenant Xiang had given him when he'd arrived. By this time on an ordinary day, he's drunk at least twice that much coffee.

This is not, however, an ordinary day.

He gets into the SUV and is backing out of his parking spot when a text buzzes his phone.

Lieutenant Xiang.

Already?

He pulls back into the spot and opens the text. It contains just two words.

Come back!

Chapter Fourteen

The tropical storm bound for South America has undergone an unprecedented intensification overnight, transforming into a Category 5 hurricane. It's also made a right turn, now heading for Cuba.

Rob and Barnes learn these astounding facts from their tour guide at the Catedral de Nuestra Señora de la Asunción. The young man mentions it nonchalantly, in Spanish, as they're gazing at the country's oldest artifact, the Cruz de la Parra, a large wooden cross planted by Christopher Columbus in 1492.

Rob and Barnes exchange a look.

"Did he say . . ."

"He did," Barnes replies, "but that's not possible."

"*Si.* It is possible," the guide tells them.

"I thought you didn't speak English."

"I do not speak it well."

He speaks it well enough to inform them that meteorologists have now issued a hurricane watch for the southeastern provinces, including Baracoa.

"But I thought it was going to hit Venezuela," an older woman protests as if the guide has some say over it. She's American, with a sunburnt nose, and she's wearing khaki cargo capris and a wide-brimmed hat with a chin cord knotted tightly under her double chin.

The guide shrugs. "Changed direction. But it is a few days away. Please do not worry."

She looks worried. "We flew here on a tiny plane. It was bad enough in nice weather."

Sing it, sister. Barnes asks the woman when she's leaving.

"Sunday night. We fly back to Havana, and then connect to Miami."

"You will be out in plenty of time," the guide assures her.

Barnes and Rob are also flying to Havana Sunday night, but they don't return to New York until Monday.

Remembering that there's Wi-Fi in this area, he reaches into his pocket for his phone. Damn. He'd left it back at the house.

There's something to be said for pulling up the AccuWeather app whenever you're wondering whether Mother Nature is going to send rain. Or unleash a Category 5 storm the likes of which the world has never seen.

It'll be four years next month since Hurricane Sandy had hit New York. He'd helped search for the missing, many of whom had failed to evacuate the coastline. Eventually, they'd all turned up, one way or another.

The guide has moved on, winding down the tour, telling them that Baracoa is the chocolate capital of Cuba and then waxing on about the chocolate factory.

Enough already, Willy Wonka.

Barnes has no desire to be swept away and drown in a ferocious storm surge. He wants to talk to Rob about trying to get out sooner. Maybe there's a flight back to the States on Sunday, ahead of the storm, or even tonight.

After the tour, the guide suggests that they linger in the centuries-old cathedral for a few moments of quiet prayer. Barnes kneels beside Rob in a pew.

Unlike his friend, he's no longer a churchgoing man, as he'd told Miguel last night. But as he kneels here, some of it comes back to him—bible verses, joyful hymns, prayers. He asks God—and his friend Wash, if he's listening and has any pull—to help this island and its people weather the storm.

Rob is still kneeling, head bowed, hands clasped. Barnes sits back and looks around.

Brilliant red and golden light falls through stained-glass windows, illuminating ancient tile floors where his forebears might have walked, and the altar where they might have worshipped, hundreds of years before he was born. Christopher Columbus haunts the place, according to the guard. Maybe his ancestors' spirits do, too.

Barnes wonders about them, about all the people who have come and gone in his own lifetime—the ones he's loved and lost, the ones he hadn't known as well as he could have, should have, or had thought he had; the ones he longs to know . . .

The ones?

The *one*.

Yesterday, after the dream he'd had on that perilous flight, he'd considered trying to find his daughter again. That had been mortality talking, reminding him that one day he'll be all out of chances to make things right. He'll be gone, just like his father, Abuela, his friend Wash . . .

Gone. All of them, just about everyone he's ever loved.

Even his mother, still hanging in there, health-wise, but never the same woman after Dad died. And Sully, and Stef, even the strangers he's tried to find over the years . . .

Rob nudges him and motions for the door. He rises and slowly makes his way down the aisle, haunted by the ghosts and by Ana Benita's prescient parting words about Baracoa.

"No one goes there unless they want to get lost . . ."
"You really want to get lost?"

Maybe he really does. Maybe, when you spend your life mourning loved ones and searching for the missing, you start to feel a little lost yourself. Maybe you relate more to the departed than to the ones they've left behind. Maybe—when you realize there's no one in your own life who would be shattered if you disappeared—then maybe you, too, want to just . . .

They step out into sunshine so bright it blinds him before he can pull his sunglasses from his pocket. Barnes closes his eyes, and when he opens them, he sees her.

There across the square, beneath a building's pillared overhang, is Gypsy Colt.

AMELIA'S SNEAKERS RASP fallen leaves along the concrete sidewalk as she heads downtown, phone pressed to her ear, ringing . . . ringing . . .

Voice mail.

Aaron's probably in the shower, or on a plane.

She forces an upbeat note into her voice. "Hey, it's me! Call me back as soon as possible because I've got big news."

The DNA match—again, front and center.

No. It's not just that.

She takes a deep breath. "Aaron, I miss you, and . . . if you're already gone, have a great trip, but if you're not . . ." Throat aching, she adds simply, "I love you."

She disconnects the call and presses a forefinger to the damp corner of each eye, walking on. She needs to regain composure before she dials her Georgia cousin.

She's spent her career helping clients make these calls—rehearsing with them what to say and how to say it. Occasionally, she'd even made the calls for those who can't muster the strength. Now that it's her own turn, she gets it. Let someone else be the buffer, on the front lines of rejection.

She lets it go for now, having reached the Commons. The wide pedestrian mall is already filled with families, students, and sightseers, strolling in and out of stores and browsing beneath the white vendor awnings that stretch for two blocks. The air is fragrant with foliage and festive food.

Passing a student band doing a sound check—curtailed electric guitar riffs and squeaky-miked "testing, testings"—she's transported back to her 1990 audition to be a lead singer for South Hill, a local band. When they'd hired a white girl for the gig, Amelia had told herself that it was about race and not talent. But that woman now sings backup vocals for a Grammy-winning rock band.

And this one has no one to blame but herself for not pursuing a musical career.

She rarely regrets having chosen a different path—Aaron, and genealogy work. But now she wonders what might have been if she hadn't been so hungry in those pivotal years for love and stability and family, so hell-bent on the quest to discover her biological roots. Where would she be now?

"It's never too late," Jessie had told her.

She hopes that's true, but she isn't so sure.

She toys with her phone as she moves along with the crowd, looking for a quiet spot where she can call her cousin Lucky. Once she knows the truth about what happened, she'll be able to figure out what to do about her life, and her marriage, and maybe she can—

No! You're doing it again!

Making the future about the past by fixating on the thing that's haunted her all her adult life.

She's also just walked past the packing and shipping store.

She backtracks, clutching the white envelope, and steps inside.

The woman behind the counter is helping a college student fill out the paperwork to mail a large package overseas, and there's another customer in front of Amelia. He turns and raises his eyebrows at her as if to indicate that this is going to be a while. Then he does a double take.

"Are you Amelia?"

"Yes . . ." He's a little younger than she is, Asian, with a sleek ponytail and a nice smile. As she tries to place him, she wonders, as always, if she's about to close the gap on her past. Then she remembers that the search for her birth mother has come to an end.

"We've never met," he says, "but I'm a huge fan of the show."

Amelia thanks him, aware that the clerk and the college student have turned to gape at her, expecting a celebrity.

"I was adopted from Vietnam," the man goes on. "Sometimes I wonder about my biological parents—what they were like, how they met . . . you know?"

"I do. If you ever decide to look for them," she says, opening her wallet to find a business card, "I might be able to help."

"Oh, thanks, but they were killed when Saigon fell. Ever hear of Operation Babylift?"

She nods. He must be one of the thousands of orphans evacuated from the war-torn country in April 1975.

He confirms it and tells her about the American family that adopted him. "I count my blessings every day," he says. "When I watch your show, and see all those people searching, I know I'm one of the lucky ones. There are some questions I'll never be able to answer, but I've had a great life."

Amelia nods, remembering what she'd said to Jessie back at the house. She'll be okay now, even if she never finds out exactly what happened back in May 1968. She can call Bettina's cousin in Marshboro, but she doubts Lucky will shed any more light on her past than she had the first time they'd talked. For all she'd known then, Amelia had been Bettina's biological child.

And so I am.

Already she feels the burden shifting, lifting. She no longer has to go through life looking back or looking hard at strangers' faces. From here on in, she can focus on the ones she loves.

As BILLY SPEEDS toward the Stoltzfus farm behind a sheriff's department SUV, with another one coming up a little ways behind him, his thoughts spin and scream more wildly than the red dome lights ahead.

Levi is dead.

Murdered.

Billy's heart aches for the gentle farmer, for his family, especially his sons, who had found him.

Billy's heart . . . *aches.*

He shifts his weight uncomfortably in the seat, picturing the young men he's gotten to know over the years at the farmer's market, so soft-spoken, hardworking, and respectful, with their simple clothes, bearded smiles, kind blue eyes. He imagines them searching for Levi when he'd failed to meet them in town, imagines them finding his abandoned horse and buggy out at the orchard, finding their beloved father . . .

He doesn't yet know the details. Lieutenant Xiang had briefed him as she prepared to rush to the scene.

It's where Prewitt had been found.

That can't be a coincidence.

The press should never have published Levi's name in the article about the child being found.

But they hadn't considered it a criminal case, hadn't thought it would put anyone in danger.

His chest constricts.

Anxiety, pulled muscle, indigestion . . .

He needs to let Jessie know. Tell her to stay home with the doors locked, just in case . . .

Driving with his left hand, he dials the house with his right. It bounces right into voice mail.

That's right. The landline is down, and the Wi-Fi.

He calls her cell instead. It, too, goes straight to voice mail.

He curses.

"Jess, call me as soon as you get this. I . . ." He thinks better of leaving an explicit message. Not just because she probably won't get it, or because he doesn't want to scare her, but because his voice sounds a bit strangled. "I'm following a lead, and I need to talk to you. But just . . . lock the doors and stay home and keep the kids inside."

He hangs up, Dave Carver's voice dropping into his whirling brain like a felled tree sweeping into a tornado.

You and Jessie are fostering the little kid they found out in the boonies yesterday . . .

The press hadn't published the child's whereabouts, only that he's in temporary foster care. But the information is out there, churning the local gossip mill.

The sheriff's vehicle flies around a corner ahead. Billy clenches the wheel with both hands, preparing to follow, but something is wrong.

He misses the turn, feels himself losing control of the SUV, careening toward a utility pole on the shoulder, and all he can think is that he should have listened to Jessie, and Theodore, and the cardiologist . . .

But it's too late.

His arms are burning, his chest is burning, and he can't breathe, he can't breathe, he can't—

BARNES SHOVES ON his sunglasses and zooms in on the spot where he'd seen Gypsy Colt.

She's vanished.

He turns to Rob. Maybe he noticed her.

His friend is squinting in the glare, and rubbing the lenses of his own shades on the hem of his silk guayabera, asking, "You hungry?"

Barnes again scrutinizes the bright pink stucco building across the square.

Had Gypsy gone inside, been enveloped by a troop of uniformed schoolchildren, taken cover behind a concrete planter . . .

Or maybe she hadn't been there at all.

"Barnes?"

He blinks, looks at Rob.

"You hungry?"

"We just ate breakfast."

"That was a couple of hours ago."

They'd eaten at a small *paladar*, not Miguel's. Upon their arrival, the smiling owner had presented them with complimentary *chorote*, a thick hot coconut milk flavored with cocoa and banana. It, along with pastries, fruit, and strong Cuban coffee had chased away the last vestiges of drowsiness, but not the lingering realization that something could have—or perhaps, had—gone dangerously wrong last night.

"Come on, I know a place down on the *malecón*, near the Museo Municipal del Fuerte Matachin," Rob says, gesturing to the east, where a wide stone embankment runs along the water. "We'll grab some lunch and then walk over to the museum."

They leave behind the church and the square and the building where Barnes had imagined Gypsy Colt. Imagined her, because he's certain he'd seen Wayland, gotten a good look at him, at the tattoo, but in her case, it was fleeting.

Then again, could he have imagined Wayland as well? If someone had drugged him, maybe he'd hallucinated all of it.

"The museum traces the Taíno history. We can swing

by the *casa particular* for Kurtis on the way. I want him to come with us and learn about his roots," Rob says as they round a corner and pass a group of barefoot, bare-chested boys playing soccer in the street.

"If he's there, he might just want to sleep."

"I don't care what he wants. He should have let me know where he's been. Lord knows what he's been up to. If I decide he's coming with us, he's coming with us."

Barnes shakes his head. "Look, we all have our rough spots, growing up. Even you."

Years ago, when he'd introduced himself as "Rob," he'd said it wasn't his first name, nor his last. *"Just a reminder of something that happened. Something I never want to happen again."*

It hadn't. He'd done his time for holding up a liquor store, and had come out with a new name and a new attitude.

"Barnes, my son isn't growing up. He's *grown*. But when he acts like a man, and lives his life like one, I'll treat him like one. For now, he gets treated like a kid, because—"

"He's not a *kid*, no matter what he's doing. And I'm not defending him, I'm just relating," he adds quickly, before Rob can accuse him of it yet again. They'd already discussed Kurtis at length this morning on the way to the cathedral. "Do you know how long it took me to grow up?"

"He isn't you, Barnes."

"*I* wasn't always me, either."

"Yeah, yeah, I know, you were *Gloss*."

That had been his nickname in the '70s on the mean Harlem streets, where nobody really gave a damn that his beloved father had dropped dead at thirty-nine. Barnes had been so slick and smooth back then—or so he'd believed—that nothing would ever stick. Warnings, charges, people—everything and everyone slid away and he moved on, unencumbered. Gloss.

One night, an old man had caught him breaking into cars and reached out to him with a handshake instead of a fist, with sympathy for Barnes's loss instead of a threat to call the cops. Turned out Wash *was* the cops. Retired NYPD.

Wash had stuck.

If not for him, Barnes would have wound up in juvy and jail, instead of on this side of the law.

But Barnes wasn't necessarily talking about his years as a juvenile delinquent. Even after that, after Wash had saved him from the streets, after he'd joined the force . . .

Yeah. Even after that, he'd had a long way to go before becoming a responsible, respectable man.

Maybe that's true even now.

"Gloss was a long time ago," Rob reminds him. "Different times, different place. Kurtis is—hey, look out."

Barnes turns just in time to catch a wayward soccer ball flying toward him.

One of the boys races to retrieve it with a shy apology and thanks. Barnes hands it back, and he darts away after flashing a smile. "*That*," he tells Rob as they walk on, "was a *kid*."

"And Kurtis might as well be. By the time you were his age, you were an NYPD detective. I was married with a couple of kids, a couple of mortgages, a booming business . . . You can't blame me for worrying about what's going to happen to him. He won't let me parent him; he won't let me help him."

"He lets you help him."

"Financially. But he doesn't want to follow in my footsteps, or—"

"Did *you* want to follow in *your* old man's footsteps?"

"—or hear what I have to say about anything, not his clothes, his music, TV, the weather, politics—"

"Hell, Rob, *I* don't want to hear what you have to say about politics—or my clothes," Barnes cuts in, smiling to show that he's teasing—sort of. He changes the subject, looking up at the cloudless sky. "What do you think about that crazy storm?"

"Doesn't seem possible."

"That's what people said back home before Sandy slammed the coast."

"At least this one is a few days away," Rob tells him. "By the time it hits, we'll be back home."

"Yeah . . . I was thinking maybe we should try to get out early."

"What happened to staying here forever?"

Perry Wayland happened.

Gypsy Colt happened.

Or even if they hadn't happened . . .

Something had.

Barnes can't shake the suspicion that someone, somehow, had slipped something into his food or beverage. Miguel, most likely, or his son . . .

Why would they do such a thing? Because they wanted to rob him? No one had stolen his money.

Because I asked too many questions?

Because I saw what I wasn't supposed to see?

It all comes back to Perry Wayland. To October

1987. Everything, for the past three decades, comes back to that.

Something Miguel had said last night is troubling him now.

"What if it ends tomorrow . . . This life. The world."

The words had slid right past his alcohol-lubricated brain at the time, but now . . .

Oran Matthews, the notorious Brooklyn Butcher who'd slaughtered several families back in the sixties, had been obsessed with biblical Armageddon.

A lot of people are, Barnes knows.

But they aren't all serving dinner to Perry Wayland— and then feigning ignorance when questioned about the man, who'd been linked to the Brooklyn Butcher copycat murders in October 1987, and to Gypsy Colt, Matthews's daughter.

SITTING AT THE kitchen table, Jessie hears Theodore descend the back stairway, wearing shoes. Ordinarily, he lounges around in slippers and pajamas till noon on a Saturday. Today, she'd been counting on him to do that, and watch Prewitt and keep an eye out for the repairman while she goes upstairs to take a shower. Maybe that will revive her energy, since a boatload of coffee and maple syrup haven't done the trick.

But Theodore is wearing a jacket and heads straight for the back door without a glance into the kitchen.

"Hang on! Where are you going?"

"To check Espinoza!" The back door squeaks open and he barrels outside.

Jessie gets up and goes to the sink, watching him through the window. He unlatches the hinged chicken wire door and stoop across the small mesh-enclosed pen to peer anxiously into the wooden nesting shelter. Even from here, she sees his body relax.

Good. Espinoza must be there.

Come on, of course he's there.

Dave Carver might be a first-class jerk, but he wouldn't trespass, vandalize their property, or harm a living creature.

Then again, maybe he would.

Maybe Billy *should* buy a padlock.

She reaches for the wall phone to call and tell him to pick one up on the way home.

No dial tone.

Damn. She forgot.

Forgot, too, to plug in her cell phone. The battery is dead.

Can one thing go right today? Just one small thing?

She sighs, closing her eyes, shoulders burning with exhaustion. She needs that shower. Now.

She opens the back door. Ordinarily the squeak doesn't bother her, though fixing it is on the long household to-do list. Today, the sound grates her like foam packing peanuts crumpling in dry hands.

"Theodore? I need you!"

"I'm busy," he calls back, muffled, his top half still poking around inside the rooster's house.

"Now!"

He backs out and turns toward her. "Mom! I said I'm busy!"

"And I said . . ." Her voice breaks—not because she's going to cry, but because she's going to collapse if she doesn't get five minutes alone under a hot, soothing spray. "I said, come here. I need you to do something for me."

Her son—so rarely capable of interpreting body language—pauses to give her a closer look before responding with a shrug. "Okay."

He closes the coop and reenters the house. "What do you need?"

"I made pancakes for breakfast."

"I'm not hungry. I want to stay outside with—"

"No, Theodore. I need you here right now. The Wi-Fi repairman is coming and I have to go upstairs for a few minutes. If they think we're not home, they'll leave." In truth, she left the front door ajar, so that if anyone knocks on the storm door and no one answers, they'll be able to see lights on in the kitchen.

Theodore starts for the living room.

"Wait, no, I need you to be in the sunroom with Prewitt."

So much for the flash of empathy. Her son's gaze narrows.

"Tell him about Espinoza," she suggests. "Maybe you can get him to say something. I've been trying all morning, but you're the only one he'll talk to."

"That's because I'm the only one who speaks French."

"Right. He needs you. And *I* need you. I'm so glad I can count on you."

He grudgingly heads for the sunroom—one small thing going right for a change—and she hurries up the back stairs.

Billy's toolbox is still sitting in the hallway outside Chip's bedroom. It's not like him to leave it lying around. She remembers how he'd huffed and winced as he'd installed the bolt on the door. He probably hadn't been up to lugging the heavy case back to the basement.

On Monday, she'll tell him to call Dr. Varma. No, she'll call herself, make an appointment for Billy to be checked out again.

In the bathroom, she turns on the hot tap, strips off her clothes, and jams them into the hamper with the never-ending pile of laundry.

The shower does help, though not as much as she'd hoped. The tension ebbs a bit in her muscles, but her brain is still clouded with exhaustion, stress, and nagging worry about her husband's health.

Back in the master bedroom, she looks for the jeans and hooded sweatshirt she'd worn all day yesterday. She'd draped both over a hook on the back of the closet door, but they're on the floor. Billy must have knocked them off and left them there. She puts them on anyway and is looking through her sock drawer for a matched pair when Theodore shouts up the stairs.

"Mom!"

"Be right there!" Jessie gives up on matching socks and pulls on two black ones that are close enough, then goes back to the closet to find her ancient pair of UGGs, hand-me-downs from Petty. She'd begged for them in middle school and grown tired of them after a season.

"They're so out of style," she'd scolded Jessie when she'd caught her wearing them a year or two ago.

"You're kidding, right? For what we spent on these, I'm going to be buried in them. Maybe they'll be back in style by then."

The UGGs are on the closet floor, buried beneath a couple of her sweaters that have fallen off the hangers. Billy again.

"Mom!" Theodore's voice is in the front hall.

"I'm coming! And you're supposed to be in the sunroom!"

"Someone's here!"

Oh—the repairman. She'd forgotten.

She hurries to the stairs, finger-combing her wet hair. "Sorry, I was just—"

She stops short on the landing, spotting Theodore below with a uniformed police officer. He's young, had played high school baseball with Chip.

"Mrs.—Jessie. Sorry, I tried to call, but the phone was—"

"What happened, Shawn?"

She waits for him to tell her that it's not about Billy, or her kids, that nothing horrible has happened, that he's just stopped by to visit, maybe looking for Chip, or even Billy . . .

But she's seen that expression of regret and sorrow before, on her husband's face, whenever he leaves the house in uniform to deliver bad news to a family whose lives are about to shatter.

Chapter Fifteen

In a rocky wilderness that lies just a few blocks from the Ithaca Commons, a gorge trail follows the rushing Cascadilla Creek all the way up to Cornell's campus.

As a student, Amelia had walked the path in all seasons. Its incline can be treacherous in icy weather, and the access points are officially closed in winter. In spring, the ice thaws to release majestic waterfalls, and in summer, you can cool off in the rippling pools beneath them. But autumn is by far her favorite season in the gorge, like stepping into a luminous impressionist canvas.

For a while, she simply walks, ascending the ancient bedrock trail and stone stairs, thinking about Aaron, and Saturdays. How they used to live for them, reminding each other all week that Saturday was coming. They could sleep in and dine out, see movies, shows, friends—or just lounge around the apartment in sweats, watching TV or trading *Times* sections across the couch. They'd load their favorite CDs into their high-tech—for the time—stereo and sing along to household chores or meal prep.

Those cozy weekends are as long gone as the stereo and CDs. Now music, like dining and television, is a solitary experience in their disquietingly quiet household. They listen to their own playlists plugged into earbuds, even when they're in the same room at the same time. Now he schedules business trip departures for Sunday evenings instead of Monday mornings, returns for Saturday mornings instead of Friday nights.

"I hate getting stuck in rush hour traffic on the way to an airport," he'd said when it all began to shift. *"And I can't miss any more early meetings."*

But what about me? Do you miss me, Aaron? Do you miss us?

They have some decisions to make when they're both home again. But she can see the familiar stone footbridge looming ahead, and she wants to call her mother's cousin before she leaves this peaceful oasis.

She dials the Georgia phone number, prepared for a voice mail greeting or even a recording telling her the phone has been disconnected.

A woman answers, though, with a pleasant "Hello?"

Lucky. She sounds like Bettina. Not just the rich drawl, but the pitch.

"Hello? Hello?"

"I'm . . ." She swallows. "I'm sorry. It's Amelia. Bettina's daughter."

"Who?"

"Amelia Crenshaw. My mother . . ." She clears her throat, begins again, stronger this time. "My mother was your cousin Bettina, up north."

"New York City." She draws out the words in wonder, as if she's there, marveling at the urban skyline.

"That's right. How have you been?"

"Just fine, just fine. It's been a lot of years since your mama passed, and mine, too. I've seen you on television," Lucky adds, without quite as much warmth and depth, like a hearty soup cooled with a touch too much water.

"Oh . . . yes. Part of my job," Amelia tells her. "As an investigative genealogist. You know."

"Oh, I know." A pause, during which Amelia imagines the woman might be about to add that they're proud of her—the whole Georgia family, proud of their successful, famous cousin. Or maybe she'll ask whether Amelia has made any progress in trying to find her biological parents.

But she doesn't do that. Is it because she herself had been illegitimate, and she doesn't approve of Amelia delving into the family's ancestral roots?

Or because she knows the truth?

The water rushes and Amelia's feet climb and the footbridge looms, and she has to say it. Just say it. Just ask.

"I'm calling because I'm wondering what you know about my birth?"

"Your birth?"

"Yes. I just found out that Bettina was really my mother after all."

A long pause. "Did you now."

She waits for Lucky to ask how she knows that. Having already decided that Quinnlynn's role in this can wait, she isn't sure quite how to answer.

But Lucky says only, "Well," like she's sitting in a porch rocking chair with all the time in the world to ponder.

"Why do you think Calvin told me that story? About finding me in the church?"

"I don't know, child. I only met your daddy a time or two."

"And my mother . . . Bettina . . . do you remember when she was pregnant with me?"

"When was that?"

"It would have been back in mid-1967, into '68."

"I didn't see Bettina at all during those years. The last time I ever saw her was in '65."

"Do you remember hearing anything about me being born?"

"Oh, I'm sure she wrote and told us about it, but I don't remember."

"Are you sure? I'm just wondering because . . . because my father told me that crazy story about being abandoned, you know?"

Does she even recall that phone call back in 1991, when Amelia had offered her condolences and her story, and Lucky had chosen to call her abandonment an "adoption"?

Silence on her end, so Amelia goes on, "For all these years, that's what I've been thinking. That he found me in a church. And now I don't think it's even true."

"No, I don't suppose it was."

Amelia pauses. Nods. Wants to cry.

"I was thinking . . . you know, if you wouldn't mind . . . maybe I could come down there. To Georgia. To get to know the family. I think my mother would have liked that."

"I'm sure she would have," Lucky murmurs. "You'll have to do that sometime."

"I was thinking maybe . . . soon."

"Okay. Of course. That would be right nice."

"Okay." She bites her lip. She's stopped walking, allowing herself to sink onto a low stone ledge in the shadow of the arched footbridge, so close to the falls that the cold spray dampens her face.

"I don't want to cut this short, child, but I have to get to—"

"One last thing," Amelia says, "and then I'll let you go. My mother gave me a ring. I was wondering if it was some kind of . . . family thing. Heirloom. Do you remember a little gold ring with sapphires, and a blue *C* etched into it? Not—"

"'Fraid I don't."

"But it was—"

"I don't know anything about any initial rings for babies in this family," Lucky says firmly. "I'm sorry, child."

"All right, then . . ." Amelia hesitates. "I'll call you in a few days, to see when would be a good time."

"A good time?"

"For me to visit."

"Oh, of course. You do that. And you take care now, you hear?"

They hang up.

Amelia heaves herself to her feet, dries her damp cheeks on her sleeves, and walks on, going over the conversation. The Collegetown trail entrance is in sight, the rickety old wooden staircase replaced earlier this year by new concrete and stone steps.

Everything changes. Everything—

She stops short.

"I don't know about any initial rings for babies . . ."

Amelia had told her the ring was small and etched with a blue *C*. But Lucky had cut her off before she could clarify the description. For all she'd known, Amelia could have been talking about a small-sized ring for a grown woman, etched to depict a blue sea—a scroll of waves, or something like that.

Initial rings for babies . . .

Something else comes back to her now. The last time they'd spoken, after Auntie Birdie had died back in '91, Lucky had told Amelia that Birdie might not even have known who Lucky's father had been, and that she had never asked.

"There were certain things you just didn't talk about back then. Shouldn't talk about them now, either, or ask questions. Just count your blessings and move on."

All right, then.

Amelia's counting, and she's moving.

But she may not be done asking after all.

In the spot next to the one where the Angler had parked the stolen car, a young couple is loading a pair of pink-clad toddlers into a double stroller. Both girls are munching cookies. His stomach growls, still empty after he'd deserted his diner breakfast, now flitting with butterflies.

He's found the boy. He's actually found him—here, close by. All he has to do is figure out where the foster family lives.

He climbs into the car and finds the cell phone he'd left in the console, powered down so that Cecile can't bother him. Now he turns it on. When it lights up, there are a barrage of texts from his wife, which he ignores, and a pop-up window asking whether he wants to allow data roaming while he's out of the country.

Only for a few minutes, and just the applications he'll need to find local real estate listings, and the names—Hyland, Hanson—along with a map to figure out where to go from here.

He opens the phone's settings and scrolls down the list of apps. An unfamiliar red icon jumps out at him.

Wait a minute. What the hell is this? He clicks on it, heart racing.

Something called . . .

Stealth Soldier?

The app is tracking him.

Cecile must have gotten her hands on his phone and guessed the password to unlock it so that she could install it. It wouldn't have been hard: 1–9–3–7—the four corners of the keypad. Easy for him to remember; also easy for her to guess if she'd seen him crisscross tap the phone.

But why? Why would his aloof wife, who'd basically encouraged him to take a mistress, suddenly care where he goes when he isn't with her?

People don't change character from one day to the next. Not that drastically.

Anyway, she'd have nothing to gain from knowing where he'd been.

Who would? Who else in the world has access to his phone and would have had any reason to track him?

The police. They must be onto him, must be following his every movement.

But no, that can't be possible. They'd have arrested him in the all-night supermarket parking lot, or they'd have stopped him from leaving the country.

Then who else . . . ?

Monique.

Monique, making a run for it on that last desperate night . . .

He'd wanted to believe that something had finally snapped inside her, that she'd chosen to save herself and sacrifice her child. Women do that. They run away, they leave their children behind, leave them at the mercy of cruel, violent men.

His own mother had done it. Why wouldn't he expect Monique to do the same?

Because he'd so often seen her tenderly cradling her son, rocking him back and forth to soothe him, doing whatever she had to do to keep him safe, healthy, alive. Because . . .

People don't change character.

He stares at the tracking app on his phone, remembering how she'd told him, on the night they'd met, that she'd run away from home because her boyfriend had been cheating on her with her best friend.

Charmed by her adolescent outrage, he'd asked her how she could be sure. *"Vous l'espionnez?"*

She'd smiled a smug little smile, and told him that yes, she'd been spying on the boy.

He'd teased her, asking if she'd followed him around wearing a sexy trench coat and dark glasses. Not like that, she'd said. No need for sexy trench coats with modern technology.

A pity, he'd said at the time.

Modern technology.

Monique hadn't been leaving her child behind the night she'd escaped; she'd been trying to save him. She'd been going for help because she'd had a way to locate the boy without the Angler's cooperation.

How, though, *when*, could she have gotten her hands on his phone? He wants to believe that it would have been impossible, yet he knows it had not. A brief distraction on his part, a moment of recklessness on hers . . .

"Imbecile!"

He sees the young couple turn to gape, then hastily push their pink toddlers away in the stroller.

Reckless, reckless . . .

She'd betrayed him.

"I'm sorry," she'd said when he'd caught her. *"Please. I lost my head for a second there, I just didn't think."*

Oh, yes, she had. She'd thought about it, for far longer than a second. She'd planned, and schemed, and spied. If she'd gotten away, she'd have flagged a passing car, called the police, and they'd have found him, arrested him, taken his phone . . .

The tracker would have led them straight to the kid. Maybe they wouldn't even need the phone for that—or him. He'd been as dispensable to her as bycatch—he'd taken the bait and she'd been about to throw him away.

Catch and release.

She only cared about herself, and the kid.

This time, there will be no reckless mistakes.

This time, the kid will die.

"EVERY LIVING CREATURE is equipped with natural instinct, Stockton. Listen to yours."

Wash had given Barnes that advice years ago, when he'd been an aspiring detective. It's served him well on the job, even better in his personal life . . . and today?

Every time he looks over his shoulder, he seems to catch a stranger's scrutiny. He isn't seeking an elderly man, an adolescent boy, a young woman. Nor, presumably, are they looking for, or perhaps even at, him . . . are they? Is he under surveillance? Do they think they are?

Paranoia all around.

Kurtis still hasn't returned to the *casa particular*, unless he'd been there and left again.

Barnes grabs his cell phone on the way back out.

"No public Wi-Fi along the *malecón*," Rob tells him.

"I just want it for the camera."

"Good idea. It's a beautiful spot."

Yeah, he's sure it is. But scenic pictures aren't what he has in mind. If he spots Perry Wayland or Gypsy Colt again, he wants photo evidence.

The midday heat sears the top of his head as they walk single file down the narrow street toward the turquoise sea in the distance, Barnes glancing into every shadowy nook, Rob brooding along behind him.

"Where is he, do you think?" he asks Barnes.

"Kurtis? Probably the same place I was the other night."

"In Santa Maria del Mar with Ana Benita?"

Barnes laughs. "I wouldn't blame him. But I'm sure he was out in some bar and he met a hot woman, and he's just—"

He stops short.

Rob slams into him from behind. "Barnes! What the hell are you doing?"

"Sorry, I was just . . . I thought I saw . . . Kurtis."

"Where?"

"Never mind. It wasn't him."

"It wasn't anyone," Rob says, following his gaze down a cobblestone alley.

It's empty, lined with brick walls and garbage cans and strung overhead with laundry on clotheslines like a vintage Lower East Side movie set. Yet Barnes could have sworn he'd seen a furtive figure duck into the shadows. Not Wayland, though, and not Gypsy, and not Christopher Columbus's ghost.

A young man, maybe planning to rob them. It's a foreign country; they're tourists. That's probably all it is, but . . .

"Barnes." Rob lifts his sunglasses above his forehead and studies Barnes's face. "Something's wrong, isn't it? And you don't want to tell me?"

Can he possibly know? About the Wayland case, Stef, the bribe . . .

"You don't think he was just out on the town last night, living it up on vacation, do you? You think something happened to him—that gut instinct of yours, right? You think he bought some drugs, got arrested, thrown in jail, or—no. You're a missing persons detective, and you think he's missing."

Barnes stares, digesting words that make no sense . . .

Until they do. Rob isn't talking about Wayland. He's talking about Kurtis.

"Oh . . . no. I don't think that at all. I mean, I think you two have some things to work out. But right now, here, I'm sure he's fine. It's not like he could text to let you know he was staying out all night even if he wanted to, which I'm sure he didn't. And at his age, I don't think he should have to."

"Yeah, well, you don't know the worry, Barnes. You're not a parent."

The words sting, but he can't blame Rob for stating

the truth. Biology and one-night stands aside, he isn't a parent, and he doesn't know. Not that worry.

He'd had a taste of it, though, in the hospital when Charisse was in the neonatal ICU. He'd stepped up, paid for her care.

That wasn't the only time he'd felt the gut sear of paternal concern.

One long-ago night on a whim, he'd found his way to the Marcy Houses in Bed-Stuy. He'd been relieved when Delia's roommate Alma told him that Charisse and her mother had moved on.

Yeah, you really think they landed in a better place? All sunshine and white picket fences and backyard swimming pools?

They reach the *paladar*, a wind-battered two-story structure with tables on the upper deck, facing the water. It wouldn't stand a chance in a Category 5 storm surge. The owner, a rotund, smiling woman named Ramira, greets Rob like long-lost family and hugs Barnes as well. Her daughter, in her early twenties, shows them to a table overlooking the sea and leaves them to examine their paper menus. Both women speak English.

"That's why I like to come here," Rob tells Barnes. "A lot of Americans do."

Indeed, at the next table, two older couples with Southern accents are fretting about the approaching hurricane. And a nearby tour group is talking about— well, arguing about—the presidential candidates back home.

"Can't escape the election even here," Rob notes with a sigh.

"Can't escape anything these days." Barnes isn't talking about politics.

After they place their orders, Rob is drawn into the conversation and Barnes promptly excuses himself, not just because he isn't in the mood for debate.

He can see two women chatting with each other while waiting to use the only restroom, and the owner's daughter is bussing a table beside it.

He joins the line, catches her eye, and smiles. She smiles back.

"I ordered the grilled *pulpo*. Good choice?"

"That depends. Do you like octopus?"

"Love it," he says.

"Then it's a good choice."

He asks her about the *paladar*'s other specialties, and whether they get a lot of American tourists here. When she tells him that they do, he asks about ex-pats.

"A few," she says with a shrug, swirling a rag over the table.

"Last night in town, I could have sworn I saw an old friend from New York. His name is Perry Wayland. Do you know him?"

Her hand goes still, clutching the rag, and then she starts scrubbing the spotless table as if trying to remove a stubborn stain. "No. I don't know any Perry Wayland."

She's lying.

Why?

JESSIE PACES THE corridor outside the surgical waiting room.

"There's been a car accident."

She'd been braced for those words ever since Chip and Petty had started riding around with older teens at the wheel and then gotten their own licenses.

But she'd never worried about Billy on the road, not even when he was out on the job in a blinding snowstorm. He's the world's most capable driver.

She'd done her best to stay calm when Shawn had delivered the news, hearing Billy in her head, telling her not to frighten Theodore, telling her . . .

"You know, Jess, if our lives had a theme, it's 'just roll with it.'"

Shawn had confirmed that her husband had survived but been injured; he wasn't sure how badly.

But it wasn't good. Otherwise, Billy would have told her about it himself—he'd call from the hospital, or pull into the driveway in a dented car.

Shawn had given her the name of the hospital, and she'd headed straight for the door.

"I can take you over there, Mrs.—Jessie."

"No. Thanks," she'd added, already searching pockets on the coatrack for her keys.

"But I'm supposed to—"

"It's fine, Shawn. I need to drive myself." She wanted to be alone in the car where she could let out the screams and sobs. Focusing on a task would keep her from stalling on the heart-stopping what-ifs.

Heart stopping.

Billy's heart, the chest pains, the cardiologist's warnings . . .

Jessie has been blindsided, like a pedestrian who'd cautiously checked for traffic from the left, stepped off the curb, and been mowed down by a wrong-way bus.

She'd found her keys and her phone and instructed Theodore to stay with Prewitt until Mimi got back. Yes, it's against the foster rules to leave him in the care of a minor, but this is an emergency and she'd planned to call Mimi immediately. She was just in town. She could be back at the house in ten minutes. Fifteen, tops.

Jessie hadn't realized until she was en route and trying to call that her cell phone battery was dead. Naturally, she'd forgotten to charge it. Naturally, she couldn't find the charger she usually keeps in the car.

But Mimi is probably home by now, and the kids are fine, and right now Jessie's main concern—her only concern—is that Billy pull through.

He'd already been in surgery when she'd arrived. Someone is supposed to come talk to her and explain what's going on, but so far, she's been left alone to wait, and worry, and wonder what she'll do if . . .

He has to make it. He just has to. Having him for all these years is the one thing that's kept her sane— though he might argue that point.

Losing him is the one thing she can't fathom.

"Nobody rolls with anything—everything—in this crazy world the way you do, Billy."

A door opens.

"Mrs. Hanson?"

A man in a white coat beckons her.

She takes a deep breath and walks toward him, steeling herself for whatever is coming.

It isn't what she expects, and not just because Billy is alive and can stay that way for a good long while, the doctor believes, as long as he learns to take care of himself—and as long as the surgery is a success.

They aren't treating his injuries from the accident—
mere bruises, lacerations, a concussion, none of it life
threatening. No, they're doing an emergency angio-
plasty. He'd suffered a heart attack at the wheel.

"He's a lucky man, Mrs. Hanson. It happened at a
high speed on a remote road, but there were sheriff's
deputies traveling behind him. They witnessed the
accident and were able to assist your husband and
administer CPR at the scene."

She digests this. "You mean . . . were they chasing
him?" she asks, imagining Billy hunting down Dave
Carver like a wild man.

But the doctor smiles and shakes his head. "Not that
I'm aware. I was told they were heading to a crime
scene out on Cortland Hollow Road."

Cortland Hollow Road.

Prewitt had been found out there.

Prewitt, frightened, telling them about *l'homme
dangereux*.

"Do you know anything about it? The crime? Was it
a robbery, or . . ."

His smile fades. "A homicide, I'm told."

BEFORE LEAVING THE stolen car in the parking garage,
the Angler had removed every bit of evidence that
might possibly link it to him. He'd thrown the passports,
one by one, into separate trash cans along the crowded
Commons. He'd pushed them down into the waste, so
blinded by rage that he didn't see, or care about, the
filth his bare hand encountered. The tackle box, too,
had gone into the garbage, sans the knife.

That, he carries in his pocket as he walks up North
Cayuga Street, seething and searching, Monique's

betrayal shadowing him like the damned tracker itself.

The street is humming with leaf blowers, people doing yard work as kids ride bikes and scooters or shoot hoops. No one seems to pay him any mind. Student housing is sprinkled through the neighborhood, kids congregating on porches with beer even at this hour. And there's a tag sale down the block, so it's not unusual for a stranger to stroll past.

He spots a For Sale sign on the plush green lawn of a stately brick Tudor. Directly across the street, beyond a yard thick with fallen leaves and downed branches, is an enormous yellow house.

The architecture is distinctly Victorian, like his father's place back in Ottawa. Does the boy feel at home here?

He hopes so. The barb will sting that much more.

He walks on past, noting that there are no cars parked in the driveway. Someone must be home, though, because the home's elegant wooden front door is ajar beyond the storm door, revealing a wallpapered stair hall and lights on in the back of the house.

At the top of the street, he looks around to see if anyone is watching before he does an about-face and backtracks. He pretends to be scanning the sidewalk as if he'd dropped something the first time, though he's reasonably certain the show has no audience.

This time, though, there will be no reckless mistakes. After he's done what he has to do to the kid—and to these Hanson people, who were foolish enough to take him in—he'll put this all behind him for good.

He thinks of Cecile. By now, she must realize he's gone. Had he told her about his mother—that she'd run off and left her family—Cecile might not have been surprised that he'd do the same. She might assume he was merely following in her footsteps.

But he'd told his wife only that his mother had died when he was too young to remember her. He'd wanted to think it was a lie, but by that time, he'd seen the brown paint spill hidden beneath the carpeting in his father's bedroom, and on the dusty floor of the secret room above, and in the damned ceiling . . .

He hadn't torn it out, hadn't confirmed that it's there, but he knows. He's always known.

He stops in front of the yellow house and looks around to see if anyone is watching.

A college-aged couple has just exited a house two doors up. He's wearing a Cornell hoodie; she's wearing a short skirt and stiletto heels. Both are perhaps still drunk from last night, weaving a little as they walk arm in arm to a car parked at the curb. Ah, the morning after, and they see nothing but each other.

The girl reminds him a little of Monique.

Monique, dead in the bottom of the lake.

Monique, who betrayed him.

He spins away, and strides toward the yellow house. Boldly, up the walk, up the steps to the door. He'll knock, and ask about the house across the street as if he's an interested buyer. He'll ask about things other people care about—the neighborhood, about the schools, the stores, the student housing, noise, taxes.

Nice. Friendly. He can do that. He can talk his way inside, and then . . .

As he lifts his fist to rap on the door, a teenaged kid appears on the other side as though he were waiting, watching, for trouble. But when he spots the Angler, his eyes seem to widen in . . . relief? Yes, unless his glasses are distorting his expression. He reaches out and opens the storm door.

"Are you the repair guy?"

He barely hesitates. "Yeah."

"My mom said you were coming yesterday." The kid stands back, holding the door open, expecting him to come in. He's wearing sneakers, pajama bottoms, and a baggy hoodie. No Cornell colors, and no Ithaca College. It's gray, and shapeless as the kid himself.

"Right, sorry, I couldn't make it yesterday." He steps over the threshold. The house smells like a mother lives here—homemade cooking, warm laundry, maybe one of those scented jar candles women like. Not Cecile. She turns up her nose unless they're the hundred dollar ones imported from Paris.

"Where's your mom?"

"She had to go to the hospital. My dad was in a car crash. How long will it take you to fix the Wi-Fi?"

"Not long." The Angler quells his excitement, keeping his voice steady. This is so easy—too easy. It might be a trap. The kid refuses to make eye contact, as if he's hiding something.

The Angler takes a few cautious steps over the threshold, looking around. "Are you here alone?"

"No. Espinoza is here. I thought you were the guy who's trying to steal him, but you're not."

"No, I'm not. Is Espinoza your brother or sister?"

"No. They're away at college. He's a rooster."

Right. The rooster.

"You and Espinoza are the only ones home?"

"Yeah."

Crushing disappointment. So close . . . but not close enough. They must have moved the kid to another foster home.

Then—a shrug and afterthought: "There's a boy here, too. But I'm the only one who can talk to him because I speak French."

A French boy.

The Angler takes another step into the house. "Where is he?"

"Espinoza?" The kid is suddenly wary. "Do you know Dave Carver?"

Dave Carver. The real estate agent who doesn't like the rooster.

"Yeah. Can't stand that guy."

The kid is pleased. "I hate him."

"Me, too." He reaches back casually and closes the big wooden door. His fingers itch to turn the bolt, but he doesn't dare. "I wasn't talking about Espinoza, though. I was talking about the French boy."

"He's doing puzzles. Why do you hate Dave Carver?"

"Because he's a jerk. How about you? Why do you hate him?"

As the kid launches into a tirade about Espinoza and Walmart and fried chicken, the Angler sees movement at the back of the house.

"Why don't I start working on the Wi-Fi while you finish telling me?" he cuts in when the kid pauses for a breath.

No argument there. He doesn't miss a beat, talking on as the Angler leads the way down the hall toward the kitchen, and . . .

Voilà.

The boy, Monique's son—*his* son—is there.

"Prewitt!"

Theodore whirls on him.

"Hey! How do you know his name?"

"Où est Maman?" The boy, small and fierce, lifts his chin and glares at the Angler.

"Maman est morte." The Angler smiles, watching the child wither at the last word.

Dead.

"Hey! You speak French, too?"

He ignores the kid and walks slowly toward his son. Only then does he see that he's clutching a silky lavender garment.

Monique . . .

There she is, alive again, her strength, her mistrust, her treachery glittering in her son's blue eyes.

There, too, is Pascal, his other son—frail, hurting, begging for his mother . . .

And there is the Angler himself—young, vulnerable, weak. Too weak to fight back the way he should have. Too weak to confront the man who'd tormented him all his life.

No. He closes his eyes, not wanting to see his own face looking back at him, or his son's face, or Monique's . . .

Or his dead father's.

Voices break through.

"Are you really here to fix the Wi-Fi?"

"Il est l'homme dangereux!"

"You killed her!" He presses his palms to his temples, seeing it. Him. *La bête noire.*

The black beast is killing his mother in the secret

room. His mother's blood seeps down through the ceiling like rain. The beast lies that she'd left, blaming him for that, for every ounce of misery in his life.

His eyes snap open. "You should have fought back! Why didn't you—"

The kitchen is empty.

The boy had slipped through his fingers once again.

He screams in rage, rushing to the back door. He throws it open. It squeaks so loudly that there's no way it had already opened without him hearing it. The space where he'd been standing, between counter and chair, would have made it impossible for the brats to get to the front of the house without brushing past him. There's only one place they could have gone.

He sprints up the narrow stairway, reaching the top just in time to catch a flash of movement down the hall—someone diving through a doorway, too large a figure to have been Prewitt. Reaching the room, he's not surprised that it appears to be empty. The older kid is there, probably hiding under the bed, but is the boy?

Turning to scan the hallway, the Angler sees the other stairway, the grand, polished one that leads straight to the front door, and freedom.

But what if he's still up here, in the room with the kid? He spins back to the bedroom, and he senses him nearby, can almost hear him breathing. But almost isn't evidence enough. He can't be sure he's here unless he searches the room, and if he pauses to do that—and he's wrong—the boy will get away.

He can't escape this time. *I have to stop him, like I stopped her.*

And then he sees it, like a gift: a slide bolt on the outside of the door—just like the attic chamber in his father's house.

He locks it in a flash, trapping at least one of them in the room.

"Faites confiance à vos sens."

He's a child again, fishing from a rickety pier with his uncle, prey lurking just beyond the surface.

He clenches the filet knife, remembering the slick of guts and blood on his hands, how he'd pretend the blade was slicing into human flesh instead of silvery gills.

"C'est comme une prison!" Monique's ghost wails in his head.

"Oui," he says aloud. *"Les prisonniers sont condamnés à mort."*

Then he hears another sound. This time, doesn't almost hear it; this time, it's loud and clear and unmistakable.

The front door at the foot of the grand staircase just opened . . . and closed.

Barnes ...

Chapter Sixteen

Deserted stretches of beach are in no short supply in Baracoa.

Barnes found one after the museum tour, while Rob went back to the house to get his phone and make arrangements to leave the island tomorrow morning.

It seems like a wise move. The surf is already raging. Barnes is watching it, lying on his back, elbows propped in the sand, when a shadow falls over him.

"Heard you've been looking for me."

He looks up.

The sun's glare obscures the man's features, and he's fully clothed, but Barnes doesn't have to see his face, or his chest tattoo, to identify him.

He gets to his feet, facing Perry Wayland. No trace of the hedge fund millionaire at a glance. But there's a self-consciousness about the beach bum vibe—his shaggy hair and beard are well-groomed, board shorts and white tee shirt unrumpled, flip-flops made of leather, not rubber, sunglasses an expensive brand. He's holding a crude bamboo walking stick.

He appears to have come alone, but Barnes senses he has not. He scans the narrow beach, bordered by vegetation. He suspects someone is watching from a clump of coconut trees.

"Who told you that I was looking for you?"

"It's a small town. NYPD comes sniffing around—people have your back."

"Yeah, don't worry. I'm not here looking for anything but a vacation."

"That's what I hear. A nice family vacation. Your friend's family, not yours. Yours is . . ." He trails off with measured deliberation and smiles, his eyes hidden behind the glasses.

He's baiting you. Don't say a word.

"Hmm. Where is your daughter these days?" Wayland asks.

There's no way he can possibly know about Charisse. Stay cool.

"What are you talking about? I don't have—"

"Sure you do. Born back on . . . let's see, I know it was a memorable day for me. October 24, 1987, correct?"

The words hit Barnes like a knockout punch on an invincible champion about to be taken down by a nobody. Dazed, reeling, he can only stare as Wayland hits him again.

"I guess you're pretty protective of daddy's little girl, aren't you? Wouldn't want to see anything happen to her . . . I know how that goes."

Barnes recovers to deliver a jab of his own. "Do you? Because you took off and left your three children."

"They didn't need me. They're all grown-up now, doing just fine. But your daughter . . . how's she doing?"

"Just fine."

"A lie."

His heart stops. "What do you mean by that?"

"You just said you didn't have a daughter, so you lied to me. And now I see . . . are you worried about her?"

He shakes his head slowly.

"So you know how she is, then, your daughter? Where she is? Who she is?"

"Of course I do."

"Well, good. That makes two of us."

It's impossible.

Yet Wayland knows that Charisse was born, knows when she was born . . .

Does he really know where she is? Or . . .

Who she is . . . the phrasing is peculiar.

"You look surprised, Detective. Maybe you thought you were the only one who likes to keep tabs on people, just in case . . ."

"In case what?" Barnes takes a step closer.

Wayland isn't a large or muscular man. Barnes is.

Barnes sees his hand clench the walking stick a little harder but catches him giving a little nod at something over Barnes's shoulder.

Turning, he sees that as he'd suspected, they aren't alone on the beach. Ah, the coconut trees. Not one, but several people have emerged from the clump. They stand shoulder to shoulder like jungle warriors, holding bamboo walking sticks like spears. All are long-haired, and the males have beards. Scrutinizing their faces, Barnes recognizes one. The man with the caterpillar eyebrows had been at the *paladar* last night with Wayland, had given a bleeding Barnes his bandana.

He turns back to Wayland as if they're old friends in the midst of a casual conversation. "You were saying?"

"That a man will do whatever it takes to protect his family. Isn't that right, Detective?"

"I'd say you failed miserably in that regard, Perry."

"And I'd say you're as clueless about my family's whereabouts and identification as you are about your own."

It's Wayland's turn to step closer. Coward. He wouldn't dare if he didn't have a posse there to back him up.

A large wave crashes at their feet.

Wayland turns to look at the sea.

"It's coming. A storm of mighty, overflowing waters. If I were you, Detective Barnes, I'd leave Baracoa before it arrives."

"Don't worry, I'm going to."

"A wise move. And after you've left Cuba, forget about it. Don't ever come back, or look back, or tell anyone about your time here. Because if you do . . ." Wayland lifts his walking stick with both hands, snaps it in half, and tosses the pieces onto the ground. "Are we clear?"

"Perfectly."

"Good." Wayland walks away to join his friends, leading the way as they slip into the trees.

"*A destroying storm, as a flood of mighty waters overflowing . . .*"

Isaiah 28:2.

Barnes had learned about the biblical prophet back in Sunday school, and is familiar with the verses about God's wrath and judgment day.

So, it seems, is Perry Wayland.

Back when Barnes was investigating his disappearance, his wife had mentioned that he wasn't particularly religious. Something seems to have changed in the decades between—decades presumably spent with Gypsy Colt, daughter of the doomsday zealot Oran Matthews.

Another ferocious wave sweeps in, this time ankle deep. Barnes moves toward dry ground as the broken bamboo pieces are swept out into the raging sea behind him.

AMELIA CLOSES THE front door behind her and leans against it, eyes closed.

This is her haven, has been since the first time Silas Moss welcomed her into his home. She absorbs the hush—her own breathing, the ticking antique mantel clock in the next room—and then it's shattered by an anguished, guttural scream from upstairs.

Her eyes fly open.

It's not Jessie. Her car isn't in the driveway, and the voice is male.

She rushes for the steps. "Billy? Theodore?"

Neither. The man at the top of the flight is a stranger.

Terror detonates and an inner voice screams at her to flee even as she meets and holds his gaze, some part of her brain noting details.

He's blond . . .

Wearing a brown coat and a startled expression . . .

Holding a knife. A knife.

Be fierce, Bettina had told her years ago, teaching her how not to become a crime statistic.

The man will descend and attack.

Unarmed, she will die if she doesn't flee.

But if she flees, then someone else will die.

Jessie's husband, her son, Prewitt . . .

Amelia will not flee. She will be fierce.

She holds her ground. But the man turns and re-treats down the upstairs hall, away from the stairs. He shouts something, words she doesn't understand. They're foreign—French, he's speaking French, and she knows now who he is: Prewitt's dangerous man.

If he's talking to someone up there, then someone is still alive.

Moving toward the stairs, Amelia slips her cell phone from her pocket, slips the button to silent mode, and dials 9–1–1 as she ascends. About to hit Send, she reaches the empty second-floor hallway and sees that the door to her own room is ajar. She'd left it closed, bolted, with her kitten inside.

Again, her feet carry her forward, her thumb hover-ing over the Send button as she peers into the room.

He's there, in a frenzied search, checking behind the curtains, under the bed, alongside the wardrobe. Clancy's carrier lies on its side on the rug, high-pitched mews coming from within. The man doesn't seem to hear them, or notice Amelia there in the doorway, but if she connects the emergency call, he'll most certainly hear the operator's answering voice.

She opens a message window instead.

Jessie might be driving, and her phone's battery had been almost dead.

But Aaron . . .

Even if he's on a flight, he'll have Wi-Fi. He'll see a text.

She quickly types, life & death, need police @ Jessie's NOW, and sends the message as the stranger yanks open the closet door.

He thrashes through the hanging garments, shoving

them aside. Then he stops short with a chilling staccato laugh.

He's found Chip's treasure cave.

He tugs the panel and pulls it from the closet.

Amelia's heart lurches when she hears a child's frightened cry. The intruder laughs again, this time louder, longer. He exclaims in French and reaches into the closet.

She turns away, searching the hall behind her as if the rescue she'd summoned via text might have instantly, silently, materialized. But no, she's on her own, unarmed . . .

Fierce.

There's a gun safe in the master bedroom. She knows the combination. But even if she had the time to find it and open it, she doesn't know how to shoot.

Her gaze falls on Billy's toolbox, where he'd left it on the hallway floor. She backs stealthily toward it and bends to grasp the metal latch. She gives it a tug, certain it will be locked.

She's wrong.

The lid lifts, and she sees a hammer lying right on top.

"Let him go!" Theodore shouts. "Or I'll shoot you!"

Amelia grasps the hammer and spins back to the room.

The intruder is clutching Prewitt, and Theodore is . . .

Oh, Theodore, no!

He's in the closet, arms straight out, both hands aiming a gun.

Billy's gun? It must be. Theodore must have overheard the password, or guessed it.

"Let him go!" he shouts again.

For a moment, it seems as though the stranger is going to obey the command.

But even Amelia can tell that Theodore's entire body is trembling. He barely has a grasp on the weapon.

In one swift movement, the man drops Prewitt to the floor and plucks the gun away from the boy. Seeing him take aim, finger on the trigger, Amelia hurtles herself forward and swings the hammer. She misses, and the gun goes off, but she'd thrown him off balance and the bullet lodges into the wall. Enraged, he reels toward her.

Be fierce.

She swings again with all her strength, and this time, the hammer's iron head slams into his shoulder. The man staggers. Theodore tackles him from behind, making a grab for the gun, and they both tumble to the floor and roll. Amelia sees Theodore's glasses fly across the room. The man's finger fumbles again for the trigger, finding it.

"No!" she screams.

He jams the muzzle against Theodore's skull just as she brings the hammer down on his.

She feels the crack of bone beneath steel.

Blood spatters from the gaping split in his forehead; his eyes close; his body goes slack.

Theodore, breathing hard, struggles to his feet. He opens his mouth but can't form words.

Amelia, too, is dumbstruck. Even the kitten seems to have been stunned to silence.

In this moment, in this room, only one voice, Prewitt's, emerges, loud and clear. *"Il est mort."*

"DAMN, BROTHER," KURTIS mutters under his breath to Joaquin.

"Told you."

"Yeah, you did. You sure did."

In all his twenty-nine years, Kurtis has never seen a woman so fine. He sure wouldn't expect to find her in what must be the most isolated spot in Cuba's most isolated town, or rather, outside of it.

To reach this place, Joaquin had poled a small boat across a gleaming shady green lagoon surrounded by a dense tangle of mangroves. Then they'd hiked a steep, serpentine trail through lush rainforest to this small shack in a sun-dappled cove alongside a waterfall. Joaquin kept promising him that it would be worth it.

It is.

Framed against a backdrop of lush green foliage, she's like some wild jungle goddess, willowy limbs bared in a soft-looking earth-toned garment.

At a glance, she appears Latina. But she's white, with sun-bronzed skin. Her delicate features are framed by a mane of dark hair, and she has the most unusual eyes he's ever seen, like purple glass.

She's older, he's aware, but not old—not like his father.

Then, moving closer and getting a better look, he realizes that she might, in fact, be even older than Rob.

But that's cool. He can tell just by looking at her that she's the kind of person who, unlike his old man, understands that age is just a number, no matter whether it's low or high or higher. She wouldn't think that just because he's about to turn thirty, he should have his shit together. She'd believe it's a tragic waste for someone like him to take the damned train to a damned corporate job in the damned city every damned day.

He knows this about her, knows it deep in his gut, at a glance, because there's something about her that's just . . .

She smiles at him, only at him, and croons in good old American-accented English, "I've been waiting for you, Kurtis. Come on inside and we can get better acquainted in private."

Damn.

He turns to Joaquin and is dismayed to find him stripping off his tee shirt, revealing a lean, muscled torso and a small horse-shaped tattoo on his left pec.

Whoa, hold on now.

If Joaquin is planning on joining them inside, then, well, Kurtis needs to speak up and say that it's cool and all, but threesomes aren't his jam.

Seeing his expression, Joaquin grins and motions for him to go ahead into the shack. "It's okay. I'm just taking a swim."

He heads off toward the pool of rippling water at the base of the waterfall, and Kurtis exhales in relief.

Joaquin had brought him here to get high, acknowledging that his country leaves a lot to be desired when it comes to that. He'd guaranteed that she'd have excellent drugs, and that she'd be more beautiful than any American movie star he'd ever seen. The second promise is certainly true. Kurtis suspects he's about to verify the first—and judging by her provocative invitation, maybe something far more enticing that Joaquin had hinted at.

Kurtis isn't one to turn down excellent drugs or a beautiful woman. But he hesitates, urban street smarts kicking in. Maybe his old man's warning, too, about what happens to you if you're caught with drugs in Cuba.

"There is zero tolerance, son. Zero tolerance! You will rot in a Cuban prison and regret it for the rest of your life."

"They give life imprisonment for drugs?"

"They give twenty, thirty years, and believe me, you will not survive that hell, Kurtis."

He'd bristled at that. He could survive in prison. Sure he could. Better here in Cuba than in some New Jersey shithole . . . right?

He sure as hell doesn't want to find out from experience.

What if this is some kind of elaborate setup? A few times, over the past day or so, he's felt as if someone might be watching him, even following him. Not that those had been sober moments. Drugs might be off-limits here in Cuba, but alcohol flows freely. Still . . .

He thinks back to Friday afternoon. He'd gone into town to score some weed to take the edge off his nerves after that flight.

Turns out the scene is way underground here, and it had taken some cautious finagling, his father's words of caution about undercover Cuban cops ringing in his ears. Finally, he'd connected with a couple of American backpackers, college kids who'd been willing to share their hard-won stash.

Making his way back to the *casa particular* after dark, he'd found that his old man was still off climbing some stupid mountain, and Uncle Stockton had gone out, probably in search of the bottled water Kurtis had promised him. He'd brought back a case—too late. He'd lit up a blunt and was loading the water into the fridge when he'd heard a knock on the door.

Figuring it was his father or uncle—and, truth be told, a little worried that it might be the police—he'd hidden the joint in the freezer and fanned the air. He'd been relieved to open the door to a young Cuban man about his age. He was wiry and lean, with shaggy dark hair, and clad in a black tee shirt, jeans, and sandals.

He'd greeted Kurtis with a casual *"Que vola?"* and flashed the friendliest smile he'd seen in ages.

Turned out Joaquin was looking for an *acere* who'd been staying at the house, but he didn't seem disappointed to learn that his friend had moved out. Sniffing the air, he'd invited himself in to smoke some weed, and Kurtis was happy to share. They'd gone out to a local bar, where Joaquin had introduced him to a group of tight-knit friends, all of whom had embraced Kurtis as if he were a long-lost member of their group, though they'd teased him about being a *yuma*.

"What is that?" he'd asked Joaquin.

"It's what we call people who are from somewhere else."

"Am I the only one who is?"

"No. In fact . . ." After seeming to weigh what he'd been about to say, he'd shrugged.

But after hanging out all night and well into the next day, Kurtis had discovered that there were a couple of other Americans in their midst. One, he'd met last night—a fair-haired older dude.

"Are you coming, Kurtis?" She beckons him to join her in the shack.

Yeah. He's coming. Following her over the threshold, he asks how she knows his name, as Joaquin hadn't introduced them.

"I heard it through the grapevine, I guess."

"Oh, yeah? Hella long way for the grapevine to reach."

Her laugh ripples like the water falling from the stone cliff beyond the door, and she runs silky fingertips over his bare arm.

"What's your name?" he asks.

"Gitana."

"Gitana. That's beautiful. What does it mean in English?"

Those translucent violet eyes study him intently before she answers, as though she's deciding whether to trust him with a secret password. Leaning so close that her lips brush his ear, she whispers, "It means gypsy."

Epilogue

Wednesday, October 5, 2016
Washington Heights

Barnes takes a mighty sip of Jack Daniels before consulting the small spiral notebook and beginning to dial. He'd written down the phone number with paper and pen, long before the electronic era of simply updating contact information on your phone.

"Hello?" Frank DeStefano's gravelly growl is familiar and yet not—thinner than it had been the last time they'd spoken, many years ago, and harried.

"Hey, it's Barnes."

"Barnes! How the hell are you? Everyone's been calling this morning. Listen, I really appreciate it, but I'll be fine. Just finished packing, and the car's already running, so no need to worry about me."

"I'm sorry . . . what?"

A moment of silence. Then, "Carolina coast is being evacuated ahead of the storm. Isn't that why you called?"

A storm of mighty, overflowing waters . . .

Hurricane Matthew.

He'd glimpsed a newspaper headline on the subway, and he'd meant to look it up online, but when he'd sat down with his laptop, he'd picked up right where he'd left off the night before, preoccupied by something far more important than the weather in a place he'd left behind.

"Yeah, I've been worried about you," he tells Stef. "How bad is it?"

"I'll put it this way. Remember how you always wanted to go to Cuba? I hope you got there."

"After you've left Cuba, forget about it. Don't ever come back, or look back, or tell anyone about your time here."

"Why is that, Stef?"

"Because it's about to drop off the map. Eastern end of the island, anyway—it's taking a direct hit. Looks like we're next, and the governor says I've got to go run for my life," Stef adds with a chuckle. "Listen, I'll call you when things get back to normal after the storm. And thanks for checking in."

Barnes wishes him well and hangs up.

After mulling it over for days, he'd intended to ask his former partner about that night in 1987. He can't stop wondering whether Stef might have known more about Wayland's disappearance, Gypsy Colt, and the copycat killer than he'd let on.

He turns on the television and flips to the Weather Channel. There's a commercial. He settles on the couch with his drink, thinking of Baracoa. Of the sensation of being watched and followed, of the way Perry Wayland had spoken about his "family," of the people who'd emerged from the clump of coconut trees. Of Wayland's warning about what might happen if he didn't forget about it once he was back home.

The programming returns, and he sees that the monstrous Hurricane Matthew is indeed headed for the Carolinas. Right now, however, the eyewall is directly over Baracoa, and the city is by all accounts being decimated by what the anchor refers to as "an epic storm of biblical proportions, the likes of which we haven't seen in this century or even the last. The damage is catastrophic and the death toll continues to rise."

Barnes is fortunate to have made it home in the wee hours Monday morning after a grueling twenty-four hours spent in airports and on planes, brooding about Wayland, Gypsy Colt, and Charisse. Neither Rob nor Kurtis had asked him what was on his mind. They, too, had been quiet throughout the long day of flying and waiting, delays and cancellations stacked from Cuba on up the East Coast.

Father and son had had a loud argument when Kurtis returned to the *casa particular* late Saturday evening. Rob had accused him of being high, which he'd denied, and had told him to pack his bags because they'd be flying out at dawn. Kurtis had protested, to Barnes's surprise, and asked to stay behind. He must have met someone.

Rob wouldn't hear of leaving him on the island. When the plane took off from Baracoa, all three of them were on it. In Havana, they'd boarded a charter to Miami, and from there, had caught a roundabout commercial flight back to New York, connecting through Atlanta and Detroit and landing at LaGuardia just before midnight.

Gazing at the footage of the storm-ravaged Cuban coast, Barnes grasps that he'd seen the lovely ancient city in perhaps its final moments. Nothing there will ever be the same.

Biblical proportions . . .

If Wayland and Gypsy Colt survive the violent onslaught of wind and water, they'll have far more important concerns in the weeks ahead. For Barnes, the missing millionaire and the butcher's daughter can be relegated to the past, where they belong. As for the future . . .

His phone vibrates with an incoming text.

Rob, responding to the one Barnes had sent earlier.

Good for you. Here you go. When you call, tell her I sent you.

The message is accompanied by a screenshot of a business card.

It might be too late to walk Charisse down the aisle, or make amends for all the years he'd missed, but he wants her to know that he's lived every day of his life with regret, wishing he'd had the strength, the character, to be the father she deserves.

He remembers holding her in the hospital for the first time, and the last. Delia was there, of course, having counted the money and tucked it away. Barnes stared down at the sleeping, perfect little face, convincing himself that she'd be better off without him in her life. At that time, he'd truly believed it.

"I want her to have something to remember me by," he'd said, taking from his pocket the precious object he'd found at Morningside Hospital back in March of that year, while he'd been visiting Wash.

Upset and distracted by his friend's illness at the

time, he had never tried to find the rightful owner. Only after Charisse had been born had he realized it was meant to belong to her. He'd found it the very night she'd been conceived.

"Someday, I want you to give this to her and tell her it was a gift from her daddy," he'd told Delia, and handed over the gold baby ring studded with tiny sapphires and the initial *C* etched in blue enamel.

Upper West Side

THE FIRST MEAL Amelia is preparing in her nearly remodeled kitchen should probably be something more elegant than buttered toast and macaroni and cheese. But there's a gaping hole where the twin wall ovens are slated to go, and the custom cabinets— installed just yesterday—are nearly bare. Aaron had texted her that he can pick up takeout on the way home, but she'd prefer to make do with a loaf of bread and a box mix.

He'll be home any minute. Time to put Clancy back behind closed doors.

She turns to see the kitten romping across the floor with his new best friend, a twist tie Amelia must have dropped from the bread bag.

"It was fun while it lasted, right?" she asks, scooping Clancy into her arms and heading down the hall. "I think Aaron's going to love you when he gets to know you a little better, and then we'll tell him you're here to stay."

Clancy mews as she sets him on the floor of her office.

"I know," Amelia says, "but he's trying to change. We all are."

She'd been shocked when Aaron had shown up in Ithaca on Saturday night, instead of flying away on his business trip.

"I'm not flying to California when my wife needs me," he'd said, and she'd realized that she had, indeed, needed him. Not just because he was an attorney, and the police had still been there, taking witness statements and crime scene photos and filling out reports. No, she'd needed someone to lean on, someone who loves her.

He does, after all. He loves her, and she loves him, and no matter how complicated their marriage has become, they—

Her cell phone rings. She pulls it from her pocket to check the caller ID.

Roger Hendrickson!

He's a lab tech at Lost and Foundlings.

"I don't do this for just anyone," he'd said when she'd asked him to expedite Prewitt's DNA sample.

"I wouldn't ask if it weren't a matter of life and death."

"Everyone says that."

"This time it really might be." She'd explained the situation, and Roger had agreed to help. "Just this once, though, Amelia. I can get into big trouble."

"You can also send a lost little boy back to his family."

When she'd spoken to Jessie this morning, her friend had just come from visiting Prewitt in his new foster home. He'd been moved as a precaution following Saturday's incident.

Jessie had told her that Billy is recuperating, doing well. So is Theodore, who'd passed his French test and seems to have put the terrible incident behind him.

Still, little is known about the armed intruder. He'd carried no identification and left behind not a single clue to his identity.

They'd hoped Prewitt might be able to provide something, but in the aftermath, he'd reverted to silence, traumatized anew.

Amelia answers the call she's been waiting for, surprised it's come so quickly. "Roger?"

"Hey, Amelia. Got the results on your little John Doe."

"And . . . ?"

"I wanted to talk to you directly instead of just sending them, because I found something really interesting."

"A match?"

"A few, actually. First, how much do you know about the Bourbon DNA Project?"

"I'm an investigative genealogist, Roger."

Launched a couple of years ago, the search for the male descendants of the French Capetian Dynasty is centered around a surprising and rare Y-haplogroup discovered in three known Bourbon descendants. The resulting effort to collect DNA samples from males with a suspected ancestral link has been met with considerable controversy and press coverage.

"Just wanted to be sure you were well-informed," Roger says, "before I told you that your young friend has the Y-chromosomal variant."

"You mean he's—"

"Yes. He's got royal blood. And he has a half brother who's already in the system."

Her jaw drops as Roger explains that Prewitt's DNA is linked to a child whose mother had submitted her son's sample for a recent round of free testing offered to suspected male Capetian descendants in an effort to confirm the Y-haplogroup.

Amelia asks who the family is and where they live.

"Not that simple, sorry. Those results were just generated a few days ago, and they're still being processed. They haven't been released yet to the family, so I can't give you any information."

"I understand. At least he has a home waiting, and a mother."

"See, that's the thing . . ."

"Oh! I was so excited I forgot that the genetic variant is patrilineal. So if the child in the system is a half sibling, his mother can't be Prewitt's."

"No, the boys share a father, and since they seem to be the same age and they're not twins, it's possible that one or both mothers are unaware that their sons have half brothers."

It wouldn't be surprising if that apple didn't fall far from a family tree ripe with mistresses and illegitimate offspring.

"I just wanted him to have a happily ever after. A family waiting to welcome him home."

"I wouldn't rule that out, Amelia. See, there's another match here—to a maternal grandmother."

"What?"

"Yeah. And when I checked her out, I found . . . wait, I'm texting you something."

A second later, her phone buzzes. She clicks on the attachment from Roger.

ENDANGERED MISSING reads the caption above a photograph of a girl who appears to be in her early teens. Sweet faced and smiling, she has blond hair and blue eyes.

Amelia recognizes her instantly.

Not because she's seen her, but because she's seen Prewitt. He looks so much like her that she might have guessed, even without the scientific evidence.

She presses the phone to her ear again, hand trembling. "Is this . . . ?"

"The child's mother," Roger says. "It looks that way, because her mother's DNA shows that she's Prewitt's grandmother, and she's desperate to get her daughter back. She's been searching for her since she went missing over four years ago."

Four years . . . before Prewitt had been born. The family likely doesn't know about him.

Amelia wipes tears from her eyes, imagining the circumstances of his birth, remembering the murderous man who'd found his way to Jessie's house on Saturday.

He's gone forever.

So, most likely, is Prewitt's mother.

She asks Roger to send her the full report, and they hang up with the promise to discuss it after she's gone over it later.

Back in the kitchen at the new six-burner stovetop, she stirs dry pasta into boiling water, thinking about Prewitt. He won't remember her, but it's for the best. He won't remember these dark days, either. Soon, all of this will be lost to him, and he'll know only the new life that lies ahead.

She recalls Silas Moss's scientific theories about why children can't retain autobiographical memories until they've grown past infancy and toddlerhood, and how many times she's wished that weren't the case.

"My birth mother must have held me," she'd said. "I must have seen her. Why can't I remember her?"

"Our brains aren't developed enough to recollect our earliest days on this earth, but that doesn't mean our hearts don't retain them."

She's been frustrated over the years, imagining an impression of her real mother's face locked deep in her mind, like a hidden room that would never see the light of day.

Now, when she closes her eyes, she sees only Bettina. *My real mother.*

When at last she'd had a chance to tell Aaron about the DNA match, his reaction had been predictable. "So now you know."

"Not everything."

"But you're not ever going to get all the answers, Amelia. I think it's time to forget the last thirty years and focus on what you want out of the next thirty."

Their lives together are a long way from perfect, but where they go from here can't depend on what she's learned about the past, and her parents. Moving on is about letting go.

It's time.

Her phone rings again. Aaron?

No. Pulling it out of her pocket, she sees an unfamiliar number. Manhattan.

"Amelia Crenshaw Haines speaking."

A deep voice greets her. "Ms. Haines, my friend

Rob Owens gave me your number. My name is Stockton Barnes, and I'm wondering if you might be able to help me find my daughter."

Bedford-Stuyvesant

THE EMAIL HAD arrived overnight on Sunday.

> *Dear Lily,*
>
> *In advance of our appointment this coming week, I thought I should let you know that I recognized your baby ring . . .*

Amelia had gone on to explain that her own mother had given her a similar ring many years ago, and how she'd lost it. Now she's wondering whether the two of them—herself, and Lily—might have some connection. Maybe even a biological one.

> *. . . If you can fill out the DNA release forms and bring them to your appointment on Thursday, we can do the sample and possibly both find out more information about who we are and where we came from.*
>
> *Sincerely,*
> *Amelia Crenshaw*

Three days have gone by, and she still hasn't responded. She isn't sure what to say, how to say it . . . whether she should say, or do, anything at all.

Clutching the blank release forms, she stares out

the window, absently listening to sirens in the street, a screaming baby somewhere above, angry shouts below.

When the *New York Times* had written about the gentrification of Bedford-Stuyvesant, they sure as hell hadn't been referring to this block. There are no renovated brownstones, yoga studios, or wine bars in this southeast corner of the neighborhood. If anything, it's gone downhill since she was a little girl.

That's why you have got to get yourself out of here once and for all. Do whatever it takes, even if—

She hears a key in the door. It opens, and the doorway fills with a large woman jostling plastic Key Food grocery bags.

"What are you looking at, girl? Get off that pretty little ass and help me."

She stands, folds the papers, and shoves them into the back pocket of her jeans—not the designer ones she'd worn to her appointment on Thursday, with the tags tucked into the waistband. Those had gone right back to the store, along with the blazer, sunglasses, and leather bag that had cost more than a month's rent on this place. Only the white tee shirt had been her own when the charade had begun.

"Do you have the receipt?" the clerk had asked at the returns counter.

"It should be in the bag . . . isn't it?"

The woman had looked, shaking her head.

"Oh, no! It was in there," she'd said, feigning confusion.

"Did you buy it on a credit card?"

Yes—one she'd slipped from a woman's purse on the subway.

"No, I paid cash. Look, the tags are on everything . . . is there any way . . . ?"

The clerk shrugged and scrutinized the merchandise for tags and evidence of wear. "I can't give you cash without a receipt. It'll have to be store credit."

"That's fine."

She'll use the credit to buy another fancy outfit for her next appointment with Amelia Crenshaw. And when this is over, she'll have more than enough reward money to buy all the clothes she wants, and move out of this miserable place, and—

"Move it! This stuff isn't going to put itself away," Alma barks, and she obeys, still thinking about the designer jeans and blazer she'd returned to the store, imagining herself wearing them when she sails out the door forever.

Then again, they're really not her own style, are they?

No. But they're Lily Tucker's.

Barrow Island, Georgia

"R-E-S-P-E-C-T," PENNY SINGS along with Aretha as she turns into the gravel driveway.

She plays this song every time she visits. It fits. If anyone in this world has earned respect, it's the ancient mistress of this little blue antebellum cottage.

Tucked beneath a massive live oak tree draped in pewter-colored Spanish moss, the house is low and wide, with a porch along the front. Once part of a rice plantation, it's been in the family since the owner's widow turned it over to their emancipated slaves soon after the Civil War. A quarter of a mile down the road, the white-pillared main house is now an inn rumored to be haunted by the dead planter and his wife.

"That big ol' house has got plenty of room for him. We don't need no ghosts hangin' around here, lookin' for attention and whatnot. I got enough to do," Tandy had told Penny not long ago, when a breeze they hadn't perceived had slammed a door somewhere inside as they were chatting right there on the porch.

If anyone's haunting the old cottage, it's probably not a nineteenth-century spirit. The last few generations have endured more than enough premature deaths and unfinished business to keep the afterworld plenty busy for years to come.

Penny turns off the music and the engine, hearing her daughter's voice in the whoosh of silence.

"You're still using a CD player?" she'd asked the last time she'd ridden in the passenger's seat, home from Atlanta and plumb full of big city swagger. "We need to get you into the twenty-first century!"

"I don't want one of those iPod things, if that's what you're thinking."

"You don't need an iPod. You can get a new phone and play music right from there. If you'd get a car with Bluetooth, you wouldn't even need to plug it in."

She'd just shaken her head. That girl never has been content to leave well enough alone. Penny's perfectly happy with her trusty flip phone and sedan, even if the odometer is edging toward two hundred thousand miles. She likes to have a good, sturdy hunk of car around her when she drives down here from Marshboro. The interstate is chockful of trucks and crazy drivers these days, and the island bridge makes her nervous, with orange cones and concrete construction barriers and fancy cars that tailgate you across.

She doesn't like it, any of it. But soon enough, her reason for coming here will be gone, and then, she supposes, she'll miss it.

She gets out of the car, grabs the bouquet she'd bought on the mainland, and peels the Publix price sticker from the cellophane.

Her feet crunch on the gravel as she heads toward the cottage, wading through evening air as thick with humidity as it is with humming insects and the scent of bacon and black-eyed peas.

A Creamsicle-colored kitten lolls on the pathway beside a crepe myrtle. The branches are stuck with upended glass bottles in the same bright cobalt shade as the cottage. *Haint blue*, the Gullah Geechee call the color, believing it wards off evil spirits. Maybe, but it didn't work on a certain blue-eyed man Penny will always remember as evil incarnate.

She steps over a second orange kitten on the steps, and past a third littermate watching flies buzz around tuna fish dregs in a couple of shallow metal bowls. A spry black cat springs from the porch rail to join her on the mat as she knocks on the screen door.

Tandy comes bustling from the kitchen, wiping sweat from her forehead with a dish towel, then slinging it over her shoulder. She grins, her few remaining teeth gleaming white in her plump Black face as she unhooks the screen door and opens it with a welcoming squeak.

"There you are! I was startin' to worry. Was there an awful lot of traffic?"

"More and more every week. Used to be not a lot of folks knew about this island."

"Now they're building condos and beach houses that sleep two dozen," Tandy tells her, holding the door wide. "Come on in out of the heat, child."

If anything, it's hotter inside the cottage, where paddle fans twirl from a beadboard ceiling so low it's a wonder no one's been decapitated.

She follows Tandy through the sitting room, with its slanted wide-planked floors and hand-crocheted doilies, and Billie Holiday croons Cole Porter on the old stereo. In the steamy kitchen, Hoppin' John bubbles on the stovetop in a black-rimmed white enamel pot with more scratches and dings than the old sedan out front.

A window above the sink faces the deep backyard bordered by dense vegetation tangled in greenbrier vines. Gators occasionally emerge to bask in remarkable harmony with the property's feline population, a fact that has never surprised the resident cat lady.

"They all leave each other alone and get on just fine. People should do the same out there in the world," she's often said in her Gullah accent, pronouncing both *they* and *there*, "day."

Tandy unwraps the flowers. "Well, aren't these somethin'. Daisies, cornflowers, lilies—a big ol' kiss from summertime."

"This weather feels more like August than October."

"That it does, child. That it does." She clips the bottom inch from the stems, puts them into a waiting mason jar already filled with water, and bustles to the fridge. "Now let me pour you some cold lemonade. And I made your favorite for supper."

"Oh, I can't stay. Nighttime driving is getting harder and harder with these old eyes of mine."

"Almost full-on dark out now, so guess you'll be going home in the dark either way. Might as well do it with a belly full of home cookin'."

"Might as well," she agrees with a grin. Tandy never takes no for an answer.

She hands over the jar bouquet, along with lemonade in a tall, moisture-beaded glass and calls toward the back bedroom, "Penny's here now, honey!" No response. Tandy shrugs. "You just go on in there while I get our cornbread into the oven. She had a restless night and a drowsy day with the heat, so she might'a dozed off again waitin' for you."

"Maybe I should let her sleep."

"No, you go on and wake her up. She's been askin' about you all the livelong day. If she misses seein' you, she'll be heartsick."

So will I.

She wonders, every time she visits, whether this will become the last time—the occasion she'll look back on years from now, thinking of all the questions she should have asked, though they're no more likely to earn deathbed answers than they were decades ago. Still, if she fails to ask, she'll remember the final conversation with regret, just as she does the final one she'd had with her mama, gone more than twenty-five years now.

She crosses the threshold into a tiny bedroom shadowed in dusk, setting the lemonade on a folding wooden tray table, and the flowers on the windowsill. A fat calico cat stares back at her from the ledge beyond the screen. Ignoring a lizard crawling along the frame, the feline keeps vigilant watch over the room as if intent upon witnessing the old woman's last breath.

A kitchen chair is pulled up alongside the hospital bed that had arrived with Tandy about a decade ago to accommodate a stubborn ninety-eight-year-old woman who wouldn't hear of going to a Marshboro nursing home. She's grudgingly grown accustomed to both, though she remains inarguably fonder of the adjustable mattress than she is of her home health aide.

Poor Tandy, Penny and the rest of the family often say. She surely has her hands full here, and for more years now than anyone other than the patient had ever anticipated.

Above the bed, a framed photograph captures the newly minted centenarian eight years ago, beaming before a towering cake ablaze with a hundred birthday candles. She'd shared her secret to longevity with the guests at her family party.

"Y'all have got to stay away from buckrahbittle. You need supshun if y'all want to live to see one hundred years."

"Buckrahbittle? Supshun?" one of the great-grand-nephews had echoed, helping himself to a handful of chips and Cheetos from the snack table. "What the heck is she talkin' about?"

"Buckrahbittle is what you got there in your hand," she'd retorted in that lazy growl of hers, old ears, eyes, and tongue still sharp as ever. "And supshun is all that good food your mama is always tellin' you to eat."

Nowadays, she spends more time in bed than she does in the folded wheelchair propped against the wall. Her hearing and vision are waning, and her throaty voice warbles with age whenever she deigns to speak. She's often silent, steeped in introspection, though she still occasionally picks up on things you wouldn't expect—or want—her to notice.

"Watch that mouth of yours, missy," she'd snapped just last week when Tandy had emitted a hushed cuss after bumping her shin on the footboard.

The nurse had rolled her eyes at Penny, whispering, "Can't get away with anything around here, even when she looks like she's sound asleep."

"Heard that, too," the patient muttered, eyes still closed as if deep in slumber.

She looks the same this evening, chest rising and falling in a steady rhythm. Despite the heat, she's swathed in two sweaters and tucked beneath a quilt she'd hand-pieced seventy-five, maybe eighty years ago for a newborn niece who's long dead now.

Having outlived not just everyone she'd ever known and loved in her own generation as well as many who came after, she's acutely aware that her time on this earth is drawing to an end. Her mind remains astute as ever, though her waking hours are dwindling and her robust physical presence is no more. Her thick mass of cornrows has been replaced by gray wisps, that rich ebony complexion is now whitewashed in chalky pallor, the once sturdy hands reduced to wizened bones clasped as if in prayer, resting on what's left of her bosom.

Planting a kiss on her withered forehead, Penny whispers, "Auntie? I'm here."

The old woman's eyelids flutter, but she doesn't awaken.

"It's all right. I'll just set a spell and let you rest."

Now she stirs, almost defiantly. Her gaze, behind thick red-framed glasses, is unnervingly bright, like a sinking ship's beacon gleaming on the misty night sea. It's impossible to imagine, in moments like this, that this bold light will soon be extinguished. When she goes, a trove of family secrets will be lost with her. Time is running out.

She gives an approving little nod. "Lucky."

There aren't many people left in this world who remember the childhood nickname bestowed by her own late mama.

Lucky Penny, Birdie used to call her, and the name had stuck, if only within the family.

The eyes scan the room and settle on her face again. "Where's Cyril?"

"Cyril?" Wide-eyed, she shakes her head. "I don't know."

A troubled frown. "What time is it?"

"About six thirty."

"How are you comin' all this way so early in the day, child? Don't you have to work?"

"It's six thirty at night, Auntie."

"Night!" She turns her head toward the window.

Beyond the screen, the backyard's shadows have deepened, and the feline sentry has disappeared into the palmetto jungle—for now.

"Thought I'd slept right through to dayclean," the old woman mutters. "The sun was comin' up over the ocean, and the dolphins, they were dancin' around like crazy, and Cyril, he was just laughin' and laughin', and . . . you sure he's not here?"

"No, he's . . . no."

"Guess it was a dream." She shakes her wispy gray head, lost in thought.

Penny clears her throat. "I got a phone call, Auntie. Bettina's girl, askin' questions I couldn't answer, or didn't think I should. I thought maybe you—"

"Maybe later, child. Maybe later. I'm goin' to rest up a little bit until it's time for supper."

With that, Marceline LeBlanc closes her eyes and drifts back to a place where sunshine sparkles on the water with her lost boy's laughter.

Don't miss the rest of the story in

THE BUTCHER'S DAUGHTER

Coming in 2020!

Chapter One

It's the silence that gets her.

Strange. It's not as though Aaron goes banging around the apartment, blasts music and television, or speaks in a booming voice. These last few months, he's hardly spoken at all. Yet on this particular morning, six weeks into his absence, stillness hangs in the Upper West Side apartment as if it's been wrapped in acoustic foam. Even the Manhattan streets far below their— *her*—bedroom window are oddly quiet, as though the whole world has decided to sleep through the dawn of the new year.

Amelia Crenshaw Haines had intended to do the same, having lain awake long after watching the ball drop—on television, not the real thing forty-odd blocks down Broadway. But it's not quite seven a.m., and she can tell this isn't going to be one of those Sunday mornings when she can slip back into slumber. Might as well get up and get moving, as if she has someplace to go, something to do. Or maybe even go somewhere, do . . . something.

"Child, it's Sunday morning and you can just get yourself to church," Bettina Crenshaw drawls in her head. When Amelia had been growing up in Harlem, her mother had never missed a service at Park Baptist Church.

She never let me miss one, either, as long as she was alive.

How tickled Bettina would have been to see Amelia sing there every other Sunday, in the gospel choir. This was supposed to be her week, but she's been on hiatus since November. You can't resonate uplifting spirit when it's been depleted from your world.

She reaches for her phone on the nightstand. She'd expected Aaron to get in touch at midnight, but had reminded herself that 2017 was arriving three hours later for him, on the West Coast. He'd been invited to ring it in with a client at the Billboard Hollywood Party, but hadn't been planning to attend. Yet Amelia, watching the LA live feed interspersed with New York's coverage, had found herself scanning the crowds for him. No glimpse.

No call, either, and no text. Not then, and not overnight. She plunks down the phone and gets out of bed.

Maybe he'd changed his mind and gone to the party after all. Maybe not.

Maybe it's a simple case of out with the old . . .

"And *I'm* the old," she tells the lump of drowsy fur on Aaron's former pillow.

Allergic to cats, he hadn't been thrilled when Amelia pulled a kitten from a kill shelter a few months ago. It was supposed to be a temporary foster situation, but when the time came for little Clancy to go, Aaron was the one who left.

Amelia pads to the bathroom, plucks the lone

toothbrush from the holder, and tries to find perverse pleasure in squeezing a tube of Crest in the middle.

Babe! From the bottom!

Why?

Because that's how you're supposed to do it.

Says who?

Aaron and his rules.

"It's going to be okay," she tells her bleary-eyed self in the mirror, and drowns her own oddly hushed and echoey voice in a roar of tap water. But these new pipes don't creak like the old ones did, and when she turns off the faucet, it no longer continues to drip.

She pads barefoot from the sleek, just-remodeled bathroom to the sleek, just-remodeled kitchen. True to his word, the contractor had finished it in time for Thanksgiving.

Aaron had moved out the week before.

It's a trial separation. Nobody'd had an affair. There had been no dramatic argument. In fact, they'd been actively working on their relationship. But couples' counseling had only confirmed that they'd grown apart.

Amelia measures grounds and water for a full pot of coffee out of habit, and then waits for it to brew, glaring at the gleaming white subway tile backsplash. She'd have preferred a vibrant, intricate mosaic one, but Aaron got the last word, saying simplicity had better resale value. At the time, it hadn't made sense. She'd still assumed this would be their forever home; that their marriage would be, well, forever.

"Who knows? We might find out we can't live without each other," her husband had said, zipping his suitcase on that chilly November morning.

"I hope so."

"Do you, Amelia?"

She couldn't answer the question then for the fierce lump in her throat. She can't now, because she's not sure.

Her life has gone on much the same way it always has. Ever since Aaron had made partner at his corporate law firm, he'd traveled more than he was home. She's accustomed to being on her own. In fact, her loneliest moments unfolded when they were here together.

Clancy is affectionate company, her investigative genealogy business is busier than ever, and her social life is unchanged. Childless by choice, Amelia and Aaron hadn't hung out with fellow couples in years. The ones they'd enjoyed early in their marriage had long since embraced parenthood, more interested in preschool and potty-training than late-night reservations at hot new restaurants. He's cultivated his circle of pals and colleagues; she has hers, though her longtime friendship with his sister has grown slightly strained.

"You're part of the family. My parents still want you to come for Thanksgiving," Karyn said back in November.

"I don't think that's a good idea."

"Oh, Aaron is fine with it. He knows we all love you. He loves you, too. I'm sure you guys will work things out. I know he can be difficult, but he'll come around."

"It's not just him, Karyn. I have some stuff of my own to work out, too."

"You mean, the thing with your mother?"

The thing with your mother—as if it's some innocuous To-Do List detail that needs tending. As if Amelia hadn't finally clawed her way out of a gaping bomb crater, scarred and dazed, only to be hit again.

She'd been eighteen years old when she'd discovered, at Bettina's deathbed, that she wasn't her parents' biological daughter. Her father—Calvin Crenshaw, the man she'd grown up *believing* was her father—had admitted that he'd found her as an abandoned newborn in Park Baptist Church on Mother's Day 1968. He and Bettina had raised her as their own.

Amelia had bought that traumatic tale and spent three decades building an investigative genealogy career, helping other people uncover their biological roots while searching for her own. She'd anticipated that the recent surge in autosomal DNA testing might lead to some answers in her own bloodline. Sure enough, four months ago, she'd finally received a genetic hit.

However, the long-awaited biological match hadn't resolved the mystery. Far from it.

Her DNA test had linked her to a woman in Marshboro, Georgia—Bettina Crenshaw's tiny hometown—and to Bettina's own biological family tree.

"I thought that if my wife found out who her parents were, she'd finally be able to put this stuff to rest and move on," Aaron had told their therapist during their final counseling session in November. "But she's more obsessed than ever."

"Because I still don't have answers! If Bettina was my birth mother, why would Calvin have told me I was a foundling? Was he lying? Or did he not know the truth himself? Was he my father, or was it someone else?"

Aaron shot the therapist a *see what I mean?* look and then shook his head sadly at Amelia. "You said you were ready to move on. That's why we're here. That's why we're trying—but you're not."

"Of course I am. Whose idea was it to come to counseling? Mine! And if that's not trying, then I don't know what—"

"No, I mean you're not *moving on*. I don't think you can. I don't think you want to. And I don't think either of us can live like this anymore."

He was right. He deserves to be spared the burden of her unresolved past, and she deserves . . .

What? To lug the damned past around like a lifetime's worth of locked luggage without a key?

Back in September, she'd thought she'd found a clue to the key, if not the key itself. Lily Tucker, a fellow foundling, had hired Amelia to help track down her own birth parents. The young woman had shown Amelia a gold baby ring she'd had on when she'd been found years ago in Connecticut. It had been identical to one Calvin claimed Amelia herself had been wearing when he'd discovered her in the Harlem church.

She pours a cup of coffee, takes it to the living room, and gazes out at the towering skyline view, rigid rectangles against a swirly swath of gray, broken by thin patches of blue.

Is the weather supposed to be decent today? Maybe she can get outside for a bit—go for a long walk in the park, clear her head.

She turns on the TV and settles on the couch, making room for her feet on the coffee table amid the remnants of New Year's Eve dinner, drinks, and entertainment for one—a protein bar wrapper, an empty wineglass, half a bottle of Cabernet, and the remote control.

Sipping coffee, she channel-surfs for a weather report, flipping past images of cozy flannel-clad couples and merry multi-generational gatherings. At least she's almost made it through this season of homey, twinkle-light-lit commercials that remind her of happier holidays with Aaron and her in-laws.

Spotting a familiar face, she pauses to watch a few minutes of *The Roots and Branches Project*, a cable television show hosted by African American historian Nelson Roger Cartwright. As a genealogy consultant for the program, she appears in some episodes, and shows up a little later in this one. But she doesn't need to watch it again, and anyway, it'll be on all day. The network is airing a marathon, hoping to reach a new audience among the hundreds of thousands of people who received DNA test kits this Christmas.

That boom is sure to make her job easier in a couple of months, as their lab results are processed and loaded into online databases. She might even find more links to her own past—perhaps a biological connection to Calvin's family tree.

Or not.

Unsettled, Amelia flips more channels until she finds a local newscast. Waiting for a meteorologist to appear, she considers the long, lonely day ahead. In years past, she and Aaron would curl up and watch bowl games into the night. She supposes she can do the same this year, but . . .

Maybe she should have spent a few more days in Ithaca after all. With Clancy in tow, she'd celebrated

Christmas there with her old friend Jessie and her family, just as she had Thanksgiving. She'd been invited to stay on through this weekend, but Jessie's husband is recovering from a recent heart attack, her youngest son is afraid of cats, and both her college kids were home with pals coming and going at all hours.

Amelia had been more than ready to come home, but this is one holiday she probably shouldn't be spending solo. New Year's is about nostalgia for auld lang syne and resolution for the year ahead. Her own future—and yes, her past, too—couldn't be more uncertain.

She stares at the television, where a newscaster returns her bleak gaze.

"In Bedford-Stuyvesant," he announces, "where the violent crime rate continued to drop last year, a double homicide at the Marcy Houses yesterday left a mother and daughter dead and neighbors looking for answers."

The scene shifts to an elderly man standing on a Brooklyn street, with a yellow-crime-scene-taped brick doorway behind him. "Don't know why anyone would do something like that to decent people," he says, shaking his bald head. "They didn't bother nobody, and they didn't have nothin' worth stealin'."

The screen shows a pair of photographs. The older woman is obese and smiling and vaguely familiar; the younger is . . .

Also familiar.

Amelia gasps and sloshes hot coffee over her hand as the reporter's voiceover continues, "The bodies of fifty-three-year-old Alma Harrison and her thirty-one-year-old daughter Brandy were discovered late yesterday in their apartment by relatives who'd grown concerned when they failed to show up at a family gathering. Police are seeking information and have ruled out robbery as a motive for the brutal slayings, believed to have taken place early yesterday morning . . ."

Brandy Harrison?

Amelia shakes her head. She'd know that face anywhere.

No, the dead woman's name—at least, when Amelia had met her in September—had been Lily Tucker.

Not only that, but . . .

Alma Harrison?

Stunned, she hurries into the bedroom to find her phone.

At half past nine on Sunday evening, Stockton Barnes gets off the subway at Eighty-Sixth Street. A smattering of headlights zip south along Central Park West, mostly vacant yellow cabs cruising in search of a fare. Across the street, every bench along the low stone wall is vacant, the park beyond fringed by tall, bare limbs, and splotched with glowing lampposts.

Barnes checks his watch, late, and strides north, making a left onto West Eighty-Seventh. Pedestrians are few—a dog-walking matron wearing more fur than her Pomeranian, a jogger in a headlamp, a pair of teenaged girls sporting matching thousand-dollar down parkas with red arm patches. The jackets had been designed for arctic explorers, but are all the rage in Manhattan's toniest neighborhoods, which don't include Barnes's own, a hundred blocks north.

New Year's Day is just winding down, and already he counts more bedraggled Christmas trees tossed at the curb than are lit in the brownstone windows along the street.

Yeah, he gets it. For many, the holidays are steeped in loneliness, depression, and stress; overspending, overtiredness, overindulgence; fighting off the flu or still fighting with family over the November election results; coping with weather woes and travel snafus. None of those scenarios apply to Barnes, but this isn't the merriest of seasons for him, either. A longtime detective with the NYPD Missing Persons Squad, he'd spent December chasing down people who weren't where they should be, or where their families expected them to be.

'Tis the season for reflecting on the year behind, assessing the one ahead—and for some, resolving to make significant changes that don't involve significant others. Precious few disappearances at this time of year—at any time of year—involve foul play, though it does happen. He's in the midst of a case involving a Midwestern college kid who'd flown to New York last week and planned to spend New Year's in Times Square with friends, but had disappeared. Barnes had located him this morning hospitalized on life support, having been mugged and left for dead in a neighborhood where no tourist should wander.

The kid's distraught parents are on a flight from Cedar Rapids, and Barnes will meet them back at the hospital around midnight. Between now and then, he's got personal business to tend to, and as he rounds the corner and heads up Broadway, his heart isn't just racing from his quick stride.

He reaches a jittery hand into his overcoat pocket for his cigarettes, then remembers he'd given up the habit more than three years ago. Damn. He sucks deep breaths of chilly night air into lungs that are growing healthier and pinker by the minute now that he's kicked the pack-a-day habit. But if ever there was a time he could use a calming smoke, this is it.

Spotting his destination on the opposite corner, he waits for the light to change and wonders whether he's ever been there before. Probably. He's eaten at most of the all-night diners in the city. This one doesn't appear to be an old-school greasy spoon like some, or cater to hipsters or tourists like others. It looks like your basic counter-booths-and-tables joint that will have pie behind glass, ketchup bottles on the tables, and a laminated volume offering everything from hash browns to seared mahi-mahi.

The place is nearly empty when he steps inside. Forty minutes late, he figures she must have given up on him and left.

Then he looks more closely at the lone African American woman way back in a corner booth, intent on her cell phone. That's not her . . .

Wait, yes it is.

He's seen Amelia Crenshaw Haines on television many times, and met her in person twice. But she'd always worn business attire, fully made-up, with her sleek dark mane falling to her shoulders. Tonight, she has on a navy hoodie emblazoned with gold letters, her hair is tucked under a Yankees baseball cap, and her face, when she looks up, bears no evidence of cosmetics. She's even prettier, he decides, without all the trimmings.

"Trying not to be recognized?" he asks.

"Recognized?" She puts her phone facedown beside the nearly empty mug of tea sitting on her paper place mat.

"You know . . . you're a celebrity. On TV and all. People must bother you when you're out in public."

"Oh, yeah. Me, Halle, Taraji, Beyoncé . . . pesky fans go with the territory for gals like us, you know?"

He grins. "Anyway . . . happy new year, and I'm sorry I'm late."

"Get hung up watching the big Rose Bowl comeback?"

"I wish. I was working a case. What comeback?"

"Penn State was a scoring machine—twenty-eight points just in the third quarter. But USC tied up the fourth with a minute left and won with a forty-six-yard field goal."

Ah, a fellow football fan. She's precisely the kind of woman who might have convinced this longtime ladies' man to give monogamy another try . . .

If their paths had crossed in another time and place.

If she didn't already have a husband.

And *if* Barnes, who'd been briefly, reluctantly married and long divorced, hadn't promised himself that he'll never go down that road again.

He slides into the booth across from her. "Sounds like a great Rose Bowl game. Thanks for waiting for me."

"It's fine. Like I said, I have something to discuss, and anyway, I have nowhere to go, except bed."

Barnes doesn't want to picture her there. No, he does not.

Nor does he want to wonder why she needed to meet with him on a holiday, though he suspects he knows the answer. Is he ready to hear it?

She clears her throat, about to speak, but he cuts her off.

"I. C.?"

Amelia looks puzzled. "You see?"

He points at the letters appliqued on her sweatshirt.

"Oh—I. C. That's Ithaca College," she explains. "My alma mater."

"I see."

She smiles at that. "By the way, I caught a glimpse of your pal Rob on TV last night. He's out on the West Coast, right?"

"Right. One of his artists was performing at the Billboard Hollywood Party."

Rob Owens, founder and CEO of Rucker Park Records, is responsible for having led Barnes to Amelia in the first place. Rob had met her when his own ancestral story had been featured on an episode of *The Roots and Branches Project*, and had become obsessed with genealogy thereafter—with his own, and with Barnes's.

"This woman specializes in reuniting long lost family members, Barnes," Rob had told him. "You should hire her to find your daughter."

"I've made a living for thirty years now finding missing people."

"Well, you haven't found her."

"Who says I want to? Or that she wants to be found?"

That was before their autumn trip to Cuba, where Barnes had an unsettling encounter he'd never shared with a soul, including Rob. He'd flown home and immediately hired Amelia to help him find Charisse, whom he hasn't seen since she was born in October 1987.

A skinny young waiter ambles over carrying a plate and a wineglass. Wrong table, Barnes figures, but he sets them both down in front of Amelia and she thanks him.

"Need a menu, or know what you're having?" he asks Barnes.

"I'll have what she's having, which is, uh . . ."

"Cabernet," she says, "and cheese fries."

Oh, yes. A woman like her could have gotten the old Barnes into all sorts of trouble.

"Cabernet and cheese fries. Perfect. Thanks."

The waiter walks away, and Barnes watches Amelia tilt the stemmed glass and swirl the maroon liquid before taking a thoughtful sip, as if they're at a Napa Vineyard. "Well? How is it?"

"The wine? Not bad, for diner cab." She sets down the glass, adds a liberal pool of ketchup to the plate, and asks if he wants some of her fries.

"No, thanks, but go ahead. I'll wait for mine," he says, though his empty stomach protests loudly. He hasn't eaten since the buttered roll he'd grabbed from a coffee cart early this morning in Hell's Kitchen, on a block littered with the remains of midnight revelry—confetti, garbage, and a few stray drunken tourists.

But sharing food strikes him as an oddly intimate thing to do in this moment. Plus, he's too nervous to eat.

He watches her slowly dredge a cheese-sauce coated fry through the ketchup, staring down at her plate, and is unsettled by her energy. He wants to think it's just that they're here on a holiday, and it's late, and she's dressed down, but . . .

Every living creature is equipped with natural in-

stinct, Stockton, a wise old detective had once told him. *Listen to yours.*

His instinct tells him they aren't here because she's found his daughter alive and well and none the worse for his having removed himself from her life.

She eats a couple of fries, and then pushes away the plate and looks up at him.

Here we go.

"Detective—"

"You can call me Barnes." Again, he finds himself cutting her off. *Coward.*

She shakes her head. "How about Stockton?"

"Nobody but my mother calls me Stockton."

Not anymore, anyway.

He hears that same wise detective's voice in his head, the night Barnes had told him he'd gotten a woman pregnant during a one-night stand.

"You make a choice, Stockton, and someday you're either going to regret it, or congratulate yourself that it was the right one."

"There is no choice. I'm not going to help raise a kid, period. It'll be better off without me."

"Were you better off without your father?"

"Hell, no. It's the same thing, whether you drop dead, or take off because the stock market crashed, or because their mother is a pain in the ass, or because you're not cut out for being a dad and you never wanted kids in the first place. The kid gets hurt in the end."

"So it's better to hurt them in the beginning, is that what you're saying?"

It was exactly what Barnes had been saying. Charisse couldn't miss or grieve or hate a man she'd never known.

Barnes had held his baby girl just once before handing her back to her mother, Delia, along with enough cash to raise her right. Amelia doesn't know about that, though.

"Barnes," she says, as if trying out the name, and then again, as if warning him to brace himself. *"Barnes."*

"What is it? Did you find her?"